The PRIEST
The STEWARDESS
And The
CHURCH PICNIC

MICHAEL DILL & RAY POLANSKI

This is a work of fiction. The names, characters, incidents, places, plots, businesses, events and locales are products of the authors' imaginations or are used in a fictitious manner. Any resemblance to actual persons, living or dead, or actual places, companies or events is purely coincidental.

No part of this book may be reproduced or transmitted in any form or by any means, electronic or mechanical, including photocopying, recording or by any information storage and retrieval system, without permission in writing from the authors.

If you purchased this book without a cover you should be aware that this book is stolen property. It was reported as "unsold and destroyed" to the authors and they have not received payment for this "stripped book."

Copyright © 2018 Ray Polanski
All rights reserved.
ISBN-13: 978-1-7241-2671-9

STORY BY: RAY POLANSKI

CONTENTS

Dedication	i
Chapter 1: Ray and Patty	1
Chapter 2: Jeremy and Evelyn	11
Chapter 3: Aaron and Joey	16
Chapter 4: John and Father Feeney	24
Chapter 5: Phyllis and Charlene	32
Chapter 6: The Girls	36
Chapter 7: Tom and Jill	46
Chapter 8: Sharon, Melissa, and the Kids	50
Chapter 9: Boarding	60
Chapter 10: The Flight	82
Chapter 11: One Day Later	123
Chapter 12: One Month Later	150
Chapter 13: One Year Later – The Church Picnic	192
Chapter 14: The Ride Home	267

This book is dedicated to everyone who is living in the darkness and seeking the light.

CHAPTER 1: RAY AND PATTY

It was just another meaningless meeting about our company's profit margins and future, many of us thought, as we all entered the meeting room and sat in our usual chairs. It wasn't official, but we all had our own little seat at the big table and we all knew that. Best to always sit there, we knew. Little did some of us know that at this time tomorrow, some of us would not be part of this anymore. Profits were not as high as expected and a few of us would be dismissed from our employment with the company after the meeting. My manager had asked me to stay for the meeting knowing that I was taking time off that afternoon for, as far as he knew, a friend's fathers funeral in another city. I did not like lying, but in this case, it seemed warranted.

They would have never permitted me to stay if they knew I was seeking employment elsewhere. In their minds, this was a perfect haven for those seeking a successful career. Why anyone would ever want to leave this place is something they could never understand.

Entering the building this morning, before the meeting, some of us noticed the unusual amount of security at the entrance to our skyscraper. Security was always present, but today it seemed like there were more than usual and they seemed to have a purpose. Most of the time it seemed like they were just showing up and going through the motions. Sort of like the rest of us. Going through the motions.

Some of us knew what lay ahead shortly. We had been here longer.

As we all sat there and listened to our vice president, Mr. Brunner, talk about declining customers and lower profits, my mind drifted off to another place. A place where profit and loss were of no concern. Dreaming of younger days, when the almighty dollar did not rule my daily schedule as it seemed to now. I thought I always wanted to be a stockbroker. My father had continually entered that thought into my psychosis from an early age as he was a "successful" stockbroker and he wanted me to follow in his footsteps. He thought that was what was best for me. Little did he know what I thought was best for me. Nobody ever asked me, not that I would have told them.

My father, being the successful broker, always had clients over for dinner parties. This left little time for him to play catch with me or other things that I saw other fathers doing with their kids. I guess I was bred to be a stockbroker, I thought to myself. So that was the position I found myself in as I graduated from the university with honors in business and finance and took a position with his former company as one of their new eager and hungry stockbrokers.

And I was eager. Working twelve-hour days to build my clientele up and bring home more and more money as a sign of my success. Everyone seemed so proud of me, except me. But I continued on this path. It always seemed like it was my only option.

By meetings end, it was clear to all of us. Some of us would not be here anymore. I almost hoped it would be me. But my upbringing kept me from wanting this too much.
They told us those who would be let go would be notified as we left the meeting and they wished all of us continued success at their company or at their new job as this is how it had to be.

As we left the meeting room, individuals were pulled aside as they were leaving and asked to stay in the room. I started to hate this room even more so as this was going on. As I was not asked to stay, I felt a small sense of relief for myself, but I felt a stronger sense of a strange happiness for those who were going to be let go as I new they would eventually come to terms with their fate and may even find happiness in their new endeavor, which they were forced to go find. I actually felt sorry for those of us who were going to continue our employment here as it seemed so meaningless in the overall realm of life.

But monetarily profitable.

I was happy to see my group's secretary still seated at her desk when I headed to my office to pack up for the day and go on my "vacation" for a few days. Darlene was the only one in the office who knew of my real destination. A chance to move on and start over. She was like me, tired of the endless parade of fake smiles and handshakes. Tired of the profit and loss statements. Tired of the rich and richer attitude of some of the principals of the company.

She was the only one who called me Raymond, instead of Ray, since Raymond was my birth name. Raymond Daniel Rossi.

But she, like me, had bills to pay and needs which cost money. Our little secret of disgust was well disguised from all of our coworkers, as it should be. One can only trust so many in a place like this. Who knows how many others were looking to move onward. Maybe Darlene and I were the only unhappy ones. Maybe not.

She helped me pack up my briefcase as we talked about her children. One was at a young age, so she needed to be taken to a day care everyday. The other attended a local catholic school. She said the children were doing well but she always wished she could spend more time with them. Her husband, Allen, was a great guy who was a local delivery driver and knew the area well. Living in the city required them both to work. But he seemed to be able to limit it to 40 hours a week and spend time with his family. It seemed, I could never afford to do that. They were always happy together when I would see them out. No dreams of vacation homes and fancy cars were ever on his mind, I told myself. I wish they were never put into my mind.

Darlene walked me to the elevator and gave me a good luck wink as I left. Wishing me a nice trip. There's not too many like her working in this place as the elevator took me downstairs, I thought to myself. We stopped at the floor below mine and a security guard and one of the "unfortunate" ones who were just let go entered the already full elevator. All of his important belongings in one small briefcase. It seemed so pathetic. His whole life's work in a briefcase. I did not know him well, hardly at all. But I knew he had a family and this situation would undoubtedly make his life harder for awhile. I wished him well, and gave him the usual, "Let me know if there's anything I can do" line that seems to come out of everyone's mouth at times like these. What else can you say? There we were in the elevator together. Inches from each other. But all of us with our own little issues and desires, locked up inside of us. None of us willing to share our real thoughts with each other, for fear of who knows what. So close physically and yet we were like foreigners to each other just passing the day. The elevator stopped at one more floor as we descended and, as the door opened, I could see other security guards and now former employees waiting to take their last ride. Some of them were tearful, others, I could sense a feeling of relief in them just from the look on their faces. As maybe they knew it was coming.

We were to capacity already and the door just opened and closed quickly for them. Doors in life seem to open and close quickly. It seems we are afraid to go through the door sometimes because of the fear of the unknown on the other side. So much safer to close the door and stay put. I was at least going to listen to somebody about what was on the other side of the door. Maybe open the door and go, maybe stay.

I wasn't sure what I wanted.

The elevator continued its flight down to the first floor not caring about any of this.

We arrived at the first floor and filed out accordingly. Something all of us had done thousands of times here. This time seemed different. Maybe it was because of the layoffs or maybe it was because I was going to explore another door and try to see what lies beyond it. For whatever reason, it seemed different.

I exited the building and got in line for a cab with everyone else. Something I have also done many times. It seemed I got to know the cab drivers better than my own work colleagues. They weren't afraid to share their thoughts and their personal trials in life with their customers. Quite different than my coworkers. Maybe we all thought that our coworkers would use this against us one day, if we said the wrong thing about the wrong person. For whatever reason, it was always a breath of fresh air to talk to someone who had no alternative motive in our conversation but to help pass the time as he took me to my destination and then get paid for it.

As I got in the cab the weather started to change from a fairly sunny day to a cloud covered day. Nothing unusual, but I knew it would change some peoples plans for the day. Most likely the plans of the well to do at the local country clubs. I never liked golf. I never would, I thought, as I smiled at the possibility of them getting rained out.

My cabbie was a foreign man. One who I immediately recognized from the pictures of his family on the dashboard and the cross and angel he had dangling from his rearview mirror. I was never very religious; my upbringing wasn't like that. There wasn't anything to gain in that my parents thought. You can just pray at home if you want. So I, like them, avoided the churchgoers. Any church, they were all dreaming of something we could not find in our financial sheets. I would pray occasionally, most of the time for the wrong things.

His name was Miguel. He had two daughters that he sent to St. George Catholic School. I had learned this previously from him during our other conversations. His wife, Anita, cleaned rooms in the local Hilton for a living as well as donating her time to one of the churches' causes. I wondered how she could find time to do that as Miguel and I chit chatted about the local sports team and their struggles. We both agreed those over paid ballplayers did not know what a real struggle was. I was pretty sure that Darlene also sent her child to St. George School as I had purchased many raffle tickets for fund raisers for her little boy.

It seemed like a weird coincidence, that two of the people who I really enjoyed spending time with and listening to belonged to that church.

Miguel knew the fastest way to the airport and that's the way we went. It took us past the city ballfields.

After a little small talk, I asked Miguel why he always seemed so happy. It wasn't something I was used to seeing while I was at work. Somebody smiling at work usually meant somebody made a financial deal and now had much more money. How could he be so happy all the time, I wondered to myself, since driving a cab could hardly be the most profitable occupation in the world and driving in this traffic all day would make any sane man crazy. He looked in the rear-view mirror and smiled at me when I asked him that. A pure true smile, one you do not see often in others you barely know. "I enjoy meeting and helping people with their problems," he responded. "It gives me a purpose. Sometimes my riders listen to what I have to tell them, while other times, my passengers are too caught up in their struggles to pay attention. We must all learn to listen to those speaking to us," he reiterated a number of times. "Our solutions in life are usually only a few feet from us but most of the time we can't see that. We only see the bad we are experiencing, and it is hard to see the good through these bad clouds. New paths in life are always available," he said. "It is like driving to the airport. There are many routes to the airport and we just need to seek the right path."

It sure seemed to me that he should have been a psychologist. But that wasn't his style, sitting in an office with four walls surrounding you. Taking notes as someone was talking about their issues. Then sending them a bill, a rather expensive bill, just for listening to them and giving them some advice. That wasn't Miguel's style at all.

We finally were to the city park and there were a number of baseball teams practicing that afternoon, young boys and girls having fun. No agendas but to play baseball. It made me think how much I enjoyed helping out my son Ron's baseball team when he played. It was a shame I had to miss so many games of his because of late afternoon work meetings. Meetings about nothing. Things that could have waited. Not like a baseball game that was going to come and go in a blink of an eye. It made me think how often, or rather how not so often my own father would play baseball with me. There never seemed to be time. When there was time, we enjoyed playing frisbee. He would say, "Ray, grab the frisbee." My father, with such a big house and yard, was a surprisingly exceptional frisbee player. It seemed like when we were out there throwing it, he finally seemed to be looking at me as a son and a friend and truly enjoying our time together. Those were the best memories I have playing a sport with my father. Phone calls, financial news, stock markets, texts, all seemed to make those occasions few and far in between. It made me think how much I was like him in this respect as we passed the group of ultimate frisbee players enjoying the day which now seemed was going to be a rainy one as the sun had virtually disappeared and clouds covered the sky. I'll bet Miguel will never miss his daughter's baseball game, I thought to myself.

Miguel told me we would be there in ten minutes as I stared out the window at the impending rain. He always liked to have music on the radio. He would ask if that was okay as soon as a passenger would enter his cab as he would not want to offend anyone. It was either one of his CD's or an oldies station he liked. He would sing sometimes, and I couldn't help joining in occasionally when one of my favorite oldies would come on. I would even ask him to turn it up when that happened. The song, Peaceful Easy Feeling, came on as we neared the airport. It made me at ease a little as I never really did like flying but I loved the Eagles and especially that song of theirs. We both sang together for the duration of the song, not caring if anyone heard or saw us singing.

Miguel dropped me off at the airport in a rainstorm. He had an umbrella and politely made sure that neither my luggage nor I saw a drop of water. I paid my fare with a generous tip and he smiled and told me to listen to those trying to speak to me. "Remember," he said, "The birds in the sky and the animals on the ground all have food to eat and He loves us immeasurably more than them, so have no worries about those issues." Smiling, he wished me a successful trip and drove off with the music blaring from his cab. He had put on Amazing Grace and turned it up as loud as his speakers would allow him. It seemed to Ray that whenever Amazing Grace came on that Miguel would turn the volume up a notch or two and just listen. I guess he just likes listening to that one, I told myself.

It seemed he was on his way to having another nice day. Most, if not all, his days were nice, I assumed. I wondered what that would be like. Having a nice day everyday.

At this point, I wasn't sure what I was seeking from this trip besides a job interview in a city that I may not want to live in and for a company that probably would be similar to the one I was currently working at. So, what is success, I wondered. I know that I currently didn't feel successful. Too many wrong choices. Situations which make you choose the wrong answer. Either way, there I was at the airport. Seeking something I wasn't sure was out there for me anymore.

I headed in to the airport and waited in line to use the kiosk for checking myself in as I didn't have much luggage since it would be a quick trip. So many people heading somewhere, I thought, as I wondered if I was the only one seeking to make a change in their life. I doubted that though. There was probably more unhappiness floating around this place than I thought. People looking for a new path. There were so many paths to choose from.

No matter what though, I was going to look for and choose the right one this time. No matter if my father approved or not.

She knew eventually the right candidate would pop up. It was getting tiresome flying back and forth from Pittsburgh to Atlanta and then home to Dallas to manage the Pittsburgh facility since the previous manager had abruptly quit. Being in charge of a day care corporation with over 10 large day care centers in as many cities was a great job, but not when one of the managers was missing, as she would be required to fill in for him until she found the right replacement. With over 100 employees and nearly 800 hundred children to care for at each facility, the manager at each facility was an important cog in the wheel.

He had left without warning and Patty had to go there immediately that night after she found out. She knew she had to go as the staff would need direction, with a sense of calmness, and she would need to begin the process of finding the right individual for the manager's position. Every day counted. Her family understood what she had to do, but that never really made it easier for them. They accepted it, as there was really nothing they could do about it.

This was the fourth week in a row she had flown to Pittsburgh and was always happy when it was time to fly back home. She was getting tired of it, but she was always way happier flying home than flying there, and today she was heading home. So, she was happy. She never liked to waste time, being the busy executive she was. Time was the only thing we all have in life, some more than others, and she liked to use it wisely. She would keep going through the resumes in the airport and then settle into her seat on the airplane and continue to read through the resumes she had received for the position. At least she hoped she could do that. She had to do it sometime this weekend, before she flew back there again, so it might as well be on the plane. Hopefully, she thought to herself, the plane ride or rather the passenger sitting next to her will leave her alone and let her continue this process.

The four individuals she interviewed this week for the position did not give her the good vibes she likes to feel when she hires someone. Getting the wrong person will only make matters worse, she knew, so she would continue her search until the right one appeared.

She thought how lucky she was when she hired the last manager for their Denver facility. Who would have thought I would have met the right candidate on the treadmill right next to me as I worked out? Overhearing the girl's conversation, with who appeared to be a friend of hers, led us to talking in the locker room. Next thing you know, I hired her! She has been the perfect fit. So glad I was listening to their conversation at that time or I might be looking for two managers. Maybe I'll luck out again she thought as she smiled to herself while watching the children playing in the holding area for her flight. It was a private little area at the end of a long slew of flight gates. Everyone here, she thought, must be boarding this plane. It started to rain as she looked out the window and what seemed like a sunny day early in the morning had now turned to a dark cloudy rainy day. Hopefully it doesn't get worse, she thought, and my flight could get delayed.

After she rolled the ball back to the children playing together, the airport lights flickered slightly.

It would be a shame if the lights went out. Valuable work time would be seemingly wasted as she continued to read through the resumes making notes on each one as she read them.

The children were all enjoying their preflight time as a number of them had grouped together for a little fun before hand. She could tell a few of the adults were relieved they had a moments peace and did not have to keep their children occupied themselves. It could be a tiring job, she thought. Probably not as tiring as the woman caring for the girl who appeared to have cerebral palsy. A 24 hour a day job for sure she reasoned. She wondered how this woman could do this everyday of her life and not be bitter that her child wasn't a "normal" child, playing with the other kids. It made her realize even more how important it was to find the right individual to lead the Pittsburgh facility and spend as much time with her children as she could this weekend. Someone who loves children and can manage a number of adult employees would be rare to find.

It was nice to see the middle-aged man playing with the children. It didn't seem to Patty that he was responsible for any of the children, but it seemed like everyone was at ease. Nowadays, she thought to herself, one needed to keep a watchful eye on their children as there were so many predators in the world. Nothing could happen here though as many eyes were on the children. You could sense that not only the children, but the man playing with them, were all enjoying the moment as they all knew that soon they would be sitting in an airplane for an extended period of time. A number of times, while reading my resumes, I found myself handing the ball back to one of the children and a few times to the man playing with them. He was an average looking man, on the fitter side, she thought to herself. He was very nice and apologetic for intruding on my "space". I told him that I appreciated the break from what I was doing, and he seemed to understand what I was saying and smiled at me as I handed him the ball. He was the kind of guy that you could be comfortable with. I think he was having more fun than the kids.

Patty watched them all for awhile and then got a little more comfortable in her chair. She continued her resume reading as the lights flickered briefly again causing some of the younger children to scurry back to their respective adults. Everyone in the seating area seemed in awe as the clouds covered the sky in an eerie darkness but a ray of light seemed to be shining on our plane.

Boarding time was creeping up as three of the stewardesses, with their overnight luggage bags rolling quietly behind them, strolled through the waiting area. They all seemed to be in a good mood and they all seemed to know each other as they professionally walked through the gate waiting area and checked themselves in at the gate and then proceeded to enter the tunnel to the awaiting plane. They to, seemed to notice the ray of light. They were pretty ladies, one younger than the other two who seemed to be in their 40's. They had all probably been doing this for awhile. It didn't seem like too bad of a job as long as you weren't afraid of flying.

Patty looked up briefly at them as they walked back, not really paying much attention. She needed to focus on her task at hand. Find the right candidate, she thought. Keep working.

A few minutes later she overheard a young girl talking to a man who was probably her father about the stewardesses. The two of them seemed to be by themselves and he did not have a ring on his finger to signal that he was married.

Patty always wore hers as did her husband, Dylan.

She heard the little girl tell her dad that the last stewardess gave her a smile and a wink as she went by and that she recognized her from somewhere. He asked her which one it was as he, I'm sure, also watched the stewardesses go by. Why not, she thought, they were his age and were nice looking in their flying uniforms. Not checking them out would seem foolish for an unmarried gentleman or even a married man. Heck, she thought, I checked them out. It's what you do when they walk by. The little girl told him it was the fourth one. The father looked perplexed as he did not see her. I didn't either, but maybe he was looking at the newspaper and I was probably looking at boring resumes for some of the time. We probably did not see her go by. Anyway, I thought the girl looked happy about it all. Her eyes now fixed on the next resume.

CHAPTER 2: JEREMY AND EVELYN

It had been almost a year since her mother had passed away. A routine checkup led to one thing which led to another. I'll never get over how quickly she went and how hard it was preparing myself to tell our daughter that mommy was going to die shortly after we got her last prognosis.

Nothing more they could do, we were told.

Jeremy thought to himself, how relieved he was that day when Evelyn told him, "Mommy already told me daddy," as he set his newspaper down. Boarding would be starting in a few minutes for those needing assistance or those with young children. He wasn't sure if he would take advantage of the early seating due to having a young child as Evelyn had matured way beyond her years these last months and could take care of herself. Sometimes she even scared him how strong she was about losing her mother. They were so close. It was nice that the hospital let her sleep there with her mom many nights toward the end. It was hard for all of us, but it seemed so much harder for me than the two of them.

We couldn't all sleep there, so I would leave Evelyn there and go home to sleep myself as I had to continue working. Life goes on and bills needed to be paid. It's a cruel part of life. Debbie knew that, and always said when I left for the night that she would see me after my work. "Take your time," she would say with a smile. "I'll be here one way or another," as she winked at Evelyn. She knew I loved her deeply and she tried to prepare me as much as possible for the inevitable end.

It would never be enough, I thought.

Evelyn began reading religious books while she was at the hospital. There was a pastor that would visit everyone on the floor every few days. Evelyn and he had gotten close, Debbie told me. It was special for her. He would spend time with her and read books to her. Her eyes would light up when he came to visit, and they would light up even more when it was time for him to go. It was like she knew she would see him again, no matter what. He couldn't stay forever in our room, but he spent many hours with her. Her books were many, but Evelyn enjoyed her book called "Heaven" the most. She would read it to her mom almost daily. They were both so happy together when they read that book.

I didn't really care for it that much. Heaven seemed like such a far away place. I prayed constantly when she was first diagnosed, but it never seemed to help. It was hard for me to dream nice things anymore and I gave up praying. But if it made them feel good, the more Heaven book reading the better.

I didn't enjoy driving past the cemetery where she was put to rest. It was just a constant reminder of what I thought was the unfairness of it all. Our house location and my place of employment made it so that I would have to drive past it daily. It seemed to fuel my anger with this harsh reality on each occasion. I used to play music on the way to work every day. A happy drive, as I enjoyed my occupation and loved my family. Now days, it was a quiet somber ride to work. It was how I wanted it to be from now on.

Nobody likes to think about their last days. Best not to. Life is for the living I always thought anymore as she was gone now.

It didn't seem to bother Evelyn. She would always coax me into stopping there for a short time once in awhile. She would keep her gravesite free of weeds and such and I would wait in the car. I would tell her I would have to check my text messages from work and she would just smile and tell me that it was okay. "Mommy understands and I will tell her you said 'Hi'," she would tell me. When she came back into the car, there was never a tear in her eye. My eyes would always be tearful as I saw her talking to her mother at Debbie's grave. I would have to wipe them dry before she got back in the car. It all seemed so unfair, but Evelyn was happier when we left, every time, so I did not mind.

I would ask her how her mom was doing, and she would tell me that, "Mommy is doing good and is enjoying heaven." When I asked her what heaven was like, she told me that it is, "however you want it to be." "There were angels everywhere," she said, "They help mommy and us." It was definitely a result of all the pastor's books on heaven, I figured, and it was better than her crawling into a "shell" of a life as I had done and wanted to do.

She would wave to the sky every time we left Debbie's gravesite. Every time.

Evelyn's favorite necklace was never far from her neck. Her mother had walked to the hospital store with her one of those days when I was at work and purchased it there. She never took it off. It was a necklace with an angel charm on it. Her mother told me that a nice lady behind the counter had suggested it when she asked her about a nice lasting gift for our daughter. Debbie said the lady also had one of the angel necklaces around her neck. The lady had a special way about her when she met Evelyn. It seemed the two of them had known each other before, Debbie told me.

The pastor had blessed it when he came up one morning and since then Evelyn never took it off. It wasn't gaudy; a simple little figurine on a chain, but it seemed to mean much more to Debbie and Evelyn. I told her it was beautiful as any father would have.

When I got the call at work to head to the hospital, it was over before I got there.

Evelyn met me in the hallway as I approached Debbie's room. She was holding her favorite nurse's hand – Maggie was her name. She was Debbie's favorite too, sometimes staying after her shift ended to spend time with them. There seemed to be tears in everyone's eyes in the nurse's area besides Evelyn's. She was sad, I could tell, and her eyes were red, but she was done crying. She held my hand as the doctor told me that she had been in no pain and that she passed away with our daughter holding her hand.

I always knew it could be anytime, but one can never be prepared for this. We had talked the night before and Debbie told me she had a peaceful feeling about everything. She told me to listen, and to be happy, as I kissed her goodbye that night.

I didn't think it was going to be our last. It was going to be so hard to be happy again.

Evelyn walked with me into the room and the doctor closed the door behind him as he left the room, so that the three of us could be together. I couldn't help but cry as Evelyn bravely held my hand in one of her hands and she clung to her angel necklace in the other. Evelyn told me mommy's last words were that she loved us both so much and that it was time to go, but she said that she would always, always be with us and would see us again. She wanted us to be happy and enjoy our lives until that time. She would be watching us.

It hurt so much that it was hard to pay attention to Evelyn.

The nurses came in after we opened the door and expressed their condolences to both of us. So many of them gave Evelyn hugs of love that for a moment I was spared of my sorrow. They had all gotten to know her "little angel" since she was there so often. Debbie started calling her that after Evelyn began wearing the necklace. It made my little girl and my wife happy, so I was good with it. I didn't call her that myself as it was hard for me to believe in angels anymore. A good angel would have cured her before this moment, I thought, so it was just hard for me to say.

The pastor came in shortly after and gave my daughter a big hug. We said a prayer together. I prayed with them, but wasn't sure why. He took a walk with Evelyn after we briefly talked. It was nice seeing her hold his hand as they exchanged smiles. I thought to myself that she would miss seeing him as we would not be coming back anymore. It was hard for me to imagine how often this scene has played out in his life. I'll never know what they talked about. Maybe it's best, I imagined. When they came back Evelyn held my hand for awhile as we both sat there.

The pastor had told Evelyn to take a few books home with her, so when we left she took her favorite book, "Heaven," with her. She said it was her mommy's favorite. She kept it in her knapsack everywhere we went, and she signed her name in the front cover so everyone would know that it was her book.

I talked to the nurses a little to understand the process to move forward from here and Evelyn and I left the hospital that day together knowing that it was just the two of us anymore.

She read her book to herself as we drove home.

Evelyn was having fun with the other children playing some type of soccer game when the preboarding announcement came over the loudspeaker. All of the children ran back to their parents and most of them headed to the restroom for one last visit before we would head off on our airplane ride. Evelyn said she was okay at the moment and sat down next to me.

It was our first flight together, just Evelyn and me. We were ready for a vacation and I wondered if she was going to be okay on the flight. Her bright attitude even in the midst of a gloomy day outside made me and others feel good. I was hoping I would meet this other stewardess. I always liked those who would bring a smile to her face. But it seemed she was always happy. Me, not so much. But I had told myself that I would enjoy this trip no matter what and go along with whatever she wanted me to do. No questions asked.

I decided, why not, as the preboarding began on the plane. Everyone let the mother caring for the handicapped girl go first. She sure had her hands full. It was good to see another passenger helping her with her luggage as she needed both her arms and hands to support her daughter as they walked to the counter. I wondered how she did it as we got in line in front of another gentleman and his little son. His son was a little older than Evelyn. He was wearing a baseball cap, but he appeared to be bald and I thought maybe he had cancer or some other unfair disease. Evelyn and he were having a good time together as we waited in line to head to the plane.

CHAPTER 3: AARON AND JOEY

Aaron had been living on edge for the last three weeks, and he wasn't sure how much more he could take. It seemed like every time he finally began to steady himself, something would come careening into him and send him teetering once again on the precipice of the unknown. It all truly started months ago, when he started experiencing severe back pains. He couldn't sleep, he couldn't concentrate on his work, and the pains didn't go away. He tried visiting chiropractors, using heating pads, and taking mild pain relievers, but nothing seemed to do the trick.

When Aaron couldn't take it anymore, he scheduled an appointment with his doctor and tried to get to the bottom of the issue and the result was far from anything he had expected. As it turned out, he had a malignant tumor on his spine that was causing the pain. The real name of his condition was schwannoma neurofibrosarcoma, but nobody knew what that meant and neither did Aaron. All he knew was that this wasn't supposed to happen to him. At 32, Aaron assumed that he still had most of his life ahead of him. He ate well, was in decent shape, and had no family history of cancer or anything else serious.

And yet, there he was, starting the chemotherapy process. There was no time to truly digest what was going on; the last three weeks had been a whirlwind. His friends were all absolutely certain he would beat the cancer – even though, realistically, his chances were about the same as a coin flip. His doctor put him in touch with a therapist that was supposed to help him cope with everything going on in his life, but the therapist was younger than he was and quite inexperienced. The therapy sessions felt more like training for his therapist than sessions designed to help him. Who was helping who?

At this point, Aaron was tired of everyone telling him he would be ok. It was all he heard from anyone, but nobody could be sure what would happen. The chemotherapy might work, or it might not and the cancer could metastasize. Everything he cared about suddenly seemed so inconsequential. The food he ate, the sports teams he rooted for, his job, and the television shows he watched every week all lost their meaning. How could he worry or care about those things when looking mortality directly in the eyes?

The worst part was that the chemotherapy made it feel like the cancer was winning. He had only been to one session so far, but he came away from it feeling incredibly tired and nauseous. He was told the rest period between chemotherapy sessions helped his body build up new healthy cells, but Aaron felt like it just gave the cancer more time to wreak havoc on his body. Aaron knew that he would also lose his hair before long, which would only make him feel worse and his friends and coworkers pity him more.

Aaron's first chemotherapy session did not go as planned. Shelley was supposed to drive him, but their recent falling out meant that he'd have to get there himself. None of his friends were able to get off of work to take him or to be there for moral support, so it was just going to be a few long, terrible hours of isolation. Aaron hated going to the doctor, even for a checkup, so going to get chemotherapy was quite overwhelming. He had so many questions. Would it hurt? Was he going to get nauseous? Would his hair start falling out after just the first session?

He knew that his friends couldn't take off work whenever he needed them to, but Aaron couldn't help but feel betrayed as he got into his car and began the trip to the hospital. Though he knew his neighborhood well, Aaron hated driving in the city. Pittsburgh was a hectic mass of bridges and roads that made navigation much more difficult than it needed to be. Shelley usually gave him rides when she could because he really did not like driving, so Aaron was apprehensive as soon as his car left the driveway.

In order to put off going to chemotherapy just a little bit longer, Aaron made a pit stop at the corner store down the road. He had been coming to this place – One Stop, it was called – ever since he moved to his apartment. It was quite rundown; it almost looked abandoned if you passed it after hours. But, true to its name, it had everything Aaron typically needed if he found himself in a pinch. Today, he wandered the aisles, keenly aware of how much time he could waste without being late for his appointment. Nothing looked appetizing to him, but that was just par for the course these days.

In the end, Aaron grabbed a pack of sunflower seeds and a Snapple, unsure of whether or not he would actually have the stomach for them. He made his way to the counter to see Shirley, who owned the store with her husband. Shirley was a squat, old woman who looked like she could have retired years ago. Even so, she was always polite and made sure to ask Aaron how he was doing.

"Is that all for today, Aaron?" she asked as he put the sunflower seeds and Snapple on the counter.

Aaron wasn't really in the mood for talking, so he just nodded.

"Now what's the matter? Usually you're so talkative, but you've hardly said a word these last few weeks," Shirley said.

"Oh, it's nothing," Aaron replied. He didn't want to pollute their typical small talk with his big problems. People like to ask what's wrong, but they are never truly prepared for someone to respond with the truth.

"I'm not sure if I believe you," said Shirley. "Tell you what – the girls and I will say a prayer for you tonight."

She gestured to the portrait of three angels she kept on the wall behind the counter. It had clearly been there for decades. The picture itself had yellowed over time, and the glass casing hadn't been given a good cleaning for much too long.

"Thanks, Shirley," Aaron said, not believing it would help but appreciating the sentiment nevertheless.

He got back into his car and threw the sunflower seeds and Snapple into his passenger seat, not bothering to open them, and finally started toward the hospital.

Aaron parked with a few minutes to spare, but he didn't get out of the car right away. Despite the anger and resentment he felt toward Shelley and his friends at the moment, he still would've given anything to have someone there with him. He didn't see how anyone could feel at home in a hospital.

He didn't know whose job it was to decorate the waiting rooms, but they clearly didn't understand the definition of comfortable. The whole place felt overly sanitized, and the bright white walls and pastel colors of the furniture were not inviting in the slightest. Aaron sat on the edge of his chair as he waited for his name to be called, acutely aware of the room being slightly too warm for his liking.

Now that he was there, everything felt very real to Aaron. There's a difference between knowing you have a malignant tumor and actually getting treated for it. He didn't know what to expect, but he knew chemotherapy could be brutal. After all, it's designed to kill a disease before that disease can kill you; there's no way it could be anything but vicious.

Aaron looked around at the others in the waiting room, who he assumed were all there for similar reasons. His heart sank as he observed some of the others. It was quite easy to tell which of them were deep into chemotherapy and which ones were just starting out. It wasn't just hair loss – some of these people looked frail and despondent. Despite all of this, some of them were smiling and chatting with one another as if they were in good spirits. This made Aaron think back to something his therapist had said to him: "Your attitude can help control this process. Your feelings follow your thoughts, and your feelings can impact how your body responds."

Were these people just kidding themselves? Were they trying to help beat the cancer into submission with positive thinking? Or were they truly happy? Aaron didn't really believe that crap. Medicine either worked or it didn't, and his feelings about it wouldn't control that outcome.

Looking around at the others in the waiting room also made Aaron a little jealous. Almost everyone there was not alone as the receptionist called out "Joey Chandler." Whether it was a significant other, a family member, a friend, or some combination of them all, just about everyone seemed to have someone to help them through this process. Even those that didn't seemed to be friendly with the others there. Aaron halfheartedly hoped that someone would talk to him, bring them into the fold of a conversation, and help take his mind off of what was about to happen. Another part of Aaron wanted to be left alone.

"Aaron Phillips," the receptionist called, pulling Aaron out of his mopey thoughts and back into the waiting room.

He inhaled sharply and deeply as he got up, his whole body tingling with anticipation and fear of what was to come. Aaron was finally about to learn what chemotherapy was all about. In his mind, he pictured big needles and a lot of pain. Now that he was there, Aaron wished he had read up more on what the process was like and how it impacted his body. He was given pamphlets that outlined everything, and his therapist had prompted him to talk about his fears leading up to his first session, but he shunned all of that. Instead of accepting that it was inevitable, he had chosen to act as if ignoring it would somehow make things easier. Turns out he was wrong.

He was shuffled down a hallway, all of these negative thoughts running repeatedly through his mind like some sort of endless infomercial. Everywhere he looked, hospital staff passed, each worker with their own agenda. They all avoided making eye contact with Aaron as he passed. It was strange, he thought. How was anyone supposed to feel confident in these people – or comforted by them – if they couldn't even look patients in the eyes?

Then, suddenly, he did catch the eye of someone. A woman around his age who was wearing nurse's scrubs was looking at him, and he sensed recognition in her welcoming green eyes. For a moment, Aaron stared back, wondering why her face seemed so familiar. She was thin, with long blonde hair loosely pulled back into a bun. Her square jaw and small, buttonlike nose framed her face well, as did the well-worn smile lines etched around her lips.

Immediately, Aaron's mind cast back to the last time he'd seen that face, almost 15 years before. He was in high school at the time – a senior. It was the end of the year, the end of his time at that school, and he was cleaning out his locker. Over the course of the year, notes and old reports had piled up inside his locker, but now he was cleaning it all out. He didn't plan on keeping any of it, but he couldn't help but look at everything as he pulled it out. Despite his eagerness to move on to college, he had a strong case of nostalgia as he looked through everything he'd accumulated over the course of the school year.

As he examined an old report on "1984" by George Orwell, he reached with his spare hand to pull something else out of his locker. The book he pulled must have loosened a bunch of junk in his overcrowded locker, and almost everything came spilling out before he could even begin to stop it. He must have looked pathetic, he thought, scrambling to try to catch it all before it hit the ground.

When he bent down to start picking up the books, pens, papers, and other junk, he realized he wasn't alone. Next to him was a girl with shockingly green eyes; she was smiling at him and wordlessly started helping him pick up his stuff. Aaron recognized her as a junior he had study hall with. She was very pretty, but their social circles didn't overlap, and he had never had an actual conversation with her. It took him a second to realize she had said something to him.

"Sorry?" he said, having not heard her.

"I asked if you were going to Paul Canter's end of the year party this weekend," she repeated, blushing slightly.

"Oh," Aaron remembered saying. "Yeah, I was planning on it. You?"

"Mhmm," she nodded. "Maybe I'll see you there?"

And before Aaron could say anything else, she got up, turned on the spot, and went back to her friends down the hall. Aaron was supposed to go to that party with a few friends, but he was relying on one of them to drive; he didn't have his own car at the time. However, that weekend, his friends decided to go to a different party. Aaron didn't mind, and he had a good time, but a small part of him had been hoping to run into that girl again.

Her name was Kate, he was pretty sure. She looked exactly the same, except for some small changes that could only be attributed to the passing of almost 15 years. He wanted to say something to her, but what do you say to someone you hadn't seen in such a long time? He didn't know where to start, but they smiled at each other as they passed. She looked busy, anyway, just like everyone else there, and he didn't want to get her in trouble by slowing her down.

He had mixed feelings about seeing her there. On one hand, he felt oddly comforted to have seen a somewhat familiar face there. It humanized the whole experience for him, in a way. Everyone there was doing their best and they were all there to help, even if they wouldn't make eye contact like Kate did. On the other hand, Aaron felt slightly embarrassed. He didn't like the attention cancer brought him. Everyone treated him differently, almost as if he was fragile. The less people that knew, the better.

That memory and all of those accompanying thoughts coursed through his mind in the short amount of time it took to catch Kate's eye and pass her in the hallway.

Eventually, he made it to where he was being led and he was given an option. If he wanted, he could receive chemotherapy in a private room, apart from everyone else. Or he could receive it in a larger room with some others. As much as Aaron didn't want to be seen, he was also afraid to be alone for this. Perhaps if a friend was able to be there for him, he would've opted for the more personal space. They say misery loves company, so Aaron decided to be miserable with everyone else for his first session.

However, as Aaron was hooked up and prepared to receive the chemo, he noticed that he was the only one feeling – or at least outwardly showing – misery. There were four others in the room, all in oversized chairs that were spread out evenly. Each chair had curtains around it that could be drawn for some privacy, but the other four people there had theirs open and they were chatting.

His nurse, who had introduced herself as Chelsea, ran some tests before she got started. He knew she was just doing her job, but she seemed a little robotic in the way she spoke. She had clearly given this talk hundreds of times before, and it almost made her seem emotionless, even if that wasn't really the case. Aaron supposed it was best for nurses and other hospital employees to not get too attached to patients, lest it interfere with their work, but he still disliked how formal everything was.

Chelsea told him that he might feel a mild warmth or burning from the medicine and not to be alarmed, as that was quite normal. She also said that it was common to feel lightheaded or tired during chemotherapy, and that many patients spend at least part of their session sleeping. While Aaron thought that didn't sound so bad, she also communicated to him that the worst part of it comes afterward.

And it turned out Chelsea was correct in that regard. He spent much of his session in silence, either sleeping or just observing the room around him. A few of the others receiving the chemo finished up and more took their place, all of them politely saying hello, but none really engaged with Aaron. It felt to Aaron like he was the new student back in grade school: He received a lot of curious looks, and a lot of people introduced themselves to him, but he didn't have a full conversation with anyone. Part of him wanted to talk to them and to perhaps make some friends – it would certainly make these sessions less lonely – but the rest of him didn't see the point. Perhaps it was the medicine making him lethargic, but he didn't see the point in putting energy into relationships at a hospital where everyone was potentially dying. If he felt alone now, he couldn't imagine what it would be like if he suddenly had a few new friends die.

Aaron left chemotherapy feeling about the same as he did on his way in, and the rest of the day was uneventful for him. He was told that the aftereffects of chemo would hit him hard, so he waited in anticipation as he ate dinner, watched TV, and got ready for bed. As soon as he thought he might have avoided some sort of side effect, Aaron was yanked from a pleasant dream and thrust himself into his master bathroom. His mouth filled with excess saliva and his stomach squirmed beneath his hands. He barely had time to lift the lid of his toilet before he was expelling the remains of his microwave dinner into it.

His stomach heaved again and again, as if it was trying to regurgitate meals it has long since digested. Aaron didn't know how long he had been bent over the porcelain, but it seemed like it was never going to stop. Once his body had decided there was no use in trying to cough up any more bile, he collapsed to the cool tile of the floor, sweaty and out of breath. So this is what they meant, he thought. This is what he had to look forward to for the foreseeable future? He didn't know if he could go through with it.

After he calmed himself down and dried himself off, Aaron tried to get some sleep. It had come so easy to him when he initially got into bed, but now he couldn't seem to keep his eyes closed. His body ached, either from the chemo or from selling Buicks to his toilet bowl. He was afraid to take Tylenol or anything else to help him get to sleep for fear that it would trigger another session in the bathroom, so he just lay there for hours, unsure of what else to do.

It wasn't until the pale light of the early morning started to seep in through the curtains that he was able to nod off. The birds had awoken and started to chirp, but his body finally decided it was exhausted enough to submit to some much-needed sleep.

Perhaps the worst part of it all was that he was taking a taxi to the airport today because his girlfriend decided she needed some space. Aaron and Shelley had been dating for almost two years without a hitch, and the first bump in the road disintegrated what they had within the first few weeks. Aaron felt alone everywhere he went – home, work, therapy, you name it. Even at the airport, surrounded by thousands of people, Aaron felt alone. All of the children were too young to know this sort of pain or to understand their own mortality, Aaron thought. Everyone older than him suddenly seemed lucky, too. He had no idea if he would even live to see his next birthday.

This sense of supreme loneliness was the reason Aaron was at the airport in the first place. When Shelley told him she needed her space, Aaron broke down, feeling like he had lost the last person in his life that could be a foundation to cling to. He simply couldn't deal with his problems alone. Luckily, he had plenty of vacation and sick time at his job, so he was able to take some time to get away. Although he couldn't say he had the best relationship with her, Aaron decided to go home and visit his mother. She was so overbearing that he actually contemplated not telling her about his cancer for fear that she would move into his apartment with him, but now he realized that he did need her. She was probably the only person who would be more worried about this situation than Aaron.

The airport made Aaron uncomfortable, but so did most crowded places these days. The abundance of talking and laughter, as well as just the sheer number of people, made these places seem so full of life. Walking through the airport, Aaron almost felt like he was a cancer cell among many healthy cells. He felt contagious, as if he could pass on his condition to anyone at any time. He knew these thoughts were irrational, but they frequently popped into his head nevertheless.

Aaron guessed that most people in the airport were going on vacation, traveling for work, or else moving forward with their lives as they should. He felt like he was one of the few – perhaps the only one – who was taking a step back. Instead of being independent, he was heading home to his mom so she could comfort him. His mom would tell him there's no shame in that, that nobody ever stopped needing their parents.

CHAPTER 4: JOHN AND FATHER FEENEY

It was a long week for John, burying a son is something nobody should have to endure.

A call from his sons' workplace was his initial notice of the accident. The local authorities must have noticed, from something in his car, the name of his workplace and that led them to me.

He was driving to work as he had done many times before, John imagined. Probably the same route every day. Just like the rest of us on our ride from home to work.

One missed red light by a young girl eager to answer her meaningless text and "Boom", Kevin's life ended in an instant. I prayed it was quick, as I couldn't pray for anything else. It was over. The accident happened. He was gone. She was still alive, her name was Alice McGregor, he knew from the police report. But his son was gone. He had a strong sense of hate and anger for this girl named Alice.

There was nothing any of the emergency personnel could do. He died instantly, the coroner had told me. At least he didn't suffer they said.

All of the suffering was going to be on my shoulders, I knew, when I had met with the authorities that day to discuss what had happened. I was sure I would be suffering for the rest of my life.

I'm not sure which trip would be worse. The trip to Pittsburgh to arrange for his burial and take care of all the other numerous tasks which needed to be attended to or this flight back home to Atlanta which would never happen again as I would never be back to Pittsburgh and see a ballgame with my son.

His apartment and furniture, all of the banking institutions and such all needed to be addressed accordingly. Bills would have to be paid and utilities closed. It was an endless array of tasks that had to be finalized.

Every time I called or personally had to attend to a matter, it seemed I had to relive what had happened to my son. They meant no harm. It was just something we would talk about as we ended the business transaction that my son had set up for his everyday life.

I will always remember the older manager lady at the bank he used. Her name was Angela Brown. She had read about the accident and loss of life in the paper, I imagined, and she needed no background story. A Christian lady, I could tell, from the items on her desk. A nice picture of her and an older lady in a wheelchair seemed to be her favorite picture as it was upfront of all the other pictures. She had everything ready for me when I arrived that day to end his accounts there. She had told me to come in anytime as she knew this was a trying time for me.

Boy was she right about that.

We talked about my son and his life. She listened intently to my words as I told her about him and the things he had accomplished in his life.

Kevin was an engineer and enjoyed complex problems. He had worked at the same place for over five years and it gave me a sense of peace that he would be able to take care of himself and be a good citizen. He must do a good job, I thought. I wish, I would have told him more how proud I was of him because of this. He seemed "bugged" about it when I would say that, so I didn't say it anymore to him.

There were many things I now wished I had said to him the last time we talked.

I told her that Kevin acted as a big brother to two young men, LeVon and James, who had no father. He surprised me one day when I came to visit him and the four of us went to a Pirates game together. He had never mentioned it before that day. The boys and him were a good fit, I thought, as I remembered that day at the ballpark. They were both black boys and my son was a white man, so it was always interesting, John thought. He would see them once a week he had told me previously. I could tell the boys loved my son. I was proud of Kevin that day.

I told Angela that I had just come from their place. They were staying at an institution that housed these young men with no homes. They had already been told about the accident by the facilities personnel, so I knew I didn't have to be the bearer of bad news. We talked and cried together, I told Angela.

There would be three of us suffering for awhile over this tragedy. The good thing for them was that they were young and time heals all, they say. I wasn't sure if I would ever heal from this, I told Angela, as it seemed she wanted me to talk about it all and no one else could hear as her office door was closed. I was sure there wasn't enough time in my life to heal.

After signing the appropriate documents and such, and after my outpouring of my son's life, it was time to go. I felt comfortable talking to her. My wife had died years ago, so it would just be me now. So, it was nice to have someone to talk to. At least for a brief moment in time. Angela assured me that all of the banking issues would be directly taken care of by her and there was no need to be concerned about any of these matters. Every little bit helps at this time, I knew, so I was appreciative of her words. Plus, I believed her.

As I got up to leave, Angela presented me with a little wrapped box. She told me it was just a little something to help with the days that lay ahead of me. She also told me to listen to those speaking to me. They might be sitting right next to you. There are people out there who care about others. I shook her hand to say goodbye, but she embraced me with a hug instead. I needed a hug. It was really the first one I had received since hearing the news. I could sense the sorrow in her heart as we embraced.

I put the box in my briefcase and left to attend to the next matter at hand. I would open it later, I thought, as I got into my rented vehicle and drove away. I hated my phone anymore as I knew this kind of device had played a role in my son's death and that I would no longer receive any texts or phone calls from him. My common sense kept me from throwing it out the window as I knew I would need it.

The funeral was over so quick. It seems that we come into this life quickly and we leave even faster.

I cried often this past week. I couldn't control myself. It would take every last bit of strength that I had to not cry on the plane ride home. I would just have to think of something else or maybe try to read a book.

But I couldn't concentrate enough to read a book, so I just sat there in my seat at the gate looking out the window, wondering why this had to happen as the clouds started to block out the sun's rays and would soon fill the sky with darkness.

As I watched the children playing in the open space at the gate area it made it harder for me to keep from crying, so I moved to another portion of the seating area where happiness seemed to be missing. It would be so hard now and it hurt too much to watch them play as Kevin and I had done so often in his early years. I would never be the same. I knew that for sure.

The box from Angela was still in my briefcase, but I didn't want to open it here. I would wait until another time or maybe never I thought. What could she wrap in a small box that would give me any peace for what I would have to endure?

My little corner in the gate area was a little darker than the other seating areas. One of the lights that had flickered never came back on. So, it was nice for me. I wanted to be in a dark place by myself. I was tired of retelling my son's fate and why I was on this plane ride. I didn't really think anyone cared. Except for maybe Angela. In my heart I knew she cared. But, she could only do so much, we both knew. Kevin was gone, and I was still around to trudge through my daily life without him. My life seemed more meaningless now, I thought to myself.

I sat back in my chair and continued to watch the clouds roll in as I noticed an opening in them allowing the sunlight to cast its glory on our plane. It wasn't long before my dimly lit area had a few more customers looking for a quiet corner to sit. For whatever reason, we all seemed to want to be by ourselves.

For whatever reason.

I couldn't imagine anyone else having a better reason than me.

I wondered why the priest sat in this area. Maybe, I thought to myself, he wanted peace and quiet so he could read his bible or pray for something. Maybe he didn't like the commotion of the children playing in the other areas or the seemingly drunk guy stumbling around flirting with the young girls. He sat down a few seats from me, leaving a few seats in between us so as not to get too close. There was no sense in sharing my story with him. He has probably seen and heard too many stories like this in his time as he appeared to be in his fifties.

He politely said "Hi" to me and sat down slowly. We both seemed worn out and it felt good to just sit there.

After thirty-two years of priesthood, one would have thought, I didn't need any more training. They sent me to the conference in Pittsburgh, anyway, against my subtle suggestions that we could save money by keeping me here in Atlanta and attending to my duties at our church instead. God knows it's a never-ending job. Let one of the younger priests go, I even suggested to no avail. The bishop, I was told, thought that it would be an enlightening trip for me. Tell Father Feeney to, "listen to what they have to say," the bishop had said to his assistant. I was still waiting to be enlightened as I sat down in a seat in a quieter section of the gate area.

It was obvious that I was a priest. Who could mistake my black wardrobe with my little white neck collar. Sometimes I thought in jest, it would be better to be dressed in white with a black collar. But I guessed that would look too gaudy. After the first few weeks, many years ago, I got used to wearing this outfit.

There was never a doubt about what I did for a living. But, after so many years, it was a wonder that I was still unsure about my own faith and if I really did help others seek God. So many confessions. So many funerals. So many instances of pain and remorse. It had been wearing on me for some time now. I had prayed for enlightenment at the conference but it did not seem to appear to me quite yet and I was almost home. Listen to him speaking to you, they told us at the conference. I couldn't hear anything anymore it seemed.

Not like when I was younger. I listened and knew my direction at an early age. It seemed like this is what I was meant to do since I was in high school. The years went by fast and next thing I knew I was the pastor of a small church in Atlanta, Blessed Sacrament Church. We didn't have a huge cathedral of a church. It was old and small, but charming. The church was located in an old Italian and Polish area and the members were all wonderful people.

There would always be good times and bad times, I knew, but sometimes I thought my faith was weakening. It was not my faith in God.

It was more my faith in the knowledge that I was actually making a difference in our members' lives. They all seemed to pay attention intently as I delivered my weekly sermons, but due to my own feelings, I wasn't sure if they were actually listening to me. Were we all going through the motions of just going to church because that's what we were trained to do or were we there because we have faith. Sometimes I wasn't sure anymore.

Enlightenment, yes that's what I needed. But I didn't find it at the conference. I would try to listen more though, maybe I just wasn't paying attention anymore I reasoned to myself as I relaxed in my chair after saying "Hello" to a few of the people seated in my area.

A little girl, whose name she told me was Evelyn, came over to say hi to me as the ball she was playing with rolled close to me. She told me about the priest, who dressed just like me, who read to her at the hospital where her mother had passed away. She wasn't quite sure where in Pittsburgh his church was. She showed me her little angel necklace and told me how she talks to her mother and still listens to what she tries to tell her. I could sense her belief and honesty and could see her radiant smile when she showed me her angel necklace.

She told me angels have helped her mommy now that she was in heaven and that they also want to help us here on earth if we listen to them. Her mother told her to keep telling her father to listen, she said. The girl seemed to know that her father, maybe did not believe in heaven and angels as much as her, if at all. I would have liked to have met the priest at the hospital as he left a lasting impression on this little girl. He might have been the enlightenment which I desperately seemed to need.

She scurried away to play with her friends as quick as she came over.

It almost seemed like she should have been my enlightenment. A little girl who believes in angels and heaven. I just couldn't see that thought, though. I thought my enlightenment would be coming from some scholar. Somebody schooled on faith.

I thought to myself, after she left, how it must have felt for the little girl when her mother had passed away. It was a feeling I probably could never know. My parents were both alive, old, but alive. Having to deal with such a situation at an early age would seem to be tragic to me, I thought. She sure seemed to be happy though. That was what was important.

I didn't like to read while sitting in an airport. Even though I never flew much, I knew there would be too much commotion. So, I had purchased a newspaper and was glancing at the headlines occasionally as I mainly watched our gate area slowly fill up with other passengers.

There seemed to be an endless array of different individuals and ages on this flight.

The group of girls, most likely in their mid to late twenties, seemed to be heading on vacation somewhere together. They were all dressed in their summer beach wardrobes and were chatting away with each other closer to the check in area. It had been decades since I went on a vacation like that with friends of mine. My vacations anymore seemed to be quiet affairs. But they were enjoyable. The girls were loud, but not obnoxiously loud. They were just young and happy. They should be enjoying this trip, I thought to myself.

The obviously drunk gentleman was having fun trying to flirt with the girls. He was much older than them. The girls knew he was harmless and seemed to enjoy his attention.
I wondered why a man would want to drink so much before taking this flight. I had seen so many lives damaged by the after affects of alcoholism. Families torn apart. Jobs lost. Children ashamed. It was a terrible disease. Sort of like cancer. I'm sure cancer can be a slow disease also. It would start small just like alcoholism and after so long would just consume oneself with its emptiness. I couldn't cure the world, I knew, so I just said a quick prayer to myself for him and his family, if he had one.

The children playing seemed to be having the most fun. They were all so vibrant and quick. One little boy with a Pirate baseball cap on seemed to be a little slower and more cautious than the others. Maybe he just wasn't feeling good today. They didn't seem to mind the rain which seemed to be coming.

Unfortunately, not all the children were so vibrant. There was a girl who seemed to be in her teens that appeared to have cerebral palsy. She was there with whom I assumed to be her mother. They had gotten there a little after me and I noticed them because they were brought here on one of the little cab carts as she could not walk herself. Her mother had supported her from behind as they got out of the cart with the help of the airline employee and slowly walked her over to a seat close to the window. It seemed like such a struggle just to get her from the cart to a seat in the waiting area. A gentleman had walked over to help her with her luggage once the cab stopped in our area. It brought a smile from the lady's face when he offered to help. After sitting the girl in the seat, the man and woman talked for awhile while the girl seemed to enjoy the window scene with the planes coming and going in the distance. The woman gave him a quick hug for his help and he continued to play with the children a little until he sat down by himself.

I often wondered why these things happen. One child born "perfect" and another with some type of disability. It was a cruel disease. Cerebral Palsy. The girl, I'm sure required 24/7 care and didn't appear to be able to do much herself. But she would smile at her mom occasionally when she saw something she liked outside. She smiled when she saw her mom hug the gentleman who helped her. I wondered if she knew he was being nice or if it was just a random facial expression of hers. Anyway, it was always a mystery to me how some of us were luckier than others. I didn't try to ever figure it out, because there was no solution. It was just life.

Maybe, for all I knew, the girl was happier than the rest of us. Anything is possible with God I thought so I did not dwell on it.

Other adults were working away on their laptops and such, while others like me just sat there, enjoying watching all of the people.

CHAPTER 5: PHYLLIS AND CHARLENE

He introduced himself as Ray, when he quickly rushed over to help me get my carry-on luggage off of the cart and over to a comfortable location for Charlene and I. Our taxi driver appreciated this as he helped me get Charlene out of the cab. With so many people needing assistance, he drove away after giving Charlene a quick hug and he told me to have a peaceful trip. Charlene smiled. Not too many people ever wanted to get too close to Charlene, or I, as her mumblings and overall features would frighten many people. It was just easier for them not to get involved and I knew that.

I remembered when Gil, my husband, had passed away, and my very small circle of friends would ask me how I was going to get through all of this as they knew taking care of Charlene was a major effort.

"Phyllis," they would say, "maybe it's time to take her somewhere where she could be taken care of by others." They meant well. But I could never do that to "my little angel."

I stopped trying to figure out why Charlene was born with cerebral palsy, many years ago. It had bothered Gil more than me at first, but he eventually got over it. The stares from other children and adults was just the way it was going to be. Most people just didn't know what to say when they would meet the three of us. It's not like you could ask if Charlene liked sports or played a musical instrument. So, it was always awkward for everyone. We knew that and would always take everything in stride.

We were going to visit my sister and her family for awhile as we had not flown anywhere in years. I was glad the airline was very accommodating to us once we arrived at the airport.

Peter had always been there for us once Gil had passed. His wife had passed away a few years before Gil and we knew them from our neighborhood. He only lived a few houses down from us and would help me with anything I ever needed. A nice-looking man about my age. Always smiling, he was. Charlene enjoyed it when he would take her on short walks down the street. She would smile and look around as he did this, giving me time to prepare the next meal, do laundry or just sit and relax for a few minutes.

Sometimes, I thought to myself, he kept me going more than I would ever let on. I liked him, Charlene liked him, and he liked us. It was only me who kept things from getting too close. A boyfriend would just never seem to work for me, I always thought. Charlene needed me and there was no room for anyone else in my life.

Peter had driven us to the airport and would pick us up on our return flight. As we pulled into the unloading area at the airport, he took care of making sure that we were properly taken care of. It made me feel so good as I was a little bit apprehensive about it all. I actually hugged him goodbye after we were all set to head into the airport.

It was the first time I had ever hugged him. It was well overdue.

He seemed to enjoy that hug more than I did as he then gave Charlene a big hug and smile. Nobody ever hugged Charlene besides me anymore. The smile on her face was so evident as she stared into Peter's eyes that I thought it was almost magical. He squeezed my hand gently and wished us a good trip.

We had each other's phone numbers, but never texted or called much. Most likely my fault. For sure my fault, I knew. I told him, "thank you so much" and told him that I would text him when we arrived there. A smile came to his face and he said he would be waiting by the phone for it and told me to stay in touch while on vacation. It was a wonderful feeling to know someone actually cared for Charlene and me.

I thought to myself that I was going to miss seeing him for the time we were away.

Peter drove off as the airline personnel helped us get through the checkout line and over to our gate. Charlene was in awe of all of the people in the airport.

The gentleman who helped us onto the transport cab which would take us to our gate was a big man. He gladly helped me place Charlene into her seat on the cab. Or rather he pretty much did it himself. There were no seatbelts for the ride, so I sat next to Charlene with my arm wrapped tightly around her.

His name was Marvin. He seemed to be around forty years of age. It has gotten harder and harder to determine one's age as I have gotten older. I don't ask anybody that anymore and I hope they don't ask me as the years have slowly drifted by. Marvin told me he has worked at the airport for about fifteen years now as he placed my carry-on luggage next to him in the front seat. He enjoyed the job and it had enabled him to provide a nice little life for his wife and their three children. Making sure we were all set to go and that my luggage was secure, he turned on the blinking lights to signal others we were going to be proceeding through the aisleways. Charlene smiled when the lights came on and she continued to look around at all of the new sights.

I told him we were in no hurry as our plane wasn't due to leave for quite sometime and he thanked me for that information. We began slowly as it was a crowded section of the airport with passengers scurrying back and forth. Charlene seemed to like the automatic walkways that whisked people past us as we slowly and safely made our way to our gate. It was going to take us about 4 minutes he said, due to traffic. We both laughed as he maneuvered his way in and around other passengers while honking his horn occasionally to let others know we were approaching.

We didn't talk much on the ride to the gate as he needed to pay attention to his task at hand. Lord knows we didn't want to hit anyone. It would have made me feel uncomfortable forever if that were to happen.

Passing four younger girls, who were all dressed in beach attire, made me think of my younger days. Life was simpler then. Back then, my friends in high school and I never thought about the things of which I think about now. Our conversations usually centered around school, boys or girls in our class who were just not with it, we thought. Boy were we wrong about some of those people. As I look back now, I guess it's just what teenagers talk about. I don't ever remember any of us wondering what it would be like if we had to take care of a handicapped individual the rest of our life. It was just something you don't think about often when you were young. There're better things to talk and dream about. That's how it should be. Take the so called "bad" when it comes and enjoy the good every day.

These girls were well beyond their high school years, somewhere in their mid-twenties. They seemed to be having fun at the Airport Bar, as it was affectionately called. I knew my Charlene would never experience what they seemed to be experiencing. It looked like four young women going on vacation for sun and fun. Maybe even find romance. Nothing wrong with that. I didn't long for her to be "normal" anymore. She was a happy girl. For all I knew, happier than some of those girls.

The ride to the gate was fun for her as it would have been a long taxing walk for the both of us. I always knew I had to stay not only mentally strong but physically strong as well.

If I ever became weak, I always thought, who would take care of Charlene. It was my biggest worry in life. I didn't worry about anything else but her and what would happen to her if I was not around. These facilities that take care of people like Charlene can only do so much for her. An occasional walk I imagine and that would be it. She would mainly be laying in her bed watching television I reasoned. I could never let that happen. So, I prayed daily that I would always be able to be there for Charlene.

She enjoyed it when I would read to her. So after we sat in our chairs for awhile and the rain began to come down, I pulled out some children's books and began to read to her as I thought she would enjoy that. She was more enamored by the ray of light shining through the clouds onto our plane.

Using her arms and hands was something Charlene did not do well either. But, for some strange reason, she made a gesture toward the ray of light peeking through the clouds and smiled at me as she stared at the light. She always rocked back and forth more when she was happy. It always made me feel good when she was rocking. Like listening to your favorite song and moving to the beat. She wouldn't do it much. Mainly when she saw Peter or a rabbit in the yard. She was smiling and rocking back and forth like I had never seen before while trying to point at the light. I wondered what was going through her mind as she did this.

I was already thinking about Peter and looking forward to texting him when we landed.

CHAPTER 6: THE GIRLS

We had known each other for nearly ten years but never had taken a vacation together. It was long overdue as we had all matured in so many ways since first meeting our freshman year in high school. The years have gone so fast. This has made me appreciate not only my time here on earth but also the time of those with whom I spend my time. Our time in life varies, some live long into their nineties others are taken at birth. I know how precious time is now and I have looked forward to this trip for awhile. I knew that I had a lot to share with my friends. A secret that needed to be told. I thought they would also have small secrets to tell me, only there's was probably happier than mine, I imagined, as two of them were married and the other was close.

I had met Karen first. She was next to me in our science class. We had never met before our first class but talking to her was easy. It made both of us feel good, as we were both on the quieter side, as far as being outgoing. She lived about a mile from my parent's house and over the years we would spend countless days together at either her house or mine. Her father loved music, so it was always fun to go there as he had a set of drums in the basement and a microphone for us to sing. He didn't mind us playing them either. Or at least trying to play them. He would say "The Karen and Barbara Duo, what a nice name for a band." We both knew it was for fun. Neither one of us ever took lessons on a musical instrument or took singing lessons. But we would put on our favorite songs of the day and try to at least sing with them with the volume up as loud as he would let us, and we would do it with our wildest clothes on.

She told me that first day that she didn't mind dissecting a frog if we have to do it. From that point on she was my partner in science. It wasn't my style to cut open a frog. Blood and guts dripping out of a frog. No thanks! I loved her for many reasons but that was sure one of them.

Karen had gotten married about 3 years ago and had a 2-year-old boy and a 2-month-old boy. We had planned this trip around her as nobody else was pregnant at that time, we all thought. She had married a man she had met in college and they seemed happy together whenever we would get together. Her friends changed a little after having the boys, but we always saw each other whenever we could. I enjoyed babysitting her boys when the two of them would head out themselves. The boys and I always had a great time together.

There house was so big and their cars always so new. Her husband, Tom, must do quite well for himself, I thought, as Karen did not work. Good for Karen, she deserved it.

She would try to set me up with dates every so often. But nothing ever came of it. The sparks just weren't there for me most of the time and when they were it seemed like it wasn't there for him. It never bothered me though. What's the hurry, I thought back then.

Lori, Samantha and I met while playing soccer. Sam and I weren't so good, but we loved to run around the field. We always thought we should have joined cross country instead, but we never did. We had other friends on the team and we enjoyed playing with Lori.

Lori was a little ball of fire. Always on the go. Not laid back like Sam or Karen. She was fast and rugged and usually scored at least one of our goals. It's hard to remember some things that happened so long ago but I'll always remember my first and only soccer goal of my "career."

It was a beautiful pass from Lori.

She had intercepted a pass from the other team and quickly pointed to me which direction to run towards. I ran as hard as I could in that direction, the sweat pouring off my brow. Then there it was; I saw the ball coming towards me. Lori had led me perfectly. As soon as the ball and I met, I made a quick kick as hard as I could towards the net and that's all she wrote. It was my first and only goal. To this day, I'm not sure who enjoyed it the most, Lori or me. We were all happy that day as I had never scored and never would again.

Lori was still single, but she had been dating the same guy for over a year now. We knew him from high school. She had met him again at a company function they attended as they both worked at the same place. It was a big company, where they worked, so they never really saw each other there until that day. And then "Boom," sparks flew right away, and they have dated since then. I'm sure she is going to marry him, I thought. It all seemed so perfect as Adam was a handsome man and everybody liked him. The other girls always seemed to admire him whenever we went out together. He never seemed to mind and was always the social one of the group. Girls or boys, he would talk to them all. Lori never minded as that was just him being himself. They were always hanging out at our favorite watering holes. There're outgoing people and there are quieter people. We all need to accept ourselves for who we really are, I knew. I'm more of the quiet and jealous type. I guess quieter girls want their man all to themselves, I laughed to myself.

I also knew Sam from cheerleader tryouts. We were standing in line together, waiting to be "judged" on our appearance and acrobatic talents. She was more nervous than me as I was only doing this at my mother's beckoning. She was a cheerleader in high school and told me it would be fun. "If you make it, you make it, if you don't, it doesn't matter at all," she told me. She was pleasantly surprised when I told her I was going to try out for it.

Neither of us made it on the team that first year. We both made it our junior year, but I decided not to do it our senior year as it took up too much time. It was just something I didn't want to spend my time on. My mother hugged me when I told her that I was not going to tryout again. She remembered it being not so fun sometimes, but was so happy I did it for awhile. My dad and her were big believers that we should try as many different things in life as we could, "as life is short," my dad would say. So, we were all okay with one of my first big decisions I had made myself on how I really wanted to spend my time and lead my life.

Sam did it her senior year and it was nice to know somebody on the cheerleader squad as they always knew where the parties were. The four of us hung out a lot together that senior year and summer before college. It was a special time for us and strong bonds were formed.

Sam was a hair stylist now. She was the only one of the four of us who didn't go to college. She just didn't want to go and went to a hair stylist school for a year before joining a salon and cutting hair full time. We all went there for our hair styling needs. Sam was a good listener. She had to be. Always with a full day of different women and men, telling her different things and issues about their lives. She didn't mind, she told me one day. It gave her a good perspective on life and its shortcomings. I could only imagine some of the stories she had heard.

With one little boy to take care of on her own and a full-time job, it couldn't be easy for her.

Sam was the first one to get married. She had actually met him at her grade schools five-year anniversary get together. She had just started cutting hair and we were in our sophomore year in college. Mark was a machinist at a local company. They started seeing each other after reuniting at the anniversary get together and have been together ever since. There son was six years old now and a handful, she would tell me. No different than most other six-year olds, I thought. But, heck, I didn't know what it takes to raise a little boy. After some thought, I knew that I agreed, I'm sure he kept her busy. Her job as a stylist worked out well for her as she would set up her appointments around his schedule sometimes. He attended the same day care facility as Karen's children, but their age differences kept them apart there and Karen's children were only their sporadically when she needed someone to watch the children while she was out and about. Some of her appointments would sometimes be at nighttime, but that didn't matter, Mark was home to babysit.

They all seemed so happy with their lives, as I looked back at the table which we were lucky to get. The Airport Bar was full of people, drinking and seemingly having fun. It didn't matter what time of day it was, Lori said, we were going to have our first drink of the trip right now, right here.

A little smile, from four pretty girls, and those two older gentlemen gladly gave up their table. Nothing wrong with that.

As there was no service at this bar, I offered to get the first drink and sprang up to get it before anyone else had a chance to make that gesture. It was what I needed to do.

I was pregnant!

Single and pregnant! Only my doctor and I knew of this as I had found out just days earlier.

My parents didn't know, the child's father didn't know yet and my three best friends didn't know. It was like I had this heavy weight on my shoulders, hidden from sight, but weighing me down, nonetheless. Heavier than anything somebody would lift that day. I would have to be strong.

So here I was, standing at a bar to order drinks for the four of us to start our long-awaited vacation. This trip was going to be full of sun and alcohol, we all knew. A few days of fun for the girls.

"Barbara," he said, "you're pregnant." Whammy! He was a great doctor and advised me to give up drinking any alcohol from here on in and I knew in my heart that it was good advice for me and my baby. Advice I would adhere to. Dr. Ruffa knew that I was going on vacation in a few days, so we made another appointment to spend more time together a few days after I got back.

He was an assuring kind of doctor. Someone who you would recommend to someone else. He was calm, understanding, and only wanted the best for me and probably the best for all his patients. I had been going to see him since I was a child, living at home. We sort of grew up together, it seemed, as he would tell me about his kids and his life as the years floated by both of us. We were friends. His life wasn't perfect either and he helped me understand that it was okay that way. None of our lives are perfect, he would say. But we needed to appreciate everyday. His job wasn't perfect, his kids weren't perfect and other things in his life weren't perfect, but he was thankful everyday. He had told me he was originally going to be a priest but at the seminary things happened and he decided it wasn't for him. That's all he ever said about it. He was much older, but I learned it was okay to be friends with older people. They have seen much more of life's difficulties and joys. When willing to listen, one can learn a lot. I always listened to him.

His practice had many pictures and sayings on its walls. It wasn't overly full, but it seemed the "walls" wanted to tell us as much as they could while we were there. My favorite picture was that of an angel holding the hands of a little girl and boy as they were walking on the clouds. No words ever need to be said on a good painting. It speaks for itself. I always prayed that there was an angel helping me through my life. I would surely need him or her now, I thought, as I was leaving the office.

As I awaited my turn to order our drinks, I could see the girls flirting with an older man who was definitely here to have some alcohol. For whatever reason, he seemed like he wanted to be a little "under the bag" when his plane was ready to takeoff. He wasn't harming anyone but himself, I thought, and the girls were laughing, so it gave me time to figure out my little dilemma. He was mainly socializing with Lori and that seemed perfectly fine with Karen and Sam.

Obviously, the girls are going to want me to drink and have fun, I knew. Should I tell them now. Should I tell them individually. My hands were sweaty as I grabbed my pocketbook out of my purse as it was now my turn to order.

I knew what each of the girls liked to drink, so I quickly ordered their drinks first.

This guy was fast. He was definitely used to pouring drinks efficiently for his patrons. Why not I thought, the more orders he takes the more tips he gets. It only makes good sense.

He placed the third drink in front of me and that's when I ordered a gin and tonic for myself, but without the gin, I told him. Jokingly, I said to him, "I'm flying the plane" as I gave him a wink. He went right to work, pouring the tonic in a glass full of ice and adding a green olive and a stir straw for me just like a real gin and tonic. It seemed he and anyone else around me could care less what I was drinking or why. I was just like anyone else here. It was pure business and I liked that. We should all care a little less about what others might think about us, I pondered to myself. Who cares what someone might think, it's not their life.

I had positioned myself nicely to block the view of my girlfriends as he had poured it. It wasn't time yet. No need to let them see this yet and damper the mood. I tipped him nicely and he gave me a wink and a smile. This wasn't the first time he had "mixed" a drink like this. I took two drinks over at a time and sat back down at the table. Nobody was aware of anything. The mood was festive.

Karen said she wanted to make a toast so we all gave her a second to come up with something and did not take our first sip yet.

"To our vacation, our families, our hopes, our past mistakes and dreams and to us," she said, as we all chimed our drinks together. They were all so happy and I made it out that I was just as happy.

It was hard to be happy in my circumstance. What would friends, relatives, coworkers and others say once I broke the news?

I was having this baby; there was no doubt about that. I prayed for strength often these past days. It at least made me feel better even if it wasn't going to accomplish anything.

A lady and her daughter passed the bar on one of those taxi services the airport provides for those individuals needing assistance. Her daughter was handicapped and appeared to have cerebral palsy. The girl was looking at all of the commotion as they drove by as was her mother. The driver was concentrating on his job at hand as there were many passengers in front of him. He was moving slowly though, he has probably done this a thousand times, I imagined. His horn sounding occasionally.

That lady must be strong, I knew, or how else could she take care of her daughter. Mentally and physically, I would bet. I wondered if my baby was going to be born with some type of issue. It just created more stress inside of me so I didn't think about it. Rather, I would try not to think about it. The road ahead is a winding road with many different paths. I hoped mine would be an easier path.

As we sat there with all of the other patrons reveling in the day, I wondered to myself when I was going to tell them. Should I tell them now. Individually? Later on? It was something I was contemplating as soon as I found out that I was with child. This moment wasn't the right time, I knew. But I would eventually have to tell them as I was not going to endanger my baby by taking any alcohol. Vacation or not, I wasn't going to endanger my baby. They would eventually find out as I couldn't hide the "no alcohol" policy all vacation. I would figure it out I told myself.

Karen's toast made Sam think of her past near mistake a few years go. It has always depressed her. She wondered how many people in the bar here were near to heading down the wrong path in life?

She had met him in high school and by chance ran into him a few years later when he came in to get a haircut. Dave and she had formed a little bond as he would return every time he needed a trim. He had asked for a night appointment that one time and I told him that would work for me.

We talked as usual that night while I cut his hair and then he told me he was going to "The Last Stop Café" for a drink if I wanted to stop by after I got through with his haircut. It was her husband's golf night, so what the heck, she thought. She went. They had a few drinks and went to another bar and had a few more. When a slow dance song came on they both were willing to dance tightly together as they were both tempting themselves with the thought of sleeping together that night. I was so stupid, she thought to herself. Only the two of them ever knew, she imagined, as he was married also. It was something that probably weighed them both down, she thought. She had finally come to her senses and told him that she had to go as it was getting late. She left him at the bar and headed home alone that night.

She didn't do it, but she always felt like she had committed adultery. She knew she didn't commit adultery, but in her mind, it sure seemed like she did. What would Mark have done if he had seen us, she thought to herself. It was a mistake she would have to live with for the rest of her life and she knew it. She knew this mistake was the cause of her depression. A depression she hid from everyone. She needed to take pills everyday to combat this strained feeling in her head.

We continued to chat about life and finished our first and only drinks when we heard the preboarding call for our airplane ride. We all knew it was time to use the ladies' room as none of us wanted to have to get up to use the plane's bathroom on our flight. I knew I wouldn't be drinking anything on the plane because of this, so I had some sense of relief in that matter. No drinks to secretly disguise.

Lori headed to the bar to grab a quick shot with the loud gentleman. "He's buying," she said. Waving a twenty. She said she would catch up to us as we still had a good amount of time before we would be boarding. "You go girl," Karen told her, as the three of us headed to the girls' room.

I knew that I would have to tell them before our first bar visit in the Bahamas.

We filed into the ladies' room with so many other ladies as that's what you do before your flight. I wondered if anyone else in here had as much on their mind as I did. We were all so close to each other, but who really knew who. I hoped none of my friends were in such a state of disarray as I thought I was in.

We had been dating for a number of months. Meeting online was a new thing for me. He was nice though. He worked at the local post office and had a good paying job with nice benefits. Toby and I had slept together twice so far. It was always enjoyable to be with him. Whether in the bedroom or out and about. I wondered what he would say once I told him as soon as we got back. There wasn't this big set of sparks for either of us, but sometimes all it takes for a large fire is a small spark.

Karen and the others had met him on numerous occasions and she liked him, she told me, as did her husband, Tom.

After finding out that I was pregnant with his baby, as it could only be his, I obviously wondered to myself if he was the one. Someone with whom I would spend the rest of my
life with. Someone who would be there to support me and my children, no matter what.

What had I gotten myself into I thought as it was finally my turn in line to utilize one of the many stalls.

But here I was, pregnant, scared and on vacation with my best friends. Who better to tell first than your best friends, I thought.

The three of us arrived at the gate in plenty of time as the preboarding had not even started yet. Our friend from the bar was also taking this plane as he quickly headed over to where we were sitting to continue flirting with us. It was hard for anybody else not to see this. He was rather loud, but not obnoxious. The children were all playing in another area so they didn't witness any of his flirtatious comments. That was good, I thought, as I would not want my child to witness his advances.

I had changed in the past few days, more protective of myself and my unborn baby.

Karen and Sam always told us they wished we would get married soon and have a little girl. As they had three boys between the two of them, they thought it would be nicer that way. A little girl to dress up. Be the things we all wanted to be. I didn't know the baby's gender yet. Nobody did.

I couldn't wait to get this deep secret off my chest and out in the open. I was sure none of them had such a secret weighing them down.

Seeing the teenage girl with the disability frightened me a little. I wasn't sure if I would be strong enough to raise a child with such a handicap. This woman must be strong, I thought again to myself, stronger than me I'm sure. I prayed again quietly to myself for this girl and my unborn child, wondering to myself if anybody was listening.

Those of us born "healthy and normal" could never imagine being like this girl. Her face though, with her uncharacteristic features, seemed to be so content and peaceful. Smiling and happy I would call it. She had been looking out the window for the duration we had been here, admiring a ray of light shining on our plane.

It was good to see another passenger helping her mother with her carry-on luggage as she needed to support her child with both arms as they started their preboarding. I could never be so strong. I'm sure of that.

My friends were all so happy as we had all been looking forward to this. I appeared as happy as them.

Seeing the priest in the section down from us made me realize that I would need to make a choice in life as far as my religion goes. I slipped away from the church once I had moved out of my parent's house a few years earlier. It wasn't that I did not believe anymore. It was more a bad choice, I knew now. Only an hour a week and I couldn't do it.

No wonder He doesn't seem to be listening to me, I thought.

As those with children and others needing assistance lined up to get their boarding passes, the flirting continued. I hoped he wasn't sitting next to us. We had two seats next to each other in back to back rows. Sort of like a four pack we laughed when we ordered the flight tickets.

It didn't matter to me which one of the three, I would sit next to. But I was glad it was Karen though. I was never quite sure why as we were all close friends. Maybe because she dissected the frog for me, I smiled to myself remembering that day.

The children were running back to be with their parents at this time, so they could board the plane accordingly. They all looked like little angels to me. No evilness in life had affected them yet, I reasoned. To young to hurt someone over money or anything else. Some of the children were with both of their parents, while others seemed to have only one. They seemed to be okay with only one parent. I wondered if my child would have a father when he was born.

CHAPTER 7: TOM AND JILL

Tom and Jill Witchkoff sat in an airplane terminal as they waited for their flight home. They didn't enjoy traveling and avoided it whenever they could. On this occasion, however, they had set out with a glimmer of hope. They met with a doctor who was supposed to be able to help them. Many people had told them she was the best they would be able to find, but the trip ended up being fruitless and they headed home more dejected than ever. Neither Tom nor Jill knew what to say or how to process the information they had been given, so they sat in silence as everyone else in the airport seemed to bustle on endlessly.

The most frustrating part of the wait was seeing the children playing in the aisles of the terminal, but not for the reasons most other passengers might be frustrated. Jill looked on in envy as an older woman animatedly told a story to two young children. She couldn't take her eyes off of the scene, but she knew she would only get more upset the longer she watched.

Just hours earlier, they had met with Dr. Barber, who was one of the best doctors in her field. The warm colors and cozy furniture that made up the office were meant to look inviting and calming, but Jill was not able to keep her body from shaking with anticipation as they waited for the doctor to see them. Tom kept one arm around her shoulders and his other hand was clasped around hers in her lap, but even he could not hide his doubts; his sweaty hands betrayed his calm demeanor.

They had been trying to have children for years, only to experience wave after wave of disappointment. Tom and Jill had been one of those "love at first sight" couples, though they didn't immediately realize it. They met in kindergarten and were friends from the start, and at one point Tom had even given Jill a plastic ring he got for a quarter from a corner store. By the time they got married at 27, they had been together longer than most couples who were years older than them. Everything seemed to come so easily for them, which almost made their current situation more difficult to accept. If they were made for each other, why were they not able to have children of their own?

It seemed cruel, Tom thought, to deprive them of the joy of parenthood. The worst part of the situation was that Jill somehow blamed herself for what was happening. Their first time getting pregnant was actually on accident. Though they were married, Tom and Jill had decided to wait a little before starting a family. Tom had just started a new job in commercial banking and was putting in a ton of extra hours, so he preferred to let things settle down before adding more responsibility to their relationship. Jill was at a good place in her career and didn't want to have to take time away to have a child.

It's funny how things work, or at least they thought so at the time. When they first realized Jill was pregnant, all of their previous thoughts and misgivings about starting a family so soon vanished. With every simple task – whether it was working out in her garden or cooking up supper – she imagined a pudgy child toddling along behind her and couldn't help but want to give her the world.

Tom got lost in similar thoughts, especially when pulling late nights at work. The office would fade away, and he would be in the back yard teaching his little boy how to throw and catch or perhaps watching his daughter at her first softball game. Their unborn child was immediately the most important part of their lives, which made them both work all that much harder at their jobs; they wanted to give their child the best life they could.

But then everything changed one night, still fairly early in the pregnancy. Jill woke up in pain, and before they knew it, it was over. They had been told that miscarriages were not all that uncommon for first pregnancies, but the thought of one had never entered either of their heads. The weight of the miscarriage hung on them for weeks, affecting them both at home and at work. Tom felt like someone dumped molasses into his mind; everything moved so slow and he couldn't gain any sort of traction. Jill experienced an emptiness that felt so real, she could've sworn she was hollow.

In time, they recovered, but they had bought into the idea of a child and it was difficult to go back to the way their lives were before. It took a few months, but Tom and Jill eventually decided to try again, only to experience the pain of another miscarriage. The pain was exactly the same as before, perhaps slightly numbed this time.

Each miscarriage took a part of Jill with it, almost like part of her soul was torn from her; physically, she was fine, but she didn't think she could recover. The longer this went on, the more Jill blamed herself for what was happening. Though her doctor explained to her that miscarriages were common – even normal – it was becoming increasingly obvious that something was wrong.

Tom and Jill's relationship had always been stress-free. They got along very well and rarely fought, but now things were more strained than ever before. Tom tried his best to be there for Jill, but he often found himself at a loss for words when it came to comforting her. What could he say that would actually help?

Jill believed she was failing as a woman, that she wasn't doing her part to actually have a child. Eventually, Jill became stuck in a sort of limbo. She wanted desperately to have a child, to fulfill the thoughts and desires that had flooded her mind since she first learned she was pregnant. But she was also terrified of trying once again, for fear that her body would fail her. Jill tried to keep these thoughts from Tom because she knew exactly how he would react, but she couldn't keep those thoughts from herself.

As time passed, Tom and Jill watched as their brothers, sisters, and friends all started happy families. Jill wanted nothing more than to carry her own children, but came to the conclusion that it just wasn't going to happen. Although they considered a surrogate mother, Jill decided she could not bare to have another woman deliver her baby. Perhaps it was selfish or elitist, but it seemed like a simple request to Jill to be able to have her own child.

That was why they met with Dr. Barber, and that was why they temporarily ignored their distaste for travel. Everything they had tried up until that point had not worked, but they hoped a second opinion could give them the answer they were looking for. Dr. Barber began by running a few tests, and then performed an examination herself. All in all, the appointment took about an hour. Traveling all this way for something that was over so quickly seemed silly, but Tom and Jill needed only to hear one thing to make it worth it.

"Well, the results of the original tests we ran were inconclusive," Dr. Barber began, "but the examination led me to believe that there is nothing I can do."

Tom put his arm around Jill as she buried her face in her hands.

"I'm sorry, Mr. and Mrs. Witchkoff," Dr. Barber said. She truly did look sorry, but Tom and Jill were devastated. With everything that had transpired over the last few years, they knew their chances of achieving a successful pregnancy were slim, but Dr. Barber was so highly regarded that they hoped something could be done.

They sat in stunned silence, not knowing what to say and not prepared at all to leave. Dr. Barber began to tell them what their other options were, but this was the only option they truly cared about. It just wasn't fair that they were unable to have children when everyone else they knew had no issues whatsoever. What had they done to deserve this? Why did God want to punish them?

Back in the airport terminal, Jill and Tom continued to feel mocked by the presence of other families waiting for their flight. It was a constant reminder of what they were not allowed to have, and Jill could not keep the tears from forcing their way past her eyelashes as she surveyed the scene.

Tom felt guilty thinking about it when his wife was next to him hurting, but he thought about work back in Atlanta; he was really struggling lately. His boss knew of their troubles, and he had been sympathetic, but sympathies eventually run out. Tom could tell that his boss was getting tired of him letting his home life impact his performance on the job. When Tom had asked for some time off so they could meet with Dr. Barber, he could tell that his boss was reluctant.

This whole thing had been difficult on Tom as well, even if Jill was the one bearing most of the pain. When they first got pregnant, he fell head over heels at the idea of being a father, and he still longed for the opportunity. Tom noticed that a girl with cerebral palsy was waiting to board the plane, and he wondered what would be worse: never having a child of his own, or having a child and seeing him or her suffer. There are no guarantees in life, Tom knew. Up to this point, almost everything had gone well for both Tom and Jill, so how could they be so upset.

CHAPTER 8: SHARON, MELISSA, AND THE KIDS

"Alright, everyone say goodbye to Nana."

A chorus of goodbyes echoed from the back of the van as Sharon Kuhn's grandchildren waved from their seats. As she returned their waves, she once again noticed how they all shared their mother's eyes. For a moment, Sharon was transported back to a time when she herself was a young mother with three kids. It was often overwhelming to have the lives of three children in your hands, but she reveled the feeling at the time and longed to experience it just once more.

She thought visiting her daughter would bring her happiness and fill the void she'd had in her chest since Alan, her husband, had passed away. It was a blissful week as she spent every waking moment with her three beautiful grandchildren while her daughter and son in law got a break for once. But now that they were at the airport and she was set to return to her empty house, Sharon couldn't help but feel that void begin to creep back in.

Sharon and her daughter got out of the van in unison and headed around to the trunk to take out her luggage. It was a beautiful, sunny day with a slight breeze – the kind of day that everyone longed for and the worst kind of day to be cooped up on a plane. In the distance, Sharon saw black, foreboding storm clouds and wondered if the rain would arrive before her flight took off.

"Are you sure you don't want me to help you with your luggage, Mom?" Elise asked as her mom stared off at the impending storm.

"No, no, don't worry about me. You and the children have to get going anyway," Sharon said, snapping out of her daydream.

Truth be told, Sharon wanted her daughter and grandchildren to stay with her as long as they could, but she knew she would only be temporarily delaying the sadness she was already beginning to feel.

The two hugged, said their goodbyes, and Sharon walked into the airport with her suitcase wheeling behind her. Elise was her oldest child, but even so, Sharon sometimes still had trouble seeing her for the adult that she was. All three of her children had grown up so quickly and now they lived in big cities where they started their careers and families. They say this is the sign of successful parenting, and Sharon was truly proud of everything her children were accomplishing, but she selfishly wished at least one of them had stayed at home with her.

Sharon's life had been so busy for years, first with Alan and then with her kids, but now she didn't have anything to occupy her time. She tried picking up some new hobbies and reconnecting with old friends after Alan passed, but nothing seemed to work for her. Her kids didn't visit often and, while they did ask if she wanted to move and be closer to where they lived, she couldn't bear to leave the place she'd called home her entire life.

As Sharon walked through the airport, the void seemed to take a stronger hold with every step. Despite the countless people surrounding her, Sharon always thought airports were one of the loneliest places a person could go. Whether you were leaving someone or going to visit others, the airport was always the in-between – a kind of purgatory that nobody wanted to spend any more time at than necessary. Even the employees seemed to be in a sort of limbo where they constantly repeat the same actions, like an assembly line that pushes people toward their destinations. Going through the motions.

Before joining everyone else in the security line, Sharon took one last look back at the entrance. She knew her daughter and grandchildren had already pulled away, but she felt a strong desire to run back out to try and catch them. She didn't do it, of course, but the thought remained.

The line for security was long and moving slowly, and Sharon occupied her time by seeing who was waiting around her. Most of the younger people in line were constantly staring down at their cell phones, almost as if they were afraid of making contact with the strangers they were standing with.

Eventually, a small trio caught her eye. A young mother with long, auburn hair was a few feet ahead of Sharon. Her slight frame was weighed down with bags, and an exhausted expression was etched across her face as she tried to keep her two young children under control. Her daughter was slightly taller than her son, and she appeared to be teasing him. They were making more noise than anyone in line, and their mother seemed unable or unwilling to get them to calm down.

Sharon smiled ruefully as she observed the scene. She knew exactly how this young woman was feeling, having traveled with her children many times back in the day. It was always an ordeal trying to keep children occupied in an airport, and she was tempted to go offer the auburn-haired woman some help. She knew the woman could use a break, and she had some tricks up her sleeve that she picked up over the years. But it wasn't her place to get involved in someone else's affairs, so she just watched and shuffled along as the line periodically moved forward.

The void continued to creep in as she watched the mother and her children, so she tried to turn her attention elsewhere. However, it seemed as though everywhere she turned, there were young families or individuals that brought back memories of her earlier, busier years. It was nice to spend the last week at her daughter's. For the first time in a while, she didn't struggle to keep herself occupied throughout the day. Now, as she got closer and closer to the flight that would take her home, she wondered what she would do this week. She had nothing planned, and knew that the days would pass much slower than the ones spent with her grandchildren.

Despite the long line, she made it through security with plenty of time to spare before her flight. She had visited her daughter a few times before, so she knew the airport fairly well and knew it wouldn't take long to get to her terminal. She had eaten just before leaving for the airport, and she wasn't a drinker, so she didn't know how she would pass the time leading up to boarding. She used to try and make conversation with others at airports, but she learned over the years that people didn't often enjoy talking to strangers. Now, she just sat quietly and sometimes read a book to pass the time.

There was one author in particular that she enjoyed reading, especially because she always seemed to be coming out with new books. As sad as it was, reading these books was often the highlight of her day because they provided an escape for her. The stories were so well written, and they painted such vivid images in Sharon's head, that she was able to escape her life and her troubles for hours at a time. Her love for reading was one of the many things she passed on to her children, and it all started when she

THE PRIEST, THE STEWARDESS, AND THE CHURCH PICNIC

would tell them stories just before bed.

Just as Sharon was getting into the story of the book she was reading, her attention was yanked back to the dull airport terminal she was sitting in. Looking up, she quickly realized what was making the disturbance that kept her from enjoying her reading. Sitting across from her was the auburn-haired woman, and between them were her two children, who were playing some sort of game most adults wouldn't understand or care to understand.

The young mother made some feeble attempts to get them to quiet down and rejoin her in the seats, but they were much too rambunctious to settle down and sit still. Sharon smiled slightly at the sight, even though it was disturbing her from her new book. It was a scene she had seen play out countless times, first with her children and more recently with her grandchildren. Children were fickle, and it wasn't always easy to get them to behave appropriately. Despite their mother's efforts, the children were much too excited by the prospect of flying to stay still.

While Sharon didn't mind too much, she did begin to notice others waiting for the flight look around at the children and quietly make remarks to each other. Nobody really enjoyed flying with loud children, so Sharon decided to try something out.

She made eye contact with the auburn-haired mother, who was looking apologetic, and smiled. Sharon put down her book and called softly to the young boy and girl.

"What game are you two playing?" she asked. The two children were caught off guard by this sudden intrusion to their game, and shyly stopped before looking down at their feet. The young boy mumbled something, but Sharon was not able to hear it. She did not intend to embarrass them or make them think she was angry at their antics.

"You can continue playing if you like, or we could try something else out. What are your names? My name is Sharon," she said.

The two children shared a quick look, and then looked back at their mother in unison. Their mother gestured back toward me, as if instructing them to answer my question.

"I'm Julie," said the girl, who looked quite a lot like her mother.
"My name is Philip," said the boy, a little hesitantly.

"Those are two very lovely names," said Sharon. "Now, like I said, you can continue to play the game you were playing earlier, or we could try something different. Do you two like stories?"

The two children nodded their heads, easing up a little at the softness of Sharon's voice. It was clear that they were unused to talking with strangers, but they also seemed intrigued at the prospect of hearing a story.

"Well, I know some great ones, or at least that's what my children always said," Sharon said. "Why don't you two sit over here and I can tell you one of my favorites?"

Julie and Philip quickly sat down in front of Sharon and craned their tiny heads upward, so their eager eyes met her face. Behind them, Sharon saw their mother relax her shoulders a bit and look on as her children quieted down. She could tell that their neighbors appreciated the quieter atmosphere of the terminal. While that was a bonus, Sharon couldn't deny that she was mostly doing this for selfish reasons. She wasn't ready to say goodbye to her grandchildren, and this allowed her to keep the illusion going for a little bit longer, albeit with another woman's children.

Across the aisle, Melissa Cuneo looked on in appreciation as the older woman began telling her children a story she had clearly told hundreds of times. Melissa herself wasn't much of a storyteller, so this was a rare treat for Julie and Philip. Melissa's parents didn't make a habit of telling her stories while she was growing up, so she didn't really use that as a tactic for quieting her children down.

Melissa kept an eye on the situation, seeing her children get more into the story and the older woman grow more animated by the minute. While she felt as though she could never truly relax, Melissa did feel more at ease than she had in as long as she could remember. As the tension seeped out of her, Melissa's mind wandered toward home and what awaited her there.

The truth was, there wasn't much at home, but it was still their home. Melissa was a social media coordinator for a small technology company. While it was a foot in the door of the industry she wanted to be in, she had to admit that she wasn't where she always dreamed of being. She had no trouble working full-time when the kids were in school, but daycare and babysitter costs added up in the summers. The only way to advance in her career was to dedicate more time to the job, but she couldn't afford – nor did she want — to be away from the kids too much.

It was supposed to be easier, and she supposed it was easier when she was with her ex-husband. They were a team, and it made raising two rambunctious children much easier. But Melissa's world came crashing down when she discovered that her husband had been cheating on her for years. As much as she wanted her family to remain intact, Melissa couldn't handle being with someone who put himself before Julie and Philip.

This was why Melissa had made up her mind to pack up everything and move to Atlanta, bringing her two children with her. She didn't know what to expect once she got there; she didn't know how she was going to handle living in an entirely new city while also experiencing the rigors of being a single parent.

But ever since she found out about Ted's infidelity, Pittsburgh felt tarnished. Her home was no longer the safe space it used to be. Everywhere she looked, she saw reminders of her broken marriage. Beyond that, her neighbors somehow found out what had happened. She felt ashamed to talk to them, or even to talk to her friends. She felt judged in every capacity and just needed to get away.

On a whim, Melissa started applying for jobs in far-away cities, dreaming of starting fresh where nobody knew her or her children. Somewhere far away from Ted. Surprisingly, she got a few nibbles and eventually a bite: A marketing company in Atlanta wanted to hire her! She explained her situation to the hiring manager and was assured that she would have the necessary flexibility to still be a single parent. Melissa still wasn't sure if she could afford to hire a babysitter or put Julie and Philip into a daycare, but she had faith that everything would work out.

Melissa still remembered the day she found out that Ted had been cheating on her. It was a pale, cloudy fall day with a bit of chill in the air — one of Melissa's favorite types of days, sadly enough. She enjoyed summers, but they got to be so hot and humid that the days could be unbearable. Fall was her favorite because of the cooler weather and the beautiful colors of the changing leaves.

On this occasion, Melissa had taken Julie and Philip to Zuck Park, which wasn't too far from their home. Ted was still at work, and the kids were bored, so she finally gave into their pleas and they ran out the front door to wait by the car. In truth, Melissa didn't mind getting out of the house on a day like that. She just felt guilty knowing that she would be getting a late start on dinner, and Ted didn't like waiting to eat.

Melissa sat on one of the rickety park benches as Julie and Philip's tiny feet carried them over the old bark that covered the playground. They were racing to the top of the biggest slide, and both tried to claim victory before calling out to Melissa to see who actually got there first.

"I think that one was a tie," Melissa called back to them. She stretched out in her seat before settling in with her hands squeezed between her knees for warmth. Melissa wore a light jacket to combat the cold, but her exposed hands had quickly grown cold due to her lack of movement.

She momentarily considered getting up and joining Philip and Julie in whatever games they were playing as they waltzed throughout the playground. Part of her still really enjoyed participating in these childish activities. They were always a great temporary escape from reality, a time for her to enjoy being with her children without having to worry about her many responsibilities.

But Melissa was feeling a bit sore today and decided against it. She didn't even know why she was sore in the first place. She thought back through the last few days, trying to find the culprit, the reason why she was in minor pain, but she couldn't place the cause. That was one of the worst parts of getting older, she thought. Your body hurt for seemingly no reason, and it took forever for it to heal itself.

Melissa looked back over at her children, jealous of their endless supply of energy. Perhaps this would at least tire them out some so she and Ted could get them to bed on time. They never did go to sleep without putting up a fight, but the nights were easier when they were tired out. One of their last-ditch efforts to stay up later was to demand that Ted or Melissa tell them a story.

Ted and Melissa usually drew straws to see who would have to tell the story because, truthfully, they weren't any good at storytelling. Neither of their parents had told them stories growing up, so they didn't know where Julie and Philip got the hankering for bedtime stories.

The shriek of a tiny dog brought Melissa out of her daydreaming about bedtime stories. The shrill bark startled her for a moment before she realized what it was; at first, she was worried Julie or Philip had gotten hurt.

As she peered around for the source of the bark, something she saw made Melissa frown. Across the park, on the other side of the playground, Melissa saw a rusting, silver Bonneville, the same car Ted drove. She squinted over at the car, which was parked along a side street in front of a quaint little house. It really did look like Ted's car – it had the same stupid spoiler that he liked so much – but it couldn't be. He was still at work, he had told her, and he didn't know anyone that lived on this block – at least Melissa didn't think he did.

She tried to put the thought out of her mind and returned her attention to her kids, who were now trying to get all the way across the monkey bars without falling. However, she couldn't help but steal occasional glances back at the Bonneville and the house it was parked in front of.

Julie was doing much better with the monkey bars than Philip was. She kept calling out to Melissa to watch her as she swung from bar to bar. Philip couldn't get the swinging motion down and kept losing momentum about a third of the way across. Melissa couldn't help but chuckle as she watched him flail his legs before ultimately losing his grip and falling to the soft ground below. He got up and brushed off the bark that clung to his pants.

Suddenly, Melissa heard the faint sound of voices and a screen door creak open. Her eyes shot back to the house with the Bonneville parked out front, and she saw two figures on the doorstep – a woman and a man. She couldn't make out their faces, but the man quickly walked across the lawn toward the car and he slowly came into focus.

He was wearing a tan trench coat, and she could just make out the color of his tie in the fading light. It was green, the same pale shade of green that stuck out to Melissa when she was buying ties for Ted a few months prior. It was him.

She couldn't make out the expression on his face as he climbed into the car, but her eyes trailed back to the woman still standing just inside the door. Surely this was all just a big misunderstanding, right? Melissa hoped beyond hope that her eyes had deceived her or that there was a perfectly logical explanation for this, but all of that hoping couldn't stop the tears from coming to her eyes.

Philip fell to the ground once more, drawing Melissa's attention away from the woman in the door. Her tears blurred her vision, but she could hear Philip say he was OK. A million different thoughts poured into her mind at that moment. What would happen? Why was Ted cheating on her?

Would the kids be alright?

She knew Ted would be home before her, probably wondering why she didn't have dinner ready for him. Melissa sat frozen to the spot as shadows of the trees in the park grew longer, and she wondered if she would have the strength to go home and confront her husband about what she had seen.

Finally, Julie and Philip ran on over to her and her bench. They were done playing and were starving. As much as she didn't want to go home at that moment, she couldn't say no to her two beautiful children as they grabbed her hands and pulled her to her feet and back toward their car.

For a while, Ted begged for forgiveness and talked about how he was "led astray by the devil," but Melissa did not relent, and he eventually gave up trying to win her back. Even if the devil did lead her husband astray, she couldn't help wondering what she did to deserve it. His actions ruined their family, put her career on hold, and made everything so much more difficult for Julie and Philip.

Melissa's parents had already passed away, and she was an only child. Although she did have a few great friends that helped her whenever they could, they had families of their own to take care of. In the end, Melissa felt like she was trapped on an island that she would never be able to get off of. This isn't to say that she didn't love her children; they were the two bright spots in her world and they brought her happiness every day. But Melissa still felt stranded, and being stranded had started to take a toll on her.

Her biggest fear was that it would also take a toll on Julie and Philip. She never considered that she would be raising two children all on her own, and she frequently felt as though she wasn't doing enough for her children or wasn't doing everything properly. Melissa felt that way before the divorce, too, but she had someone else to lean on during the difficult times. Now, she wasn't so sure she could always handle things. Melissa made sacrifices time and again for her children, but they also took a toll on her.

Snapping out of her daydream, Melissa continued watching the older woman tell her children a story. She had Julie and Philip wrapped around her finger in a way Melissa could only dream of, and Melissa couldn't help but wonder if she would ever be able to do the same. This lady had clearly raised a few kids of her own, and judging by the scene splayed out before her, she had probably done a magnificent job.

CHAPTER 9: BOARDING

The call came over the loudspeakers that preboarding for those needing assistance would begin in 15 minutes was a harsh reality to John that he would never be back in Pittsburgh. John knew that. His wife was gone. His son was gone. He would have to get used to that. He wondered if the priest sitting down across from him was from a church in Atlanta. He had tried to join a number of churches over the years but never really found the right one.

Why join one now, he thought to himself. All he had was gone.

He thought about the gift box from Angela. Too many people around now to unwrap this gift, John thought to himself. Let it stay in my briefcase. He enjoyed his talk with Angela. It was a good way to rid oneself of some grief. It's a hard thing to handle and sharing that with her eased his burden, he thought to himself. He imagined the priest has had to deal with similar circumstances for countless people.

John wondered how he could do that for so long. He must be quite the believer. John still believed but his sorrow was deep and painful. It would take more than one man, even a priest, to ease his pain.

Ray had been playing with the children for awhile before preboarding started. Anytime one of the children scored a goal, most of the kids were all happy for that child. Little hands, high fiving each other. It almost didn't matter which team scored. They were excited. Somebody scoring a goal in his world meant that someone just made a big money deal. Others were happy for the one scoring the deal, but it was always a fake happiness. We were all a little jealous when that would happen as it would raise him higher on the "totem pole." Closer to the top, we all thought, and that seemed to be where we all wanted to be. No matter what. But, we would shake his hand and show our happiness for him anyway. We all wore a lot of different masks there. Putting on the one that would most suit us in the situation at hand.

I wondered how many of us getting on this airplane were hiding behind some type of mask. A problem, desire or secret not shared with anyone. Hidden away inside of us and lessening our enjoyment of our day. We all have issues, I knew. It certainly wasn't just me, I was certain of that.

Ray's hands were full as he had his carry-on luggage as well as Phyllis's and Charlene's.

He had heard a page for Phyllis Terry at the gate and watched her as she went over. The counter was close so there was no worrying about Charlene. They talked a little and she looked my way and pointed at me and they both smiled and she sat down. They must have been asking her if she needed additional assistance. It will be nice to help her out, I thought to myself. A small little thing to make her life nicer.

Phyllis mentioned the ray of light to Ray as they got in line. Ray hadn't noticed it yet as he was busy the whole time playing with the children. They just looked at each other after looking at it one last time and smiled. Ray said that, "Maybe it was a good luck sign," and they both laughed. "We could all use a good omen," Phyllis said. Ray hoped that the two of them would both have some good luck.

This interview was with a large outfit. Worldwide. His current place of employment was small compared to it. They had sought him out as he was making a name for himself with the rich and richer. It was all about the money. That was their business, though. I didn't hold it against them. I just wondered if that was the business I wanted to be in anymore. The phone call with them went rather well and I was heading there. Most likely they would offer me a job on the spot. Time would tell. He wondered whether that was going to be his "good luck."

I better put my papers away now Patty thought as she watched Ray help the lady and her daughter through the boarding procedure. She watched him for minutes as he did this. The girl even seemed to like him. Maybe she could tell he was helping her mother out and that gave her a smile. It's hard to tell what a person in her condition really knows. Was she aware of this or not, none of us will ever know, but it seemed to me that she knew he was special compared to all of the other people she saw at the airport.

Nobody else seemed to care, although I am sure the airline would have assisted her. This lady, Patty thought, does things on her own. She couldn't depend on anyone and would probably only ask for help if she was desperate.

She could tell that he was good with all kinds of kids and she wondered what he did for a living. She was happy it was almost boarding time as she was tired of reading resumes. I got a bit done, she knew, so she was happy. Happy to be heading home. The right one will come up. It was just a matter of who and when. Organizing her papers and grabbing her carry-on bag she headed to the ladies room for one quick visit before the flight took off.

Seeing the girls who looked like they were heading on vacation to have fun made her even more aware of her need to find the right candidate for the job. She needed a vacation too and would take one after she found him or her.

The girls were all lively and happy as she noticed them talking to the "tipsy" passenger. Patty figured they had no major problems in life, at this time in their lives, as she headed to the restroom. She passed another girl their age, dressed like them, as she headed to the restroom.

Little did she know about their lives.

Evelyn was excited as we were proceeding through the preboarding line. The boy with the Pirate hat on was just as excited as her. They had been playing together for some time with the other children and it seemed like they had been friends forever, her father thought.

He remembered when he first met Debbie. She won his heart the first time she said "Hi" to him. His heart was torn now, though. She was gone. His anger at the "unfairness" of it all would never go away.

He didn't dream about her anymore. He did at first. Not anymore. He wanted to, but it hurt too much.

Evelyn had brought her knapsack as her carry-on luggage. It held all of her favorite things. Her books were always the most important thing to her when we went somewhere. She would read in the car sometimes or we would listen to music. I spend so much time with her now that Debbie was gone that talking in the car faded away as we would talk at home and in the yard all of the time. She knew I had to do housework, yardwork and other things her mom used to do. So, she would help me with these chores and that gave us nice times together where we could talk. I needed a break sometimes though, so it was usually when we were in the car.

I think Evelyn prayed for me daily.

Something I didn't do, for sure.

I told her that she would have plenty of time to read and to bring as many books as she likes as long as they fit into the knapsack. She filled it up nicely with books and other items to keep her busy.

She never took off her angel necklace. I was glad it had a nice strong chain on it for her.
Her life had been hard enough. If I prayed for anything anymore, it was that she would not lose that angel charm.

It would hurt me too. Maybe as much as Evelyn. When I would see it on her it would remind me of her and her mother. Those were Evelyn's best days, I thought to myself. I wondered how she was really doing. She seemed happy and we talked often. But I knew it was hard for even Debbie's "little angel" when she passed.

I just do the best I can for her, Jeremy thought to himself.

A few of the stewardesses were there to greet us as we entered the door of the plane. They were pleasant girls. I wondered how many flights these girls had taken so far in their careers. The older one of the two probably has logged thousands of trips, Ray imagined.

"Hello," they said to Charlene as Phyllis capably assisted her thru the doorway of the airplane. Charlene was all smiles as she was greeted.

It is a job for them, I knew, just like mine. It made me wonder what they really thought as we entered the plane. But that didn't really matter. I said "Hello" back and ducked my head as I entered the plane.

Phyllis knew to fly first class with Charlene as she needed the space. So, we were shown their seats as soon as we came in. The passengers behind us were not aggressive to get in. They understood the difficulties Phyllis endures. Most of them couldn't dream of it. Why would they want to, though? Their children were probably all healthy, I thought to myself.

While Charlene was getting buckled in, I let Phyllis know that I would help her as much as she needed. I was in no hurry. I had extra hours to kill once we landed. She seemed happy at the gesture and told me she would like to get off last, so they wouldn't hold anybody else up. I told her as I placed her carry-on luggage above her, "no worries there, as I'll be the last one off."

They laughed and smiled together.

As I was closing the overhead luggage door, and wanting to say bye to Charlene, I noticed the ray of light on our plane. Charlene was rocking back and forth slightly as she was staring at it out the window. She was enamored by it.

So was I.

I was brave and gave Charlene a little hug. Her hand grabbed my hand and squeezed it slightly as she turned and smiled at me. That hug was worth something. Something more than a lot of money, I thought to myself. I headed down the aisle to my seat as I was well back in the plane and had a clear shot all the way there as it was empty besides a few more stewardesses. The only nametag I could read was a pleasant looking lady's named Maria. She let me walk by with a wonderful smile on her face as I headed to my row.

The ray of light was shining on both of us as I walked past her.

The next group behind me was closing in as Charlene was all situated and some of the children were eager to get to their seats. So, I hurried to get my luggage up and in a cabinet and get into my seat. I wondered if someone would be right next to me or not. I wouldn't bother them, I thought to myself, and maybe they won't bother me. I needed to do a little reading about the firm I was going to interview with. Boring stuff.

I got a few "Hi's" from some of the children and their parents as they were situating themselves. It was fun playing ball with them. A version of soccer that I could have played all day if I had the time.

Barbara saw Lori heading to the women's restroom from the Airport Bar as Sam and Karen were texting somebody. It seemed she stayed at the bar longer than we all first thought but it didn't matter to any of us. We were all here to have fun. While the girls were texting, I just sat there.

THE PRIEST, THE STEWARDESS, AND THE CHURCH PICNIC

Thinking.

Who would I tell first when I got back? Toby, who was my baby's father, my mother, my father or maybe my parents at the same time. It was going to have to happen so I reasoned I might as well give it a little thought. My father had always told me to be strong and face the cold accordingly when we would do our weekly walk together in the winter. He told me to think about other things. "Don't think about the cold," he would say. It would actually help during those cold days. "If you don't think about it, it won't affect you as much."

I was going to try and do that with this baby on our vacation. Just not think about it too much. My friends and I had been planning this for so long as we all needed a break from our "normal" lives. There was no way I was going to ruin this.

I would tell Toby first, I reasoned, as this is his baby also. He should be told as soon as I get back. I didn't want to tell him right before I had to go and then be gone for awhile. He'll know the day I get back, I thought. Then my parents.

Lori finally got back with us and said how long of a line it was in the girl's room. As I had noticed one of our fellow passengers go in and come right out, I didn't think it was so full that there was a line. It seemed empty to me as I saw other girls go in and out. Maybe Lori didn't want us to know she had a few more drinks than just one more. I laughed to myself. It didn't matter to me. We were here to have fun.

Sam and Karen were probably texting their husbands. I had texted Toby, when I left for the airport. He was always nice to me, I knew. I wondered if their husbands were excited about them leaving for awhile too. We all need a break sometime, I thought to myself.

Lori dropped her phone as she was going to text Adam. Something we all do. She had to keep from swearing as there were young children still in the seating area. A couple of the kids laughed a little. She grabbed a seat and sent her text.

My phone was put away for awhile.

Evelyn and I entered the plane and her excitement was evident in her joyous looking face. We were on the front of even the preboarders, so it was a little calmer. The stewardesses were very cordial as we walked past them going through the first-class section. I wondered to myself if one of them was the lady who smiled and winked at Evelyn. No matter, I would never see her again, I thought to myself.

Seeing the handicapped girl in a happy state and peering out the window made me, and I think Evelyn, happy for her. It probably has not been so wonderful for her all the time, I reasoned. Her mother appeared to be a calm woman. So many people walking past her and staring. It never bothered her from what I could see. She was polite and enjoyed seeing the young children in a good mood as she imagined they were all going somewhere fun.

Evelyn noticed a few books on the lady's lap and told her that she liked to read books also. The lady said she loves to read books to her daughter as she could not read them herself. Smiling at her, Evelyn told her, "She probably loves listening to you read books to her just like I read to my mother in heaven." The lady gave her a nice warm pat on the arm as Evelyn proceeded to look for our row.

I told the lady to have a nice flight and that it looked like a special one as the sun was glaring on our plane.

I hurried to catch up to Evelyn, she had found our row. I was going to sit by the window and she wanted an aisle seat. We had worked that out previously. She was looking around as I got comfortable in my seat and I figured she was looking for her favorite stewardess or just checking all the different people out.

We buckled ourselves in and watched as the other passengers with young children were starting to fill up the aisle.

The boy with the Pirate hat on and his father were further back in the plane. Evelyn couldn't help but "high fiving" him as he walked past us. His father had a wedding ring on his finger, so I assumed the boy still had his mother to care for and raise him.

Getting remarried and falling in love was something I wasn't sure I wanted to do. Actually, I thought to myself, I'll never do that again. They say sometimes "love hurts," whoever said that was right, I knew. There seemed little time for me to look for love. Something maybe I really didn't want to find anyhow. It was Evelyn, I needed to love. So those, "nice to see you again" words Lauren would tell me, when I would see her at the grocery store never really sunk in to my head.

THE PRIEST, THE STEWARDESS, AND THE CHURCH PICNIC

Lauren was a little younger than me and worked as a cashier at the grocery store where Evelyn and I shopped. We all seemed to enjoy our short conversations together while I was checking our groceries out. She always gave Evelyn a free lollipop, which she pulled out of her jeans, whenever we would go there. I wondered if she did that for all the children. They liked each other. I liked her. But, I never would let those thoughts stay in my head too long. I wanted to stay in my dark place.

After they had passed us to find their seats, Evelyn told me that the little boy had cancer. It took me aback as I didn't know how to respond. I was glad he was already passed us and settling into his seat further back, when she told me. I didn't want to have a face of pity when he would have walked by. I remember that "pity face" people would give me when I told them about my wife's passing. I hated it. But, it's hard not to have one some time when you see someone and know of their situation.

She seemed so "matter of fact" about it. She said the boy told her when they were playing together after she asked him why he didn't have any hair. Evelyn had told him everything would be alright when he mentioned this to her. Maybe she knew something, or maybe she was just trying to make him feel better, I thought. How could she ever know something like that? Either way, the boy seemed in good spirits.

Evelyn told me he was going to the baseball game on Saturday and that he was trying to see as many as he could. I imagined this would give his mom a little break. I knew that feeling of needing a break. It was always wonderful for me whenever Evelyn would have a sleepover at one of her friends' houses. Her friends' parents all knew the situation and they knew I appreciated it. It was my little break.

I guess one of my fondest recent memories was when all her friends came to our house for a sleepover. The girls rotated every month and there were usually seven to ten girls, depending upon who could make it. The girls all had asked for sleeping bags on the same Christmas and they started that tradition right after that Christmas.

Debbie and I enjoyed that time together alone when she left for a sleepover. Able to go out and do the things we did before our "little angel" came into our lives.

Evelyn had thought it would be fun if all the girls made dinner that night instead of the usual pizza they would have at all of the other sleepovers. Pizza was the way to go. Quick and easy for a parent. But she thought it would be fun and she was right. Many of the girls never really helped out in the kitchen yet as they all had mothers to do this for them. It's what mothers do. But Evelyn had become quite the cook. I wasn't sure if she wanted do it this way to "show off" or because she wanted to teach them something good and useful. Either way, I was good with it.

We had decided on chicken, potatoes, salad, beans, and a few other different side dishes. Plus, she wanted to bake a few pies. I remember it as being apple and pumpkin. When we were checking out of the grocery store that day, Evelyn pushed the cart into Lauren's line, like she always did. Lauren could see we were having quite the little party. Evelyn told her about the sleepover party and how they were all going to cook dinner together and then do whatever comes next. I could see the happiness on her face when Evelyn was telling her all this and explaining how she knows how to cook. She was happy for Evelyn, as they had previously talked about Evelyn's mother. Lauren was most impressed with the pie mixes. She told Evelyn her favorite pie was apple and Evelyn told her she would remember that. With a grape lollipop in her mouth that day, we told Lauren goodbye and she winked at Evelyn and told her she wished she could taste some of Evelyn's cooking one day. Evelyn just smiled.

The girls had so much fun cooking. They just all chatted away as Evelyn would bark out orders as to who was doing what and how to do it. None of the girls minded, though. I think because they didn't know yet and were excited to know. It was a couple hours of good bonding time for them all.

It all tasted so good, since they made sure to make enough for me. Evelyn, being Evelyn, made sure everything was cleaned up perfect after the dinner. I thought they probably all learned something there also. She always tried to do as much as she could to make my life easier as she knew it was harder now that her mother was gone for me. She would have no part of me spending my time cleaning up her mess.

It made me a little angrier inside my head after Evelyn told me about the boy. More unfairness, I thought to myself. I was glad, I gave the boy's father a nod when he passed by. It really didn't mean anything, but it was some form of communication with him. One of those have a good trip nods. I was thankful his son and my daughter enjoyed their time together. Maybe, that's what the nod meant.

Patty finished packing her resumes back into her briefcase at just about this same time. I better head to the restroom, she thought to herself. She was a coffee drinker. Her coffee "habit" had grown since she was younger. Two or three pots a day she would consume now. It kept her going but made her have to use the restroom more often. It was a fair trade off, she always thought, as she could get more accomplished by being on a coffee "buzz."

She figured the young "party" girls would be going there shortly so she headed to the restroom now, before they could get there.

John saw the young couple sitting alone in the corner. They were young by his standards and seemed to be in their late twenties or so. Just about Kevin's age when he died. He figured they were happy and ,who knows he thought, maybe they just got married and wanted to be off to themselves talking romantic things.

Maybe they liked the darker seating section for this reason. A little more romantic. It couldn't be because they would want to be in a "dark place" like me, he thought.

It made him wonder if Kevin had many girlfriends or even any, while he was in Pittsburgh. Kevin didn't discuss that subject when I would see him, and I wasn't going to bring it up. He was on his own on that, John new. He had done his part in Kevin's maturing process and those were his choices in life. No matter now though, John understood, that he would never know.

John knew that he would want to use the restroom before it was time to board but he would keep an eye on how fast people were coming out of the men's restroom and judge it from there. No sense going to early.

He had noticed the one gentleman going for the third time in less than a half hour. John understood the need to use a restroom more often as one aged, but this man was younger.
It might be some type of physical problem, he thought, but it didn't really matter. He would wait until that gentleman returned before he would make his move.

Lori asked the other girls if they needed to go to the restroom one more time as the boarding call for the remaining passengers was starting. "We're all good," they responded, as they began to shut off phones and prepare to head to the check in gate for their boarding passes. "Sounds good," Lori said, as she headed to the restroom one more time.

She didn't have to wait in line to get her stall in the women's room. Lori was glad about that. She could take her time. Heck, she thought to herself, I'll have time to have one more drink as I sit here.

Her purse was large, just like her three best friends'. The bigger the better they would say to each other when they would go purse shopping together. Lori's reasons were the same. You can put more stuff in a bigger purse, they all mused.

She liked to carry small bottles of alcohol with her anymore.

A couple swigs of her favorite vodka going to the store or shopping never hurt, she would say to herself as she quickly drank one while quietly hidden in the bathroom stall. Her big purse had wonderful compartments in it for her "habit." When she bought it with Karen and Barbara that day, she knew what she would be putting inside the purse. It would hold whatever she would want, discreetly, even a mixer, if she needed. The bag was perfect for her, she told the girls at the checkout counter that day. They laughingly agreed.

She knew she had a problem. But she thought it was a small problem. She never had been in an accident. Never missed work. Never did something that only a drunk would do. If she had a problem, it was small, she would tell herself. A small bottle of mouthwash hidden away in her purse always hid her drinking odor. It was standard routine. Finish the bottle, have some mouthwash, spit it into the empty bottle and then throw the bottle out at her first opportunity.

She was a "smart drinker," she thought. Never let the bottles pile up. But she had plenty of room in her purse if they did, she always knew.

After rinsing her mouth out with her favorite mouthwash, she wrapped the empty bottle in toilet paper and left the stall to wash up before leaving the restroom. As she left, she discreetly placed the bottle in the trash bin. No evidence left in my purse, she laughed to herself, as she headed back to her friends.

Karen was just finishing her last text to her husband as Lori was coming back from her final stop in the restroom. She wouldn't want the girls to be reading these texts, she thought, so she was glad when she shut her phone off before her friends became too nosy.

They would find out soon enough.

THE PRIEST, THE STEWARDESS, AND THE CHURCH PICNIC

She had texted her husband to tell him their only option was to declare bankruptcy.

Years of living over their heads and keeping up with their so-called friends, led them to be financially under water. The big house, new cars and other items were things they could never really afford. They bought them anyhow. Using credit card after credit card to pay the minimum charge, there was never an issue. It worked for years. But the masquerade was over. She couldn't go on this way anymore falling deeper and deeper into debt. She told him to put the house up for sale. Put a for sale sign on the seldom used expensive car and call a lawyer to start the bankruptcy proceedings. Karen thought how ashamed the others will probably be of her when she tells them. They're going to find out, she knew.

Karen also knew that the best thing for her to do was also get a job. Maybe something at night time so that her husband could watch the kids and no babysitter was needed. They couldn't afford one. She placed the phone in her purse. Her texts safely hidden away.

Groups of people were now huddled closer to the gate area, as they all knew the preboarding process would be over shortly. There were only a few more groups with young children and regular boarding would be beginning soon.

Patty gathered her stuff and headed over to one of these areas. She found herself next to the four girls going on vacation together and enjoyed chatting with them. She learned some of them had children, just like her. They were taking a much-needed break, they said. Patty's break from her kids had now been too often. She wished that this was her last trip, but she new it wasn't over yet. The right person will appear, she'll hire him, and then, hopefully, no more airplane rides for awhile. She was eager to get on the plane, settle in and continue her resume reading. It was what she needed to do. The girls all seemed so happy, she thought to herself.

Father Feeney and John got to talking a little also as they inched their way closer to the gate area. They would stay towards the back of everyone as that's how they both were. No need to be upfront. The plane won't leave until we're all onboard, they both knew.

John was glad Father did not ask him about why he was flying today. He figured Father was smart. Most of the times conversations can lead to awkward situations and the priest, he figured, would rather just not know about it. John could tell the priest was tired looking. Maybe from his trip or maybe from the years of these kinds of conversations. He wasn't going to make it harder for either of them and kept the conversation simple. Sports, world affairs and that "ray of light" shining on our plane was what they talked about. He was not going to bring up his son's death.

Barbara, after seeing the priest, knew that she would have to tell her priest also. She thought of all the people who were going to eventually find out about her pregnancy. It was a heavy burden thinking about that. Her family, her neighbors, her relatives, her coworkers, everyone she knows will be finding out. She took a deep breath and remembered what her father said about thinking of something else. Think of the beach, she thought to herself. But it didn't really help much. The burden was too big.

Melissa was thankful that the airlines were smart enough to have preboarding as her kids were a handful for her. She was also thankful for Sharon, the kids and her seemed like old friends and she offered to help get the kids on board. Julie even held her hand as they waited in line.

Sharon had told her that she lived in Atlanta and that she was in Pittsburgh to visit her children and grandchildren. Melissa asked her how she liked Atlanta, and she told her she liked the weather better there than in Pittsburgh but sometimes she would get lonely as she lived alone now.

Melissa understood that alone feeling. She was moving to Atlanta and didn't know a person there. Well, she knew one, she smiled to herself. She knew Sharon now. It was going to be such a big undertaking for her. New city, new job, new apartment, and most importantly a new beginning for her and her children. She was glad she would have a week to get things settled before she started her job. The children would need to go to a day care while she was at work. This would be the most important thing for her to take care of as soon as she got there. Her kids were not going to be left in a place that wasn't full of love and happiness. She wondered if that was possible.

While Julie was latched onto Sharon's hand, Philip was having fun with the other children in the line. They were about to enter the plane and Melissa was happy about that. Get our lives back on track, she hoped. It was hard for her to imagine ever forgiving Ted for what he did to her. She had no time to think about that anymore, she had too much to do, she knew, when she would get to Atlanta.

Sharon felt at ease with Julie and Philip. Julie was quieter than Philip.

She was used to that. Michael, her grandchild, was very active and hard to keep still. Philip was much like him, so Sharon knew how to deal with that. It would never bother her, she thought to herself. He was a little boy, and that's how little boys are.

As Melissa entered the plane, the stewardesses gave them all a warm welcome. Julie admired their nice attire and Philip just wanted to scurry down the aisle to find their row.

One of them asked Julie if Sharon was her grandmother and Julie looked at Sharon and said that today she was, and they all smiled. Sharon's smile was the proudest. Melissa could tell she enjoyed being with them and imagined she missed her own grandchildren. They hurried to catch up to Philip as it seemed to them he found their row.

Julie was a little sad when she realized that Sharon would not be sitting with them. Melissa could see her eyes swell up a little when Sharon said that she hoped we would have a nice plane ride and that her seat was a little further back. She helped her get the kids situated and their luggage put away and gave each one of them a hug as she told them she would be a few rows back.

She left as quickly as they had met as other passengers were filing in behind them and Sharon had to find her seat. It made her sad to leave the kids, especially Julie.

But there wasn't much she could do so she found her seat. It was next to the emergency exit door. She didn't think it would be a problem and sat down there because that's where her boarding ticket placed her.

Just then a stewardess came up to Sharon as she was getting comfortable in her seat. Her nametag said Maria, so Sharon said, "Hello Maria," as the pretty stewardess sat down in her row. She explained to her that whoever sat in that seat would have to be physically able to open the door if necessary. It most likely would not be needed but she asked Sharon if she could indeed do this or maybe it would be better to move to another seat. Sharon thought that would be the best for everybody else and gladly told Maria that she would sit wherever she took her.

Maria told her she would be getting back to her on that once more of the passengers were onboard and the seating arrangements more fulfilled. Sharon just smiled and told her "she would be waiting right here."

Dan was happy to see Joey high five the little girl. She seemed so full of life, as did Joey. He thought to himself how lucky he was to be able to take him to see the Braves baseball game on Saturday. His workplace was aware of the situation and accommodated him as best they could. He appreciated that. It would also give Joey's mother a little break. She needed it to as it was a heavy burden for all of us. Mostly it seemed for her and I as Joey was unfazed by it all. All the visits to the hospital were like a little vacation trip for him. Nothing bothered him. It bothered him though.

Joey loved baseball and so did I, Dan thought to himself. When he concocted this crazy idea to visit all the major league baseball stadiums, I immediately fell onboard with the idea. This would be our eighteenth different stadium. We never got bored doing it. We both brought our baseball mitts to each game in the hopes of catching a baseball. That hadn't happened yet and probably wouldn't, but I didn't let on about that. The odds were small to get a ball. Even one that you didn't catch but either bounced your way or was given to you by someone who caught it. Not too many people give away a caught foul ball though, I knew.

He loved his Pittsburgh Pirates and it gave us something to do as a family. We all loved going to the games.

Joey and I had taken a picture in front of each of the stadiums we had been to so far and he had them plastered all over his bedroom wall. I prayed that it would be something he would enjoy for decades and decades of his life. Not months or years.

His favorite stadium was Fenway. It seemed to be most boys favorite. I didn't have a favorite. I was going to enjoy them all with him. No matter what place or who was playing. Most of the times we didn't see the Pirates at these stadiums, but Saturday's game was going to be the Pirates versus the Braves. He must have packed four Pirate shirts besides the one he was wearing. He would figure out which one to wear on Saturday, I thought. He was good at packing by now. I was saving my favorite Pirate shirt for the game. It was a "Willie Stargell" jersey. He was my favorite. Joey had a few favorites. Baseball players often change teams, so I was glad that it didn't seem to bother him. He knew that's just how it goes in life. Just like the cancer. It's just life.

Dan knew that his son had accepted that more than he ever would.

Aaron heard loud crashes of thunder as he got in line to board the plane. The once beautiful day had very quickly gone south, just as their flight was scheduled to do. The sky was full of dark, foreboding clouds that seemed so solid, Aaron wasn't sure their plane would be able to fly through them. Although he never had any fear of flying, Aaron was a little apprehensive as he made his way to his seat.

He preferred a window seat, but the last-minute nature of his trip meant only aisle seats were available when he booked the flight. Aaron wasn't sure how long he would be at his mother's house, so he packed heavy and had some trouble squeezing his suitcase into the overhead compartment.

As he worked on getting his luggage into the compartment, an impatient man with a strong smell of alcohol on his breath pushed past him while loudly complaining about him holding up the line. Normally, Aaron would say something to him for being so rude, but he really wasn't in the mood to argue with anyone at the moment.

He sat down, buckled himself in, and reclined his seat as he waited for the rest of the passengers to file in. There were a few children on this flight, which always seemed to make flights loud and unenjoyable, and also a group of young women who were likely going on spring break based on their excited chatter.

He hadn't been sleeping well since Shelley left, so he was hoping he could nap while the plane was in the air, but everyone passing his row made him feel like this would be a sleepless flight. Plus, the limited legroom and the storm outside had him expecting an uncomfortable and turbulent time.

As the plane's passengers continued to get settled, a man slightly older than he was and a young boy sat down across the aisle. The father looked like he could fall asleep at any moment, even with the raging storm, but the boy seemed to be full of energy. Aaron hoped the boy would not be loud or obnoxious; even if he couldn't manage to sleep on the flight, he wanted to at least be relaxed.

He took another look at the boy, who was wearing a Pittsburgh Pirates cap, and noticed that he was quite thin and might be bald, or at least had very little hair. It made him think of his own future, as the chemotherapy would soon rob him of his curly, jet black hair. He'd been tempted to just get it over with and shave his head himself, but he wanted to cling to normalcy for as long as possible.

The boarding had now begun for those sitting towards the back of the plane. That's where we wanted to sit, Lori thought to herself, when we purchased the tickets together that day many weeks ago.

The girls entered the plane and passed Charlene staring out the window at the light and rocking her upper body back and forth, gently, as to a slow beat. Her mother was very pleasant with everyone as they passed her and her daughter. We couldn't stop to chit chat or anything as everyone needed to be seated so we just kept moving. Like cattle going through the corral.

Just going through the motions.

Lori and Sam were first, with Karen and I right behind them. The gentleman that had bought Lori a drink at the bar after we left was a few people in front of us. He took his seat in the very back and we were just a few rows in front of him.

He probably wanted to be by the restroom, she thought, as he would most likely need to rid himself of some of those drinks he had. Lori and he were two of a kind, it seemed, as they were both in a happy state of mind. He told Lori if she wanted that he would buy her another drink if she sat with him and played a game of cards later on during the flight as the seat next to him was open.

Lori smiled and agreed with him. No hesitation on Lori's part. She knew the only thing better than a drink is a free drink and it was going to be a two-hour flight. She would need a drink or two.

They all placed their purses under their seats. Dark secrets hidden away for the time being.

John knew that it was time to head to the restroom as he told the priest he had better use it now. The gentleman who had been in and out of the bathroom a number of times was leaving the restroom, so John headed that way. Get rid of some of this waste inside me he thought. Every last bit. He wished he could get rid of some of the waste that was now in him due to his son's death this easy. It couldn't be that easy though, he thought.

The passengers were moving more quickly now through the boarding pass line.
Tom and Jill were happy about that. Their hopes for good news from the Pittsburgh specialists was not the answer they were looking for. It was time to get out of this city. A gloomy city they both thought as they looked out the window as they were in line.

Tom was happy that the children were all aboard the plane now. He knew it bothered Jill to see them. She longed to have a child and they had done all they could too have their own. It just wasn't going to happen. He was sure that they weren't the only ones in this situation. But their problems didn't matter to him.

There wasn't too much to smile about as the two of them boarded the plane. A short smile and nod was all he could muster to acknowledge the stewardesses' greetings as they entered the plane. He knew life wasn't perfect, as he glanced at Charlene, but he couldn't understand why they had to be the ones who couldn't have their own child. He or she would have been loved and well taken care of. So many children were being neglected by their mothers, and many of them were growing up without a father figure. He saw this scenario happening all the time. He wondered if these mothers were having babies for the benefits they would get on welfare. The whole system seemed to be a mess, he thought.

Jill wondered how Tom really felt about everything. Seeing the children playing in the airport and some of them in their favorite teams' jerseys was a stark reminder that Tom may never have a son to play with. She knew he longed for that. But what could she do? They tried and tried, to no avail. Maybe it was time to accept this as she found her row and seating on the plane. They were sitting next to a younger lady. She looked like she was Asian.

Jill introduced herself to the woman and found out that her name was Sonya. Jill sat down next to her as Tom closed the cabinet on their luggage and took his aisle seat. Sonya introduced herself to Tom as he was buckling himself in for the ride. She seemed like a well kept smart young lady as he noticed the book she had with her. It appeared to be a book someone studying to be a doctor would have.

By this time, John had gotten back from the restroom and was looking for his seat. Maria, the stewardess asked if he needed help as he was looking around. He told her not really but that any seat would work for him as he wasn't picky about things like that. Maria smiled and told him it would be wonderful if he would trade seats with a woman who was next to the emergency exit door. She was older and more on the frail side and the airline would prefer to have someone a little more physically capable next to the door in case the door was needed to open. She smiled and told him that it has never occurred on any flight she has been on, but they always needed to take care of that.

He said, "No problem," as he followed her to the door seat.

Sharon got up for the man and Maria directed her to sit where John was going to sit. Julie's eyes lit up when Sharon showed up in that seat. Right across from her. It was hard to believe for both of them as it made Sharon as equally happy. She buckled herself in and gave Melissa a nod and smile.

John sat himself down in the seat next to the emergency exit door and began to read the instructions on the door. He figured if indeed he did have to open the door, he better know how it works. It helped eat up the time as the other passengers were finding their own seats on the plane.

Father Feeney was pleasantly happy when he realized he was in the same row as the man he was talking to during the boarding wait. He liked an aisle seat to stretch his legs some as he was a taller man and he was happy to see this familiar face reading the instructions on the door.

Father jokingly asked John if he would be able to open the door if needed. He looked away from the door and saw that it was the priest preparing himself to sit in their row. "Let me read it a few more times," John said, "and then I think I'll have it," as they both laughed. They never really exchanged names while they were in the airport, so they greeted each other again with a handshake and exchanged names.

They both felt comfortable with their seating arrangement.

As did Sharon.

Julie couldn't wait for the plane to take off as she thought it would be the most exciting part. She kept saying, "one, two, three, liftoff," as she pretended her little hands were actually the big plane we were on.

Sharon could see that Melissa did not have a ring on her finger, so she had not asked about anything like that earlier in the airport. Maybe she was never married, maybe he died or they divorced. It wasn't really any of her business. She was just passing time with the lady's children and helping her out a little. Sharon knew that we all needed to help each other out more in this world. Maria the stewardess came by and gave Sharon a smile and she gave Julie and Philip each a lollipop which she pulled out of her uniform.

Melissa gave her a friendly smile for that as the ray of light continued to shine through the windows of the plane. Clouds seemingly forever in the distance while rain continued to fall gently on the plane and the rest of the runway. It was a sight to see, Melissa thought to herself.

Patty found herself in a row with her seat being in the middle. She was going to have a harder time reading her resumes, she thought, as she was placing her luggage in the compartment above their row. The gentleman in the aisle was pleasant enough as was the lady next to the window but she was hoping for a little more room. She noticed the stewardess giving the two children lollipops and told her it was a nice gesture as Maria passed by.

THE PRIEST, THE STEWARDESS, AND THE CHURCH PICNIC

Maria smiled and, out of the blue, asked Patty if she wanted to move to another seat towards the back of the plane as there was a row with two empty seats and it would make everyone a little more comfortable. She quickly thanked her, as did the two passengers Patty was going to sit by and she grabbed her luggage out of the compartment and followed Maria to a different row of seats.

Ray was by the window, he liked to peer out the window at the clouds as his mind drifts away to other thoughts. He was slightly startled when Maria introduced Patty to Ray. She would be sitting in the aisle seat, so Ray and Patty knew that they would have plenty of room. They both remembered each other from the "soccer" game as he had noticed her reading resumes and she had noticed him playing so wonderfully with the children.

After Maria had left and Patty was buckling herself in, she wondered to herself, how the stewardess knew her name. She thought maybe she did her homework on who was sitting where, she imagined, and she really didn't think about it anymore.

"I hope I'm not intruding on your space," Patty quipped to Ray with a wry smile on her face. "Not at all," Ray laughed back at her remembering that he had said the same thing to her in the airport when he was playing with the children. He told her the middle seat was all hers and could use it accordingly to set some of her papers. She appreciated that and took advantage of it by setting her briefcase there. He could see her company's logo on the briefcase as well as her business card dangling from it with her name and company title. He recognized the name of the company as it was the same day care where Darlene's child currently goes daily while she goes to work. Darlene always said nice things about it, he thought to himself as the stewardesses were preparing to give us their usual instructions on how to buckle up and how to use the oxygen masks if needed. They also explained to us where the exit doors were. In case the door was needed, I knew at least to head towards the priest. Hopefully that wouldn't ever be necessary.

The doors were now closed as the plane was being pulled in reverse out of the staging area it had been in for loading all the passengers. The ray of light seemed to get bigger as we backed out, in the rain, as it looked like the sunshine was starting to cover the entire runway.

The stewardesses had given their little preflight instructions to all of us as Jeremy was looking attentively at the two stewardesses who gave the instructions. He asked Evelyn if one of them was the stewardess who winked at her. She was reading her book at the time, as she was already bored of looking around at the other passengers, so she just giggled and told me, "No daddy." The stewardess who was in front of us giving instructions resembled Lauren a little. She was pretty in her uniform, Jeremy thought to himself as the vehicles pulling the airplane were almost where they would be unhooked and we would be on our own. "Pretty soon, Evelyn," I said as this was going on. I told her, "Next thing you know we will be in the clouds, sort of like being in heaven." She just said, I was silly and continued to look at her book and occasionally tried to see all the way into the first-class area.

She's probably trying to see the pilots or maybe she's looking for her stewardess friend, Jeremy thought as they, along with everyone else, were being checked to insure they were all properly buckled up. I double checked Evelyn's and mine and just sat back and relaxed looking forward to our vacation together.

The plane was now on its own, as we were slowly getting into the small line of planes ready to enter the main runway and take to the sky. The stewardesses had been told to take their seats by the captain and he informed us all that we would be taking off shortly.

Phyllis was holding Charlene's hand as the plane began to move as it was a little jerky to start. She knew Charlene had watched the other planes taking off, but she wasn't a hundred percent sure that Charlene understood that we were going to be doing the same in a few minutes. Charlene always liked it when her mother would hold her hand, she thought to herself, so she did it often. She hadn't held anybody else's hand, besides hers, since Gil had passed away. It was nice for the both of them.

Lori would have liked to use the restroom one more time before they took off, but that wasn't happening. She would have to hold it until they were in the air, she knew. Something she has done before.

Barbara and Karen just peered out the window together at all the goings on in the gate areas as they were heading to the main runway. Planes were being refueled and maintained. Luggage was being taken off and onto several planes while other luggage carts were scurrying towards who knows where. Planes, some bigger than others, were being pulled or pushed to their appropriate locations. Quite a lot of activity, they both said to each other.

THE PRIEST, THE STEWARDESS, AND THE CHURCH PICNIC

Ray was wondering what Atlanta would be like as Patty was getting herself prepared for a little work. He imagined it would be similar to Pittsburgh. A hassle to get to work and a hassle to leave work. From what he understood, Atlanta was much bigger than Pittsburgh and he figured their traffic situation would probably be just as bad. He quietly wondered to himself what kind of a position or person Patty was looking for. Obviously, it would seem if someone was looking at resumes, they were probably looking to hire someone, he thought. He laughed to himself as he thought maybe he should slide a copy of his resume into the pile. Give her a laugh.

Julie and Philip were also trying to look out the window as they were preparing for takeoff. They hadn't traveled much, so it was going to be exciting for them. She was glad they understood why they had to move to Atlanta. They were only children, but they knew. Kids probably know more than they'll ever tell us, Melissa thought. Her interview at the company, the month before, was perfect as her boss was also a single mother and could relate to her situation. She had told Melissa it would work out well for her and she believed her. So here she was, she thought, heading to Atlanta. She prayed to stay healthy and strong for her children's sake as she was all they had. She wished she knew at least someone in Atlanta to help her occasionally.

Joey had been on so many flights for our baseball journey that the plane ride didn't really excite him much anymore. After the first few flights, Dan imagined, it gets old hat for all of us. Even the stewardesses, he thought to himself, must get tired of it. It's their job though, they must trudge through it just like the rest of us at our jobs, he knew. Dan could see Joey checking out the Pirate book the gentleman across the aisle from us had on his lap. This guy must love the Pirates as much as Joey, he figured, with the Pirate jersey on and a book about the Pirates. He was sure of one thing about the guy, he loved his Buccos.

CHAPTER 10: THE FLIGHT

Julie told Sharon to "hold on tight" as the captain announced that they were next in line. Sharon smiled at her as Julie kept flying her make believe plane in the air in front of her cute little face. Sharon didn't mind flying, but she was always happier when they landed.

She thought most people probably were like her, happier when the plane was safely landed.

Barbara afforded herself a small smile when the plane started to speed up down the runway. By the time they flew back, she knew, her three best friends would know her secret. How they reacted in the many days to come about her baby would be up to them. She wasn't perfect, and she knew that no one else was either. But she figured that she was the least perfect of the bunch. She shouldn't judge herself though, she thought, as the plane finally soared into the sky.

The clouds had all but disappeared in the direction we were heading, and the blue sky was more and more evident as the plane began its ascent to its traveling elevation. It seemed like the clouds opened up for us, Jeremy thought, as he peered out the window. Not that he minded. He was looking forward to just sitting there for awhile.

Sometimes it was hard for him to just sit there. He would feel guilty if he knew Evelyn was bored or wanted to do something and he would be in no mood for it and would just sit there. He did that once and vowed not to do it again. He had to spend as much time with her as he could; she deserved that, having been "forced" into having only one parent. It made him tired though sometimes. Always on the go with her or the chores that needed to be done for her and him. The grass wouldn't cut itself. The food wouldn't cook itself. He had to always keep going. His favorite part of the week was when the two of them could just stroll slowly through the grocery store. A mellow nice thing they did together. And at the end of it all he knew that most times they would see Lauren. He knew that made Evelyn happy and to tell the truth, it made him happy also. But, he didn't really want to allow himself to be happy again. He may smile on the outside, he would tell himself, but he was angry. Angry that his "little angel" didn't have a mother.

It wasn't long before the captain took the plane to its required altitude. We were above the clouds at that point, the sun shining everywhere. He came on the loudspeaker and told us it was okay to unbuckle our seatbelts as we had clear sailing. Joey laughed when he said that. "We're not on a sailboat," he chuckled to his dad. "I know that," his father said as he checked the tickets he had previously purchased for the game on Saturday. Since the Pirates were playing, he got better tickets than they normally got. Joey didn't know that though. He thought we were going to sit in our usual cheap seats and move up if we could. He didn't mind. He knew the costs of all this. We were lucky to be able to swing it. Our church friends helped financially and it's something we'll never forget they did for us. Joey knew, the odds on getting a real baseball were slim in the cheap seats, but we both never gave up hope.

Joey never gave up hope.

Despite the extreme winds and heavy rain, the plane took off without a hitch. Take off was Aaron's least favorite part of a plane ride; his ears always popped and there was that moment of unease as if the plane might not actually get off the ground.

Just after the plane reached altitude, a flight attendant named Maria, according to her nametag, walked down the aisle checking on everyone. She was tall, with dark hair and a peaceful aura about her. Her calm smile and soft voice were not uncommon among stewardesses, but something about her made Aaron feel at ease.

As she passed Aaron's row, she smiled and gestured to his Pirates shirt and the boy's Pirates hat and said, "Looks like you two will get along."

Aaron groaned internally at her comment. The last thing he wanted to do was talk to this young boy for the entire flight. Of course, the boy immediately turned to Aaron to inspect his shirt. The boy's father was already fast asleep, so he couldn't tell his son to leave Aaron alone.

"My dad and I are going to the Pirates game in Atlanta," the boy said. "My dream is to visit every stadium before I die."

While Aaron thought it's never too early to have a bucket list, he was surprised this kid was talking like his days were numbered.

"How many have you been to so far?" Aaron asked, intrigued. "You should have plenty of time to visit them all, but that's great that you're starting so early."

"This will be the 18th city I've been to," the boy said proudly. "I'm not sure how much longer I've got, though. I have cancer."

The words hit Aaron like a 98 mile per hour fast ball. This kid has cancer? And here Aaron was thinking he got the short end of the stick. This boy couldn't have been older than nine. Aaron thought back to his preteen days and wondered how different things would've been if he had cancer then.

Not quite sure how to respond to that revelation, Aaron decided to keep the focus on baseball. "Wow, that's quite a lot of trips you've taken. Which stadium is your favorite so far?"

"That's easy. Fenway Park in Boston. The Green Monster was so cool to see in person," he said excitedly.

The boy kept on going, talking about all of the stadiums he had visited and which ones he liked and disliked. Aaron kept nodding and smiling at the boy, but he couldn't focus on what he was saying. Everything about this seemed so sad. His days were seemingly limited, and yet he spoke with the breathless excitement of any boy his age. Was he not worried about dying? Did he not care that he might never complete his goal?

"What's your name?" Aaron asked when he was finally able to get a word in.

"Joey," said the boy. "What's yours?"

"My name is Aaron. If you don't mind me asking, what kind of cancer do you have? How long have you had it?"

"I have leukemia," Joey said, "and I've had it as long as I can remember. I think my dad said I was born with it, but I don't remember that far back."

Aaron looked over Joey's head to examine the sleeping father. He wondered what it must be like raising a child with leukemia. It was difficult enough for Aaron knowing that he could die soon, but he didn't know if he could handle having a son or daughter with cancer.

Why did bad things happen to good people? It was all Aaron could think about over the last few weeks, and now he was sitting next to this child who was given a death sentence before he could even walk or talk. Aaron had been lamenting the fact that he got cancer at such a young age, but at least he'd been able to go through adolescence without having to worry about dying.

This whole situation had driven Aaron into a funk, a sort of depression that he could not seem to claw his way out of. He just kept thinking about missed opportunities. Just like everyone, he had goals and desires and plans, but he thought he'd have all the time in the world to follow through on them. Would he ever get a chance to visit the beautiful national parks he'd seen online, particularly Yellowstone and Yosemite? He had never even been out of the country, save for Canada. Now he was frequently reminded just how large the world really was and knew he would likely never get to see the vast majority of it.

Beyond travel, Aaron had plans to start his own marketing company that he had been putting off for years. While he enjoyed the work he did, his ambitions were greater than being a piece of someone else's puzzle. But now, he couldn't justify putting the time into that endeavor because work seemed so inconsequential when faced with the possibility of death.

Most of all, Aaron feared that he might never have the opportunity to settle down and start a family. He observed the little boy next to him and thought about the rest of the children on the flight, and he wondered what it would be like to be responsible for another human's life. Shelley was supposed to be the one he would settle down with, but now that was out of the question. As devastated as he was by her leaving, he supposed he was bitterly happy that she showed her true colors before they started a family together.

Aaron looked back across the aisle at Joey, who seemed content playing with a toy he had brought with him. So many thoughts and emotions coursed through Aaron's mind and body – how could this kid be so calm in the face of such an intimidating disease?

"Can I ask you something?" Aaron said to Joey.

"Sure," Joey said, giving Aaron his full attention.

"Aren't you scared? I imagine having leukemia has to be very tough to deal with," he said.

"I think it's tough for my dad and my mom," Joey said. "They worry a lot. I can tell they get nervous whenever I go to my friend's house or when they drop me off at school or when we have to visit the hospital."

"Well, that makes sense," said Aaron. "I'm sure they care about you very much and worry that something bad could happen."

"But don't you get scared?" Aaron pressed on, almost embarrassed that he was essentially asking this child for advice on how to deal with the prospect of having cancer.

"No. I am at peace with my life," Joey said, pausing to smile at Maria the stewardess, who was passing in the aisle. "What is there to be scared of? I know that God is watching over me."

The answer struck Aaron momentarily speechless. This kid was braver than he was. Aaron couldn't go more than a few hours without feeling sorry for himself, and meanwhile Joey was living his life as though he had no problems.

Aaron had always been what he called a lazy catholic; he was raised in the church, but as an adult, he didn't go to mass and really didn't pray like he should. Now that he had cancer, he felt further from God than he ever had before. How could he put his faith in a God that let this happen to him?

"There is plenty to be scared of," Aaron said.

"Do you have cancer?" Joey asked.

"Yeah, I have a tumor on my spine," Aaron said. "I found out a few weeks ago, and things aren't looking so great for me."

It felt weird to be talking to a child about his problems, but Aaron also oddly felt at ease. Throughout everything that had happened over the last few weeks, he had never actually talked to someone in the same boat as him.

"I know I'm not as young as you," Aaron said, "but I'm still young. I always thought I had my whole life ahead of me, but now I might not make it to my next birthday."

"You need to have faith that it will work out for the best," the kid said. "God is here for you, even when you might not realize it."

"It sure doesn't feel like he's here for me," said Aaron, realizing he sounded more like the child in this conversation.

"My mom always told me that God doesn't shout – he whispers," said Joey. "So, I try my best to stay calm and listen when I'm scared, and that's when I find God."

For the last three weeks, Aaron had been shouting "Why me?" at God, almost as if he was assuming God would shout back at him. Perhaps, if he had calmed down enough to listen, he would have heard what God was trying to tell him. He was looking up at the sky for an answer, almost as if he expected God to hire one of those planes that wrote messages in the clouds.

Aaron's mom also used to give him advice like that, but he had moved away years ago and didn't talk to her as much as he should. He hadn't had high hopes for this trip. More so, he was visiting his mom because he felt like he was out of other options. His life suddenly lacked direction, and this was a last stitch effort to help him gain some semblance of control back. Oddly enough, his conversation with Joey was helping reassure him that this was the right thing to do.

Deciding to try and turn the conversation toward something more lighthearted, Aaron asked Joey who his favorite Pittsburgh Pirate was.

"Well, it used to be Andrew McCutchen before he left, but now I guess it's Starling Marte," Joey said excitedly. "Who is your favorite?"

"I also liked McCutchen, but my favorite player of all time is Roberto Clemente, hands down. Do you know who he is?"

"I've heard of him. My dad told me about him. Why is he your favorite?"

"I actually never got to watch him play – he was before my time – but my dad would always talk about him when I was growing up. He was a real good guy off the field, too."

Despite his initial reluctance to talk to this kid, Aaron couldn't deny that he was having a good time so far. It didn't hurt that they were now discussing baseball – a subject Aaron could talk about for hours and hours. Most people got bored with his long-winded talks, but Joey seemed to hang on every word he said.

As a special treat for Joey, Aaron fished a book from the bottom of his carry-on bag and presented it. He had found it in one of the airport shops on his way to the terminal. It was a book detailing the history of the Pittsburgh Pirates. Aaron thought his mom might be interested in it – after all, he hated to visit her empty-handed – so he paid for it and hastily put it in his bag.

With Joey being as young as he was, pretty much all of the Pirates history was way before his time. Though Joey's dad had taught him well about the history of the game, Aaron enjoyed filling in the gaps and talking about some of Pittsburgh's greatest players and sports moments.

Joey was surprised to hear that the Pirates had won five World Series.

"The last time they won it all was in 1979," Aaron told him.

"Wow, that's like forever ago! That's before I was born," Joey said, mouth agape.

"That's before I was born, too, you know," Aaron said, chuckling. "I'm not that old."

When they started looking at the book, Aaron was holding it across the aisle for Joey to see, but it wasn't long before the book was nestled in the little boy's lap. He eagerly flipped through the pages, looking at the pictures and reading about legendary players and games.

"You know, I was originally going to give that book to my mom as a gift," Aaron said, "but she knows even more about the Pirates history than I do. Why don't you keep it?"

The book almost toppled out of Joey's lap at the sound of this offer. He clutched the book in his little hands so it didn't hit the floor, and he looked back and forth between Aaron and his father, his mouth open wide.

"You mean it? I really can keep it?" he asked.

"Sure thing," Aaron said, smiling. "As long as you promise to read the whole thing."

"That won't be a problem!" Joey said, still smiling widely.

The captain also said that the stewardesses would begin distributing beverages and a snack shortly. The gentleman that Lori, and the rest of us, met at the bar was happy to hear that and offered to buy us all drinks. Karen and I passed on his offer but Lori and Sam took him up on it. "Heck, since you're buying, I'll have a double," Lori laughingly told him.

"We have plenty of time to drink it as the flight just started," she told Sam. Sam just stuck with one. A beer. It would be enough for her, she thought to herself. She, along with probably everyone else in the plane, didn't want to have to use the restroom during the flight. Plus, it was still early in the day, she thought, I don't want to get too tipsy before we even get there.

Lori figured she would play a game of cards with him after the stewardess gave them their drinks. Sam didn't mind. "He paid for the drinks, so why not?" she told Lori. "Go for it!"

Sam knew that this would give her an opportunity to take one of her depression pills. It made her feel better, for whatever reason, so she fumbled through her purse and found her bottle of relief. Nobody knew about this, not even her husband, and she was going to keep it that way. She got good at faking happiness. A feeling she longed for, happiness.

She wondered how her friends always seemed to be so happy. It made her feel more depressed thinking about it so she always chose not to. They were her best friends and she was glad they were happy.

Lori headed back one row to sit with him, purse in hand, as he grabbed his cards out of his briefcase. "We'll play a game of gin rummy," he told her as he searched for the cards. Lori could see in his briefcase a few small bottles of vodka in there as he was going through it. She was glad it was vodka, she thought to herself, as that's what she likes to drink. They thought alike on that, she mused to herself. A can of soda and some vodka, safely hidden away. She hoped she didn't appear to be in the same heightened spirits as he was. She was a good drinker, she knew. She would never be like that. "Gin rummy it is," Lori said, as the man began to deal the cards.

Karen had asked for water. It's what I was going to order, so I was glad she ordered first. "Two waters, on the rocks," I told the stewardess as all three of us laughed accordingly. Barbara knew that from here on in her eating and drinking habits would need to change. Mainly her drinking habits. She didn't overdo it, but she was young, and they would go out to the bars and nightclubs with friends and have a few drinks. That would change now. Today. She would drink just water and juice until the baby was born. She wondered to herself again, if she could handle a handicapped child and the issues associated with it. She thanked the stewardess, took a small sip and took a deep breath and sat back in her chair.

Think of something else, she told herself. This will be a lot easier telling them than my parents, she knew. It was inevitable, that she would have to tell them. Her parents had met Toby a number of times before and liked him. They were short visits, the two of us would make, when I needed to grab a few things and Toby enjoyed the visits as well he had told me after we left there on numerous occasions. So, at least they had met. He was my baby's father and there was no way around that.

Evelyn ordered an orange juice once the beverage cart got to their area. She knew I would like a water, so she ordered that also. Neither of these two girls were the stewardess whom Evelyn seemed to be enamored with. It was a brief walk by and wink, the lady must have given Evelyn, as I never saw her. But, a father can tell when a child is genuinely excited about something or someone. So, I figured she had to be there somewhere. She usually only had that "glow" about her as we would be waiting in Lauren's line at the grocery store.

I never knew if it was because she always gets a lollipop or if it was because they genuinely liked each other. When Lauren found out about her mother, from her priest Father Mayer one day when he was a few customers behind Evelyn and had seen the two of them talking, she had made a special card for her and gave it to her the next time we saw her. She never showed me the card, but I knew of its importance. We had made a pact a long time ago that I would not go through her things and that she wouldn't go through mine. So, I never rummaged around for it to read or anything like that. It was probably one of those "sorry to hear about your loss" cards.

I had gotten tired of those. You have to read them all, but that doesn't mean you have to like it. After the first few, I grew weary of opening another card, but I pressed on accordingly until I had read them all.

I always figured that it was between the two of them and I left it at that.

The beverage cart had moved further up the aisle as Evelyn continued slowly sipping on her orange juice. She liked to use a straw and we were both glad that the stewardess gave her one. Next thing you know, kneeling down in the aisle next to Evelyn's chair was another stewardess; it was Maria.

She was like I had imagined in my mind after Evelyn had described her. Quietly pretty, with a certain calm radiant aura around her. She said "Hi" to me and started to talk to Evelyn, as I listened while looking out the window. Maria asked her what book she was reading, as Evelyn smiled at her, showing her the cover of the book. It was her favorite book about heaven. She knew it by heart, she told Maria. A priest had given it to her when her mother was in the hospital, shortly before she died, Evelyn explained to Maria. She told her that the two of them would read it at least ten times a day, taking turns reading. One of us would read while the other would turn the pages she said. It was not only her favorite book but also her mom's.

Maria said that she remembered that book when she was younger. Just a little older than you are now, she told Evelyn. After describing the very last pages and the pictures on them, Evelyn knew that she had also read the book before. Maria told Evelyn that it was also one of her favorite books. I thought it sure was a coincidence that they both had read and liked the same book. She couldn't be lying, Jeremy figured, because Evelyn never showed her the pages in the book. At least not in this plane or in the airport, he figured. Just a strange coincidence.

Maria, still in a semi kneeling kind of position, moved closer to Evelyn so as to allow a passenger to walk down the aisle to utilize the restroom. Jeremy had remembered him from the airport, as it seemed to him that the gentleman had used the airport restroom a number of times while he was sitting there watching the people wander around the airport.
He figured he had a health issue and that was that.

When she got closer, Evelyn noticed the necklace and charm Maria was wearing around her neck. It was exactly the same as hers. Evelyn pulled her charm out of her shirt so that Maria could see it. "Indeed, indeed it is the same," Maria said as she pulled hers out so that Evelyn, and I, as I was looking now, could see it. They were the same. I could see that.

I would tuck Evelyn into bed after she said her prayers every night, so I had seen that charm hundreds of times before. It was just another one of those weird coincidences one sees in life every so often. It made Evelyn happy, so in turn, it made me happy, if nothing else.

They both tucked their charms back into their shirts as Maria told Evelyn that she would bring her a nice blanket for her nap. "Give me a few minutes," she said, and she would be back before you know it.

I thanked Maria for looking for some blankets for us as there were none in the luggage compartment above us. Those who travel frequently probably all knew to grab one when they could. I had told Evelyn, "Daddy was tired and might take a nap on the plane," and she said if I was going to take a nap so was she. "We could nap together," she laughed. Maria just smiled and walked toward the back of the plane. The other stewardesses were still busy pouring drinks and handing out snacks.

I was looking forward to a little nap as it was a busy morning getting everything packed for the trip, driving to the airport and the whole airport check in process. Evelyn said she was going to dream of her mother. I just smiled at her. It was all I could do, as I knew my dreams would be more of the nightmare type. No heaven dreams for me, I thought.

Father Feeney was comfortable in his seat. They were better than the chairs in the gate area, as he slouched back a little in it. The sun shining through all the windows creating a bright scene throughout the airplane. It reminded him of when the sun would shine through the windows at his little church. The sunshine would come in from up high and shine down on the pews and some of the statues in the church. The statues and for that matter, the church itself, was old. But the statues were impressive. Hand crafted years ago, he imagined. Not only of Jesus and Mary, His mother, but also of various saints and angels. He didn't have a favorite. They were all wonderful works of art and he was always proud when he could show someone new, the inside of the church. Visitors were always impressed by them.

He couldn't help but seeing the pile of mail that John had set down between them. He had asked if it was okay as he was thinking of going through some mail on the ride home. Father didn't mind at all, "It's all yours," he told John, with a smile, leaning back comfortably. John thanked him for his kindness and as Father nodded back at him, he noticed that the mail seemed to be addressed to someone in Pittsburgh. He could see the words, Kevin McDonald, clearly, on the top envelope of the stack. He knew his flight friend's first name was John, or at least that's what he said it was, Father thought to himself. Maybe it wasn't John. Maybe he didn't want me to know as it wasn't my business. He was a quieter kind of man, Father thought, and actually he knew that it wasn't any of his business.

But Father couldn't help but noticing the top envelope was from St. George's Church in Pittsburgh. He wasn't trying to be nosy, but there it was, inches from him. He couldn't help but notice the church's logo on the return address. He had just met a priest from there, at the conference. His name was Father Mayer, he now remembered. That was his church. He was the pastor there and was one of the presenters at the conference. They talked for a short time that day, but Father Mayer said that he had to go as there were a number of patients at the local hospital he still needed to visit that day. I remember thinking that he must be quite the priest and wondered, as I sat in my chair, if the little girl who told me about the priest, who read to her, was actually referring to Father Mayer. Small world, he thought to himself, as John was finishing his drink, staring out the window at who knows what, Father thought.

John knew that he would have to read the mail sometime. He had collected it all that week and had gone to the post office to stop anymore mail from going to his son's old apartment. It was one of the many things he did that week. Depressing things. Any further mail addressed to his son would be forwarded to John in Atlanta. He wished to himself that this pile would be the end of it as each letter from Pittsburgh would be a fresh reminder of his son.

Finishing his drink, he handed it to the stewardess collecting things needed discarded. He decided it was time to open the mail. The first envelope, he noticed, was from some church in Pittsburgh. He wondered what that was about as he began to open the letter. John hadn't gotten into the habit of going to church anymore and he wasn't aware that his son had attended that church or any other church, he thought to himself.

After carefully opening the envelope, John pulled out a two-page handwritten letter. He was surprised as he hadn't seen a handwritten letter in years. It seemed nobody wrote anymore, they just type, he thought quickly to himself. Before reading it though, he looked at the second page to see who it was from. He knew it was from St. George Church, but he wanted to see who it was actually from before he read it all. It definitely wasn't a copy of a generic letter a church might send to everyone in their parish or something like that, he knew.

It was signed, Father Mayer, pastor of St. George Church.

After placing the empty envelope back on to the top of the mail pile in the seat next to him, he sat back a little more comfortable in his chair and began to read the letter.

Father Feeney noticed the St. George logo on the envelope again after John placed it back down onto the empty seat next to him. But he kept to himself, as he knew John was about to read the letter. He could also see that it was a handwritten letter, something he hasn't seen in awhile either.

He wasn't being nosy, he knew, because whether it was a magazine, book or letter that someone was reading almost right next to you, it's hard

THE PRIEST, THE STEWARDESS, AND THE CHURCH PICNIC

not to notice.

The letter was addressed to the father of Kevin McDonald. It said that, he, Father Mayer, wanted Kevin's father to know a little more about his son and offer his condolences. As he had never met him, it was the best way for him to get a message to John about his son, Father said in the letter.

Father explained how Kevin started going to his church many months ago. He would bring two young men with him every Sunday morning and he had introduced himself to Father on one of those occasions. Kevin had found "God" one day and just started going, the letter said. Father Mayer knew that Kevin, not only loved but was very thankful for his father who lived elsewhere. His father, he had told the priest, made him the man he was today. Father stated that, "He knew that Kevin loved his father deeply." It was something John wished he had said more to him now. "I love you son," that's not too hard to say he thought to himself quietly. He wished he would have said it more.

It seems Kevin also began helping out at the church on many additional occasions. Father said that when he needed help, "I always could depend upon Kevin." He also would take walks with those needing help due to being in a wheelchair. The letter said his little group would meet once a week after church and he, along with the two young men he was mentoring, would always push someone. The elderly folk all appreciated him, loved him and prayed for him, the letter said.

It was hard for John to fight back the tears, but he did. He knew he had to.

The letter ended with Father Mayer writing that he needed to continue to lead his life accordingly, as Kevin would want you to. Look around and listen, the letter said, and you will feel your son's glory in all that you do.

With prayers and love, signed, Father Mayer.

John just sat back in his chair and glared out the window. A smile came to his face as he began to really understand the man Kevin had become. He was prouder than ever. When he got home, he would write this pastor a letter. He wished he could have shared this with Angela; when she gracefully listened to him tell her about his son. Maybe she knew how wonderful he was, he thought.

It was time to open that little wrapped box from Angela now, he thought to himself, just as Father Feeney, seeing that John was finished with the letter, asked him if that letter was from St. George Church in Pittsburgh. He knew the pastor there, he said. He had just met him this weekend at a conference and he seemed like quite the man, Father Feeney said.

As John carefully put the letter back inside of the envelope, he smiled at Father and said, "Yes, it is. It's from a Father Mayer."

"A wonderful man," Father said.

"I wished I could have met him," John said to Father. "It seems my son went to that church and had gotten close with Father Mayer. I wasn't aware of that," John said, "until this letter."

"I had to bury my son, last week," John told Father Feeney, holding back the tears.

Father Feeney, after hearing this, adjusted his chair to the upright position and grabbed John's right hand. Father blessed himself, closed his eyes, and said a short prayer for Kevin. It was a homemade prayer so not knowing the words, John couldn't pray with him, but he blessed himself also when he finished and thanked him.

"I didn't want to bother you with my troubles," John told Father, "but you had asked about the envelope and such, that it just came out."

Father put him at ease quickly about that and it was a relief for John to hear.

He further explained how his son had passed away and that he lived in Atlanta but didn't get to church much anymore. The churches that he tried going to were just not right for him. Father nodded his understanding and asked about the letter. John let him read it as that was the easiest way to do it. It was a letter that he would be proud to share with anyone. What better description of his son then that, he thought, gazing out the window.

After putting on his reading glasses, Father read the letter himself and then placed it carefully back in the envelope.

"Truly blessed you are, to have raised a man like that," Father said. "Truly blessed." They sat there quietly for awhile, taking it all in.

Jill and Tom were glad they were finally heading back home as Tom struck up a conversation with Sonya before she began reading her book. As he had been sitting there for awhile now, he definitely knew that her book was about the anatomy of humans. He couldn't help but noticing that as the book was large, and the cover had a bright picture of the human body with the big words, "ANATOMY," on it. "That looks like a book only someone smart would read," he said to Sonya as she glanced his way. She laughed and said that she didn't know about that, but that it was a book about the anatomy that she was reading as part of one of her courses in college.

She was studying to be a doctor, she said. She wasn't quite sure what kind of doctor yet, but she would have time to figure it out. Tom told her that he would bet she would be a wonderful doctor one day and that her parents were probably so proud of her for going the route she was going. What parent wouldn't be, he knew.

Sonya told him that she believes both sets of her parents were happy about her decision to be a doctor. Tom thought quickly to himself that her natural parents must have gotten divorced and that they both got remarried. That would be two sets of parents, he thought.

"My parents had died when I was only eight years old," she said. "They were both innocent victims of an accident, it wasn't their fault," she said, "but they paid the consequences for someone else's actions. I paid for the accident also."

It pained Tom to think of it. He wished he would not have said anything and told her he was sorry about that.

She smiled at him and said that it was okay. Her pain and anger faded away many years ago over the unfortunate incident.

She told Tom, while Jill also listened, that she was blessed to have another chance in life.

"After the accident, I was homeless. Homeless people in my country have nothing. They are treated worse than the dogs," she said. "I would go to the shelter for children, and that was how I ate. It was when I joined the church there that my luck changed. The church was affiliated with an adoption organization in the United States. Most of the times, the only ones who would get adopted were the real young ones. Older children, as old as I was back then, were usually passed by on being adopted. After so many years, the child would usually turn to the streets for a living. Anyway they could," she explained.

"But for some reason, a family chose me. A family in the United States, that lived in Atlanta, Georgia, wanted to adopt me. They had two children of their own and wanted to adopt a child. Any child. Someone who needed to be loved and taken care of like anyone else. Before you knew it, I had been blessed with new parents and a brother and sister," she chuckled.

"That was about ten years ago," she said. She continued to say that she donates some of her spare time to the adoption cause now, not only in Pittsburgh but also in Atlanta at one of the adoption agencies in each of the two cities. She had promised herself, when she got adopted, that she would do that when she got older. She was good to her word, as she knew she was so fortunate and tries to help out others who are currently in the same kind of situation that she had found herself in many years ago. "I like helping people now," she said. "That's probably why I decided to become a doctor. My second set of parents are proud, also," as all three of us smiled at each other when she said that.

"That's a wonderful story," Jill told Sonya as Sonya began to page through her book to begin her studying. Earlier, Sonya said that she went to the University of Pittsburgh for medicine and worked at the Catholic Charities adoption center.

Jill knew where the center was located in Atlanta. She drives by it occasionally when she goes to visit her parent's house. A modern looking building, clean and well kept. She never really thought about a situation like Sonya's before. As she looked back on her life, she suddenly realized how lucky she was.

Just when Sonya was about to begin her studying, a stewardess came by. She said she overheard Sonya say that she was adopted, and I guess wanted to say something about it.
Her name was Maria, and she said, "Keep up the good work, Sonya," and told her, or maybe us, I wondered after she said it, that "God loves those the most, who sacrifice their time, talent and treasure to help a child, that isn't even their own, in need."

She left as quickly and as quietly as she came. Sonya told her that she knew that and she hoped her parents knew that. Maria, smiled, when she left, and told Sonya, "They'll find out for themselves one day."

THE PRIEST, THE STEWARDESS, AND THE CHURCH PICNIC

Jill and I just sat there holding each others' hands after Maria left.

Sonya went to reading her book and the two of us thought to ourselves about what Maria had just said.

Evelyn was finished reading her book again. Not that she needed the book, she had it memorized. She liked looking at the pictures, I thought to myself, because she definitely knew all the words. She carefully placed the book back in her knapsack, zipped it back up and placed it under the seat. She must have known Maria was coming with the blanket, because there she was. Blanket and smile in hand.

Maria gave the blanket to Evelyn and asked her who or what she was going to dream about. She answered that she was going to dream about her mother. It was her favorite thing to dream about and she told her that now that we were way up in the sky and closer to heaven, she wondered if her dreams would be louder. Maria laughed and said, "Debbie would like that," as she looked at me also before she left. "Sweet dreams to both of you," she said, heading back down the aisle. I didn't remember, Evelyn or I, telling her Debbie's name. At least, for sure, I knew that I hadn't told her, and I was pretty sure that Evelyn didn't either.

Since it was her trip, and that I had told her she was in charge, Evelyn told me that I would have to dream about mommy on our nap just like her as I tucked the blanket around her. I told her I would try, but I wasn't sure if she believed me. Dreaming of Debbie only caused me more pain when I would awake, I thought to myself.

The two of us bundled up in the blanket made it nice and warm for both of us. It was a little cool in the plane, I thought. Evelyn closed her eyes and seemed to nod off faster than me. She was probably tired of the plane process as much as I was. She was a big help, I knew, with packing and everything else. I was going to listen to them both and try to dream of Debbie; I would do anything for Evelyn, as I thought about the three of us when we took Evelyn to the ocean the first time. We always enjoyed going to the ocean, and that's where Evelyn and I were eventually heading after a quick layover in Atlanta. I would think about that as I shut me eyes, hoping to drift into a deep sleep for awhile.

The ocean trips were what he was hoping to dream about. He remembers the first time Evelyn felt the cool splash of an ocean wave bouncing off her legs. She couldn't get enough of the ocean after that, he thought to himself. It had made Jeremy feel good when Evelyn held his hand before she closed her eyes.

He loved to hold her hand, he thought as he fell asleep.

Phyllis was glad that Charlene fell asleep on the plane ride. It would give her a chance to take a nap also. Without even being asked, the stewardess was nice enough to bring over some blankets for them once we were in the air. They were small, but they gave Charlene a comfy feeling when she wrapped it around her upper body. The sun was shining bright through the window next to Charlene, but Charlene didn't seem to mind and had closed her eyes and dozed off into a deep sleep shortly after the captain notified us that we could unbuckle our seat belts if we needed to.

She looked at her phone before she got more comfortable in her seat and was pleasantly surprised that Peter had sent her a quick text. He said to enjoy the trip and he missed her already. It was a nice feeling to know, as she closed her eyes and thought about Peter.

Barbara and Karen were both happy to sit in their chairs without having to say much. They would be together for a number of days and would be able to talk later, they acknowledged. "Lets just relax and enjoy the peaceful ride," Karen said with a wry smile as they both knew that it was a little louder in the card game a few rows back.

Lori and Paul, the drinker guy, were heavily into their card game. They weren't overly loud, but they were having fun. "What the heck," Karen said to Barbara, "let her have some fun. Better her than us," they joked to each other. Karen's thoughts were about their impending bankruptcy. It was going to be a shameful thing, she thought to herself. She wishes that she never bought some of the things that she did. They couldn't afford them and she knew that when she bought them. She'll never forgive herself for what they did. Trying to be something, they weren't. All for appearances sake. Who cares anyway, she now imagined. She hoped that her friends wouldn't care.

Lori was happy when Paul, her new card playing, drink buying friend reached into his briefcase and pulled out some small bottles. She knew, though they were labeled mouthwash, that they were actually full of alcohol. He didn't even ask, he just poured some into her glass. She gave him a wink when he did this. They both knew their styles. Do it quietly. Keep it hidden. But do it. Nobody around them saw him refill their glasses. Keep it coming Lori thought, I'm on vacation as she shuffled the cards to deal the next hand.

Sam just stared at the window enjoying the view from way above the planet surface. It had become clearer now and she could see the ground below. An occasional cloud would obscure her view but on the whole it was clear. She was glad Lori was having fun. But she was glad they were in a plane and not a bar at home. She knew what could happen when a man and a woman share a lot of drinks together. Bad choices are made. At least Lori won't have a bad choice to make with this guy, she thought to herself. She'll never forgive herself for that night. It was a bad choice to meet a man for late night drinks when your husband is away even if you didn't sleep with him.

Sam wondered if she was the only one on the plane that suffered from depression.

Out of the blue, Barbara asked Karen what it was like to have a baby born from inside of you. Karen had thought that it was an interesting different kind of question for Barbara to ask but thought that she asked it since they both saw the pregnant lady a few rows in front of them. Barbara had helped her with her luggage, Karen had remembered, so she figured it wasn't too crazy of a question.

Karen went on to tell her everything about it all from beginning to end. Barbara listened intently as she told her, almost in awe of the whole idea. At the end, Karen said that it was wonderful. "Heck," she said, "that's why I did it twice," as they both laughed.

Barbara thought about Toby and his reaction when she would tell him. He wasn't a perfect catholic, but he was a catholic, and premarital sex was just not something they condoned, she thought to herself. She knew he went to church most of the time. It was probably going to be hard on him also as he would have to tell his parents and everyone else. He had made his choices though, just like her, she knew. He would have to learn to live with them. Most of us don't know the consequences of some of our choices in life. Go to college or don't go to college. Marry him or marry him. Buy this or buy that. Drink this or drink that. Each choice, she knew now, could have a lasting profound impact on one's life. She would start to make the right choices from here on in, she promised herself.

Despite sitting next to Joey, who was excitedly flipping through the pages of the book Aaron had given him, Dan was sound asleep for much of the flight, until a small patch of turbulence roused him from his peaceful slumber.

"Where'd you get that book from?" Dan asked sleepily, rubbing his eyes.

"From Aaron!" Joey said, pointing across the aisle. Aaron cast a look around at Dan and waved.

"Hello," Aaron said. "Your son and I were talking about the Pirates, and I figured he could get a lot of use out of that book."

"That's very nice of you," Dan said, surprised at Aaron's generosity. "Are you sure you don't want it back?"

"Not at all!" Aaron replied. "Like I said, he could get a lot of use out of it."

"Thank you very much! What are you headed to Atlanta for?" Dan asked Aaron.

"I'm just going to visit my mother." Aaron said. "Speaking of the Pirates, we are planning on going to the game tomorrow night."

"What a coincidence," Dan said. "Joey and I are going as well!"

Father Feeney and John talked a little more about John's son as the flight continued. John was now glad that he had been seated next to him as the two of them seemed to talk like old friends who actually cared about each other. You don't see that happening anymore, he knew. Father told John that unfortunately bad things happen in life. God doesn't like it either when that happens, but he lets us make our own choices. The girl who caused the accident made the wrong choice and Kevin had to pay for it. She made the wrong choice that day. He has seen it so many times over his career, he told John. Young children dying tragically. Families torn apart by divorce, drugs or alcohol. Relationships ruined due to infidelity. An endless array of sad stories. "It's just part of this thing we call life," he said. "We are granted only so much time on this earth and we need to use that time wisely. Never waste someone else's time either," he said. "That's worse than wasting your own time. Time is precious."

I knew now how time was so precious. I wish I would have had one more day with Kevin, John thought. Just a little more time.

He wondered to himself what they would have done together if they knew it was going to be the last time they saw each other. Go to a baseball game? Who knows he thought. John knew that going to the church that day would be one of the things Kevin would have wanted to do together if they knew it was their last day. He could sense that from the letter.

"Truly blessed, you are," Father said again. "I'm sure Kevin has found glory with God. It was apparent from the letter from Father Mayer, the kind of man Kevin was," he said. "Not all men are like that. Some men would never spend their time with a couple of young men who had no father themselves. Some men would never donate their time to help the elderly enjoy the short time they have left on this earth. Both you and Kevin were truly blessed," Father said with a smile.

John thanked the priest in such a way that Father Feeney knew he had helped this man out. A grieving man, maybe with a new outlook on it all. He was unsure sometimes, in the past, how well his sermons went over with his parishioners. It's something that is hard to tell. But this time, he knew. This man had been changed by that letter and my words, Father thought. Changed for the good. It made Father realize that small victories are good victories and that he shouldn't judge himself so harshly. Tell them the truth, tell them to lead a holy life and hope they listen and act accordingly. That's all he could really do. They'll all make their own choices. We all do. Father relaxed back in his seat as he saw John grabbing a small wrapped box out of his briefcase.

Angela had told him, "Listen to those close to you," he remembered. He hadn't felt this good since hearing of the news of his son. The letter and Father Feeney's words were inspiring. Actually, he hadn't felt this good in a long, long time. He knew Angela was right as he began to open the wrapped box she had given him. He didn't like to call it a present. Presents were for good, happy occasions, he thought to himself. So, he just called it a wrapped box.

The paper came off easily, as it always does, from around the box. It was so perfectly wrapped that John was careful when he unwrapped it, not wanting to tear the wrapping paper. She was quite the special person, he thought, as he opened the box.

Inside it was an angel figurine made of glass and shaded blue. It was no more than 4 inches high. The light shining through the window shone nicely on the figurine as he held it in his hand. He knew now who the angel was looking after him. It was his son. His wonderful son. It seemed to him that Angela must have had a sense of this. One way or another, he was glad he did not just throw it away. He would place it on his nightstand, next to a picture of him, his late wife and Kevin. He closed his eyes and said a short prayer. It was the most meaningful prayer he had said in some time. He prayed to his wife and son. He was at peace.

It was hard not to notice John opening the box and revealing what was inside of it. Father was intrigued by the figurine as he asked if he could hold it. It reminded him of one of the statues in his church. Much smaller, obviously, but it was similar. Father asked him who had given him that as they were now it seemed good friends. John told him the story of Angela and again remembered that she said to "Listen." Father said again that he was truly blessed.

He told John about the resemblance of his figurine with that of a statue in his church and John was listening now. The sun would shine on that statue every morning, he said. That's when John said, "Father, I would like to come visit your church sometime soon."

John was listening.

As they were now to altitude, Patty figured it was time to open her briefcase and continue her resume reading. She had taken this flight so often that she knew pretty much how long she had before the captain would give us the buckle up message. That was her cue to stop working, put her things in order and buckle up. Destination within reach, she knew. So, she unbuckled her seatbelt and started taking resumes out of her briefcase.

Ray knew that the logo on her briefcase was from the day care facility that Darlene was taking her children to. He wasn't really sure if they both went now but he knew at least one of them did. "ABC Daycare" was the name of it. Nice little logo, he always thought when he would drive by it occasionally. He mentioned to Patty that his secretary, Darlene, and a few other friends of his take their children to "ABC Daycare" and that they have never complained. "That's a good thing," he said, "as people like to complain about things." Both of them laughed at that comment. "They sure do," she said. "They sure do."

She told Ray that she has worked for the company for nearly twenty years. Starting part time in their Dallas facility while she was in college, she took a job there a few years after she graduated and had been working somewhere else. Her job, at that time before ABCD, as they affectionately called it, was not very fulfilling. "It didn't even pay that well as I was a younger person. It really felt like a job, every minute of the day. One day, when I was at home on vacation from there, I stopped by the facility that I had been working at to say hello to some of my old coworkers who were like my friends and I found out they were looking to hire somebody. It was full time with benefits. Pay was okay, not really even more than I was making, but I made the choice that day to take the job. When I left that building that day knowing that I was starting a new job, a new experience, it felt like I had just won the lottery."

She continued to tell him that she had worked her way quietly up from that position to a number of other positions at a few of their other facilities. Whatever is needed, she would do for them, as they had always been good to her. She was now actually in charge of all the facilities. She had help in the main office, she told him, and would normally visit a different facility each week. This kept her in touch with most of the facility managers as they played the key role at their respective facility. It wasn't too bad on the home life as she would fly out Tuesday afternoon, go there Wednesday morning and be home that night. They would give her afternoons off for the rest of the week as they knew her time, and everyone's time, was important, and they appreciated her doing that for them. "It has really been a wonderful tradeoff, as it gives me my afternoons with my children. Something an eight to fiver, just never gets to do," she said. "We all have to learn there are trade offs in life. So we must choose wisely. I thank God daily that I had made that choice many years ago."

Her latest main task and the reason for all of these resumes, she continued to say, was that the facility manger from the Pittsburgh office had abruptly quit, so she was looking for a candidate to fill that position. "I haven't found him or her yet," she smiled, as she began reading the resumes and taking notes accordingly. "He'll come around, I'm sure," she said with her head down.

He could see she was smart and exact. Her notes were well written, and she seemed thorough to him. When she would read through one of them, she seemed to be rating them all on a number of categories as she had a list of names and scores, with their totals.
Ray wasn't going to be nosy and bother the lady. He understood she needed to get this done or she wouldn't be working so diligently on it. She was at it in the airport and on the plane. She probably read thru some of them on the cab ride over to the airport, he chuckled to himself as he stared out the window.

He wondered what a facility manager does while he is there. Probably more worthwhile than what I do daily, Ray thought to himself, as he continued looking out the window at the things below.

Julie and Philip were happy when they could take off their seatbelts. They could move around a little more and look around the plane better from their seats. Sharon could see Melissa pointing to the buttons above them and describing what they all did. Philip couldn't reach them sitting down, but standing up was a different story. As soon as he could, he stood up and adjusted the airflow and turned on the light on his buttons and he seemed to like the air blowing on his face.

Sharon was happily surprised when Julie asked her if she would read her a book that she had brought with her. "Of course, I will," Sharon said, while Melissa nodded her head in approval with a silent thank you all along doing it with a bright smile. She loved her kids, but any break she could get, she would take. It was a long day for her preparing everything for this trip. Because, this was it. Who knows when she was going to be back in Pittsburgh?

Their father had given her approval to take the kids to Atlanta. He knew that Melissa needed to take this job for the kid's sake. He couldn't afford to give her more money than he was already giving her, so she did what she had to do.

Carrying the book she had picked out, Julie walked across the aisle and sat down next to Sharon as the seat next to her was open. Sharon had to unbuckle her seatbelt as it was still fastened when Julie wanted to come over next to her. She always wanted to be as safe as she could be when flying.

Julie sat herself down and said hello to the gentleman in the window seat. He smiled at her and gave her a hello back. There was no concern on his part having the little girl sit there. If his young child was on a plane, he liked the thought of an elderly lady taking the time to read her a book. He gave Sharon a wink and told them to enjoy their book as he was putting on his headphones to listen to some music. Julie could hardly hear the songs he was listening to so everyone was good with the situation. Philip kept adjusting his airflow knob while Melissa kept an eye on him to keep him from hitting the "stewardess needed button" needlessly. He would always listen to his mother, but she kept her eye on him anyway.

The two of them snuggled a little closer as Sharon began by reading the title of the book.

"The Elephant and the Mouse," she said, as she opened the book. It had been opened many times before, she could tell as the pages were smeared with small fingerprints. The book had very nice illustrations on each page that Julie would feel the need to describe to Sharon after she read each page. They would take turns flipping to the next page, because Sharon had said that was only fair. Julie smiled at that. She liked the idea of life being fair. The story ended well as both the elephant and the small mouse realized that they could help each other and that they were both needed. It's a good feeling, Sharon thought to herself, to be needed. They both said, "The end," after Julie turned the last page and they had finished the book. It wasn't a long book but it was a worthwhile book. Sharon knew that Julie took the book to heart as Julie made sure to explain to Sharon, what the moral of the story was really all about. It was a good reflection on Julie and her mom, Sharon knew.

While they were reading the book, Philip decided he wanted to sit next to the window, so Melissa and him traded seats. Just as Sharon was finished reading the story and was giving it back to Julie, Julie asked her mom for her animal picture book. Melissa handed it to Sharon and told her that "Julie loves this book too, but no reading is needed," winking and smiling at her. Julie took the book and sat back in her chair and began to page through it. It was a big book. There are a lot of animals in the world, Sharon imagined.

Melissa and Sharon started up a little conversation shortly after that as Philip was enjoying peering out the window. He would occasionally tell his mother what he saw down below. Sharon asked Julie if she could sit next to her mother for a short time, while she was paging through her book. "You bet," she said, as Sharon slid across the aisle to sit next to Melissa for awhile.

"You have a lovely daughter and son," she said. "Your daughter reminds me of one of my grandchildren who lives in Pittsburgh." She explained how she lives in Atlanta and that her children and grandchildren all live in Pittsburgh now. She had just spent the last week there with them and this was her flight back home. It was home for her. It was lonelier now she said, but she explained to Melissa that she wanted to stay there. She lived in a small house in the north side of Atlanta and besides her church friends; she didn't know that many other people. A few of the people in the neighborhood were also her friends and there were a number of other people who would wave to her and such, when they saw her taking her daily walk, but on the whole, that was it. There were some children who lived on her street, but she didn't really know any of them. "People seem to keep to themselves more nowadays," she told Melissa. So, she never liked to be a bother to them.

"I understand your feeling about not knowing too many people," Melissa said. "We're going to be living in the north side of Atlanta ourselves. We are moving from Pittsburgh where the children have lived all of their lives. So they are sort of excited. Me, I'm excited but it's more of a nervous scary excitement."

"I recently got divorced from my husband, their father," she went on, "and needed to take an opportunity that arose. My ex husband really can't afford to give us any more money than he already has, and he and the kids understand that I needed to take this position. Bills need to be paid. Clothes and food need to be purchased and day care isn't cheap," she mused.

"This company had brought me to Atlanta a number of weeks ago and as far as my career goes, it was a perfect fit," she said. "We talked about it, and "Boom" here I am heading to Atlanta. I came down another time, while the kids were with their father, and got situated with our apartment and with the schools. I had a mover take care of the furniture and had called the school district and received instructions from them on what I needed to do as far as enrolling them into a new school."

There were only a few things that she would need to really address when she got there, since her car was being shipped to Atlanta and the apartment was all set. She would mainly have to find the right day care center for the kids. This job wouldn't work out perfectly as far as being there for them after school and such, so that was her last item to cross off her list. She told Sharon that she had all week to take care of that and hoped that it would be enough time. She knew this would be an important decision for the children's sake as well as hers. Sharon nodded in agreement on that. She wouldn't want her grandchildren being watched over by the wrong people. Some of those places only care about the dollar signs, she knew from previous experiences. It was an important decision for sure.

Right then a stewardess came by and asked Julie if she enjoyed the book her grandmother had read to her. Melissa saw her walk by them earlier when Sharon was reading the book to Julie. Julie giggled and told the lady that she, "was silly," and that Sharon was not her grandmother. Melissa thought to herself that she wished the kids had a grandmother
in Atlanta to help out. It sure would make things a little easier, she knew. The stewardess looked at Melissa and Sharon as she told the little girl, "Yep, I'm just a silly stewardess today." Julie smiled some more as she

winked at Sharon after the stewardess headed to the back of the plane.

Barbara, Karen and Sam decided that after they checked in to their hotel, they would meet in Barbara's and Karen's room and go from there. It would be a night to remember, the three of them said, as Lori continued her card game.

A night to remember, you bet, Barbara thought to herself. That's when she would tell them her secret. She had to, she knew that. That's when she would do it. It made her feel at ease more now that she knew when and where she was going to tell them. The four of them needed to be alone. She didn't want to tell them in a place where there were all kinds of other people. No stranger needs to listen to my secret. This was something that needed to be said in a quiet place. Just the four of us. Four old friends with one new secret, she thought. A few hours from now and the cat will be out of the bag. Some of the weight will be lifted off of her shoulders. At least some of it.

Tom and Jill had thought about adoption at one time. But after a friend, or rather a work associate, had told Tom about an adoption that went haywire in his family, he wasn't keen on the idea. Jill had thought it wasn't a bad idea when they first talked about it, but never brought it up again after that. She just prayed that the two of them could have their own child.

They were both rethinking this situation to themselves after Sonya's and Maria's words about adoption. Neither of them knew their troubles, Tom reasoned. It wasn't a big setup or anything like that, he knew. It was just a conversation about a young girl, a girl without a family who was lovingly taken into another family with no guarantees of anything. Sonya could have been a problem in so many ways to her new parents. She could have had health issues to deal with or other mental or physical problems to deal with. Her "new" parents' didn't care. They adopted her without any restrictions and it seemed to Tom that the young girl had grown into a smart and wise young lady. They took a chance and went through that door. The unknown door, not knowing what the other side would bring.

Tom noticed that Sonya had stopped reading for awhile, so he thought he would talk to the young lady some more about the adoption process, it couldn't hurt, he thought to himself.

"How's your studying going?" he asked her as she closed the book and placed it in her lap.

"Good," she responded. "It's hard reading, not like a novel. Some of the words, I can hardly pronounce," she laughed. "But I'll learn them, I promise," as she smiled some more.

He asked her what the name of the agency was that she works at in Atlanta and Pittsburgh.

"It's the Catholic Charities Adoption Center. I am not catholic, she continued, but it is a wonderful organization focused on helping children get adopted. They have always been very good to me throughout the years even though I am not catholic. My parents are Baptists and that's the religion I have been accustomed to and will always follow. Both religions teach good principles and the adoption center does not care what religion you are if you go through the process to adopt someone."

Jill was also listening attentively while Sonya talked.

Sonya asked Tom if he knew of someone who may be interested in adopting a child. Tom hesitated, but Jill spoke up at that time.

"Tom and I are not able to have our own children. We had been in Pittsburgh to see a specialist there," she said. "Her name was Dr. Barber."

Sonya nodded, saying that she had heard of her. Jill continued to tell Sonya that she was their last hope and that it just wasn't going to be possible for them to have children.

"You obviously have tried everything imaginable," Sonya said, knowing that they flew from Atlanta to Pittsburgh to see this doctor. "Sometimes the things we want aren't necessarily the things we need in our life. There are so many children, not only from the United States but also abroad, that could use a caring family to love them daily. I've seen it work many times now. The joy in the eyes of the adoptive parents has only been outdone by the joy I have seen in so many children's eyes."

"I will attest to that," she smiled.

Sonya continued by saying that she would be at the Atlanta center tomorrow if they were interested in going on a tour and talking to some of the people there.

"You don't need an appointment or anything like that. You can just come in and listen to what they have to say about the options and the overall process. It won't take much time and I'll be there with you to help answer any questions," Sonya said. "They aren't pushy people at the center as they understand it is quite the commitment from a couple to adopt someone they do not know at all. Actually, their process ensures that a good amount of time goes by before a decision is finally made. They want it to be right. Not only for the child but the individuals adopting the child."

Jill looked at Tom and told Sonya that they would give it some thought as it was a big step that required much thought. Sonya nodded in agreement and told them that she would be there between 9 am and 2 pm the next day. "Banker hours," she laughed, as did Tom and Jill. Sonya went back to reading her book and Jill grabbed Tom's hand gently as they both sat there both pondering what to do.

Jeremy woke up first from his nap and looked over at Evelyn to see if she was still sleeping. She was, so he was careful not to bother her out of her slumber.

He had finally dreamed of Debbie! Jeremy couldn't believe it. It was a happy dream. His dreams had been dark for so long that he almost hated going to sleep anymore.

It was a dream about Debbie, Evelyn and himself, at the beach. There she was dressed in her pink summer sundress that he had bought her for her birthday. It was Evelyn's and Debbie's favorite dress as I had also bought one for Evelyn to match Debbie's. The three of us were walking on our favorite beach, holding hands. It seemed only Debbie could talk in his dream. Evelyn and I, both of us on either side of her, were just listening.

"It was time for me to go," she said to us, smiling down on Evelyn, her little angel. "My time here has come to an end and the two of you need to continue this walk together without me by your side anymore."

I was crying as well as Evelyn in the dream. Debbie had picked up Evelyn and gave her a long hug and told her to help her father out as this would be very hard for him. She told Evelyn, she would always be a little charm around her neck, keeping an eye on her. She also told Evelyn that it was okay to have another mommy and to help daddy find the right one and to always share with others the good things she has. Evelyn seemed to acknowledge Debbie and her words in the dream.

After setting Evelyn back down on the beach and giving her a kiss on the forehead, Debbie turned to me. She told me she was happy where she was and that she loved me very much. She said, she couldn't have picked a better husband or father for her child and that it was okay to remarry and be happy again as she was happy and would see us again. She told me to listen and love everyday of my life and I would know who the right girl was. "Don't be angry anymore," were her last words to me.

She then walked down the beach herself as Evelyn's hands and mine were clenched together. Evelyn smiled at me and said, "Everything will be alright, daddy."

I was sitting in my seat, with tears silently running down my cheek, as Evelyn awoke. I wiped them away as I did not want her to become alarmed thinking I was in pain or something like that. They were actually tears of happiness, I knew.

As soon as she sat up in her chair, Evelyn told me that she had a wonderful dream while she was asleep. She said she dreamed of the three of us walking down the beach together and talking about how mommy had to go and some other things that mommy wanted me to know. I asked her if we were swimming in the pool or the ocean, but she said we were just walking. Holding hands together. Mommy and she were in their favorite pink sundresses.

Jeremy couldn't stop the tears from drifting down out of his eyes as Evelyn was telling him about her dream. It was the exact same dream, he knew. He knew it was time to release the anger and emptiness he thought he should carry with him forever and allow the light to shine in his life. The light always shined before, when Debbie was here, and he now knew it needed to continue. Not only for him but also for Evelyn.

He felt a strange weight leave his shoulders at that moment and he gave Evelyn a big hug. She said that my hug was like the one her mom gave to her in her dream. We both smiled at each other as I noticed the sunlight create a sparkle off of her necklace charm. Now I knew why that charm was so important to Evelyn. I just couldn't see it through the darkness that I so wanted to be in. Evelyn folded up the blanket as perfectly as when Maria had given it to us.

Evelyn asked me if I dreamed of mommy too during my nap. I told her that I did and that her mom said she loved us both and would always be there with us. It brought a smile to her face as she finished her last fold of the blanket.

For some reason, I blurted out that I liked the lady at the grocery store. Evelyn said she did also and that she was special, just like her mom was, as Maria quietly appeared next to Evelyn. She asked us how our nap was and if we had sweet dreams. Evelyn and I both acknowledged that as Maria grabbed the blanket from Evelyn.

"It will be a wonderful vacation for the two of you at the beach," she said. "Enjoy your walk on the beach together because that's what your mom would want you to do."

She gave Evelyn a loving pat on the head and me a nod and smile that would break any man's heart. I told her we would and that Evelyn couldn't wait to put on her favorite sundress for the walk, as it has been too cold in Pittsburgh to wear. Maria said that was wonderful and that Evelyn would look lovely in pink as she walked away. I wasn't perplexed by this lady anymore. I knew now that she was either a psychic or an angel.

Evelyn took out her favorite book as I looked out the window, smiling and happy for the first time since my wife's passing.

Father Feeney was glad when John said that he would like to visit his church. He wrote down the name of the church, Blessed Sacrament Church, the address and phone number for him and said that he should stop by anytime. "You'll love our little church," Father told him. "I can't wait to show you the statue that resembles your new figurine."

John was holding onto the angel figurine as it was like hugging his son. He didn't feel the pain of his son's passing anymore as he thought about how wonderful his son was.

Just at that time a stewardess came by and commented on the statue as the sunshine made the statue seemed to come alive. She looked at John and seeing that it was a present, told him that "You must be a really blessed man to receive such a gift. Blessed indeed," she said as she walked by, Father smiling at her words.

His life had suddenly changed, and John was going to take advantage of his time as he placed Father's note into his wallet for safe keeping. He would definitely go see him and the church. John wondered to himself if this was how Kevin felt when he found God and went to St. George's Church the first time. There was something here, he quietly thought. Could it be Kevin's work from above? It was too magical to think about, but he now knew how Kevin felt and why he started doing the things he was doing in his life to help others in need. He promised himself, at that moment, to find a way to help others. Kevin would like that as John closed his eyes and prayed for Kevin's guidance.

Ray thought about what it would be like to work for an organization that cared for children. It seemed to him that one would get more out of life by doing that than caring for someone's money. He knew he was tired of that, but it was so hard to just change one's career at his age, he thought to himself, as he continued glancing at Patty's pile of resumes. I'm sure I could do that job, with minimal training, he thought. He opened his briefcase and took out his information on the company he was going to interview with and a copy of his resume which he had sent to them. He changed it slightly to match the qualifications they were looking for even though they already knew about him.

She was a little resume bored, as she leaned back in her chair to take a break from it all and noticed Ray looking at his resume. She politely asked him what he did for a living as they had never discussed that.

He was a stockbroker, he told her. His father was one and he seemed to, or rather did, follow in his footsteps. He continued to tell her about his job and his life back in Pittsburgh and that he was going to interview for a nice position with a bigger company in Atlanta. Higher up the totem pole, he laughed. He also told her, that he was sort of unsure about it all and that sometimes he wondered if it was time to do something else with his life. Days in the financial world were not so fun anymore to him, he told her, but that's where he's been for a long time. Too long, he sighed, with a wry smile.

Patty remembered how wonderful he was with the children in the airport. Children he didn't even know. Children he wasn't even getting paid to spend time with. She knew he was good with children and must love kids. She saw how he scurried up to the taxi to help the lady with the handicapped child and how he helped her board the plane, without even being asked. She knew that he had heard of their day care center as some of his friends sent their children there.

She wanted to know more about him.

Melissa was enjoying her conversation with Sharon as her children were keeping themselves busy on their own. Julie reading her animal book and Philip in awe looking out the window at all the scenes below. "It looks so different from way up here," he told his mom as he continued gazing out the window looking for interesting buildings or farmlands.

THE PRIEST, THE STEWARDESS, AND THE CHURCH PICNIC

Sharon had enjoyed her time so much with Julie that she told Melissa, "It's a shame the plane ride has to end shortly as I enjoyed reading to your little girl."

"I think she enjoyed it also," Melissa told Sharon, both of them smiling at each other and thinking the same thing.

It would be nice to be able to read to Julie and Philip more in the future, Sharon thought to herself as Melissa asked Sharon, "Would you like to come over to our apartment sometime for dinner or something?"

Those were the words Sharon was unknowingly waiting to hear. "I would love that," she told Melissa, as she looked at Julie paging through her book.

Sharon wrote her phone number and address down on a piece of paper and gave it to Melissa. "Here's how to get ahold of me," she told her.

Upon looking at her address, Melissa could see that their zip code was the same so she looked up directions to her house from her apartment and realized that they were only a few blocks from each other. Melissa let Sharon know that and after seeing the directions, Sharon told Melissa that she walks past her apartment complex everyday on her morning walk.

"It's about a six-minute walk from your apartment to my house," Sharon said, "and I do that walk everyday."

She told her she likes to stay as active as possible, "It's good for everybody to stay active," they both agreed. "How about I stop by your place tomorrow on my morning walk?" Sharon said to Melissa. "Maybe I can watch the kids for awhile to help you out as you get settled into your new life. I have nothing else really to do, dear," she said, "and it would be nice for me also."

Melissa told Sharon that she would love to see her tomorrow morning and they agreed on about what time as they continued talking about things to do in Atlanta. It was a stroke of luck for both of them and it all started from just a simple "Hello," Melissa and Sharon thought to themselves. "I'll be there," Sharon said. "You can always count on me."

Melissa now wasn't going to be so alone in this new city and the same could be said for Sharon.

Jill didn't want to get into a long discussion about adoption with Tom while sitting on the airplane. Too many other disinterested people sitting so close to them, she thought to herself, so she kept quiet about the whole thing.

Tom on the other hand, didn't care who was around when he would say something. If it needed saying, he would say it. He never cared what other people thought of his actions or words. They spoke for themselves. But Jill was happily surprised when Tom told her that he would like to go to the adoption center tomorrow morning and talk to the people there. Actually, happily surprised was putting it mildly. She was now reinvigorated.

The so called "hopelessness" of their situation was going to be a thing of the past. She imagined quickly to herself what it would be like to hold a child of her own. It would be her own child. This child would call her "mom," just like Sonya sitting next to her, referring to her new parents as her mom and dad. She could see a sense of solitude in her husband's eyes as he told her this. It was a peaceful easy feeling. She knew this had been wearing him down for months now. She could feel the hope in his words.

Sonya couldn't help but hearing their conversation as she was sitting right next to them. When it was appropriate, she told them her full name again and told them to ask for her when they arrived at the center. She told them where to park, what doors to come in, everything they would need to know.

"It will be a wonderful day for you both," she told them, as she was getting resituated as the captain had come on the speakers to inform them that it was time to put on their seatbelts as they would be landing shortly. All three of them buckled up accordingly per his instructions. Tom and Jill were eager for tomorrow to arrive.

Joey flipped through the book Aaron had given him for a good chunk of the flight, but he eventually turned his attention back to his new friend. Joey knew other kids with cancer from the hospital, but he had never really talked to an adult that shared his ailment.

"Do you have to go to my hospital?" Joey asked. "I go to the UPMC Cancer Center."

"Oh yeah, Hillman, right?" Aaron asked. "Yeah, I just started treatment there."

"I'm pretty much always in the pediatric ward," Joey said. "Come see me next time you're there, and I can show you my drawings!"

"Ok, that sounds great," Aaron said.

Dan looked on with a faint smile and hoped Aaron would follow through with that plan.

After her nap and dream on the plane, Evelyn knew what she needed to do with her "Heaven" book now as she took it out of her knapsack. Her mom had told her in her dream what to do with it. It was time to let it go and share it with someone else who may need to read it. Her mom told her it would be okay if she gave her book to someone else to enjoy. Evelyn knew who she wanted to give it to, so she unbuckled her seatbelt just before the seatbelt fastening signal came on and scurried to the front of the plane.

She wanted to give it to Phyllis and Charlene.

So she just walked right up there and introduced herself to Phyllis. Phyllis remembered the little girl and listened to her story, which she said quickly, about her moms passing and that it was her favorite book. She wanted Charlene to enjoy the book now, she told Phyllis as she handed it to her. Evelyn smiled at Phyllis and told her that she was sorry it was old looking as she has read it hundreds of times. Phyllis, with a smile and a small tear forming in her eye, hugged the little girl and thanked her accordingly.

"I'll read it every day to Charlene," she told Evelyn as Maria the stewardess was walking by. Maria told Phyllis that it was a wonderful book as she grabbed Evelyn's hand to walk with her back to her seat. Evelyn was happy to see the smile on Charlene's face when her mom showed her the book. Charlene began rocking back and forth as Maria and Evelyn headed down the aisle to her seat. Phyllis knew her daughter was happy about the book. She didn't know if she knew what the book was about, but she knew she was happy. That's all that mattered to her. She just wanted her daughter to be happy. She knew she wouldn't ever go on a date, she wouldn't win a trophy for something, she wouldn't do a lot of things in her life. So she just wanted her to be happy. And she was happy, Phyllis thought to herself. Phyllis said a quick prayer for the little girl and hoped their paths would cross again some day.

Maria helped Evelyn buckle up and told them both to enjoy the rest of the flight as she needed to go now. It was time for the plane to begin its landing process and she needed to buckle up to just like the rest of the passengers. Evelyn knew she had to go and put out her arms for Maria to give her a hug. The two of them hugged each other for a short time and then Maria told Jeremy to take care of his "little angel" as she left heading to the back of the plane.

"I will," he said, as he double checked Evelyn's seatbelt. He looked forward to saying bye to her once the plane landed as she was nice to Evelyn and him. There was something special about her, he knew, and he wanted to thank her one last time.

Out of the blue, Patty asked Ray if he had ever thought about managing a company. The business, she told him, was all set up and there were really only two mandatory requirements for the job.

"The first being, you have to love children, and the second is you must be a caring kind of individual," Patty said. "I can tell you are top notch in both of those categories. If you're interested, I'll tell you everything you need to know about the job.

Ray thought to himself for a millisecond and then said he would be interested in talking about it. Patty told him the whole scoop. The good things, the bad things, everything about the position. There was nothing he felt deficient on as they continued talking about it. His questions were good questions about the job and Patty addressed them accordingly. They even talked about the compensation and so forth. She let him know that there would be a one-week training program at one of their facilities and that she thought he would be right for the job. She was the only person responsible for choosing the new manager for the Pittsburgh facility and her decisions were never made in haste or frowned upon by the owners.

She offered him the job as the plane began its descent down.

Since the captain had issued the orders to buckle up our seatbelts, she knew the card game between Paul and her had to come to an end. It wasn't really a card game. It was more of just something to do while they drank, Lori knew. The drinks just seemed to go down so quickly anymore. She could probably have played for hours if they had the time and the booze, she chuckled to herself. She thanked him for buying the drinks and buckled up next to Sam.

THE PRIEST, THE STEWARDESS, AND THE CHURCH PICNIC

Sam was glad to see her friend safely back with her as the stewardesses were making sure everyone was buckled in appropriately. The smell of booze on Lori's breath was easily recognizable as she hadn't taken her usual swig of mouthwash yet as it was packed away in her purse. She didn't want to fumble through her purse looking for it, as Sam might see some of the bottles of booze she had carried onto the plane with her. She always had to be thinking about that when she was carrying her fuel. They both sat back in their chairs and enjoyed the last views of the clouds as the plane was slowly lowering its altitude with every tick of the clock.

Karen knew that her husband would do what she told them they had to do. She wondered if her family could survive this bankruptcy situation. All for what, she wondered as she looked out the window and enjoyed the sun beating down on her through the window.

Barbara was happy that the plane was going to land in a short time as she left the restroom in the plane. She couldn't wait to land, so she used the restroom on the plane. She was right after Lori's friend Paul. He needed to go also. One more plane ride and a quick cab ride to the hotel and then next thing you know she would tell her friends. As she closed the door behind her to walk to her seat, Maria the stewardess was in the back of the plane and handed her a charm she had taken off of her neck. Maria told Barbara, that this was for her little girl. She's going to be a "healthy little angel" she told her, as she placed it around Barbara's neck and gave her a quick hug and told her she needed to get to her seat and buckle up.

Barbara was in a small state of shock after she left Maria to head back to her seat. She couldn't understand how this stewardess could ever know that she was pregnant as she tucked the angel charm into her shirt and proceeded to walk down the aisle to her seat. She knew that she wasn't really showing any baby bump yet and that the stewardess could not have overheard her talking about being pregnant, because she hadn't talked about it. Yet, it happened, she knew that I was pregnant and that it was going to be a healthy baby girl.

As she buckled into her seat, Karen could notice a slight change in Barbara's demeanor. They had known each other for so long that each one of them could tell these kinds of things about each other. She asked Barbara if she was okay and Barbara just nodded yes.

"I'm better than I was a few minutes ago," she told Karen as she sat back in her chair, feeling the angel figurine around her neck.

She told me so calmly and assuredly, she thought to herself, about the stewardess. I prayed that she was right. Right, about being a healthy baby. Barbara had not cared so much about whether it was going to be a boy or a girl she only prayed that the baby would be healthy.

Barbara remembered going through her parent's storage closet in the basement, the day after she found out that she was pregnant. She new that they did not like to throw anything away; they were old school. Not like everybody nowadays, having to always have the newest of everything. Her parents were out of the house for awhile so she couldn't help but look to see what was there as she knew there were plenty of items from her childhood and further back.

They had kept it all! The crib, the stroller, the playpen, all kinds of useful items. She remembers crying that day as she was going through the items, wondering what was going to become of her life now. She cried for a long time that day as she went through the stuff. It was the last time she would cry, she had told herself. She needed to prepare for this next chapter in her life and she knew she couldn't and didn't want to go through it unhappy. A small peaceful easy feeling came over her that day when she realized that her parents had everything she would need. Children aren't a cheap date, she knew, after seeing the items Karen and Sam had needed for their children. Karen's children always had the best of everything. It would help her immensely, financially, she thought to herself at that time and forced herself to smile about that. There were boy toys and girl toys, so she knew either gender would be fine by her. She would prepare herself for a baby. Either gender would be a handful for her.

The plane was continuing its descent downward as Tom and Jill held hands both thinking about the possibilities that lay ahead for them. Tom hoped that the center would not care that they were a biracial couple. They had been through some terrible times because of it, or rather, because of how some people perceived them. A black man married to a white girl. He knew that there were still many people in the world who didn't think it was natural or a good thing for blacks and whites to marry. He had protected Jill from this hatred as much as he could, but it was always there.

He wondered to himself, if given the opportunity to choose, would he choose a white baby or a black baby. Maybe a baby born from another biracial couple. Would they choose a boy or a girl? There may be choices which would need to be made, he thought, but he would wait for tomorrow's visit. We might not even choose this path, he thought, so try not to think about it, he told himself.

THE PRIEST, THE STEWARDESS, AND THE CHURCH PICNIC

Jill was just happy that they would be going there in the morning and that there would be a familiar face at the center when they arrived there. She knew it was a stroke of luck or something like that to have sat next to Sonya. She remembered what Maria, the stewardess, had told her about those people who choose to adopt unwanted children. It made her want to go there even more. She prayed to herself that her husband felt the same way as she did.

Philip could see the ground approaching fast now as he peered out the window. He told everyone in listening distance to "hold on" as they were about to land.

The plane touched down onto the runway as smooth as silk, Jeremy thought to himself. He was a different man now. He knew that. He knew what he was going to do with his life and he knew he was going to be happy. Evelyn needed that. She always needed that, he thought to himself. His selfish anger was gone. Like a dream, disappearing when you wake up from a deep sleep. There was no time to be angry. Debbie wanted him to be happy. He finally believed what Evelyn had always been trying to tell him. He couldn't wait to say bye to Maria. She was special, he knew. They would take their time and be the last passengers off the plane, so he could do that, as the plane taxied to its gate.

Ray was a little shocked when Patty offered him the position at the day care center. She handed him a piece of paper with the offer clearly written down on her company's letterhead. Patty, dressed in her Pittsburgh Pirate T-shirt, told him that the offer was good for a week and to give it some thought. She told him to look around and listen to others and compare his opportunities accordingly. Ray shook her hand and thanked her kindly.

"No, thank you! I'm glad we got to sit next to each other and listen to each other," she said. "It was an easy decision for me to make," she smiled, as she put away her resumes.

Ray folded up the offer letter neatly and placed it in his briefcase. He knew he was going on an interview for a lucrative position, so he had a lot to think about it. He remembered that he had told Phyllis, that he would take his time getting off the plane in order to help her out with Charlene and her luggage. It was important to him. He wasn't going to forget that lady's needs.

The plane began its unboarding shortly after we had stopped.

Phyllis, although sitting in first class, remained seated with Charlene as the passengers slowly passed by them heading out the door of the airplane. She hoped that the gentleman who helped her earlier would be there again to help her. It made her think of her friend, Peter. He was so helpful all of the time and had never asked for anything in return. She would text him as soon as they were squared away in the airport. She was looking forward to texting him as Charlene was slowly rocking back and forth while watching everyone proceed to exit the plane.

Melissa, Sharon and the kids were gathering their carry-on luggage and books as it was now their turn to do so. Julie had asked her mom if they would ever see Sharon again as Melissa and Sharon's eyes met. "Mommy hopes so," Melissa said to Julie, just as Sharon said that she was going to visit her tomorrow and bring a surprise present for her and Philip. Julie's eyes lit up. Any child's eyes would light up at the thought of a present, but her eyes were aglow because she knew she would see Sharon again. Julie afforded herself one quick hug for Sharon even though they all knew they had to get going as people behind them were anxious to leave.

Tom and Jill told Sonya that they would see her in the morning. The young lady was happy to hear that, Jill could tell, as they all smiled and proceeded to head down the aisle.

John and Father shook hands while seated and then also gave each other a quick hug as they got up. John checked to make sure he had the address of Father's church and told him he would stop by shortly. It made Father Feeney happy. He listened, just like they had told him at the conference, he thought to himself, and now this man is on a better path in life. He was going to look forward to showing John his church.

The bishop was right, it would be an enlightening trip, Father knew now.

When the crowd ahead of them started to thin out, Aaron, Dan, and Joey climbed out of their seats and finally stretched their legs. Aaron grabbed his suitcase from the overhead bin while Joey placed his new book in his backpack and zipped it up; Dan was busy grabbing his and Joey's bags from the bin.

"It was great meeting you! Have fun at the game tomorrow," Aaron said as he prepared to leave the plane. "Did you bring a glove with you?"

"You bet I did!" Joey said. "I take it to every game I go to, but I haven't caught anything yet."

"Well, one way or another, I hope you get your first big league ball!" Aaron said before turning and heading for the front of the plane.

Barbara and the girls, all dressed in their summer attire, proceeded to grab their carry-on luggage and head down the aisle. Barbara was looking around the back of the plane for Maria, the stewardess who seemed to know that she was pregnant. But, she didn't see her anywhere. She just smiled and got in line with her friends, after helping Lori grab her items. She was a little tipsy, but nobody minded. They were on vacation. One more flight and they would be at their destination.

As Patty got up to exit the plane she left room for Ray to also stand up and grab his items from the overhead compartment. She noticed that he was remaining seated and asked him if he was okay. He told her that he had told Phyllis that he would help her and Charlene get off the plane and so forth. He had time, he told Patty, so he was going to make sure they got their luggage and were safely in a cab. So he was in no hurry. Patty looked at him and smiled. He was the right man for the job, this Ray Rossi, she thought to herself, as she shook his hand one more time and told him she was looking forward to talking to him further if he had any questions about the position. "Call me anytime," she told him as she proceeded down the aisle.

The plane was nearly empty as Jeremy told Evelyn it was their turn to go. As they were loading up their items, he was looking around for Maria, one more time. He wanted to thank her. There was something special about her, he knew. Evelyn knew that in the airport, he thought to himself. But he didn't see her, so he asked one of the other stewardesses where Maria was.

"There was no stewardess named Maria on this flight, sir," she stated. "You must be mistaken."

It left him stunned for what seemed like a minute. He was sure that was her name, so he asked Evelyn if indeed there was a stewardess named Maria. "You know," he asked her, "the lady with the angel charm similar to yours."

Evelyn just looked at her dad, her face aglow, and told him, "Daddy, she was an angel sent from mommy to help you. Mommy had told me that she was going to do this for you on my last visit to her grave."

I had to sit for a minute after she told me that. I would see her talking at Debbie's gravesite, but never imagined she was actually talking to someone. It made it all so surreal. My "little angel" always knew and I just couldn't or wouldn't listen. That had all changed now, I promised myself, as we walked down the aisle.

As Evelyn approached Phyllis and Charlene, Charlene eyed Evelyn inching closer to her and her mom. She began smiling at Evelyn and rocking a little more as Phyllis grabbed her hand and thanked her again for the book. "You're a little angel," she told Evelyn, "and we'll remember you forever." Evelyn smiled, as did I. I was finally understanding how angels work in our lives, and I was liking it.

My little girl and I were heading to our next flight and then the beach. I couldn't wait.

Ray was the last one to leave the plane. Almost the last one. Phyllis and Charlene were sitting there patiently waiting for him to come down the aisle. Phyllis knew that she could use the help and was hoping he would be good to his word. And there he was, standing next to them, opening up the overhead compartment to grab their luggage. She knew he was a man similar in his convictions as was her friend Peter as he smiled at Charlene and helped get her up and going. He even handed Phyllis the luggage and said that he would help Charlene walk to the luggage area and then the cab. He made sure that Phyllis knew that he was there to help until she was safely in a cab.

This made her at ease as one could imagine how hard this would be without someone to help. Someone good, someone like Peter.

She told him good things were going to come his way for being so good to her and her child. Good things indeed, she said, as they walked out of the plane and down the corridor to the inside of the airport.

CHAPTER 11: ONE DAY LATER

It was a well kept building they had passed by a number of times in their lives and the parking lot was just as Sonya had described. Tom and Jill were there just a little after Sonya had said she would be there as they were both excited at the possibilities that lay ahead of them today and were both up early to prepare for the day. "No need to bring anything the first day," Sonya had told them. So they didn't bring anything with them besides the strong desire to have a child of their own. As he parked the car and they proceeded to the entrance, Tom took a deep breadth in anticipation. They had been on so many visits to doctors and such over the last year or so that he hoped this would be the answer to their dreams. He wasn't sure if he could handle another disappointing meeting.

Just like she had told them, the receptionist desk was right there when they entered the building and the lady behind the counter greeted them both warmly. She was an older black lady, probably past retirement age, Tom thought to himself. Probably someone who likes to help out and volunteer her time to a good cause, he assumed. Her badge said her name was Shauna. After she greeted them, she asked them how she could help them. Jill greeted her with a handshake and told her our names and said that Sonya had told them about the adoption agency.

Shauna knew exactly who we were then, as she quickly dialed the phone and spoke to Sonya. "Your new friends are here now dear," she said over the phone and hung up after that. She said Sonya would be down in a minute and she handed us a general brochure about the agency and pointed us towards the waiting room where there was coffee and other delights. I thanked her kindly and headed straight for the coffee as she and Jill began chit chatting about who knows what. The waiting area was full of pictures of families. There were literally hundreds of pictures of families that were formed via the adoption process. Some white, some black, some oriental and some mixed. I could tell right away that it would not matter that we were a biracial couple. They didn't care about that, Tom knew, as he looked around at all of the pictures.

It wasn't long before Sonya appeared at the front desk. From a distance, I saw her give Jill a hug as they met each other. A warm feeling came over me that moment as I knew this was where we were meant to come. I headed over to the receptionist's area and Sonya greeted me warmly as well.

Shauna told us were blessed to have a friend like Sonya and that she has known her for as long as she can remember. Both their faces smiling at each other, after Shauna laughingly said that her memory wasn't so good anymore. It made both Jill and I relax a little bit more about the whole process. We said our goodbyes to Shauna and followed Sonya to the elevator. "We are going to head upstairs where the case managers are located," Sonya said, as the doors in the elevator opened, and we all stepped inside.

Sharon was a creature of habit but today was going to be a little different. The usual 6:00 am alarm didn't even wake her up as she was up well before that and had turned it off. She was looking forward to her walk today. She was going to stop by Melissa's apartment and spend time with Julie and Philip, but she would need to wrap the presents she bought for them last night. Sharon had stopped at the Atlanta Zoo after landing yesterday and purchased a family admission pack for Julie. It was good for up to four people and could be used over and over again. She knew that Julie liked animals as she had patiently paged through her animal book on the airplane. Upon landing she also went into a store at the airport and bought a model plane for Philip. She thought maybe it was something they could make together one day. She would like that, she thought, when she had purchased it. She took her time wrapping the presents as it reminded her of wrapping presents for her own grandchildren whom she dearly loved.

After her breakfast, it was time to head out for her walk. She had done this many times before, but today was special. She had a bag with some presents in it. So, with her walking sneakers on, she headed out the door. It was a clear sunny Atlanta morning. She loved mornings as it always seemed a little more peaceful.

Her pace today was a little quicker than usual. The bag of presents

THE PRIEST, THE STEWARDESS, AND THE CHURCH PICNIC

clutched in her hands.

Melissa had risen early also that morning. She had a lot of things to do in the next few days and time was precious. She wondered if Sharon was actually going to stop by or not. She hoped she would, for the kid's sake. They had gone through enough disappointments in their young lives and she hoped this wasn't going to be another.

Philip was still sleeping but Julie was up early also. The first words out of her mouth that morning were about Sharon. "Is Sharon coming over this morning, mom?" she asked Melissa, before even saying good morning to her. "I'm not sure, honey," her mom said, because she really wasn't sure. Maybe, she thought to herself, that Sharon was just being nice to the kids on the airplane. Make them feel good for awhile, and then move on with her own life. She silently prayed that Sharon would show up but as the minutes passed by, she became more and more unsure.

Then the doorbell rang!

Julie darted to the door and could see that it was Sharon. The room wasn't big enough for the happy feeling they all had when Sharon entered their new apartment. The sun beaming through the door and shining on Julie's face. Julie hugged Sharon as she came into the apartment and Melissa closed the door behind her, wiping the tear from her eye. She hadn't seen Julie this excited in some time and it meant the world to her.

"Where should I put these presents?" Sharon asked Julie with a smile making Julie all the more happy.

"Right on the table here," Julie told her as she ran to Philip's room to wake him. Melissa gave Sharon a long hug while Julie was waking her brother and thanked her for being here. They were both in a state of happiness. It was going to be a wonderful day, they both knew, as Julie came running back into the room.

"Which one is mine?" she asked Sharon as she placed the two gifts on the table.

"Yours is the small one," Sharon said. "The one that says, 'For Julie,'" she laughed. She looked at her mom and asked her if it was okay if she opened it before Philip got there but she said to wait until Philip came out. The anxiety was building in this little girl. Who could blame her? It wasn't Christmas or her birthday, but she was getting a present. It doesn't get better than that.

Philip finally entered the room and it seemed like hours to Julie, although it was less than a minute. He greeted Sharon with a hug also because it made him not feel so all alone either. He knew that the three of them weren't going to know anyone else in Atlanta, so it was a comfortable feeling for him.

Then Melissa yelled out, "It's time to open the presents!"

Julie smiled at that and began to meticulously open her present as Philip just attacked his wrapping. He had his opened quickly. Julie was in no hurry, she didn't want to tear the wrapping paper, Sharon thought to herself.

Philip loved the model airplane. He had never made a model himself, he told Sharon. But she told him she would help him build it whenever he wanted and today was fine by her if it was fine by his mother. Melissa nodded accordingly and needed to leave for a second as the happiness was taking a toll on her eyes. She asked Sharon if she needed a coffee as she headed to the kitchen. "Sure," Sharon said, "with just a touch of cream, please."

Melissa returned with the coffee just as Julie had finally unwrapped her present. It was a zoo pass, Julie extorted. "I love the zoo!" she said, as she hugged Sharon again. Sharon hadn't received so many hugs in Atlanta in one day since she has lived here, she thought. She was going to enjoy every second of it. Julie excitedly showed her mother and wanted to go to the zoo that instant.

Her mom looked at Sharon and told Julie that they would be going to make their first trip to the Atlanta Zoo whenever Sharon was going to be available to go. It's going to be the four of us. They weren't going there without her, she knew. Julie just looked at Sharon, waiting for an answer from her as she was so eager to know when.

"Well, let me talk to your mother first," Sharon responded. "But I have a feeling it's going to be soon," as she turned to Melissa.

"How about we go to the zoo today and have lunch there on me and we can talk about your babysitting needs?" Sharon asked Melissa. "I'm available every hour of everyday and would look forward to it. We can make it work," she told Melissa.

Melissa knew it was right. She hadn't known this lady for a long time, but she knew it was right. Once Melissa told Julie and Philip that they were going to go to the zoo later today, they were both ecstatic. Julie went to her room to grab her animal book which she had read on the plane and Philip opened the box containing all of the pieces of his model airplane.

It almost seemed overwhelming to him, all the little pieces, but Sharon assured him that the two of them would start putting it together piece by piece tomorrow. And that was okay with Melissa. They were now a family of four.

Aaron felt like a teenager again. He was in the passenger seat of his mom's old Town & Country, and they were on their way to see the Pittsburgh Pirates take on the Atlanta Braves. It was the day after his flight in, and he was feeling very nostalgic. For his whole life, he had wanted to grow up and go tread his own path, which is why he left home as soon as he could. Now that he was back, memories flooded his mind at every turn.

He had intended to take an Uber to his mother's place last night, but she surprised him at his gate when he got off the plane and didn't give him that opportunity. Though he talked to his mom from time to time over the phone, it was rare that he saw her in person anymore. As he walked off the plane, there was no mistaking who was waiting for him. She looked just as he remembered, with her short, curly blonde hair, kind eyes, and permanent smile. Everything exactly the same, though her face was a little more lined with wrinkles.

Aaron had blushed slightly upon seeing her; she was holding a sign with his name on it, as if he were someone famous. It was her idea of a little joke, but Aaron also noticed that she had a prideful look in her eyes as he walked toward her. Aaron felt guilty upon seeing her like this. No matter how long he went without seeing her, she never held it against him. He almost would've preferred it if she got angry at him from time to time for his failure to visit – he certainly deserved to draw her ire – but he was her only child and she respected his independence.

After meeting his mom at the gate, Aaron was hit with wave after wave of memories. He knew the way home so well, he could've gotten there with his eyes closed. The neighborhood, the street they lived on, and the very house he grew up in – if he had any lick of artistic ability, he could've painted everything down to the cracks in the sidewalk.

Of course, some things had changed. His mom had gotten new countertops in the kitchen and repainted the guest bathroom, causing both rooms to look slightly out of place in his mind. But his bedroom was untouched, almost as if his mom wanted to preserve it for some sort of museum.

As they headed to the baseball game, Aaron watched his mother struggle with the Atlanta traffic – the only thing that could take the smile off her face. Well, maybe not the only thing.

When they had gotten home the night before, they were both exhausted. His mom had offered to make Aaron something to eat, but he suggested they order a pizza and relax. He intended to tell her about his cancer, but he wasn't sure how to broach the subject. Aaron played out the scene in his mind over and over, his mother in tears not only because her only child had cancer, but also because he had waited weeks to tell her.

They ordered a supreme pizza from a place called Valerio's – their favorite. The pizza was loaded with toppings and gooey mozzarella cheese, but every bite Aaron took tasted like cardboard as he mulled over how he was going to break the news to his mom. She looked so happy and content as she munched on her slice of pizza and asked him about his job and life in Pittsburgh. He didn't want to weigh her down with his worries and problems. But she must've realized something was wrong.

"Is everything ok, Aaron?" She asked. "You've barely touched your pizza and I know from personal experience that you can clean a plate better than my dishwasher."

She smiled at her little joke, but it quickly faltered, and concern washed over her face.

"Mom, there's something I have to tell you," Aaron began, having no idea what to say next. His mom put down her slice of pizza and her eyes met his, analyzing them, like she was trying to decode a cypher he had hidden in them.

"I have... I have a tumor," he began. "I have cancer. It's rare. It's treatable, but it's going to be tough to beat."

"What? But... but you're so young," she said, tears welling up in her eyes. "Surely there's a mistake, or – It's gotta be a mistake. Did you get a second opinion? I know a great doctor here in Atlanta that I'm sure could help."

Aaron almost laughed at her reaction, not because it was funny, but because her words matched his exact thoughts when he found out.

"I know I'm young – I thought the same thing," Aaron said. "But it's definitely cancer. I've seen the x-rays, I've spoken with multiple doctors, and I've started chemo. It's going – "

"You've already started chemo?" She interrupted, looking hurt. "How long have you known? Why didn't you tell me about this sooner?"

"Mom, I'm sorry," Aaron said, also tearing up. "I should've told you sooner, I know, but I was overwhelmed, and I didn't want you to worry. But now Shelley couldn't handle it and she's gone, and my friends can't take off of work to go to chemo with me, and I'm just feeling very alone in this.

I just don't know how I'm going to get through it all."

"Oh, honey, we will get you through this," His mom said, pulling him into a tight hug. "I'm here for you, I'll always be here for you. Don't you worry."

A car horn from behind them made Aaron jump, and he was brought back to the present. He quickly wiped the tear from his eye before his mom noticed. They had both done their fair share of crying last night, and he didn't want to start the waterworks again. As apprehensive as he had been to fill his mom in, he was even more relieved now that he had told her. She understood how he was feeling better than anyone else had, and he finally felt like he had someone in his corner of the ring in his fight against his tumor.

Aaron's mom also knew not to dwell on the subject. They had their talk last night, and he knew she was going to be thinking about it constantly from now on, but she wouldn't harp on him about it or treat him any differently now that she knew.

Aaron was thankful to have gotten the elephant in the room out of the way, and he was actually looking forward to the baseball game. He'd been in such a daze for the past few weeks that he hadn't really been able to enjoy anything. Everywhere he looked, he saw healthy people and couldn't help but feel sorry for himself. But the conversation with Joey on the plane and the relief from finally telling his mom helped take off the blinders he had been wearing and allowed him to once again see the world around him.

The sun was high over their heads and beating down on the crowd jockeying to enter SunTrust Park. He loved living in Pittsburgh, but he did miss the hot Atlanta weather sometimes. The sweltering heat reminded Aaron of the many games he had attended as a little boy. His dad would always take him to see the Pirates when they were in town, which is why he is such a huge fan to this day. As far as Aaron knew, his dad never visited Pittsburgh before he passed away, but he was a dedicated lifelong fan. Living in Pittsburgh gave Aaron tons of opportunities to see games, and he knew his dad was jealous as he watched down on him from heaven.

One thing Aaron never grew out of was taking a baseball glove to games. You never knew what would happen, and he liked to be prepared if a foul ball or home run headed his way. Over the years, he had collected his fair share of game-used baseballs – some more memorable than others. These days, he gave any balls he caught to one of the children in his section. It was a small gesture, but it always made the kid's night.

Aaron kept his glove trapped under his arm on the way to their seats, his hands carrying an ice-cold beer and two hotdogs. His mother walked alongside him as they searched for their seats – she had picked a section down the right field line slightly past first base. His mom knew this was one of his favorite areas to sit because it was a great view and there was a decent chance of catching a foul ball.

It turned out to be a great game and, for the first time in weeks, Aaron was able to enjoy himself without negative, health-related thoughts creeping into his consciousness. He enjoyed everything about baseball, from the beautiful weather and the fun between innings to the excitable crowd and competitive players down below.

Aaron couldn't remember the last time he'd had a day like this with his mom. He was always so focused on making a life for himself that he sometimes forgot the life his mom had given him. Together, they combatted the heat with a few cold beers and any hunger pangs with some unhealthy food.

Aaron was stuffed by the time the top of the 6th inning rolled around, and he took his eyes off the game to tell his mom how much he appreciated being with her on this fine day.

"Thanks again for everything, Mom," he said. "I couldn't have asked for a better day."

"Of course, Aaron," she said. "You know, we can do this again soon when I finally come visit you in Pittsburgh."

They grinned at each other, and then a chorus of "Oohs!" made them look skyward. Starling Marte of the Pirates had popped a ball up in the air, and it was heading foul – straight toward Aaron. Like he had done so many times before, Aaron slid his hand into the well-worn leather glove and added it to the sea of hands outstretched toward the sky.

Like they were meant for each other, the foul ball and Aaron's glove connected with a crisp smack, and Aaron lowered his arm for a better look. The ball was a little worn from use, with a large grass stain and a few frayed areas of red stitching. He glanced around his section for a kid to toss the ball to, but he surprisingly didn't see any.

"I guess I'll have to give it to a lucky kid on the way out," he said to his mom, who was complimenting his nice grab. It was his first foul ball in years.

At his mom's house, Aaron had a whole collection of baseballs he'd caught at games. He had scoured his old room the night before, looking at his old collections, memories, and everything a teenage boy thought was worth keeping. The shelf above his desk was packed with all of these baseballs, some worn, some new, all with a memory attached to them. When he first started to build his collection, Aaron arranged the baseballs on the shelf, but he soon had too many to properly fit on the shelf. He had little plastic stands for each of them, but they were all squeezed together causing them to sit precariously on the shelf. Aaron was almost surprised they hadn't fallen off over the years.

He examined the baseballs the best that he could without dislodging them and causing an avalanche; waking up his mother like that would've made him feel 17 again. Aaron smiled to himself as the little souvenirs brought back memories of home runs, foul balls, and some of his favorite players.

While Aaron appreciated having those memories, he'd had enough for one lifetime. For the last few years, he always made sure to give any balls he caught to a nearby kid who was looking jealously at him. He knew these little tokens would make them much happier than they could ever make him.

The baseball game ended exactly how Aaron had hoped – with a Pirates win. The game itself was rather uneventful – there were no extraordinary comebacks or heroics by one particular player – but Aaron and his mother couldn't have been happier with how the day had gone.

They stayed in their seats for a bit after the final out of the game, soaking in the sun and the beautiful views. Neither Aaron nor his mother liked leaving with the rush of people at the end of the game. Everyone was always pushing and cutting their way through the crowds, as if they could actually avoid the traffic. It seemed that no matter how fast you were in getting to your car, there were always those who got there first.

Instead of jostling with the crowd and getting frustrated at the amount of traffic, Aaron and his mother preferred to wait in their seats and finish the last of their beers or any snacks they had bought during the game. Though they could never completely avoid the traffic, being at the very end of it saved them a lot of stress.

Aaron quickly realized that the only issue with this plan was that he had missed his opportunity to toss the ball he'd caught to a young fan. Most of the stadium was deserted by this point, though Aaron kept his eyes peeled for someone who might want the ball. He kept tossing it up in the air as he and his mother slowly winded their way toward the nearest staircase out of SunTrust Park.

Just as Aaron was holding the door to the stairwell open for his mother, he felt her gentle hand on his shoulder. He glanced around at her to find her gesturing toward a small boy, who was leaning against a railing with his father as they looked out over the field. The boy was small, no more than seven or eight years old.

Aaron let the door creak shut and started making his way toward the couple, his mother trailing slightly behind him. The closer he got, the more this pair seemed familiar to him. He caught a few words of their conversation and realized he definitely knew their voices from somewhere.

"Excuse me," Aaron called over to them, fairly certain of who they were.

The pair broke off their conversation and turned in unison to face Aaron and his mother. Joey was wearing the same ballcap and inquisitive expression as he had on the plane the day before, and his father smiled over at them politely.

"I thought I recognized you," Aaron said, smiling at them. "Did you enjoy the game?"

"Did I ever!" said Joey. "We had amazing seats, the Pirates won, and I ate three whole hotdogs!"

They all chuckled at Joey's enthusiasm, but Aaron couldn't help but agree – there's nothing better than that.

"I was wondering if we might see you here," Dan said. "Joey has been talking about you ever since the plane ride. You made quite the impression on him."

"I'm sure it's nothing compared to the impression he had on me," Aaron said, blushing slightly from having needed the advice of a boy a quarter of his age. "You're raising a fine young man, Dan."

"Oh, by the way, this is my mother," Aaron said, gesturing to his mother, who was standing a few feet behind him. "Mom, this is Joey and his father Dan. They sat next to me on my plane yesterday."

Dan and Aaron's mom quickly split off into their own conversation, leaving Aaron to talk to Joey.

"So, what do you think of this stadium? Where did this game rank for you?" Aaron asked.

"Oh, that's tough," Joey said. "It's definitely up there, especially since it's a Pirates game and they won. I'll have to think about it."

"I know what you mean. It's hard to pick a favorite. I have so many," said Aaron. However, he thought about the time he spent with his mother today and decided that it definitely made the list of his favorites, despite the game being rather uneventful.

"So, have you told her yet?" Joey asked, glancing over at Aaron's mother.

"I did," Aaron said with a sigh. "It was tough, but I'm glad I did it. I feel like it's brought us closer together, which is more than I expected or would've asked for."

"That's good," said Joey. "Nobody should have to go through this alone. I've seen so many people at the hospital, and the happier ones always have someone there to make them feel better. That's why I'm glad I have my parents."

"You know, Joey," Aaron said, "You're pretty smart for someone your age."

Aaron was still slightly embarrassed from having to take advice from someone so young, but he was finally starting to understand what Joey meant when he said, "God doesn't shout – he whispers." Aaron had been living in his own head for weeks, asking why God had done this to him, but not once had he paused to actually listen to what others were telling him.

THE PRIEST, THE STEWARDESS, AND THE CHURCH PICNIC

Talking with Joey on that flight had finally broken through his thick skull, and he now felt less alone than he had in a while.

"I just have more experience with it than you do," Joey said.

Aaron laughed, and once again tossed the ball he had caught into the air. He hadn't even realized he'd done it, it was more of a reflex or a habit, but he caught Joey eyeing up the ball as it rose and fell back into Aaron's glove.

He couldn't believe it had taken this long for Aaron to realize that seeing Joey once again was a sign. He'd been looking for a young boy or girl to give the ball to, and now here he was standing in front of the only child left in the stadium. Plus, on the flight the day before, Joey had mentioned that he'd never caught a ball at a game.

Glancing over at Dan and his mother, who were both still deep in conversation, Aaron asked, "Do you want to play catch for a bit?"

Joey beamed at him, and without a single word, ran about twenty paces away and got into position. Aaron hadn't played catch in years, but his accuracy was still there. The first toss found the center of Joey's glove, and he quickly returned fire. Catch was such a simple game; there were no rules, and there really wasn't any way to win, but it was so peaceful and enjoyable. Playing with someone as young as Joey brought back a boyishness Aaron hadn't felt for years.

He wasn't sure how long they'd been playing but, eventually, a stadium employee came by and told them they had to leave. Joey grunted with the effort of one last good toss, and Aaron reached out and snagged it before turning to their parents. At some point during their game, it was clear that Dan and his mother had stopped talking and just stood there watching the two boys play.

As they headed for the stairwell together, Aaron said, "Joey, catch!" and tossed the ball up into the air. It plopped right into Joey's glove, and the boy looked up at him in amazement.

"That's a foul ball I caught today off of Starling Marte," Aaron explained. "Why don't you keep it?"

"No way! I can keep it for real?" Joey said, smiling wide and staring at the ball.

"Of course, you can!" Said Aaron. "Besides, I already have a bunch at home from games when I was your age. It's time you have one of your own."

"Wow!" Joey said, examining it as if he'd never seen a baseball before. "Dad, look at this! Look at what Aaron gave me! It says it's official right here!"

Dan patted Aaron on the shoulder and mouthed "Thank you!" to him. Aaron didn't know if Dan realized just how much his son had helped him. Besides, that baseball would mean a lot more to Joey than it would ever mean to him.

Joey couldn't stop talking about the ball or the game as they walked down the many flights of stairs and then toward their parked cars. When they talked on the plane, Aaron was impressed with how mature Joey was for the way he was handling his battle with leukemia. But now, Aaron was reminded that he was truly just a kid at heart. The cruel disease coursing through his body may have caused Joey to have to deal with problems meant for adults, but he was still so young.

Eventually, the two pairs had to go their separate ways. Joey and Dan were heading back to their hotel so they could catch their flight home in the morning, whereas Aaron was staying at his mother's for a few more days.

"I'll see you again soon, right?" said Joey, as they started to part ways. "Won't I, dad?"

"I'll be back to the hospital for chemo for sure, plus I have to meet with a therapist from time to time," Aaron responded. "I'm sure we will be seeing each other again."

"Ok, good," Joey said, before walking over and giving Aaron's legs a big hug.

They waved goodbye one more time and then walked toward their cars in the fading sunlight.

Barbara was glad it was over, boy was she ever. Her load was lighter now, much lighter. She knew the others were also carrying a lesser load now after last night's discussion. Who would have thought that she wasn't the only one with a dark little secret?

The girls had arrived at their destination around 6:00pm after their second flight of the day. They had finally made it to their beach resort hotel and the girls were ready to enjoy it. They had decided to meet in Barbara and Karen's room that night around 7:00pm to start the festivities, so they all unpacked quickly.

Lori waited until Sam was in the restroom before she finished her unpacking. The bottles of liquor needed to be secretly stashed away somewhere safe, she knew. She wouldn't want Sam to know about her drinking. She would probably tell her that she had a drinking problem, if she knew the whole story. Drinking before work, before shopping, before anything. Lori knew she liked to have a drink at home even before she was going to go out drinking for the night. But, she reasoned, she didn't have a problem. So why worry about it, she thought to herself.

Sam quietly unpacked her bag as Lori was in the restroom. She would hide her pills in one of her outfits so that Lori would never find them. She felt like less of a human being. Having to take pills for being depressed.

THE PRIEST, THE STEWARDESS, AND THE CHURCH PICNIC

Sometimes she thought how everyone should have a reason to be depressed. It wasn't like everybody's life was perfect, she wondered to herself as she hid the prescription. Maybe everyone just masks it better than her or maybe they just aren't depressed, she mused. She knew that she always seemed to have a mask on.

After putting a few things on hangers and placing their clothes in the drawers provided, the two of them headed to Karen and Barbara's room.

Karen had taken her phone with her into the bathroom to text her husband. She didn't want Barbara, or anybody else for that matter, to know what her text was about. They would eventually find out, she knew. But she wasn't going to tell them. They would just find out themselves one day. It would be easier for her, she thought. So she texted him in the restroom to insure that he did what needed to be done. They couldn't pay their bills anymore and things needed to change. They needed to change now, and bankruptcy was the only way.

He texted her back immediately and said that it was all taken care of. He had gone to a lawyer and the paperwork was sent to the appropriate agencies. It was done.

Karen let the girls in after hearing a knock at the door while Barbara said she had to use the restroom. She needed to prepare herself. This was it; she was going to tell her best friends about her pregnancy in less than a minute. It made her stomach queasy and her palms sweaty, so she needed to get composed. She couldn't stay in there forever, so she flushed the toilet, washed her hands and came out.

Everyone was sitting on the two double beds that each room had. They were all chatting about where they were going to go that night as Barbara sat down with them. The television was on, showing some kind of oldies music video that Karen had found when Barbara finally blurted out the words she knew she had to say.

"I'm pregnant!" she said, with a few tears running down her face.

The shocking statement caught them all by surprise. The only noise you could hear was the television blaring out the beat of some long-forgotten song by the Eagles. It was Peaceful Easy Feeling.

"I found out a few days ago," she said. "You're the first one's I've told. Toby, who is the father, doesn't even know yet," as tears streamed down her face, "and I'm going to have this baby, no matter what anybody says."

Karen, who was sitting next to her, hugged her tightly and told her that she loved her and she couldn't wait to share that love with her baby as they all joined in for a long group hug.

All of them with small tears forming in their eyes for different reasons.

Barbara's weight had been partially lifted off of her shoulders. It felt good to say.

She continued by telling them how she hadn't been feeling so well and had gone to her doctor a few days ago. That's when she found out. She doesn't know for sure but she told them she has this strange sense in her that the baby is going to be a girl. "A mother's intuition," she jokingly said.

"Well it's about time one of us had a girl!" Karen chimed in. All four of them laughing together at the thought of it all.

"This little secret has been on my mind since that doctor's visit," Barbara said, "and to tell the truth, it has caused me to be depressed knowing how I will need to tell everyone. Really depressed."

"I have given up drinking," she told them, "per my doctor's good advice. The drink I had at the airport was just tonic water and it didn't taste good at all," she told them laughingly. "No more drinks for me until this baby is born. I need to take care of myself," she told them, "because everyone has their own issues to take care of and we all need to do what we need to do in order to make our own lives better."

She told them how much better she felt now that she had told them about her secret. It wasn't a dark secret anymore. It was just life. "Unexpected things and situations happen in life," she told them, and now she realized that was what it was. Just part of life. Just like doctor Ruffa had told her. Things happen in life and we just need to deal with them as well as we can. She was going to move on and be happy about it. Her baby wasn't going to have a mother that was forever guilty and unhappy about the situation, no matter the outcome with Toby.

"It was weird," she said to them. "You listened, and I spoke a little, and now I feel better."

Karen listened to Barbara talk more about her situation and so forth and decided that she also needed to rid herself of this guilty feeling weighing her down. Barbara wasn't the first girl in life to get pregnant before she got married and her and her husband weren't the first one's in life to have to declare bankruptcy, she thought quickly to herself.

Karen told the girls it was time for her to tell her little dark secret, as their attention suddenly turned to Karen. What could this be? They all wondered quietly to themselves as Karen continued speaking.

"We're declaring bankruptcy," Karen told the girls. Shifting the mood quickly from Barbara's pregnancy to her own so-called dark problem. "Tom filed the paperwork today."

The girls all called out for another group hug as the music kept playing on the television. It was all oldies, and they liked that type of music. It was the same kind of music they all heard growing up. Plus, they liked it, even if it was from their parent's generation.

She took a long slow deep breath and told the other three girls that Tom and her had been living way over their heads for a number of years now and it was finally catching up with them.

"We had gotten to be friends with a number of Tom's friends from work," she said, "and they were all financially 'richer' than us."

"Most of them had chosen to have two working parents and that was a big difference compared to how we chose to raise our children. Tom and I decided long ago that I was going to be a stay at home mom for as long as we could afford it," she laughingly said, "maybe we could never afford it, but that's what we did. But that never stopped us from keeping up with these new 'friends' of ours."

She told them that she just wasn't and couldn't keep trying to live their lives as they were. Living in a big house with all its amenities, having new cars all the time, all the best items for the kids, and all of the other things they accumulated had just put them in a bad way financially.

So they had decided that bankruptcy was the best way to go. She also told them that she was going to look for a job. It's what needed to be done now and maybe she could find a job that was a good fit for her and the kids. She told them that she had sent her resume to a children's daycare center about a part time job and that maybe she would luck out.

She told them that she knew for sure that Tom was selling two of the three vehicles and had put the house up for sale and that she had already been looking at houses in their old neighborhood. Where their parents lived. "It was the kind of neighborhood we all grew up in," she told them, "and that's why I have three wonderful friends with me right now."

Barbara laughingly told them, "Boy, I sure need a drink after all of these secrets!"

They all laughed with her, as Karen, who was up at that time, grabbed a water for everybody out of the refrigerator. They would pay top dollar for those waters, she thought to herself, but they all needed one now she knew.

The three girls all told Karen that it was no big deal. So your house is smaller, one of them said and who cares what someone might think. A house doesn't make a home.

"You had made a good choice to stay at home with your babies," Lori told her. "You just made a bad choice on some financial decisions. Sounds to me like you're going to fix that."

All of this made Lori think about her choices. She knew she needed to start making the right choices too.

"Thinking about doing something can't hurt anyone!" Barbara told her after that. "Anyone who wants to think differently about you has no bearing on your life and never will," she said. "So remember that," she told her good friend.

"I have to tell you something girls," Sam said, "It seems thinking about something, but not doing it, has actually hurt me over the past year. I have depression now, which I take medications for. It was probably the thing I almost did that has made me feel guilty for so long now."

Barbara took a swig of water as she was now understanding how they all had their own little dark secrets. Secrets that were really nothing and which could be handled in one's life rather easily with a little help from others. Her load was lighter by the minute.

Karen also felt more relieved after revealing her so called dilemma. She held Barbara's hand as they all attentively listened to Sam.

Sam told the girls about her night of drinking with a customer when

THE PRIEST, THE STEWARDESS, AND THE CHURCH PICNIC

Mark was at a golf outing. She told them that she did not sleep with him, but it weighed heavily on her mind as to why she would do this. She told them that she was really happy in her life at that time and that it was just one of those things that got her excited as the two of them were talking that night when she was giving him a haircut. She had drinks with him and danced with him and the thought had occurred to her to sleep with him.

But she didn't.

But she has been depressed since then and it just seemed to get worse as the days have worn on.

"I've wore many happy looking masks lately," she jokingly told them.

The girls assured her that she didn't do anything terribly wrong. It wasn't worth bringing you down into a dark place over something you didn't do. "Sometimes, we have to let go of these things," Karen said as she joked about getting rid of her big house and fancy car.

Barbara told Sam that she hadn't been to church or confession in so long but was going to be going there next week if she wanted to go. Her parents had always gone to St. George Church when she was growing up and she had gone there also so she wanted to join there.

Sam was like Barbara in that respect. She hadn't been to confession in awhile, but she remembered that feeling she had when she left church after going to confession. Telling someone your sins, only to be forgiven, always left her with a wonderful outlook on life and death.

Sam told Barbara that she looked forward to going with her to see the priest there.

Her little talk with her friends had left Sam with a slightly new outlook on life. It seemed to her, that for the first time in awhile, she was actually really happy. It felt good, she knew, and she was going to stay that way.

Lori knew that all of these problems were made by decisions each one of her friends had made in their lives. Decisions that could affect them the rest of their lives. She knew that she also had gotten to a dark place herself by the decisions she only had made. Her drinking was a decision and maybe it was time to start making the right decision, she quietly thought to herself as the oldies videos kept playing.

The video was so good that Barbara, Sam and Karen got up to start dancing to it. Like they did in the old days. When they were younger and their troubles smaller.

Lori thought to herself that even after all this, they were happier than they were this morning. She got up and danced with them, because after the song was over, she was going to free herself from addiction. She was going to get happy again!

They weren't sure it was coming, the three of them, but when the song stopped and the dancing dulled out, Lori crying profusely, told the girls that it was her turn.

"I'm addicted to drinking," she sobbingly said. "I drink all the time. I even drank in the restroom stall in the airport. I have wanted to quit so bad," she told them, "but I just can't do it alone and I need help. I need a lot of help," she said.

The tears were streaming down her face as she was declaring her dependency on alcohol to her three best friends. Barbara and Sam each grabbed one of her hands as she sat there crying for awhile, unable to talk.

All of the girls were shedding tears over all that had just come down in that room in the past 15 minutes.

Barbara jokingly laughed when she told the other girls "there are no more tissues in the box!" It brought a little laughter into the conversation, if only for a brief moment in time.

When she could talk again, Lori told them how it all seemed to start so innocently and slowly. Unnoticed, jut like a cancer growing in you. Her boyfriend, Adam, and her, were out at least four nights a week at various bars and events. Adam always liked that she told them. We enjoyed being out with our so-called friends, but after months and months of this type of behavior, like a cancer growing in you, she became more and more dependent upon having alcohol.

So when she wasn't out drinking, she was drinking at home.

She got good at it, she told them. "I would hide the bottles in my purse, along with mouthwash and drink whenever I wanted," she said. "It didn't matter where or when."

She was going to get help. Her three best friends were going to see to that.

Lori was finally at peace with herself. She didn't have to hide her addiction anymore. She was done with it and was going to take a different path. A winding path, but she would be taking it with her three best friends.

They would all be taking a different path than they were on before this trip. A path to happiness. A path of forgiveness and caring for each other.

They all sat there and talked about their futures together for some time until another oldie video came on that they remembered so well and they all got up to dance along with the music. It was a dance of joy for all of them. It was going to be a better vacation than all of them ever imagined. Free of the unseen forces on their shoulders bringing them down into the darkness. They were all going to enjoy the light this world has to offer.

They all talked about how much better they felt after their "coming out conversation", as they all affectionately called it now. No pills or alcohol, no big gifts or additional money, nothing physical, but yet they had all been changed for the better and were happier. None of those physical items could ever have taken them to the state they were now in.

John knew that the first thing he was going to do after unpacking was write a few letters.

He was going to start with a letter to this Father Mayer then he was going to send one to Angela at the bank and then his last one was going to be to the two boys his son had befriended. Those young men, he knew, were dear to his son's heart and he would make them dear to his heart also. One way or another, he was going to continue what his son had started. It would be his main goal in life. Help those in need.

In his hand-written letter to Father Mayer, he thanked him over and over again for shedding light on his son's endeavors. Father son relationships are difficult sometimes and since they lived in different cities, it only made it harder. "Your letter," he told Father, "helped bring me out of my despair. Words will not be able to describe this" and he continued in the letter to tell Father that he would somehow continue his son's work and hoped that the two of them would continue their correspondence as time permitted.

He also told him about his new friend, Father Feeney, who had attended the conference in Pittsburgh and had met Father Mayer there. He explained how he believed they were meant to sit next to each other on the plane and that Father Feeney was also listening to what God had been trying to tell him as this was the conference's main goal.

He ended the letter with the hope that one day they would meet in person and share more stories about his son.

His letter to Angela was more than just a thank you for the gift. He could call it a gift now. He knew that it was probably the most meaningful gift he had ever received, and it was such a simple little gift.

It was the first item he put away when he got home. Right next to the picture of his wife and son on his bedroom nightstand. It would make him think of both of them each and every night before he went to sleep. A sense of peace before falling asleep, something he hadn't felt in awhile.

He told Angela about the letter from Father Mayer, from St. George Church, and how he had sat next to a man of faith on the plane ride home. He also told her how he felt blessed by it all and told her about his son's efforts at the church.

Little did he know at this time that Angela was well aware of his son's endeavors at that church.

He thanked her again for all that she had done for him and hoped that one day they could meet and talk again. He told her it would be a wonderful day if that were to ever happen.

The letter to the young men his son had befriended was the last of the three letters. But that didn't make it his least favorite. He knew his son had taken time out of his life to help these two boys in need. Boys he didn't even know before. He could have spent his time golfing or hanging around other friends, but John knew that his son chose to spend his time nurturing these young men into becoming productive caring adults.

Men like his son.

He afforded himself a few tears remembering the day he met them at the baseball game, but at that time he wasn't fully aware of the overall affect his son had on them. He took a break from writing as his hands were trembling a little thinking about Kevin.

THE PRIEST, THE STEWARDESS, AND THE CHURCH PICNIC

It wouldn't be for some time from now before John would fully understand his son's impact on these boys.

John told the boys that he would like to stay in touch. As often as they would like, as he gave them his phone number and email. He told them he wasn't much of a letter writer but he would enjoy an email whenever time or their desire to send him one permitted them to do so. He told them he knew his son loved them and he would try to do the same.

He also sent them a little monetary gift and hoped they would spend it wisely. In his heart he knew these boys would somehow be a reflection of his own son and thus a reflection on him.

He wished he could spend more time with them, he thought to himself.

"Please stay in touch," were his last words in the letter and signed it "Love always, John."

He gathered the three letters and headed to the post office to mail them that day. John needed these to be sent and received as soon as possible. He needed these people to know how he felt about them.

Evelyn was wearing her pink summer sundress as Jeremy and her strolled along the beach, hand in hand, just like he likes it. It was a beautiful sunny day and they were both enjoying it.

She told her dad that it was just like our dream on the plane.

Jeremy looked at her, and then up into the sky, and told her, "Your mom made sure that it was going to be sunny for us today," with a big smile. She smiled back at him as they both picked up their favorite seashells they could find laying on the sand and enjoyed the smell of the ocean.

They were both happy.

Phyllis had texted Peter when they got into the cab to leave the airport to let him know that Charlene and she were all good. He texted her back, with his usual prompt reply to her, and they continued to text more and more the next day.

Even though she had just gotten to Atlanta, Phyllis couldn't wait to get back home and talk to Peter. It would be a wonderful day she imagined to herself. Wonderful for the three of them.

Ray was happy that it was going to be a morning interview. He liked the thought of getting back home that afternoon as he would have a lot to think about.

The traffic to their building was as expected. Hectic, to say the least. But, he knew it would be like that. No different than back home in Pittsburgh.

The building was similar to the one back at his current job. A tall steel, brick and concrete building with many stories neatly placed alongside other buildings similar in stature. It was really no different than where he worked besides the architectural differences.

The lady at the receptionist desk knew of his coming, and politely told him where the elevators were and what floor to get off on. They too had security guards at the entrance, similar to back home. He thanked her and headed that way. It was no different than the elevator rides he had taken everyday as a stockbroker back home. There was small talk amongst a few of the passengers about some financial deals and the baseball game that day. The Pirates were in town.

The elevator stopped on the fourteenth floor and as the door opened and he headed out of the elevator, a security guard and another man with a briefcase entered it right after he got out. Ray wondered if this was the same scenario that had played out at his firm yesterday. Somebody getting let go for whatever reason. He couldn't dwell on that as he had an interview in less than a minute he imagined. He could feel the tension in the man's aura as they walked by each other. He has felt that before with some of his old colleagues who were let go.

One door, both opening and closing, he thought to himself. For some it was an opportunity to see what lies beyond the door as it opens, while for others a door closing and an opportunity ending. Maybe for each person a good thing or maybe a bad thing. Only time would tell.

The girl at the receptionist desk greeted him kindly and asked him who he was here to see. Ray gave her his name and she immediately knew who he was supposed to see that morning. She dialed his extension and Ray could overhear her say that he was here, and she then hung up the phone. She told him that Mr. Anderson would be out to greet him shortly and asked him if he needed a coffee or water. Politely he told her that he was good and before you knew it, Mr. Anderson showed up.

THE PRIEST, THE STEWARDESS, AND THE CHURCH PICNIC

"My name is, Bill, Bill Anderson," he said, "nice to meet you, Ray."

"Pleased to meet you, Mr. Anderson," Ray said before Mr. Anderson told him to call him Bill.

"Let's head to my office."

It was a nice office. A little bigger than mine back in Pittsburgh. There were many awards on his walls and on his desks and I already knew he was a principal in the company. He asked me if I had any troubles on my trip here and before you knew it we were into our interview.

They were the usual questions, and I gave him the usual answers. We had talked for some time on the phone previously, so we were both aware of each others needs and wants. They were looking for someone to grow their financial portfolio and I was looking for a change. He knew of me through other investors he had worked with and he said I came highly recommended. "Your father was a stockbroker, also, wasn't he, Ray?"

It was a question he already knew the answer to, but he played along.

"Yes, yes he was, sir," I said. "He has been teaching me this business since I was a young child," I laughed, as did Mr. Anderson.

"Well, he did a good job," Bill responded quickly and many of us in this business have the utmost respect for your father, Earl Rossi.

Through the vast array of award plaques and such, I spotted one picture of his family. It appeared as if he was married and had two boys and a girl. He still had a ring on his finger, so I assumed he was still married, but I was a little amazed at the lack of pictures of his family. There was just the one picture of them. A photo shoot picture of the five of them hidden behind all of the other meaningless pictures. No pictures of a son in his youth baseball uniform or his daughter in a ballerina outfit.

He imagined that this gentleman was like his father.

Dedicated to a fault over his work. Sales awards and so forth were more important than baseball games or dance recitals.

It was all too familiar to Ray.

The interview was short; Bill knew he wanted me to join their organization before I even got on the plane to come to Atlanta. He offered me the job right there. It was already typed out and spelled out everything. It was a great offer. Much more lucrative than where I was at, and I believe he knew that. He gave me a quick tour of the place. It was no different than any other office, but he felt the need to. Maybe, I thought to myself, he was showing me off to all the others. Letting them know he was bringing in a thoroughbred. Somebody they would have to contend against in the race for more profit and money. Somebody who might be faster than them and hard to keep up with.

It was almost like a warning to them. Stay vigilant and keep producing.

I told him that I would just need a few days to go over things with my wife as we shook hands. He said he understood and that he was looking forward to me joining their organization. It would be good for me he said.

How could he know what was good for me? I thought to myself.

I smiled, thanked him and headed to the elevators. I could see a few of the others in the office eyeing me up as I entered the elevator, checking out the competition. Some of them probably wondering if their future was in jeopardy.

Patty woke up later then usual the morning after the flights home. They were tiring days when she had to fly back on two flights in the same day. Her kids knew that and they always let her sleep in a little. She would be off from work today and they were looking forward to spending time with their mother.

When she finally awoke she gave her kids each a big hug and asked them what they wanted to do today while she was making them breakfast. The youngest had made a list out that she handed to Patty and she just smiled and said, "Let's get to it."

It was going to be a wonderful day for her and her family.

The sun was shining bright thru the windows of his church that morning. Father Feeney hadn't said mass in a number of days, so he was looking forward to his morning mass. There wouldn't be a huge crowd at church, he knew, but every mass was special to him.

He had come to the realization that his parishioners do listen to what he has to say but being human they sometimes do not act on his words. He knew he would continue his preaching even if only just one of those in the church that day would listen and try their best to follow the words he had spoken to them all.

As mass began that morning, the sun was shining as usual on his statues creating a wonderful aura around the inside of the church. It reminded him of his friend John, from the plane ride and his gift of an angel statue. Father knew that he had touched John's soul in a good way on that flight and it gave him a feeling of peace.

He prayed that John would find comfort over the loss of his son and also prayed that he would one day come visit his church. It seemed to him that John had listened to what needed to be heard and he only hoped that he would have the hope and faith to come to church and grow his love for God and everyone else.

It was wonderful to be back at his little church, he thought to himself, as he began the mass with an opening prayer.

Tom and Jill thanked Sonya again as they were leaving the adoption center.

The case manager had been very helpful and when they were through, she had taken them to Sonya's desk as she knew they were friends. It was a pleasant place to work so Sonya had taken the time to walk them out herself.

Jill told her that it was a very good meeting and that they had been given all of the information and paperwork they needed. Sonya, knowing that it was a big decision, told them to take their time and make sure this was the right choice for them.

Deep in her heart, Jill knew that this was the right choice.

Shauna, seeing them about to leave gave them her blessings as they walked by her receptionist's desk and told them to follow the path that they felt was right for them. Jill hugged Shauna for what seemed to be an eternity before Sonya opened the front doors to walk us to our car.

The sun was shining, and it was looking like a great day.

"Thank you so much Sonya," Jill said, to the studying doctor. "It's been the best day I've had in quite sometime."

Sonya had seen and felt that feeling before from a number of other couples who had been to the agency.

"You are quite welcome," she said, as she hugged them both. "I hope our paths in life cross again," she said, smiling and waving as she headed back into the building.

Tom opened the door for Jill as her hands were full of paperwork and as he walked around the car he took one last look at Sonya and quietly thanked God for sending Sonya into their lives. He watched her go back into the building as he took one last look at one of the signs in front of the adoption agency. The sign said: FAITH, HOPE AND LOVE AVAILABLE HERE. He believed that.

The two of them were quiet for awhile, both of them just enjoying the experience and the possibilities that could lay ahead of them before Jill spoke up.

"I would like to have this paperwork finished in a few days and sent back to them as soon as possible, Tom," she said. "I want to adopt a child."

Tom kissed her hand as those were the words he was hoping or maybe praying to hear.

"We'll take care of it all in the next few days," he told her, with a small tear forming in his eyes. He told Jill that he didn't care if it was an infant or an older child; they all needed somebody to love.

Jill began crying at his words, it was cry of joy and happiness, she told him, as she told him to pay attention to his driving. She turned the music on to their favorite oldies station.

They didn't listen to music in the car much anymore. There hadn't been a reason to be sing-along happy for a long time now. But they were both in a happy mood. Tom even turned it up a little louder when she did that.

It was a sound to hear, the both of them singing to the song on the radio as they had done years ago, when they were happier. It was a song by the Eagles and they knew the words.

THE PRIEST, THE STEWARDESS, AND THE CHURCH PICNIC

Ray headed out of the building as others were also coming and going. He got in line for a cab with the others as he had done so many times before in his life outside of his building in Pittsburgh.

He laughingly wondered to himself how Miguel, the cab driver back home, was doing. He could envision him sitting in his cab, singing to himself, as happy as a lark on a sunny day. He loved Miguel, he thought to himself. He knew he was a good man, maybe not financially rich but richer beyond belief in so many other ways. Ways that truly mattered.

He got in his cab when it was his turn and told the driver to take him to the airport.

Sitting in the back of the cab, Ray had a big decision to make. It wasn't one he needed to make at that moment or even that day, but it would need to be made.

He thought quietly to himself how Mr. Anderson and his company were almost a mirror image of his current situation back home in Pittsburgh. Just a different building and different faces in a different city. Faces which were probably covered in fake masks. Masks put on to prevent someone from knowing the true reality or one's true feelings.
He often wore his own mask at work, he knew.

He remembered Bills office, decorated with awards and other plaques indicating financial success. A so-called successful man.

The others in the office were similar to faces he saw at his current job. Everyone on edge wondering how well the other guy is doing and whether he or she was doing enough to keep the principals happy, it was never enough he knew. He had been to that office before, just not in Atlanta.

Ray read the letter indicating the company's offer to him. The dollar signs were all over it. If he were to talk to his father about this, he knows he would tell him he would be crazy not to accept this offer.

He knew who he was going to call as soon as he got back home to Pittsburgh.

CHAPTER 12: ONE MONTH LATER

The sky above his apartment was a solid blanket of dark, foreboding grey; the sun was working overtime trying to pierce the thick veil, but only small patches of light could seem to break through. Aaron's face was stony under the hood of his coat as he tried to protect himself from the stiff wind that accompanied the fast-approaching storm, but his spirits were still high nevertheless.

He was on his way to his second chemotherapy session, and he sure as hell was not looking forward to the resulting sickness that would surely greet him later that night, but the last few weeks had taught him, he had been shutting off the rest of the world, convinced that he was alone and that he alone knew what it was like to have your life hanging in the balance.

But a chance encounter with a young boy on a flight the month before – perhaps some would call it fate – gave him the new lease on life he had been looking for. He had reconnected with his mother, stopped holding a grudge against his friends who were doing the best they could, and finally started to move past his ex-girlfriend who had given up on him so quickly.

It wasn't easy. In fact, it was incredibly difficult at times. But for the first time in years, Aaron had his eyes and ears open to the world around him, and that allowed him to see how far he had strayed into the darkness.

Before heading to the UPMC Hillman Cancer Center, Aaron decided to make a quick detour through his neighborhood's corner store, One Stop. He visited this rundown shop frequently because it was convenient, and he liked to snack much more than was healthy, but walking through the door reminded him of his first chemotherapy session.

He had been dreading the hospital so much that he used this little detour to procrastinate actually going; he couldn't remember what he bought that day, but he was certain he threw it out without eating it.

Today, he picked up some beef jerky and the Skittles that came in the purple bag – two of his favorite snacks. He made his way to the counter, following the same winding path through the aisles that he always took. Aaron couldn't help but tempt himself by looking at what else the store had for sale, but he stuck with the beef jerky and Skittles.

He set his items down on the well-worn counter, which was painted an unflattering off white, save for the patch at the very center where the passing of countless purchases had worn through to the wood beneath.

Shirley greeted him just as she always did.

"This all for you today, Aaron?" She asked. "Those Skittles are buy one get one half off, if you're interested."

"Nah, I don't need any more than this. I don't even need this, to be honest," Aaron replied with a chuckle.

"You've been in a better mood lately," Shirley pointed out as she scanned his credit card. "For a while there, I was worried about you."

"Yeah, I was worried about myself for a bit there, too," Aaron said, smiling back at her. "But I'm doing better. I'm glad I have you and the girls to watch over me."

I gestured to the faded and frayed picture behind the counter of three angels. Shirley always said they were looking out for her and her customers. Aaron usually never gave the picture more than a quick glance, but something about the angel in the middle stood out to him today. She looked familiar to him, but he couldn't place where he knew that face.

"You want your receipt?" Shirley asked, snapping Aaron out of his daze.

"No, thanks," he said, the moment of recognition passing. "You just keep watching over me. I'm sure I'll see you soon."

Aaron drew his hood up over his head and pushed hard against the door, which was being forced shut by the strong winds. He was surprised it hadn't started raining yet, but hoped it would hold off at least until he got inside the hospital.

The first huge drops of rain from the storm began to fall just as Aaron approached the automatic doors of the Hillman Cancer Center. He entered, removed his hood, and shook off the droplets. Thankful to finally be inside, Aaron checked in at the front desk and went to the waiting room until his name was called.

Aaron still wasn't used to the hospital setting and the overly-sterile aura that permeated every aspect of the rooms. He understood why hospitals had to be that way, but it still made him uncomfortable. Chemotherapy was scary enough to begin with, but Aaron was doing his best to maintain a positive outlook. As he waited, Aaron thought of Joey. Joey had been through much worse than Aaron, and he did it with a smile on his face. If his young friend could stay positive in the face of something so scary, Aaron had no excuse.

He wasn't in this alone, and neither was anyone else in the waiting room. He didn't know who most of them were or what their diagnoses or chances were, but he knew they were in the same boat as he was. While Aaron had felt alone the last time he was in this waiting room, this thought now gave him strength.

Aaron was sitting in a chair right next to a hallway, and he watched as various hospital staff and personnel walked in and out of rooms. He was staring down the hall absentmindedly, just waiting for his name to be called, when he realized that someone was walking toward him. It was the same nurse he had seen last time – the one he had gone to high school with. He wasn't sure if she was walking his way because he was staring at her, or if she had also recognized him.

"It's Kate, right?" Aaron asked when she was close enough, unsure of what else to say. She had to know why he was sitting there, and he still felt uneasy when talking to people about his illness.

"Yeah," she said, smiling softly at him. "And you're Aaron. Gosh, it's had to have been almost 15 years since I've seen you."

"You still look the same, though," Aaron said, blushing a little.

"Yeah, so do you," Kate said.

There was a brief silence after this. It was always awkward running into old classmates. Most of the time, Aaron had the same exact conversations – both people had boilerplate answers to basic questions, and they'd make a hasty excuse to end the conversation. But Aaron didn't really want this to be one of those conversations, and perhaps Kate didn't either.

"You know, you told me you were going to Paul Canter's end of the year party the last time we saw each other," Kate said with a crooked smile. "But I was looking for you there, and I didn't see you."

Speaking of high school like this took Aaron back to that very night, and all of the sudden he had butterflies in his stomach. He remembered that night perfectly, and he truly did want to go and see her at Paul's party.

"I remember that," Aaron said, blushing a bit more. "My friend, Chris – not sure if you remember him – had a car that night and he wanted to go to a different party. I didn't have another ride, so I had to tag along."

"Oh, I see," Kate said, almost as if she was embarrassed for bringing up the memory. "Well, you missed out on a fun party."

"I bet I did. The one we went to wasn't that great," Aaron said.

"Well, I should probably get back to work," Kate replied, giving Aaron a small smile.

"Oh, yeah, ok," Aaron said. He wanted to keep talking but knew she was right.

They said their goodbyes and Kate started to walk away until Aaron finally worked up the nerve to say something.

"Hey, Kate!" he called after her. She turned to look at him. "I know I'm about 15 years too late, but can I make it up to you for missing that party?"

She paused to consider the offer. It was only a few seconds but it felt like an eternity to Aaron.

"Alright," Kate said, taking out a pen and writing her number on a piece of paper for him. "Give me a call, but no standing me up this time."

With one last smile, she turned and left. Aaron was surprised at his luck. He came in for chemotherapy, and he would be leaving with a phone number. Another guy in the waiting room gave him a thumbs up, and Aaron couldn't help but smile to himself as his name was finally called.

Aaron was still smiling as he made his way back to the room where his chemo session would take place. Three of the four oversized chairs were already occupied, and Aaron was guided to the empty one nearest the large window at the end of the room. Aaron looked out over Pittsburgh as he clambered into the enormous chair and the nurse started the process of preparing him to receive the poison that was supposed to eliminate the tumor winding its way down his spine.

Aaron thought back to his first chemotherapy session, about how hopeless he had felt and how little he wanted to be there. He still didn't want to be there, but he couldn't stop thinking of Joey's infectious smile and how he managed to tackle this deadly disease head-on. Like it or not, Aaron knew he would be in this chair every month or so for the foreseeable future. He could spend this time one of two ways: Either shut himself off from the world and refuse to acknowledge those who were also struggling with cancer and chemotherapy, or treat it as an opportunity to grow and make friends with those who knew his struggle better than anyone else.

A month ago, he was definitely leaning toward the first option, but what Joey had said about listening to the world around him helped Aaron realize that he wasn't as closed off as he felt. Before he could change his mind again, Aaron turned to the woman in the chair next to him. She was older than him by a decade or two, and the effects of the cancer were pronounced enough to suggest that she had been at this for a while.

Aaron's nurse had just finished taking a blood sample and would soon be ready to put the IV in his arm to inject the meds that preceded the hard stuff. He knew the drugs would drain him, making him incredibly tired and ready for a nap, but he didn't want to be passive for all of these treatments. There wasn't a ton of talking going on, which meant the others in the room likely also felt the desire to sleep the hours away.

The woman was awake, however, and he was hoping to find a way to start a conversation with her. But no matter how hard he tried, he couldn't think of a good jumping off point; everything that popped into his head just seemed stupid. Just as he was about to say something about the weather outside the window – Aaron knew it was a weak opening, but he didn't have anything better – a nurse approached the woman and Aaron realized she was finishing up for the day. He might have had a few more minutes to start a conversation, but he felt like he missed his opportunity and decided to let it go.

With a huge sigh, Aaron felt the medications starting to drip into his veins and his head felt lighter; it would be difficult to stay awake, let alone coherent enough for a conversation. He sat there in a daze for a while, not really aware of how much time had passed, until someone climbed into the giant chair the woman had previously occupied.

Looking to his right, Aaron made eye contact with the man from the waiting room that had given him the thumbs up. The man smiled over at Aaron as the nurse started to draw his blood.

"I bet you're feeling pretty good right now, huh?" the man said. He was older than Aaron – perhaps in his 50s – and had dark black hair that was slowly but surely starting to turn silver. He was quite tan for a man who lived so far from a beach, and he had a round, slightly pudgy face that perfectly framed his big, toothy smile.

Aaron wasn't sure if the man was referring to the drugs that were making him feel loopy or the scene he witnessed in the waiting room, but he smiled back and nodded at the man.

"Today has been good to me," Aaron said. "I'm Aaron, by the way."

"My name is Lee," said the man. "So, what brings you here?"

Lee said it with a smile, but Aaron could tell that he was serious and actually wanted to know his story. Aaron could tell off the bat that Lee was one of those people who was more charismatic than should be allowed, but he also exuded sincerity. Aaron filled Lee in on his tumor and what exactly schwannoma neurofibrosarcoma was, and Lee told Aaron all about his colon cancer.

Despite the conversation being centered on diseases that could very well kill them, Lee spoke with a lightheartedness that wasn't common in the hospital and it made Aaron feel better about his whole situation. Everyone usually treated cancer so seriously – nobody joked about it – but Lee talked about it as if it was nothing more than the common cold. Aaron quickly learned that this was Lee's second go around with the deadly disease.

"They say what doesn't kill you makes you stronger," Lee said with a smile. "So, I should be even better equipped to beat the cancer this time. I've already done it once, so this should be like riding a bike."

"But what's your prognosis? Aren't you nervous that it came back again?" Aaron asked, amazed at how blasé Lee was about the whole thing. Aaron himself was finally starting to look on the bright side of things, but he still treated his tumor seriously.

"You need to lighten up, kid," Lee said, looking over at him. Despite being in the middle of the chemotherapy session, Aaron was impressed with how talkative Lee was. Aaron was so tired he could hardly manage to keep up with the conversation, but Lee didn't seem to be feeling the effects at all.

"I've been through it before, and maybe I'll have to go through it again if I beat it this time," Lee said. "But that's not for me to decide. Either this chemotherapy crap will work and my body will respond, or it won't and the cancer will take over. I'm going to let the doctors do their jobs and just live my life in the meantime."

"That's a good way to look at it," Aaron replied, genuinely impressed by Lee's mentality.

"It's the only way to look at it," Lee snapped back. "Or, at least it's the only constructive way to look at it."

There was silence for a bit and Aaron thought Lee might finally be feeling the effects of the drugs dripping into his veins.

"So, what was it you said you do again?" Lee said, eyes still closed.

"I work in marketing," Aaron replied.

"Do you like what you do?"

"Yes, and no," Aaron said. "I have a good job, but my ultimate goal is to open up my own marketing company. I have some big plans, but I'm not quite where I need to be to carry them out."

"You should stop dawdling and start working toward that goal," Lee said. "You might not be here next year, so why wait to start working on your big plans?"

"Well, it's not that simple," Aaron said, a little frustrated. Lee clearly didn't know what he was talking about.

"Sure, it is," Lee said. "The only way to get started is to get started. If you're waiting for things to be perfect, you'll be dead before you start – and not just because of cancer."

Aaron appreciated Lee's bluntness, but it was hard to think about leaving his job and starting a new business while simultaneously battling cancer. While he supposed nobody would hold it against him for being reluctant to pursue anything new during a time like this, Lee's words did give him pause.

The conversation shifted from work to sports and then into personal life. Even though Aaron walked into the hospital that day planning to be more talkative and meet some new people, he was still surprised at how easy it was to talk to Lee.

He was an interesting man who had an endless supply of stories to tell. Lee owned an auto body shop that he opened decades ago, but he had spent most of his younger years traveling and working any job that he could find. Talking to him made Aaron rethink how he was living his life. While he always felt like he was living the right way and doing the right things, people like Lee made him realize that there was no blueprint to life.

Growing up, everyone is told to stay in school, find a career that pays good money, and settle down and start a family. And while Lee had eventually done those things, he took many detours on his journey there. Confronted with cancer and the thought of his own mortality was quickly making Aaron realize there were many things he wanted to do that he had put off or cast aside because they weren't what he was "supposed" to do.

The conversation with Lee helped the four-hour session slip by much faster than his previous one. Before he knew it, his nurse was getting him ready to leave for the day. All the time they had spent talking kept Aaron from feeling the tiring effects of the medicine, but they hit him all at once as he tried to get out of the chair.

He felt incredibly lethargic, as if his body was half asleep and he was moving through molasses. He was sure the feeling would wear off as he got his blood flowing again, but it reminded Aaron of how powerful the drugs were that they had to put into his body. After what happened last time, Aaron was not looking forward to the nausea that was sure to follow. He just hoped that his body got more used to it as time wore on, because spending the night in the bathroom once a month was not an option.

"Well, hopefully I'll see you around," Aaron said to Lee as he started to head toward the door.

"Sure thing, Aaron," Lee responded, his eyes closed. He had talked so much that Aaron was not surprised to see he was finally succumbing to the effects of the medicine. Aaron never thought sitting in a chair for four hours could be so draining, but that medicine packed a real punch.

Aaron glanced out the window as he walked back toward the main entrance of the hospital and saw a glimmer of sunshine in the distance. Rain was coming down in sheets for his entire chemotherapy session, but it was finally starting to slow down. Still, Aaron was not looking forward to the walk to his car.

Wanting to delay the trip just a little bit longer, Aaron made a small detour to the desk in the reception area.

"Excuse me," Aaron said. "Can you please tell me how to get to the pediatric ward?"

The receptionist, whose name was Sandra, according to her nametag, looked up at him and smiled.

"Of course! If you head down the hall to the elevator," she said, pointing to his left, "and take it to the third floor, it will be on the right. Are you visiting a family member?"

"Thank you! And no, I just wanted to stop by and see a friend of mine."

Aaron did as he was told and headed to the left and made his way to the elevator. As he walked, he mulled over everything Lee had told him during his session. Ever since his first encounter with Joey, Aaron had been trying to pay more attention to the people he met and the world around him in general. So far, he'd really enjoyed opening up his mind and his heart to others, even complete strangers.

Lee's passion for life was infectious, and his words definitely resonated with Aaron. If it wasn't for Joey, Aaron might never have talked to Lee. But even though Aaron was trying to be more positive and open-minded during this whole affair, he was still struggling. Joey was so young; he didn't know what life was like without leukemia. Lee experienced so much in his youth that he was content with life, and cancer was not unusual at his age.

Aaron felt caught in the middle of it all. But, on the elevator ride up to the pediatric ward, Aaron decided he wasn't going to let these feelings of helplessness overwhelm him. So what if he'd drawn the short straw? Life is what you make it, and Joey and Lee were both testaments to that. Acting like he was already dead wasn't going to do him any good. The only thing he could do was to keep chugging along with chemotherapy and live his life the best he could.

The ding of the elevator reaching his destination sounded like the dig of the bell in a boxing match; Aaron was reentering the ring for the next round, and he was ready to put up a fight.

Aaron walked into the pediatric ward not knowing what to expect. Seeing a bunch of sick kids wasn't typically a recipe for making him feel better, but he knew that seeing Joey would raise his spirits. Quietly, Aaron wondered whether all of the kids were as optimistic and happy as Joey was, or if he was an outlier.

The first thing Aaron noticed about this floor was that it was decorated completely different than all of the other floors. The tiled floor wasn't just a dull speckled white; it had splashes of color everywhere, and all of the letters of the alphabet could be seen spread randomly across the tiles.

The walls were also painted all sorts of colors: One section was painted like a field with all sorts of flowers, another was made to look like a jungle full of animals, but Aaron's favorite was one painted to look like the night sky. He smiled at these beautiful paintings, no doubt the handiwork of some local artists, but the murals also made him sad. Some of these children spent their days and nights in these wards, which meant they weren't able to experience some of these sights first-hand. Realizations like these made Aaron respect Joey's parents even more for taking him on so many trips to baseball stadiums. Seeing all of baseball's best fields would be a dream come true for any fan, but Aaron knew Joey had to appreciate it even more.

Aaron slowly continued down the aisle, constantly distracted by the numerous paintings and pictures that filled his vision everywhere he turned. As he neared the reception area, a group of papers hanging on the wall caught his attention. They were drawings done by the children who occupied the ward.

Aaron stopped to admire their work and was immediately reminded of what his parents' fridge looked like back when he was a young boy. Though he never really did have much artistic talent, he was always drawing pictures to show his mom. She hung up each and every drawing Aaron made, to the point where the fridge was dangerously plastered with pictures and magnets.

Most of these kids were better artists than he was. The drawings included family portraits, landscapes, sports heroes, and many other surprises that children's brains can come up with. A picture in the bottom corner caught Aaron's eye. The drawing was quite good; it was a picture of a baseball field.

Despite the picture being drawn in crayon, Aaron quickly recognized it as the field of the Atlanta Braves. Off to the side of the field were two stick figures playing catch with a baseball. Below the two characters were the names "Aaron" and "Joey."

"Wow," Aaron said aloud to nobody in particular. Aaron had been so focused on the impact Joey had had on him, that he didn't consider how Joey might have viewed their little session of catch. Over the years, Aaron had given out so many baseballs he had caught that he didn't really think much of it, but that little game of catch was now immortalized in crayon.

After staring at the drawing for a few minutes, Aaron realized that his eyes were wet with tears. A boy as special as Joey deserved a full life, deserved to get better. He had no idea what Joey's prognosis was, but he knew that someone like Joey was made to beat this dreaded disease. He wanted to take the picture off the wall and hang it on his fridge at home, but he knew he shouldn't take it without Joey's permission.

Instead, Aaron pulled out his cell phone and took a picture of it. As he finished the walk over to the receptionist, Aaron sent the image to his mother with a little message telling her where he had found it. He knew she would appreciate something like that.

"Excuse me," Aaron said to the receptionist. "Is it possible for me to see Joey Chandler? He's a friend of mine."

The receptionist looked up at him with her giant brown eyes and dazzling smile.

"Oh, yes, of course you can. You know, I'm glad you're here to see Joey. He doesn't get many visitors other than his parents."

"Well, I'm happy to be here," Aaron said, a little sad to hear that Joey didn't get many visitors. "You know, he drew me in that picture over there. We played catch the last time I saw him."

"Oh, then you must be Aaron," the receptionist said. "Joey has been telling us all about you. It was very nice of you to give him that baseball you caught."

"It's no big deal. It's just a little thing I like to do for the kids at baseball games," Aaron responded, barely holding back a smile. "Actually, I think Joey did a lot more for me than I did for him. I don't think he realizes how special of a kid he is."

"He really is," the receptionist said. "I could be having a terrible day, and he knows just how to turn things around for me."

After the receptionist told him Joey's room number, Aaron smiled at her, said his goodbyes, and made his way down the hall. Knowing that Joey had been telling the hospital workers about him gave him a little extra pep in his step as he walked.

Although having cancer had impacted his life negatively in many ways, it had also given him two new friends in Joey and Lee. Aaron now believed that everything happened for a reason, so God must have brought these two amazing people into his life for a reason. Then, his heart leaping a bit, Aaron also remembered he had a date to plan with Kate. So perhaps it was three people God wanted in his life. Aaron certainly hoped so.

The cheerful artwork and wild array of colors continued all the way down the hall to the room the receptionist had directed him to. The room was large, but cramped, as if multiple people were trying to claim it as their own. In fact, that was kind of the truth.

There were four large hospital beds inside, each occupying a corner. The hospital clearly gave the room's four occupants complete control over the designs of their quadrants.

The corner where the door entered was a sea of blue, including the walls and all of the decorations. The bed was empty at the moment, but the child who normally lived there was a huge fan of the sea and everything that lived in it. The other front corner of the room was darker and full of planets, constellations, and spaceships; the girl who occupied that bed looked like she was a year or so older than Joey.

The bed next to the girl was also empty, though the child who normally occupied it must have been of superhero movies. Joey's corner of the room would've been obvious to Aaron even if the boy wasn't sitting in his bed, smiling wide at him. His area of the room was a shade of green that was unmistakably supposed to resemble the grass from a baseball field. The area was covered with baseball memorabilia – mostly for the Pittsburgh Pirates – and drawings just like the one Aaron had seen in the hallway.

"You came! You came!" Joey said, unable to contain his excitement. "I told my dad you said you would come. I've been waiting for you to visit!"

"Of course, I came, buddy!" Aaron said, also unable to keep from smiling. "Today was my first day back in the hospital for chemo since I saw you, and I didn't want to leave without saying hello."

Dan, Joey's father, was sitting in the corner of the room. Aaron and Dan exchanged pleasantries but weren't able to say much else due to Joey's excitement. He started showing Aaron everything he had with him in the hospital, from the pictures he drew to his collection of baseball trinkets. It turned out Joey was collecting one thing from each stadium he visited, whether it was a ticket stub, bobblehead, or something his dad got him from the team store. Thanks to Aaron, his prized possession was now the foul ball caught at the game in Atlanta the month before.

Aaron sat down at the foot of Joey's bed, and they caught up on what had happened to the both of them over the past few weeks. Joey was not much different than Aaron was at his age; his favorite school subjects were art and recess, and most kids his age would probably agree.

However, Aaron couldn't help but be impressed with Joey's artwork. It was clear that he put a lot of time and energy into his drawings. Despite being so young, Joey clearly had the talent of someone much older than him.

"I saw your drawing in the hallway," Aaron told Joey, when the talkative boy finally let him get a word in. "The one with us playing catch – it's very good! It was so good that I almost stole it right off the wall. Instead, I settled for a picture of it."

"You can have it!" Joey said, clearly happy that Aaron had seen it. "I can make another one. It's no big deal."

Though Aaron was tempted by this offer, he thought of something better.

"Tell you what," Aaron said. "Why don't we leave that one up in the hall, and you make me another one? I want everyone who walks by to see your drawing of us playing catch together, so they all know we are friends."

"What do you want a drawing of?" Joey asked

"Hmm," Aaron responded. "That's up to you. I trust you. You can draw me whatever you want, and you can give it to me next time I visit. How does that sound?"

"Deal!" Joey said, practically shouting with excitement.

After that, Aaron had to get going. It had been long enough after his chemotherapy session that he had started to feel under the weather. His visit with Joey, combined with the long conversation he'd had with Lee, was really making him feel drained.

He said his goodbyes to Joey, but Dan followed him out into the hallway.

"Aaron," Dan began, "I can't thank you enough for coming to visit. You don't know how much it means to him – how much it means to me."

"Don't mention it, Dan," Aaron said. "You have an amazing son, and I am happy to visit. Talking to him on the plane opened my eyes and gave me a new perspective on life when I really needed it."

"Speaking of a new perspective, I wanted to ask," Dan said. "Do you happen to go to church? No big deal if not."

"I used to, but it's been a few years," Aaron responded. "To be honest, once I found out I had cancer, I began to doubt my faith even more. Joey has restored some of that faith."

"Well, no pressure, but I take Joey to St. George's every Sunday morning," Dan said. "Joey really likes you, and I'm sure it would mean the world to him if you came sometime."

"You know what?" Aaron said. "That sounds great. Count me in!"

With that, Aaron strode back down the hallway and into the elevator. Once again, the chemotherapy kept him up most of the night and he had frequent bouts of nausea. Despite all of this, Aaron's mind was much clearer and more focused than it had been after his last session. He knew this would only be temporary; it was something he would get through as long as he kept his faith.

Jeremy was looking forward to their trip to the grocery store today as was Evelyn. He wasn't as nervous as he was two weeks ago when he first asked Lauren out for a date.

As they drove to the store that day, he was hoping that she would be there working the checkout register. He knew what shift she worked so he made sure that Evelyn and him would do their shopping during that time. Evelyn had always prayed that her father would ask Lauren out for a date, he knew now, but she didn't know that it was going to be that day.

Evelyn would always eye up the cash registers when they would first arrive at the store to see if she was working that day, and there she was, working her usual register with her usual special aura. It always brought a smile to Evelyn's face when she would see her as we walked in and grabbed our cart. Lauren would always wave at her, or now I know, at us, when we walked in. It made all three of us a little happier.

Today he was going to do it, Jeremy had told himself. He was going to ask Lauren out on a date. She might have to decline his offer for whatever reason and it didn't matter how many other people would hear him ask her even if she had to say no, because he was going to do it.

He knew as they were gathering their food that Evelyn would pick her line. It wouldn't matter to her how empty and quicker the other lines might be, he knew she would pick her line. Jeremy was counting on that.

He took his time meandering through the aisles that day. Slowly building his courage. The thought of her saying that she couldn't do it because she had a boyfriend or something like that made him a little queasy as they gathered their last items.

Evelyn always knew what groceries they needed. She had become a professional at shopping. Always loaded with coupons and knowing what was on sale. It made it a lot easier for me, especially that day. She had grown to be quite the cook and basically took care of deciding what we were going to have for dinner on a nightly basis.

After grabbing her favorite icecream, as we always grabbed that item last so that it wouldn't melt before we got home, Evelyn headed to Lauren's line. It wasn't that busy that day and we were third in line to checkout.

I remember rehearsing how I was going to ask her out so many times over and over again in my head for days before this day, but it all seemed for naught as we were now placing our items on the counter for Lauren to ring up and I couldn't remember any of the suave lines I was going to use to ask the big question.

"How's my favorite girl?" Lauren asked Evelyn as she reached into her pocket to hand her a lollipop as she always did.

"Just peachy," Evelyn responded as I also greeted Lauren.

"I bought my dad's favorite chicken today," she said to her, "and I'm going to make more than we can eat so that daddy can take some to work with him."

"You're a wise girl." Lauren responded, "wise indeed."

"How are you today, Jeremy?" Lauren asked with her usual upbeat kind of style.

"I'll let you know in a minute," he laughingly told her in response as both Lauren and Evelyn seemed a little confused.

"I was wondering if you would like to have dinner some night or something like that?" Jeremy asked her, looking straight into her pretty green eyes.

The customers behind him eyeing them up after hearing his question. Nobody staring at them, but you could feel them listening attentively to hear the answer. Even the other checkout girls seemed to take notice.

Lauren just stopped what she was doing and looked at Evelyn and asked her, "What took your daddy so long to ask me out?" Both of them with shocked big smiles on their faces.

Evelyn wasn't so sure how to answer her question as she was surprised by his question and maybe scared of what Lauren's answer would be. So, she just looked at him quickly and then stared at Lauren.

"I've been waiting to taste Evelyn's cooking for a long time now," she answered, smiling at Evelyn. "So whatever day she wants to cook, that's the day we're going to have our first date."

A huge relief came over Jeremy after hearing those words and he just looked at Evelyn for an answer to Lauren's question.

It was a friday, a friday I will never forget as Evelyn excitingly told the two of us that she was going to head home from here and start cooking because tonights the night.

Lauren and Jeremy just looked at each other as she handed Evelyn a pen and paper to write down our address. "I'll be there at 6pm tonite then," she said, as Evelyn frantically wrote down our address, all the while with a big smile on her face.

"Can I bring dessert?" she asked us, or rather she asked Evelyn.

"Not this time," Evelyn answered, "because I'm going to make you your favorite pie, apple pie."

"You have a good memory young lady," Lauren said, "but remember next time I get to do the cooking!"

Jeremy remembered feeling on top of the world at that comment as it seemed to him that Lauren was already preparing all of us for our second date.

"We could pick you up, if that works better," Jeremy told Lauren. But she told him that it would be easier this time if she just drove herself as the two of you need to get in that kitchen and get going on dinner.

After we put our groceries in the cart and paid our bill, Lauren came out of her little space at the checkout counter and gave Evelyn a big hug. Evelyn wouldn't let her go and I could see a joyous smile on the older lady behind us as she could feel the love flowing through the air at that moment. The lady had an angel pin on her blouse, very similar to Evelyn's necklace, and the old woman nearly had a tear in her eye as Lauren also gave me a quick hug and said she would see us tonite and that today was a wonderful day for her.

I answered her question from earlier about how I was doing today and told her that today sure has been wonderful and it was only going to get better.

As Lauren got back behind the register, her fellow cashier next to her gave her a thumbs up signal and all those in hearing distance all seemed to be elated at the events of the past few minutes.

Evelyn was proud of her dad that day, I could tell as we headed out of the store. It was a wonderful day for all of us and Evelyn's chicken was only topped by her apple pie she made especially for Lauren. She made sure that when Lauren left that night, that she took a piece of pie with her.

Evelyn and Lauren hugged goodbye that night after we finished our third game of monopoly, Evelyn winning all three games, as it was time for her bedtime. I walked Lauren to her car with her piece of apple pie in hand, that night, and thanked her for a great first date and asked if it we could do it again sometime.

"I'm off all weekend," she told me as she wrote down her phone number and address for me. "Give me a call tommorrow morning and we can figure out what the three of us are going to do this weekend," she said, as she handed Jeremy the piece of paper and gave him a quick kiss on his cheek. He could see Evelyn looking out the window as he politely closed Lauren's car door and he headed back into the house.

It was truly a special day.

Today, though, we were shopping for food for just Lauren and I as

Evelyn was going to be having a sleepover at one of her friend's house. Evelyn decided we should have Italian so that's what I told Lauren the two of us were going to make that night as we were checking out.

The three of us had been together at least six or seven times over the past few weeks, even going to church together on Sundays, but this was going to be the first time that it was just the two of us.

Evelyn was excited as I was, and she gave me instructions on how to cook the veal parmesan and so forth. She wanted it to be perfect. She wanted to leave a little early to go to her friend's house, sleeping bag in hand, as she knew I had a lot to do and she wanted it to be a good nite for Lauren and me. I'll always remember hugging her and saying bye that night when I dropped her off at her friend's house for the night.

She had grown to be quite the little girl. A girl her mother would be proud of. Her mother's little angel.

Jeremy and Evelyn had visited her mother's grave a few times since their vacation and anymore Jeremy would visit the gravesite with Evelyn and it no longer hurt like it used to. They would both talk to Debbie and when they left, they would both be happy and put on the music as they drove out of the cemetary.

We were all surprised when Toby showed up at the airport that day to pick me up. I had planned on taking a cab with the girls and had no idea he would be there. He was always a little shy and silly but seeing him in the airport holding a sign caught me by surprise as well as the rest of the girls.

There he was, sign in hand and it said, "BARBARA, I LOVE YOU, WILL YOU MARRY ME?"

When he saw us coming out of the exit tunnel from the airplane he had gotten down on his knees and all of the other people in the gate area had nicely formed a semi circle around him leaving him in the middle. There would be no getting around him, if I had wanted to that day.

He obviously didn't care who was going to see him, even if I was to say no, he was doing it.

Karen was the first to see him as she was slightly in front of me. Some of the other passengers in front of us had also stopped to witness what was about to happen. They had no idea who the girl was, but they were going to wait there to find out. Karen just looked at me smiling as I entered the gate area.

This magical trip was far from over, I quickly thought to myself as I now understood what all the commotion was about.

The sign was so big that I noticed it right away. It was Toby and he was going to propose to me in about 5 seconds. I looked at Karen and then at the other girls as Karen grabbed my luggage bag from me that I had taken on the plane. Lori grabbed my purse and Samantha just couldn't help but crying after all we had gone through and what she was about to witness.

My three best friends were right behind me as I approached Toby, kneeling and vulnerable, he was.

Before I could say anything, he asked me to marry him.

With tears streaming down my face and nearly 200 people anxious to see what I was going to say, I told him that I loved him also and I told him - "Yes."

He gave me a hug and a kiss and all of the people in the gate area were clapping and high fiving each other. Some of them appeared happier than me, I had thought to myself that day.

Toby hugged my friends, as did I after I had said yes, and I thanked some of the others for their kind words for the two of us.

Behind everyone in the distance, I could see Maria, our stewardess, looking my way over the crowd of people in between the two of us. I waved at her and she at me with her graceful smile. There were to many people to fight through to talk to her and the next time I looked up she was gone.

She was gone, but she wasn't forgotten, as I grasped the angel necklace she had given me and said a quick prayer, while everyone was crowding Toby and taking selfies with us. It was exciting for everyone. My three best friends were all crying at this point and I had nothing left to do but cry in happiness with them.

After all the hoopla was over, it was time to grab our luggage and head home. Hand in hand, Toby and I walked to the luggage area together and I told him there was something he needed to know. He said nothing I would say, would change his mind on wanting to spend the rest of his life with me, so I told him right there.

"I'm pregnant with your baby, Toby," I said to him, "And I think it's going to be a little girl."

He hugged me and said if it was going to be a little girl, he would like to name her Maria, after someone who helped raise him. I was nearly shocked by that and hugged him and told him that if it was indeed a girl, she was going to be named, Maria. It was all so surreal to her.

To date, that was the best day of her life, Barbara knew. It was quite the scene that day in the airport, she thought to herself as she was driving to her doctor's office for a routine checkup.

That scene played out many times over and over again the week after returning from their "coming out" vacation. Telling her parents and family as well as his wasn't nearly as hard as she thought it would be. Her dad immediately told her he had been saving our old baby stuff for this day to come as he had always prayed he would have grandchildren.

She didn't tell him that she knew he had items stored away, as he was so ecstatic to show Toby and her his supposedly secret stash of these kind of items. Toby and him went through all of the items in a bonding kind of way as the two women just sat there and watched the two of them. Her mother holding her hand and rocking back and forth in a happy kind of way.

Her mind had tricked her into thinking the worst things about other people and their thoughts on all of this. It was not at all like she had imagined. She was bringing herself down for days because of what she thought others would say. As if that had any bearing on her life at all.

Toby and she had gone to meet Father Mayer at St. George Church, where her parents belonged, and he knew them well and remembered Barbara also. He was understanding and not condoning in any way the decisions both Toby and she had made in their lives. He was happy to see and talk to them about their needs as they wanted to get married quickly in a private little ceremony with just close family and friends.

They were going to be getting married at that church and had become members. The wedding was going to be in less than a month and Father didn't see any problems with any of the issues they brought up. She knew this was how he was going to be, but until they had talked, it was a little stressful on her. Stressing out about nothing again. She had never seen Toby happier as Father embraced him with his whole heart that hot sunny day.

As they left the church that day it was hard not to notice the young black men pushing the wheelchairs of a number of elderly folk around the sidewalk of the church. They were sweating she could tell, but they all seemed to be laughing together. There were a number of them being pushed around and also a number of them gathered under a shelter which seemed was designed for those in wheelchairs.

It sure seemed to her as they drove away that this was the kind of church they wanted to belong to.

Barbara had taken Sam to St. George's for confession a number of weeks ago and they both had confessed their sins that day and had asked and received forgiveness.

Sam hadn't felt that good in years. She had told Barbara on their ride to Karen's house that day, that her depression wasn't going to get the best of her anymore. She had talked with Father Mayer for quite sometime that day, she said, and he had pointed her in a good direction. She wasn't as bad as she thought she was and there was no sense in being depressed about bad thoughts. We all have them he had told her as he had finished his little talk to her and he had told her that she deserved to be at peace with herself over this.

She told Barbara that she was no longer taking pills for depression and had began a running program to help her body and her mind. It was working she told Barbara as she not only had dropped a few pounds of flesh but had also dropped a lot of clutter from her mind on those running days. She really enjoyed it, she told Barbara laughingly, even more than the walks they all took together every two weeks. The four girl friends spending an hour together, walking around Schenley Park. Listening to each other and helping each other with solid good advice.

Sam and her family were now regular members of St. George, she told Barbara, and her and Mark were going to renew their marriage vows together at Saint George at the next ceremony. Father had suggested that to her when they first talked in confession that day and she knew this is what she wanted to do. It gave her a sense of peace and Mark liked the idea also.

Barbara told her that it was wonderful and that she could sense the happy feeling radiated out of Sam just as they sat there and talked on their drive to Karen's house. It was moving day, for Karen, Tom and their children and the four best friends and their families were all going over to help.

They pulled up in front of Karen's house and Sam grabbed the cookies they had purchased for the moving day. There would be food and drinks for everyone today as it was a joyous day. By the grace of God they had sold their house quickly to a doctor whose family was moving to Pittsburgh from another city and he wanted to get things moving fast. That was good by Karen and Tom as they wanted and needed to be out of there. They had found a perfect little home for them in their old neighborhood. Close to the playground at St. George Church and close to all the people they knew growing up. It was almost uncanny Sam said to Barbara as they walked up to the house to look for Karen or her husband.

She knew her friends would be there to help her. They were always there to help her. She just didn't realize it until about a month ago, Karen quietly thought to herself, as she saw the two girls coming up the front stairs, cookies and such in hand. They all greeted each other warmly as she grabbed the cookies and placed them with the food others had brought to the moving party.

The men were already there carrying out furniture to the rental truck and Barbara was happy to see how well Toby was fitting in with the other men. They all seemed to genuinely like each other and she was happy about that.

They only had one car anymore and many of the other items had been sold at a garage sale Karen had done the weekend before. She told her friends that it had gone well and that for once in a long time, Tom, and her, were not stressed out financially anymore. Things needed to change and they did, she continued, as she told them that her oldest child was excited about their new home as there seemed to be a number of children living on their new street.

The three girls continued their conversation until a car pulled up that they did not recognize, and Lori and her new boyfriend got out of the car. They all laughed together when they saw him open up the car door for her to get out as her old boyfriend wasn't that way.

Lori had broken up with Adam, her old boyfriend, shortly after returning from their trip. He did not want to change, she had told her three best friends, so, she was going on without him. It was the best thing she had ever done for herself, they all knew. Lori had joined Alcoholics Annonymous and had now been totally sober for a month.

The girls had never met her new boyfriend yet as they had just started dating a few weeks ago. His name was Mike and they knew just a little about him from talking to Lori.

Lori saw the girls and headed right for them with Mike before he darted back to the car to grab some food he had brought for the moving party.

Lori hugged her friends as usual as Mike was carrying nearly twenty sub sandwiches he had bought himself for Lori's and soon to be his friends. Karen was the first to greet him as he needed help carrying them all and she hugged him also and introduced herself and her husband to him. Barbara and Sam did the same after he came back out of the house as he needed to set those subs down. Each of the girls greeting him with a warm hug and also kidded him about opening up the car door for Lori. He blushed and said that he didn't do it all the time for her, but he wanted to make a good first impression, he laughingly told them.

"Put me to work, Karen," he said after a brief conversation with the girls. Karen introduced him to a few more of the guys and he just went at it from there, leaving the four best friends together on the front porch, as his assignment was to undo the swingset as that was going to the new house.

Sam kiddingly told Lori that he was a keeper, not a creeper, as they all laughed together.

Lori told them she had met him at a coffee shop after her AA meeting a few weeks back and that it was as if it was meant to be. She told him that day, where she had just come from and how she ended up there and he just listened intentively. The next thing she knew, they were going to dinner the next night on him. He didn't drink alcohol as he was allergic to it and he was an engineer at a big company in Pittsburgh. He even went to church at the local church where Barbara belonged, she said.

She told her friends she had been praying more nowadays and that she went to church on Sundays and was praying to meet the right guy when she was standing in the coffee shop waiting her turn to order. He just appeared next to her and after she ordered he quickly told the cashier that her drink was on him. And now here I am, at your moving party, with a new boyfriend. A sober boyfriend she laughingly said.

They could tell Lori was in a better place than she was before. She lost a few pounds and was looking like that girl who used to run circles around them playing soccer.

It was the best moving party ever; Karen's older son told the girls as he knew them well from their time babysitting him. He grabbed a donut and headed to the swingset to help Mike take it down.

Karen told the girls that she was still waiting to hear back from a few of the places where she had sent her resume, she had only heard from one of them so far. It was the daycare company and they had told her that they would be hiring a number of individuals on a part time basis soon and that she was near the top of the list of possible candidates. They would let her know in the next few weeks and had thanked her kindly for sending an application. She told them that she would find something but wasn't in to big of a hurry as there was a lot to take care of in the new house. She didn't need insurance so that was a plus for her as far as the hiring process, she told them, as her husband had good insurance.

They all told her good things were coming her way. Good things were coming everyone's way, they all knew.

Father Feeney's little church was just as he had described it, John thought to himself, as he pulled into the parking lot that morning. It had been less than a week since they had met on the airplane, but John was eager to visit his new friend's church.

He had telephoned Father a few days after meeting him on that flight and they were going to spend some time together after his morning mass. John hadn't been to mass much lately, so he made sure to arrive early that day so as not to come in late. He was greeted nicely by a number of other individuals who were attending mass that day and it made him feel good.

As he was sitting there waiting for mass to begin, John could now understand what Father meant when he was talking abut the statues. The sun was shining bright that morning through the stained windows and the inside of the church was heavenly looking with the light adoring the statues. It gave John a sense of peace as he sat there looking at all of the pictures and statues located throughout the church. It was more beautiful than he imagined.

A bell rang, and Father entered the church as everyone stood up and sang an opening hymn that they all seemed to know. John did the best that he could, but he didn't really know the words, though he knew no one minded. There were mostly older people at the mass and John felt at home at this church from the very beginning.

Father's sermon was powerful. He talked about forgiveness and its effect on everyone involved. It made John think to himself about those in his life that he needed to forgive. There was one person he could think of, someone who he knew he needed to forgive. Someone who had felt the same type of pain he had felt.

He knew he needed to forgive the young girl who went through the red light and crashed into his son's car, killing him that day. John knew her name and her address from the accident report and he would have to figure out the best way to do this.

John thought to himself how extraordinary it was that he was empowered to forgive on his very first visit to the church. It was a wonderful mass. He knew he would be back often.

Mass ended with Father walking down the aisle and standing in the back of the church to say hello to all those who came to church that morning. As John approached Father a big smile appeared on both their faces as they were both happy to see each other again. Father hugged John and introduced him to some of the regular church goers who were all glad to meet him.

After everyone left, John and Father Feeney walked through the inside and outside of the church and Father, beaming proudly, told John as much as he could about the church and all of its statues. He was proud of them all, John could tell, and he should be, he thought to himself.

After their tour, John told Father how powerful his sermon was for those who wanted to listen. He told him how he needed to forgive the young girl who was involved in his son's accident and that if he hadn't gone to mass that morning, he would forever carry this unneeded weight on his shoulder of anger and hate toward this girl.

Father was pleased that his sermon reached someone's heart and soul and he was especially pleased that it was the soul of his new friend, John. They talked about it for sometime and when they got done with that, John knew how he was going to approach the young girl and make sure that she knew she was forgiven.

John bought an early lunch for Father and a few of his helpers that day. These people would volunteer their time and talents to keep the church in good condition and John could only think about how his own son, Kevin, had volunteered his time at St. George's in Pittsburgh. The lunch made him even more in awe of who his son really was.

Upon leaving that day he told Father that he would see him at church, not everyday, but often, he laughingly told him. He also told him he wanted to help the church out in anyway possible. John told Father to think about how he could help, and they would discuss it in the days ahead.

As he got into his car and drove away that morning, he knew where he was going next. He was going to the local gift shop to get a card and a gift for someone. Someone who was in the need of being forgiven. Someone who was probably in a dark place. A place he was familiar with, a place he had left behind.

She had never been the same since the day of the accident. The day that she caused the death of a young man.

She had been in the hospital for a few weeks herself back then and never really could find a way to say she was sorry or even to who she should say it to. It had changed her forever. A guilty feeling always wearing her down.

The accident had changed her whole family. They all knew that a young man was dead because of Alice.

Alice knew it changed not only her but her parents and her siblings. She prayed that it would be diffferent when she would wake up every morning, but it never was. She prayed every night for the man and his family as well as for her family but every morning that same depressed mood would follow her wherever she went.

A dark unseen cloud following her everywhere.

Alice McGregor retrieved the mail from her parent's house that day like she always did. It was the usual mail but today there was also a little box addressed to her. The return address was from Atlanta and the name on the return address had the same last name as the young man who was killed in the accident she caused. She was trembling slightly as she quickly remembered how his car looked that day after she rammed him at full speed.

Her parents were home that day, as she slowly walked back to the house with the mail, so she handed them the mail but kept the box to herself.

Her mother asked her who the box was from as her father entered the same room.

"I think it is from the young man's family who died in the accident," she said.

Bringing back vivid memories of that day, tears began streaming down her face as she would have to relive it again. She was weary of reliving that day, wishing it would have been different.

The three of them sat down at the table as her parent's wanted to be there for her when she opened it. Nobody knew if it was going to be a good thing or a bad thing, so they were preparing themselves to help their lovely daughter on what may be another awful day for her.

After wiping her tears away, she opened the box to find a short letter addressed to her and a necklace with an angel charm on it. The letter was from Kevin's father.

She read the letter out loud so that her parents could hear.

It read. "Dear Alice, my name is John, I am Kevin's father. I needed to write this letter to you to let you know that I forgive you with my whole heart and soul. It is not only my desire to do this but it is most definitely what Kevin wanted. You need to move on from this and continue to lead your life as I am sure it has changed you in a darker way. A darkness that needs to disappear. A darkness that I am familiar with. It is okay to be happy again, it is okay to fall in love, it is okay to dance a joyous dance and it is okay to live a long life. I'm sure that Kevin prays for you daily from his

THE PRIEST, THE STEWARDESS, AND THE CHURCH PICNIC

place in heaven and he won't rest easy until he knows you are at peace. I learned a lot about Kevin from Father Mayer at St. George Church in Pittsburgh and listen to these words I have written and please, let any dark thoughts leave your soul. Please also tell your parents the same thing, they need to be happy also as you are most likely a wonderful daughter. A daughter who made a mistake, in a blink of the eye, just like the rest of us make mistakes on this earth. Please also accept this little gift as a reminder of Kevin as he will be always watching over the both of us to ensure that we stay out of dark places. Love, John and Kevin."

Alice couldn't move or really talk much after reading the letter, so her father, with a tear forming in his eye, put the necklace around his daughter's neck.

That letter changed them all. It was going to be a bright day for Alice and her family from now on, the darkness was fading.

She would find a way to thank John, somehow, someday.

Phyllis's life had changed for the better once she finally let Peter get closer to Charlene and her. They were heading downtown together, the three of them, to watch a parade that day. There would be bands, animals and all kinds of other various assortments of floats in the parade and Peter had suggested that because he thought Charlene would like it.

He was always thinking of her, she knew, and Phyllis was now always thinking of him. They had grown much closer in the last few weeks and she felt comfortable leaving Charlene with him to have a little time to herself. It felt good to her to be able to take a brisk walk for a change or one of many other little things most people take for granted.

Peter would take them everywhere anymore. To church, to the grocery store, anyplace they wanted to go. Today, though, they were heading to watch the parade.

With lawnchairs in hand they found a nice spot where they could see everything, and Phyllis knew that Charlene was enjoying the sights as she was rocking back and forth, smiling at all those who passed her. One young lady placed some mardi gras beads around Charlene's neck and this made her especially happy.

She always brought some books with her wherever they woud go in case Charlene wasn't in the mood for what was going on and would rather just page through a book and today was no different. Phyllis always carried the book that the little girl gave to her on the plane about heaven. It was Charlene's favorite book now, as well as her's. She prayed for that girl everytime she would read the book to Charlene.

As the three of them sat there in their chairs watching the animals from the zoo go by, Phyllis reached out and held Peter's hand for the first time.

The smile that came to his face was only outdone by the smile on Charlene's.

From the moment they met Sonya, Tom and Jill knew their lives were going to be changed for the better. For years, they had done everything in their power to have a child of their own, but it just wasn't meant to be. The miscarriages took a toll on the Witchkoffs individually, and it also put a strain on their marriage. Though their lives went on as they always had, they felt like something was missing, as if they had lost something even though they never actually had it to begin with.

They had purchased a four-bedroom house for the sole purpose of starting a family, but the extra bedrooms were mostly unused. Jill used one as a home office, and they turned another into an exercise room, but those arrangements were only supposed to be temporary and the rooms still felt empty to them. By this point in their lives, they expected the house to constantly be filled with the sounds of a family: laughter, tears, and even anger at times.

The house even came with a swing set and slide in the backyard, which they still had not taken down. It had fallen into disrepair from lack of use, the red paint chipping away and one of the swings was broken. Even if they did have children, they knew they would have to replace it, but they never got rid of it – though Tom grew tired of working around it when mowing the lawn.

The neighborhood they lived in was perfect for starting a family; many of their neighbors were around the same age, and most of them had young children that loved to play together. Tom and Jill frequently got asked when they'd be having children of their own,
their neighbors blissfully unaware of how much these questions pained them.

But, thanks to that fateful plane ride where they met Sonya, things were finally about to change for Tom and Jill Witchkoff. As soon as they visited Sonya at the Catholic Charities Adoption Center, they plunged head-first into the adoption process, eager to finally start their family. For years, Jill wanted nothing more than to be able to give birth to a beautiful daughter or handsome son, but she was now equally excited to adopt.

The adoption process was lengthy, complicated, and slower than they would have preferred, but they trudged along nevertheless, knowing that all these precautions were to ensure each child was properly cared for. Sonya kept in frequent contact with them, walking them through the process and answering their many questions. Tom and Jill called her their little angel; it was like God had sent her to them, so they could figure out what their purpose was as parents.

At the moment, Tom and Jill were in the middle of what Sonya called a homestudy. They had already gone through all of the initial paperwork and passed the regular clearances. Just a few days before, they had their first meeting with their agency worker from the Catholic Charities Adoption Center, Judith. Judith's job was to assess their readiness for adoption and also to act as their main source of information – other than Sonya, of course.

The whole week leading up to their first meeting with Judith had Tom and Jill more nervous than they had been since their first date. Jill spent hours cleaning, rearranging couch pillows, and baking cookies to ensure everything was spotless. Tom mowed the lawn three times that week – which confused their neighbors.

Tom and Jill weren't perfect, but they wanted Judith to think they were in order to ensure they could adopt, and adopt as soon as was allowed. When the day of the first meeting of their homestudy arrived, the Witchkoffs woke up even earlier than normal and tried to go about their morning.

Though their house was usually quiet – Tom and Jill weren't very noisy – it was even more quiet this morning. The only sounds in the kitchen were the clinking of spoons on bowls and the drip of the coffee pot. They had cleaned the whole house and discussed every talking point, so there wasn't much to say. Plus, their nerves got the better of them.

Judith wasn't set to arrive until 9:30 that morning, but Tom and Jill were sitting in their favorite chairs in the living room by 8:30, unable to think of anything else to do to kill the time. They sipped their coffee and tried to start conversations, but neither could think of much to say.

Slowly, the hands of the clock ticked on and the appointment time arrived. Their hour-long wait felt like an eternity, and yet they were still waiting. They had a great view of their driveway and the street from their chairs, and their faces perked up every time a car passed. But none of the cars were their agency worker's and the clock ticked on.

Around 9:45, a sky-blue Prius skidded to a halt in Tom and Jill's driveway and a frazzled little woman clambered out and ran up their walkway. Though she composed herself during the time it took Tom and Jill to answer the front door, she was still panting slightly when she introduced herself.

"Hello! So sorry I'm late," Judith said, still out of breath. "Either your neighborhood is tricky to navigate or I need a new GPS."

"Not to worry," said Jill, gesturing to Judith to come inside. "Tom and I have just been enjoying our morning coffee and having a nice chat. We are in no hurry today."

Despite Judith's tardiness and the collective nervousness of Tom and Jill, the meeting went very well. Although they were not yet parents, Tom and Jill had been preparing themselves for parenthood for years and that much was clear to Judith. They both worked and could support a child financially, but had enough flexibility in their jobs to ensure they could properly raise a family. Jill was planning on taking a reduced role at work that would allow her to work from home if they were able to adopt a child.

Although they still had a long way to go in their homestudy – this was only the first of a series of meetings with Judith – this was a fantastic start for Tom and Jill. The meeting had taken them through lunchtime and, though they offered to make something for Judith, she politely declined. Their stomachs were rumbling as they said their goodbyes to Judith, their nerves having melted away as soon as the meeting started.

"You two take care," Judith said. "Now that I know how to get to your house, I promise I will not be late for our next homestudy meeting! It was lovely meeting you and I look forward to seeing you again soon."

"Likewise, Judith," said Tom, his hand holding open the screen door for her to pass through. "And you have our phone number, so feel free to call us if you do get lost next time."

They all chuckled softly as Judith waved goodbye and headed back to her car. Jill put her arms around her husband as they looked out over the neighborhood. The sun was high in the air, the only blemish on the otherwise empty sky, and their block was full of life. Across the street, kids ran through a sprinkler to cool off as their mother looked on from the shade of the front porch. Down the road, a couple pushed strollers as they speed walked behind.

Usually sights like these reminded Tom and Jill of their empty house and inability to have children, but today they smiled as they continued to wave to Judith's departing car. Sights like these were once again giving them hope

– hope that they would soon be able to put their own baby in a stroller for a walk or perhaps set up a sprinkler for their child to run through.

There was still quite a lot that had to transpire before they could adopt, but Tom and Jill knew Sonya, their little angel, would guide them along the way and ensure they would finally have a child of their own. They were only one month into the process, but they hoped that, in a year from now, they would finally know what it's like to be parents.

Over the course of their first month living in Atlanta, Melissa and her children became fast friends with Sharon. Not only was it nice to have someone who loved being around her children, but Melissa also loved having an Atlanta native to show them around the city.

This whole experience brought back so many memories for Sharon, who couldn't help but be reminded of her own children. Whether it was taking Julie and Philip to the park or the zoo, watching them run through the sprinkler to cool off from the hot sun, or constantly replaying their favorite movies and TV shows, Sharon was constantly transported back three decades to when she was a young mother.

The day after first visiting Melissa and the children at their new apartment in Atlanta, Sharon couldn't help herself and went up into her attic to look for toys, clothes, and other things her kids had valued back in the day. Most of the clothes were out of date – though Sharon hoped some could be considered "retro" – and many of the toys were worn out and faded, but she sorted through everything to see what Julie and Philip might like.

Sharon was worried that Julie and Philip wouldn't like any of the toys she picked out for them; after all, kids these days preferred video games and other electronics over the toys her children had grown up with. But, funnily enough, Julie and Philip were very interested in these old-fashioned toys and often played with them.

One month ago, Sharon's home had looked like the home of a single, middle-aged woman, but it now looked like the home of a young family. Sharon's chores used to mostly consist of dusting, but two young children made cleaning her house much more involved. There were stains on the carpet that weren't there before, and some scratches and nicks on the walls and doorframes – mostly the handiwork of Philip, who Sharon called her "little wild man." But Sharon didn't mind the extra work, and she certainly didn't mind that her house was a little worse for wear.

For the first time in years, Sharon was feeling happy again. When her children originally moved out, she was glad for the peace and quiet and all the extra time to herself, but things changed over the years. After her husband, Arthur, passed away, she grew lonely and fell into a routine. Her children were all grown up and had built careers and started families in other cities. Though she could have moved to be closer to her children and grandchildren, Atlanta was her home and she was much too attached to the house she had raised a family in.

Sharon had always felt like she was meant to stay in Atlanta, and now she found out why. As happy as she was to have Julie and Philip in her life, she was even happier to be able to assist Melissa. After Melissa got home from work, she would frequently share a cup of tea with Sharon as the children played. The conversations they had really helped them develop a bond, and Sharon learned so much about the struggles that Melissa had faced in recent years.

Not only dealing with the anger and shame of a cheating husband and the consequential divorce, but the added pressure of finding success at work as a single mom really wore Melissa down. As their first few weeks in Atlanta passed, Melissa started looking less stressed and finally was able to breathe a little.

With everything she had been through over the last year or two, Melissa wasn't sure about her move to Atlanta. She had been in a rut for so long, that she didn't think she'd be able to get out. Though she hoped the change of scenery would help, and she knew the different job could put her on the right path, she worried every moment of every day up until the move.

However, one month later, Melissa couldn't have been happier. Her fears started to subside on the plane when she met Sharon, and they evaporated the next day when Sharon came over with gifts for Julie and Philip. She didn't know whether it was fate that they sat next to each other on the plane, or some sort of divine intervention from God, but she was thankful every day that it happened.

Another worry of hers was taking her children away from their father, Ted. Melissa's heart still ached with pain every time she thought back to the way her marriage ended, but she never wanted Julie and Philip to be without a father. Moving to Atlanta made it nearly impossible for Ted to be in their lives, but she had full custody and he understood that it was his actions and his actions alone that drove his family so far away.

Julie and Philip talked to Ted on the phone a few times a week, and they often filled Melissa in on what Ted was up to. Though she hated hearing his name, she couldn't bear to tell them that; their happiness was more important than hers. In fact, over their first month in Atlanta, Melissa's children reported that their father was working hard on turning his life around.

They told her he was going to church several times a week, donating his time to those in need at the parish. Melissa was positive he was doing this out of guilt, but a small voice in the back of her mind was hoping he truly was becoming a better man. Forgiveness was part of her faith and, although the chances of Melissa forgiving Ted were slim to none, she hoped they could at least have a working relationship for the benefit of Julie and Philip.

Though Melissa and Sharon's relationship was symbiotic, Melissa knew that she was getting a lot more out of the deal. Though the hours at her job were flexible, she originally planned to spend a lot of money on a daycare or babysitter for Julie and Philip until they got old enough to stay home alone. She also didn't anticipate having the time to meet new people and potentially begin dating again. At this point, she wasn't actively looking; after all, the end of her marriage was still fresh in her mind, and she had sworn off men at the time.

However, she knew how things had a way of working out and she made sure to keep her eyes and ears open everywhere she went. After what happened at the airport with Sharon, Melissa decided to embrace everyone who came into her life. She knew that God put everyone in her life for a reason, and she didn't want to miss anything or anyone important.

It had only been one month since her big move to Atlanta, but Melissa was happier than she ever could have dreamed. She thought back to the time leading up to her move. Melissa wasn't sure if it was right to move her kids across the country to a city where she didn't know a single person. She questioned herself constantly at the time, but now she knew this was her destiny.

It was only Ray's second week on the job, but everyone there could tell things were going to be just fine.
As soon as he got back that day from his interview in Atlanta he called Patty and told her he was accepting her offer to manage the ABC Daycare

facility in Pittsburgh.

Patty was elated at his call as she knew he was the right man for the job.

Ray's wife, Beth, and son, Ron were also very happy for him. They knew he was longing for a change but none of them knew what it was going to be. They were happy that they would be staying in Pittsburgh and they were also happy at how Ray had been in a more peaceful mood when coming home from work.

After his call to Patty that day he quietly told Darlene, his friend and secretary of his decision to leave the company. It was the first time he ever saw her cry while she hugged him as she was so happy for him upon hearing what position he had taken. As she sent her child there herself, she couldn't be happier than to know a man like Ray would be running the show at the daycare.

Ray told Darlene that when the right opportunity came along at ABCD, as he now called it, he would let her know, as she quickly typed out his resignation letter for him.

She was pleased to hear this and made sure he had her phone number and such if and when he needed to get ahold of her.

He then walked into his manager's office with the letter of resignation and thanked him for all his help. He also asked him to thank the principals of the company and told him it was best if he just left now as he didn't want to be a disruption for two weeks in the office. "It's best I leave today," he told him as he shook his hand and headed out of his office. A few goodbyes to some of his colleagues and he was heading to the elevators.

No hoopla or drama, it was time to go, he knew, as he waited for the doors on the elevator to open. It would be the last time these doors would open for him and that was alright by him. The elevator took him down to the first floor as it had done a thousand times before, never caring who was coming or who was going and as he left the building that day, he felt a strange calmness about the rest of his life.

Looking back at the tall building one last time as he got into his cab, a big smile came over his face as he knew this driver.

It was Miguel!

"Music, today?" Miguel asked as I buckled up my seatbelt. "As loud as it will go," Ray told him as Miguel asked him for his destination.

"We're heading back home, this morning, Miguel." Ray said, "Take the long way."

"Yes sir," Miguel said smiling. "You're off early today, is that why you are so happy?"

"I just quit my job today and will be starting a new career in a few days, Miguel, and I am going to be managing a day care facility, ABC Daycare. I was looking for a change and I listened, and I finally found what I really like to do. I've never been happier!"

Miguel made the sign of the cross and looked back at Ray and said that now he was going to be like him. "You're going to really help people grow now," he said, his head bobbing back and forth to the oldies song on the radio.

"It's going to be a great day," he said, as he told Ray he was going to drive wherever the music takes us.

Ray couldn't be happier having Miguel pick him up on his last day as they both began singing in unison to a song they have heard many times before over their lives.

"It was St. George Church that you belonged to, isn't it, Miguel?"

"Yes sir," he stated. "I'm the head usher there and have been for many years so far. Father Mayer, the pastor there must like me or something," Miguel continued as the music rolled on.

"It's a diverse community of people who share the same goals in life. With over half of the congregation being minorities, it's a place where everybody can feel comfortable. We all try to lead our lives as God would want us to and we all try to help each other out the best that we can to live a fulfilling happy life. Sunday's are my best days as I know that is when my family and I attend mass there and have a chance to listen to the word of God together."

"Miguel, tell me about this Father Mayer. My old secretary, Darlene, belongs there and she and her husband, Allen, have always said wonderful things about that church."

"Darlene and Allen Oliver – wonderful people," Miguel began. "I know them well. Allen's a great coach. Sit back and let me tell you a little story about the kind of man Father Mayer is."

Ray got comfortable as Miguel turned the music down a shade and began to speak.

"One day a few years ago, Father Mayer caught a priest in a sexual act with a student when he was visiting another parish. Needless to say, Father was appalled and immediately notified his superiors in the diocese. After his initial phone conversation with them, a number of days passed, and he had not heard back. Angry at their indifference, Father Mayer headed to the diocese offices and wouldn't leave until he met with his superiors. It seems they wanted to let the situation take care of itself and not make a big deal about it. Father met with numerous people that day – not all of them priests. The diocese was reluctant to face the public backlash and opted to simply relocate the priest."

"That wasn't good enough for Father Mayer. He knew that ignoring the problem would only lead to more abuse, and the revelation made him wonder if the diocese was hiding any other predators."

"He went to the authorities as soon as he left that meeting and notified them of what had occurred, knowing that his superiors might try to punish him for disobeying their orders. Detectives wasted no time, visiting everyone at the diocese Father had mentioned."

"At that point, Father wasn't sure what else he could do, so he waited. A few days later, the diocese announced a few priest relocations, including Father Mayer. Father knew this was not about his performance. He had taken our parish from a group of a hundred to well over a thousand. It was their idea of payback. The priest Father Mayer reported was also being transferred."

"After Father's sermon the following Sunday where he announced his relocation, a few of us looked into the situation a little further and found out the reason why. There were a number of high-ranking government officials that belonged to the church, so it wasn't very hard to find out that Father had reported another priest to the authorities. We couldn't believe the church was trying to cover up such a heinous act."

"Word spread fast throughout the parish. The following Sunday all four masses were completely empty. There wasn't a single person and there wasn't a single penny in the collection."

"Anita, my wife, had asked Father if he would give some of us a blessing that Sunday since a different priest was already assigned to St. George. She told him that I would pick him up and take him to her group's prayer meeting that day at a local gymnasium."

"I dropped him off and Anita walked him the rest of the way. I had to go mail a little letter to Bishop Perchman and Archbishop Persicoski, telling them there would be nobody attending mass at St. George until Father Mayer was reinstated. Close to 2,000 names signed this little letter."

"When Anita took Father into the gymnasium, not a word was spoken. It was unbelievable; it was standing room only and everyone waited for Anita to walk Father to the microphone to give them all a blessing. Everyone had decided to give Father Mayer their support instead of going to mass. They knew who they wanted to lead their church and, in the letter, they let Father's superiors know that."

"It didn't take the archbishop long to rectify this situation, especially when he learned about what Father had witnessed."

"Father Mayer was back the following Sunday, and those so-called superiors were at the mercy of the police."

"They took a collection at that impromptu prayer service, and Father received over $50,000 dollars. Father has since used all of that to upgrade the handicapped facilities of the church."

"He told the archbishop he would stay, but only if it was all the way up until his retirement and only if he could choose his successor."

"The detectives are still uncovering all kinds of other abuses throughout the church, but all of it was spearheaded by Father Mayer taking a stand for

THE PRIEST, THE STEWARDESS, AND THE CHURCH PICNIC

what's right."

"So, what do you think, Ray?"

Ray paused for awhile and then told Miguel he would like to meet this Father Mayer and visit his church.

Miguel smiled, put on his left turn signal and told Ray "we're going to head there right now if that is good by you?"

"That's good by me," Ray said, "I'm in no hurry and today has been a wonderful day so far, so lets go there."

"I'm in no hurry now either and I believe your day will only get better now," Miguel stated as the two of them continued singing to all of the oldies songs that came on as they were driving there.

Ray looked at his briefcase briefly as Miguel drove past the ballpark. All of his work for the past years all neatly packed away in a small little case. His work to date could only be measured by dollars and cents. Stocks and bonds from pharmaceutical companies to healthcare companies and so on. It was all so meaningless when one would look at the big picture, he knew. He always knew.

He would tell his father about leaving the company after this church visit, Ray thought to himself as he peered out the window at the boys playing baseball with their fathers'. It brought a smile to his face knowing that he would never miss another of his own son's baseball games.

Miguel and Ray continued there little karaoke cab ride all the way to the church parking lot that day.

It was a big church with a tall steeple with a cross on the top. There was a large sign out front that said – FAITH HOPE AND LOVE AVAILABLE HERE and there were a few statues outside of the church. The glass stained windows of the church shone brightly as the sun was beating down on everything that day. There were various pictures of saints and angels on the windows and the colors covered the whole spectrum of possiblities.

The parking lot was in between the church and a large grassy area that included a play area for the young children with swingsets and such and a baseball field. There were also two large shelters and a number of other smaller covered areas, one even had a large firepit that appeared to be well used.

A winding sidewalk around the facility seemed to encompass the other smaller buildings on the campus as well as the school and it meandered through a large garden near the church. There were a number of handicapped people in the shelter area with some of them being wheeled around the sidewalk by individuals much younger than them.

The larger shelter had enough picnic tables to seat a few hundred people, Ray could tell, and the grass was being mowed by some older gentlemen. Everyone seemed to know this cab.

Miguel waved to a few of them as they waved at him as we headed into the church area to try to locate Father Mayer. It seemed to Ray that everyone there knew Miguel, even some of the individuals in wheelchairs.

How could you not like a regular guy like Miguel, Ray thought to himself as they were both acknowledged by a number of other parishioners who were insuring that both the inside and the outside of the church were in a tidy condition. It made Ray proud when Miguel introduced himself to some of these individuals as his good friend.

"They are all volunteers," Miguel stated, "We all spend just an hour a week to help keep the church going in any of a hundred different ways. It not only saves on money but helps keep everybody connected to each other."

As we headed through the church and into another area of the building, which had various other rooms, there he was on his knees, cleaning the tile along the perimeter of this large open greeting area. "There's Father Mayer," Miguel said, as they both headed in his direction.

"So good to see you, Miguel," Father said as Miguel helped him get to his feet. They hugged briefly before Miguel introduced Father to his friend Ray.

"Father this is my good friend Ray Rossi."

He was slightly taller than Ray and appeared to be in his late fifties. His hair slightly grayed and his hands hardened by years of working on his knees, Ray thought quickly as he extended his hand out to Father.

Before he could raise his hand all the way, Father gave Ray a quick small hug instead of the usual handshake.

"Pleased to meet you Ray," Father said as he wiped his hands clean of the soapy water he was using to clean the tile.

"My pleasure," Ray responded quickly as Miguel helped Father move some of the cleaning items to the next area to be cleaned.

"What brings the two of you to our humble building today," Father said, as he thanked Miguel for his help.

"My friend Ray here does not belong to our church, Father, but I believe he may be interested in joining and he wanted to come meet you. Isn't that right Ray?"

"Yes it is, Miguel," Ray responded as Father smiled broadly at Miguel and asked him to fetch him a glass of water while he could talk to Ray himself.

Miguel nodded and headed into one of the rooms as Father told Ray to follow him so they could talk about Ray's needs and so forth.

Ray told father his upbringing and how there weren't many church days in it and how he had come to the realization that he needed to have God more in his life. He told Father about how Miguel had touched his heart and how one of his other parishioners, Darlene Oliver, whom Father knew, had always talked highly of the St. George community. He jokingly told Father that he has bought many a raffle ticket from her for different affairs from this church. Father laughingly thanked him for that.

They continued their little walk and talk for some time before Miguel came back with two glasses of water, one for Father and one for Ray. That's the kind of guy Miguel was, Ray knew, as he took a sip of the cool water Miguel had brought for him without Ray even asking.

The three of them talked together for a little while longer and then it was time for Father to get back to work and Ray to head home to see his family. Father hugged them both and told Ray to stop by anytime. "Give it some thought," Father told him, "as joining this church or any other church is a commitment to not only God but also to your family and to the other members of the church."

"God's peace be with you," he said as he headed back to cleaning the tile.

"Since we are here, let us say a quick prayer for our families," Miguel said, as they both kneeled in one of the pews for a short time and then headed out of the church and toward the cab where a few of the parishioners had taken it upon themselves to give his cab a quick wash.

Miguel thanked them kindly.

Ray knew as the two of them were getting into the cab that this was where he needed to join.

He didn't need to join a golf country club or an exclusive members-only dining facility. He didn't need to join the local yacht club or anything like that. He needed to join this church and he was going to let his family know that today.

"It's gonna be a good day," Miguel said as he started his newly washed cab backup and turned up the music as usual. He waved to the young folk gathered to assist the wheelchair bound individuals as well as to the kids playing baseball as we left the church parking lot.

"It's gonna be a great day, for sure," Ray said as he started singing with Miguel after he told him his next destination would be to his own father's house in the ritzy area of the city. Miguel knew the area and they were on their way.

Ray would have no talk of Miguel giving him a free lift that day. "You keep that meter running," Ray told him as they headed to Rays' fathers house.

He knew he would be home then as his favorite business show would be starting shortly so there was no need to call him to see if he was there. He knew his father quite well and he knew that his father would be shocked when he told him that he had quit his stockbroker job for a position that paid much less. Ray thought to himself that his father would be a little angry so as they pulled up into the long driveway, he laughingly told Miguel to keep the car running in case they had to scurry out of there.

Miguel smiled and told him that everything would be alright as Ray closed the cab door behind him. He could hear the music blaring and Miguel singing as he approached the steps of the house.

He saw his mother in the garden, so he thought he would go see her first.

When she saw Ray, she immediately got up from her gardening duties and headed his way. His mother always wanted what was best for him but she was a quiet lady. Never a bad word out of her mouth about anybody or anything.

He hoped she would understand, Ray thought to himself as the two of them hugged.

So many hugs today he quickly thought to himself, his wife, Darlene at his old company, Miguel, Father Mayer and now his mother, whom he loved dearly.

"What brings you here so early son," she said to him as they sat in the bench by the garden.

"I quit my job today and I have taken a position as a manager of a day care facility here in Pittsburgh," he told her, looking into her eyes to get a sense of her true feelings. "I wanted to come over and tell the two of you before dad hears about it from one of his financial friends. It's what I wanted to do all my life, work with children and help them grow up to be good caring people."

His mother paused for a short second and then grabbed his hand in hers and told him that she was so proud of him for moving on from "that place." She always called it "that place." She knew more than anyone else what it was like to work there as her husband, my father, had spent many decades there. Many extra hours and lost time that should have been spent with her family. She knew more than anyone else the toll it took on all our lives.

"I've never been happier for you son," she said with a small tear in her eye. "You're going to do so well at your new endeavor and I can't tell you the joy I feel for you and your family."

Ray also told her that he was going to join a church, St. George Church. It was something he had wanted to do for a long time, he told her, and his friend, his good friend Miguel, the cab driver sitting in the driveway had helped him figure this all out.

She was equally happy about this as she always wanted to join a church but she was always to quiet and to obedient to her husband to insist that they go to mass.

After Ray had talked to his mother a little longer, he told her it was time to go tell his father. "Wish me luck," he told his mom smiling as they both got up from the bench. "It's time to tell dad of my decision."

His mother hugged him and told him everything would be just fine and that he was inside watching his show. She thought it best to stay outside so she headed over to the cab to meet Miguel.

Ray's palms were a little sweaty when he found his father in his favorite recliner. Business magazines strewn on the coffee table and his coffee mug half full.

"Hey son," his father said as they shook hands at seeeing each other. "Surprised to see you here so early, is everything all right?"

"Never been better dad, how are you doing?"

"Good," his father responded, "just watching the markets a little."

"I came to tell you that I quit my job today. I haven't been happy doing what I've been doing for quite sometime now and I have taken a job as a manager at a day care facility here in Pittsburgh. It's what I wanted and needed to do with my life and I hope that you understand that."

His father grabbed the remote and shut off the television. Ray could tell he was a little shocked by it all as his father knew that he was doing well there and knew many of his clients.

"Well, well," his father said, "you have grown to be the kind of man your mother and I always wanted you to be and I am happy that you had the courage to do this. It's something I had thought about many times over when you were younger, but I never quite had the courage to seek a different path. I couldn't be happier for you."

Ray's emotions quickly ran the whole gamut: surprised, happy, shocked, perplexed and mostly relieved.

His father got up and hugged his son. Ray couldn't remember the last time his father ever hugged him. It felt good. Ray thought quickly again about how many hugs he had gotten that day and it made him confident knowing his father was behind him on this.

"That place, as your mother always called it, had always taken care of me financially," his father said, "but I knew, more than anyone else knew, that it always demanded to much of my time. Time that I should have been spending with you and your mother. I didn't enjoy sitting in a meeting when I knew you had a baseball game back then, but it seemed like I had no options. I have to tell you that I am sorry for those days when I should have been home more instead of golfing with clients or flying somewhere for a business trip."

The conversation had taken a twist as it was his father doing all the talking. Asking for forgiveness was not his father's strong suit so Ray knew that the man, his father, was bearing it all, years of remorse coming out of his mind and soul. Things that needed to be said were going to be said right there and then.

"You have nothing to be sorry for, dad," as they both embraced, his father still apologizing for not being there as often as he should have been.

He never ever saw his father cry, but today was different.

They continued their conversation for a short while and then Ray said that he needed to go as his friend the cab driver was outside, and Ray could see by looking out the window that his mother and him were having a nice conversation as she was laughing a lot.

"I'm going to pick up Ron and head to the park for a little frisbee, if you want to come dad," Ray saying this even knowing that his dad never misses his morning stock market show.

"I think today will be the last time I watch any of these silly business shows," his dad said as he was wiping the tears from his eyes after pouring out his long hidden inner feelings to his son. "How about I pick you guys up in a half hour and we all go together, but only if I get to buy lunch to celebrate your new position!"

"Sounds like a plan dad! Bring our favorite frisbee with you."

His father walked him outside and they both headed to the cab where his mother was laughing profusely with Miguel.

"Miguel has told me some good things about you son," his mother said as Ray introduced his father to Miguel. "He also told me you are quite the singer," she said smiling at her son, knowing that his life was heading in a good direction.

"I see you have met my mother, Janice, and this is my father, Earl Rossi," Ray told Miguel as Earl and Miguel shook hands for the first time.

"Pleased to meet you, sir," Miguel said, "and you have a lovely wife, who has told me a few good stories about my friend Ray when he was younger," Janice and Miguel looking at each other with big smiles on their faces.

She could tell her husband had been crying so she held his hand as Miguel and Ray got back into the cab, both of them in the front seat.

"She had hugged Miguel and told him that they would see him again, at church, at St. George Church." She was also going to do what she always wanted to do and she didn't care what her husband would say.

The two of them drove away as Miguel, who had gotten out his oldies CD, put it into the player and put on their favorite song. It was Peaceful Easy Feeling and it was by far their favorite oldies song. So with the music blaring the two of them began singing together not caring about anything else around them. When the song ended Miguel laughingly told Ray, with a wink in his eye, that they were ready for the big stage.

"I look forward to that day," Ray said with a smile.

His mother, holding her husband's hand, told him there was something she wanted to do today.

They made it home after a few more songs and Ray thanked Miguel for everything and gave him a large tip for being the best friend he could ever find. Miguel didn't argue about things like that with Ray anymore, so he

THE PRIEST, THE STEWARDESS, AND THE CHURCH PICNIC

thanked him and told him he hopes to see him at church one day soon.

The friendly cab driver took off and Ray headed into his house to see his family. It had been quite the day so far and it was just getting started.

That week went fast for Ray as he was trying to do as much as he could with not only his family but also with his father and mother. It was a special week for all of them.

But it was Sunday night now and Ray was starting his new job Monday morning. They had joined the church that week and had gone to their first mass together as a family that Sunday. Father always liked to introduce the new parishioners at church so when it came time, Father Mayer introduced Ray and his family to the applause of everyone. His friend Miguel walked them down the aisle and gave them all a big hug and this made it even more special as everyone knew Miguel and his family as they were good people. It was a wonderful morning and it was the beginning of many wonderful Sunday mornings as Ray and his family met many people that day. They knew they did the right thing and they were excited about helping out at the church in anyway possible.

It's hard not to be nervous the day before you start a new job, so Ray just relaxed the rest of the day and went to bed early that night as he was meeting Patty for breakfast Monday morning and then they were both going to ABC Daycare for his first day of work there. Patty would be staying Monday night and leaving Tuesday afternoon as she wanted to introduce everyone to Ray and get him off on the right foot. But she didn't mind having to flyout Sunday night as she knew she had found the right man for the job.

They met that morning and it was like they had known each other for years. Ray wore a jacket and tie as he was so used to dressing up for work while Patty wore her favorite Pirate tshirt. It was the same shirt she wore when he met her on the plane ride that day. She was a casual kinda lady. She didn't need to be fancy, her words and actions were more powerful than any expensive attire she could ever wear. It made him feel good when she told him that he would be the only one with a tie and a jacket there so if he wanted to leave it in the car, that would work. His transition was complete. "No more suit and ties," he laughingly promised Patty as they drove to the facility.

His first day on the job was like any other first day. He met all the workers and was given a nice tour of the facility by three of the employees. Later in the day Patty, Ray and his direct reports had a nice meeting, and everyone was very welcoming to Ray.

At lunch he asked Patty what she was doing that night and asked her if she wanted to go to a Pirate game with him and his wife. Her eyes lit up at that and he told her they would pick her up at 6pm that night and have dinner at the ball game.

The day flew bye fast as there were so many people to meet and so much to do. He wasn't sure how big of an office he would have or if he would even have an office, so he just brought two pictures with him that day. One was of his family on vacation and the other was of him, his father and his mother playing frisbee in his father's yard. He would bring more of these pictures later, but it was enough for now. Pictures that would always bring back good memories. There would never be any award plaques or such in this office, Ray knew.

It was a good first day and Ray was especially happy when he got to meet and play with many of the children. Patty could see that he was the right choice, she already knew that, but today solidified it. A few of the employees she had gotten to know rather well from all her trips to Pittsburgh had given her the thumbs up on Ray and seeing him spend time with the children was something the previous manager never did. It was going to workout for everyone.

Ray was glad he listened to what Patty had to say to him that day on the plane ride to Atlanta. He would listen to others he trusted more now also, people like Miguel, as it is by listening that we can hear how someone is trying to help us out, he knew.

Ray and his wife Beth met Patty at the hotel that night, as planned, and the two girls talked all the way there about both of their families, baseball, Pittsburgh and all of the different things to do in the city. Ray just listened as Patty told them about her husband. He was a minor league pitcher when they first met, and she grew to love baseball. His career wasn't anything special, he played a few years but then decided to move on as he was just not quite good enough to make the majors. "He was a pitcher," she said, "but his fastball just wasn't that fast," she said laughingly. "He held no regrets towards the game and he still loves it dearly and we like to take our kids to as many games as we can."

"Well one day you'll have to bring your family to Pittsburgh and spend the weekend with us," Beth said, as Patty nodded her approval of that.

It was a good game, the Pirates won 4 to 3, so all the fans were happy. Ray didn't get to talk much at the game as Beth and Patty seemed to be like old college friends reuniting after not seeing each other for awhile. They dropped Patty off at the hotel and again there were more hugs. Ray was liking this hugging thing. Patty promised Beth that one day she would bring her family to Pittsbugh for the weekend. Ray told Patty that he would pick her up at the hotel in the morning and they all went their separate ways.

"It was a great first day on the job," he told his wife, "It was a blessed day indeed!"

Over the next few weeks, Ray had made some needed changes to the daycare's employee structure as well as adding more tools for the employees to teach the children. He added a music area where kids could learn the different instruments as well as improvements in the playground and reading areas. The book drive, Miguel and he started at St. George for the library brought in hundreds of good free books for the children and he was in the planning process of upgrading the facility to handle those children with special needs.

Children with special needs, that was going to be his passion.

He was going to do his best there and everyone knew it. The enrollment began to climb as he utilized some old friends of his to help with the marketing of the facility and he would need to hire some more help shortly.

Ray never had to stay late during these first few weeks and he knew he would never have to miss a family event again due to work. He imagined to himself that he was in heaven as it sure felt different going to work everyday now.

He prayed everyday now, after joining the church, he prayed for his family, his parents, his friends and all those who were not as lucky as he was in this thing called life.

CHAPTER 13: ONE YEAR LATER – THE CHURCH PICNIC

It was the fourth year in a row that Miguel had been chosen to head up the annual picnic at St. George, his beloved parish. Actually, there was never a choice to be made, he was the right man for the job and everybody knew that and did there best to help him. Especially his friend Ray.

The weather had been wonderful on Saturday and it looked to Miguel like Sunday's weather, the day of the picnic, was going to be equally as nice with maybe rain clouds coming late in the day. The picnic was set to go from noon until 7pm that night, with a outdoor mass at 12:30 and dinner served at 2pm, so he prayed the rain would hold off. Everybody prayed for the rain to be silent that day as this was the church's favorite day of the year next to the birth and death of Jesus Christ and a few other Holy Days.

Miguel had set up a small breakfast Sunday morning for those on the picnic set up committee in the school cafeteria. There was going to be much work to be done that morning and he knew the men and women would work better with a little food in them.

So he got there early, Miguel and his cab. Everyone knew that familiar cab.

His family would be coming later as they did not need to be there that early, so he grabbed the space close to the entrance, a good free advertisement spot for his cab. Maybe get a few new customers.

Ray got there at roughly the same time as they had talked earlier that week about meeting there to get things going. They would need to put up the fencing first as the church wanted to utilize one entrance for everyone to park in and have greeters at the entrance. The picnic was free and all were welcome. There was no need to be a parishioner so there was going to be a lot of people and they both wanted it to be a great day.

They would also need to put up the sign, set up tables and chairs, get the raffle items on display, setup the food and drink area, setup the small stage and speaker system where father would say mass at noon, bring out not only the children's games but the adult games such as bocce and so forth and many many other things to do before noon so they both got there at 5am to start the process.

Miguel knew he could count on Ray and Ray knew he could count on Miguel. They loved each other.

After greeting Ray, they both went inside and began the process of preparing breakfast for the volunteers who would be coming shortly. It was just drinks, coffee and juice, and bagels and doughnuts, but they wanted it setup before the volunteers arrived at 6am.

"It looks like another beautiful day," Ray said to Miguel as they finished setting up the breakfast and headed outside to begin the task list.

Miguel, smiling, told Ray "a pretty angel that he prays to told him the weather was going to be perfect, so have no worries," he laughingly told Ray.

"I believe you Miguel," Ray said, "I believe you," as the two of them began putting caution tape around the grounds where needed so as to direct everyone to enter through one spot.

Miguel's wife would be selling raffle tickets at the entrance as there were numerous nice gifts donated by the church's community to raffle off. It would be a good fundraiser for the church.

It was Ray's father and mother, Janice and Earl, who had joined the church nearly a year ago, who provided the money for the food and drinks.

Ray was surprised that day when he and his family were at church, waiting for the mass to begin, and there walking down the aisle with Miguel was his father and mother. He was pleasantly shocked when they entered the pew with them and his father and mother greeted his family before they knelt down to pray to God before the service started. Miguel just gave Ray a wink and headed to the back of the church as Ray and his wife just looked at each other in happy amazement.

Ray couldn't have been prouder when Father Mayer introduced his father and mother to the other parishioners as he always did to new members. They stood up together, holding hands, something it seems they hadn't done often through the years, as all of the other members welcomed them wholeheartedly.

His mother and father had visited the church, the day Ray told them about his new job, and they had become members. His father, unbelievable as it seemed at that time, had become the volunteer with the most hours and would be recognized for that at the picnic. His father had also joined the finance committee at the church and had recently been elected to head that part of the church's mission.

The finances of the church had never been better.

It was going to be a great day for his family.

As more and more volunteers started to arrive that morning it was up to Miguel to point them in the right direction and manage the logistics of setting up for the picnic so he left Ray to finish the caution taped "fence" and began to bark out orders to the others after they had their breakfast.

One of the first things he would need to do was to setup the food area as the parishioners would all be bringing a side dish or a dessert, and there wasn't a volunteer who hadn't carried one of those items with him or her as they arrived that morning. There would be hundreds of dishes and desserts, so he concentrated his efforts on setting up the tables for the food first, utilizing one of the new shelters outside.

It was a large picnic pavilion, donated anonymously by one of the church members and that's where the food was going to go in case of inclement weather.

After the "fencing" was completed, Ray and a few of the other volunteers concentrated on putting up the sign as others began setting up tables and chairs as the sun's rays started to peak brightly over the horizon.

The sign said:

FAITH, HOPE AND LOVE
AVAILABLE HERE

THE PRIEST, THE STEWARDESS, AND THE CHURCH PICNIC

They placed the sign next to the main entrance road for all to see. There's never any sense in hiding the truth, Ray knew anymore. It was all here, and he wanted it for himself and his family.

It was a great win for the Pirates yesterday as Ray and his family had attended the game with his manager, Patty, and her family. Ray's wife, Beth, and Patty had become good long-distance friends and had often talked via Skype many times since he had joined the ABC Daycare Company.

Ray had suggested to Patty that she should come up some weekend with her family to take in a game and maybe make it a short work visit also as he knew she liked to visit each facility at least once a year. Beth had thought it would be a great idea to do it the weekend of the picnic as they could go to the ballgame Saturday and come to the picnic on Sunday. Beth told Ray that it would give Patty the opportunity to talk to a number of parents whom send their kids to the daycare and this would give her a different perspective on the daycare. Patty thought it was a wonderful idea, as did her family, so there we were at the game Saturday night, cheering on our beloved Pirates. Beth, my son Ron and myself and Patty and her husband Dylan and their two children Mike and Donna. Ron was a little older than Patty's kids but they all got along good.

Ray knew from previous conversations that Dylan was a minor league pitcher for awhile, so the two of them talked about that and talked about Ray's old job as a stockbroker. It was a nice day for everybody. He had never taken his wife and son out with any of the other workers or managers at his old job and again Ray knew that this was meant to be. Plus, he loved what he was doing. It made him smile as he was finishing putting up the sign, because he knew Patty's family would have a nice time at the picnic also.

By 10am that morning, with over 100 volunteers from ages 5 to 90 helping out, most of the work had been completed. The children had concentrated on bringing the nearly two hundred raffle items out of the school as individuals had been dropping off items for the past few weeks. They also made sure the young children's games and prizes were setup as each child that day would be leaving with some type of toy or memento. The baseball field was ready to go and the grills were all ready to be lit when needed.

The stage that Father Mayer would use for mass and would be used to call out the winners of the raffles as well as for a little music was in process, so it was time for Miguel to take a break. He found a quiet spot under a shade tree and just sat there himself. Ray noticed this, but left Miguel to himself, as he seemed to be talking to himself or praying. No matter what the case was, he was not going to bother him, Miguel was about to pull off another great picnic and he wouldn't do anything to bother his friend as he appeared as if he wanted to be alone.

The food kept coming as parishioners would drive by and drop off a large bowl of potato salad or some type of home cooked apple pie. It was going to be a feast and Ray knew down deep that it was probably his father who had donated the money for the new pavilion as well as the hamburgers, hotdogs and drinks galore. He knew his father would have no part of this picnic running out of either.

The handicapped area was also buzzing with activity as those needing physical assistance would have no part of not helping out in some small way. It was joyous to see them work with the children in bringing out the raffle items together and helping place the silverware in individual napkins for all the people who would be coming today.

The wheelchair bus company that brought many of the handicapped to the picnic was owned by some members of the church. They had started the business up about six months ago and now had two buses and two vans to transport these individuals not only for St. George Church but for those in need. The name of the company was KEV'S TRANSPORT and it was named after a young man from the parish who was tragically killed in a car accident.

The young man had apparently started a volunteer group with some people he was mentoring to assist those who were in wheelchairs and after the accident a few of the young men kept it going and built on it from there.

It was still two hours before the picnic was to start but people were beginning to show up with their table cloths and lawn chairs in hand. It was going to be a family event. Someone might stop by, someone who didn't belong to the church or even know a sole there, but they were going to be treated like family. Just like the sign said, FAITH, HOPE AND LOVE--- AVAILABLE HERE. Plus today there was free food for all. Another sign next to this sign showed that and also said all were welcome. Father Mayer would have it no other way and neither would the members of this church. At least for one day, they would try to provide a place for others to come and enjoy the day, enjoy the food and enjoy what God has given to all of us.

As Ray saw the stage being put up he wondered if he would ever have the courage to play in front of a group of people. If it ever happened, it would be his first time, but he doubted he would ever do it.

When he saw Father Mayer, dressed in his usual black attire walking the pathway, Ray gave him a quick wave as he also saw his father and mother pull up in their vehicle. Father was heading towards Miguel, still parked under the tree, but he knew he had to go help his parent's out as he figured his mother probably overdid it on the baking. As he got closer to them, he could see he was right, so he gathered a few of the children and led them to his father's car.

After a few hugs, his mother began handing the children some of the baked goods as well as a few baskets of wrapped gifts meant for the children. She knew Ray was in charge of the children's activities and she couldn't help but over do it, she told him, as they walked towards the entrance of the picnic together.

"Hello Anita," Ray said as he gave the woman a big hug. "Mom, Dad, this is Anita, she is Miguel's wife and she will be the main greeter here at the entrance as well as pushing the raffle tickets," he said smiling, It's Earl and Janice.

"Hi Anita," they both said together as his father pulled out a couple twenties to buy some raffle tickets.

"It's so nice to meet the parent's who raised a man like Ray," Anita said, as she took the bills and handed his father a pile of raffle tickets.

"My two girls are out and about somewhere," Anita said, "I think Miguel put them in charge of placing trash containers around the whole picnic area, he thought that would keep them busy for awhile and accomplish something that needed done."

"I will make it a point to say hello to them sometime today," Ray's father said as they continued inside as others were coming directly behind them.

"Good Luck, with the raffle tickets Anita," Ray said as the three of them and the children helping out headed to the food area to drop off the food and prizes.

"Looks like Miguel and you have things under control," his father said, nodding his approval.

"I believe so dad, and thanks for all that you have done. I think that without your help this picnic and some other things wouldn't have been as good as they are."

"We'll talk about that later," his father told him as he saw Father Mayer waving to him to come over where he and Miguel were talking.

"It looks like Father wants to talk to you," his mother said to his father, "so you better head over there, Ray and I will get these items placed accordingly."

"See you in abit," he said as he walked over to them. Ray couldn't help but wonder what that was about, but he knew it could only be a good thing, so he just helped his mother and thanked the children for helping.

His mother knew a number of the ladies helping in the food area, so he told her to have fun and went about his next task. All the ladies looked like they were having the time of their lives.

Miguel had told Ray that the two of them would share responsibilities for the music. We're going to play oldies until enough of you music men show up to play live, Miguel had laughingly told Ray a few days ago, so Ray's next task was to set up the speaker system and get some oldies on there as everything else seemed to be going well.

One of the members of the church, Stan, owned a recording studio and had all kinds of speakers and musical items. He brought all the equipment they would need to have an enjoyable music day and Ray and him set it all up. Ray was happy about that as there were cables galore, but Stan knew what he was doing, and they finished in no time.

It was 11am and all of the tables and chairs were set and more and more people were now coming through the entrance. He could see Anita at the entrance constantly handing out raffle tickets to those who entered. It would be money collected for a good cause.

People were setting up tables with their own tablecloths and many people brought small tents and portable covered awnings to shade themselves from the sun. Seeing all this develop, Ray thought to himself, made him think that this is what it must have looked like at the music festival, Woodstock, many many years ago. He would have liked to have gone there as he imagined it was a fun day in many ways similar to their picnic.

In the distance, Ray could see another priest and a man heading towards Father Mayer, Miguel and his own father. The three of them were heading back from their little conversation and he could see them all hugging as they greeted each other. The two priests took a walk together towards the flower garden, Miguel headed to the entrance, his father headed towards the food area and the other man headed to the handicapped pavilion.

Ray turned the music on, after Stan gave him the thumbs up, and put in Miguels oldies CD. He wondered how many times the old CD had been played as the music began. He started the volume low and eyed up Miguel as he could see that Miguel was signaling him to turn it up. So he did, until Miguel gave him the "AOK," signaling that the volume was perfect. The speakers were located in a number of areas around the grounds and the music could be heard throughout all the church grounds.

Everyone seemed to be moving to the beat and Ray could even see Father Mayer dancing with a few of the children.

It seemed like the music starting was the signal that the picnic was on. It might have only been 11am, but it had started. There was a continuous flow of people coming through the entrance and Ray could see another of KEV'S TRANSPORT buses dropping off some more handicapped individuals. There was a whole group of younger people waiting to assist them and push them over to the pavilions or wherever, he could see, and the man who was with the other priest also headed over there.

John had flown into Pittsburgh for the picnic with Father Feeney on Saturday and Father Feeney knew that he would be delivering the sermon at the picnic. Both John and Father Feeney had stayed in touch with Father Mayer over the past year and they had been looking forward to this visit together for quite sometime. Father Feeney had told John that there would be a nice surprise gift for him at the picnic but that he would have to keep his eyes open to see it.

After receiving John's letter about a year ago, Father Mayer let him know that the two boys were continuing Kevin's project of helping out the handicapped and John knew in his heart that he was going to help out also. Father told John that the way he could help out would be to assist with continuing Kevin's project; John had money saved up, saved up for his son, so he was going to use that money to help continue what his son had started. This was how

KEV'S TRANSPORT started. John had sent Father Mayer a large check for the purchase of a handicapped bus and van and he asked Father to help the two young men get a company started. Father knew there were many other people in the church that would help get the business off the ground and before you knew it, the young men his son had taken the time to mentor as a big brother, had a profitable business going. Insurance would pay for most of their "clients" and the two young men, with the help of a team of advisors from the church, were now fully equipped and insured to grow the business.

As John headed to the bus, a small happy tear dropped from his eye onto his cheek. He knew Kevin would have loved to have been here that day, but that was life. He would be watching from above, he knew.

As he walked to the bus to say hello to one of the boys his son had befriended, as he had skyped with them nearly a dozen times in the last 7 or 8 months and they knew each other well, he noticed that one of the younger girls pushing one of the handicapped individuals in a wheelchair had a necklace that sparkled so brightly in the sun that it almost blinded him. As he got closer to the girl, as they were both heading towards each other, John knew that the necklace, giving a sparkle only heaven could have sent, was the one he had bought for Alice McGregor.

This must have been the gift that Father had told him to keep an eye out for.

As they neared each other he was sure of it so he said, "Excuse me, young lady, are you Alice McGregor?"

She politely said, "Yes I am." As the lady in the wheelchair nodded her approval smiling at the two of us as if she knew what was taking place.

His heart was beating faster as the sun shone down on the three of them. A meeting was about to happen between two people whose paths were destined to cross.

"I am Kevin McDonald's father," he stated, not sure of what would be taking place after he said that. Would it be to much for him, to much for the young girl, he was about to find out.

The young girl and the older lady in the wheelchair both looked at him for what seemed to be awhile before the old lady spoke up and said, "Very pleased to meet the father of one of the nicest young men

I have ever met," she said, breaking the ice, for all of them.

She was a smart old lady and she obviously knew more of the story than John would have guessed she knew.

"I am pleased to meet you," Alice said, in a strained voice with a look in her eyes of anxiety and fear as to what was going to happen next.

"Not as pleased as me," John said as he embraced Alice with a hug that seemed to last for hours. The two of them both finally having one last full-blown cry fest together. They didn't care how many people were witnessing this small event in life. Even the old lady had to fight back tears.

"I'm so so sorry," Alice said over and over again as she wiped the tears from her eyes with a tissue the old lady gave to her. "I don't know what to say to you," as she continued to fight back more tears.

"You don't need to say anything anymore, to me or anyone else, it was an accident, you didn't go out that day looking to cause trouble, it's just part of the crazy world we live in with fast cars and planes and such. Allow me to push this pretty lady's wheelchair and you walk with me," he told Alice. The old lady nodding her approval.

The old lady introduced herself quickly as Marilyn Brown and asked us to push her over to a picnic table she pointed at that he guessed must be where her family was gathering.

"It wasn't until I received your letter that I had a good night's sleep," Alice said, "and when you mentioned Father Mayer from St. George Church in the letter, I thought I would go talk to him. He was wonderful and has helped me cope with what I have done, and I decided that since Kevin wasn't here to continue his mission, I would help out as much as I could. Before you knew it, my parents and I both joined the church and I volunteer on projects that I think your son would have liked to be part of. Father Mayer seemed to know your son well, so he thought that Kevin would have liked this mission the best. Helping those in need. Those who need help just to get around. It's now my mission."

"I couldn't be happier," John said, "and I am glad to see you wearing the necklace."

"I never take it off," Alice said, as Marilyn Brown was just listening intently.

"We're both done crying about the past, agreed Alice?" John said, and Alice agreed with him after giving him another hug. "We both need to enjoy our lives and help others out when we can," he said as they got to the picnic table Marilyn Brown had pointed them to.

He recognized that face from somewhere, John knew, but he couldn't quite place it as the three of them arrived at Marilyn Brown's picnic table. It wasn't until she got close and the lady gave Marilyn a hug that he remembered.

It was the lady from the bank, the lady who gave him the gift, it was Angela, Angela Brown. It was her mother he had just brought over and now he remembered seeing the picture of the two of them on her desk.

"Hello John," Angela said, "I see you have met my mother," she laughingly smiled as she gave John a nice hug. "It is a wonderful surprise for all of us," as she also embraced Alice and asked her how she was doing.

"Today has been the best day of my life," Alice said, "I feel as if a weight has been lifted off my shoulder and I now feel truly forgiven." Angela and Alice hugged again and Alice said that she needed to get back to the bus as there were others needing assistance.

"I'll be here all day," Alice told John, "and it would truly be a wonderful thing if you would stop by and say hello to my parents sometime today. I think they would not only like that but I think it is something they also need."

"There isn't anybody strong enough here to keep me from that task today, Alice, so go do your thing and I will find you later," after a quick hug she was off. The letter had helped her find her way out of the darkness and today just made it even brighter.

She told Marilyn and Angela bye and that she would see them later. It was obvious to John that they had known each other for some time.

"How are you doing, John?"

"I was doing great this morning and now I'm even doing better," John said. "The picture on your desk that day was you and your mother, and it seems the two of you had gotten to know my son."

"I didn't want to trouble you that day, as I knew it would be a hard day, but I had gotten to meet your son a few times as he had gotten to know my mother quite well in his mission to help the handicapped. Kevin was my mother's favorite, pusher, as we call them, she loved your son and we were all in pain for some time after his death. It was Father's words at mass the Sunday after the accident that gave us some peace. Faith, Hope and Love available here. Your son was well loved in this church and you should be not only proud of him but also of yourself for raising such a fine young man. Marilyn had gotten to know Alice a few months after the accident and now Alice is my mother's favorite pusher. I believe you must have liked the little gift I gave you that day as I know, from talking to Alice, about the letter you wrote her and the gift you gave her. You're a wonderful man John and there are those of us here who know how you financially supported Kevin's boys, as we call them, in their transportation business."

Marilyn nodded her approval at Angela's words and the three of them talked for awhile as more and more people were lining up to sign in at the entrance of the picnic.

Miguels daughters were now helping their mother out at the entrance with the raffle tickets as noon was approaching but it seemed as the grounds were already filling up fast.

John knew that he wanted to talk to Alice's parents so he asked Angela and Marilyn if they knew who they were. They did, and after pointing them out to him, John told the two of them that he would see tham later as he needed to meet them. They both understood that and told him that it would be a wonderful gesture and they were sure the Lord's words would work wonders. He hugged them both and headed towards Alice's parents.

The four best girl friends and their families knew to get there early so that they could put a few picnic tables together, so they all got going early that morning. They were each going to make their favorite side dishes in the biggest bowls they could find. They were going to meet at Karen's and Tom's place, so they could all arrive together and it was also close enough to the church that they could all walk to the picnic.

Karen's and Tom's lives had changed for the better over the past year and it was evident to all their friends and families. The pressures of being financially strained were a thing of the past and actually they were now to the point where they could actually save money every month. Previously every month they were more in debt. You could feel and sense a calmness in Karen's face and this calmness relayed itself into her daily life with her husband, her kids and her new job.

It took a few months, but she eventually was hired by the daycare company she had sent her resume to about a year ago. She worked about 32 hours a week, four days a week and she could bring her two children with her for free there. She was what they called part time, but this was a nice company perk for anybody who worked there no matter full time or part time. Her two boys loved going there and she could see a nice development in them during the short time she had worked there. She spent most of her time there helping handicapped individuals and it gave her a sense of peace she never had before.

These children were happy with just the little things in life and it made her appreciate her little house and healthy family even more. It was perfect for her as Tom and her could pull this off with only one car.

Barbara was the first to show up at Karen's that morning and her little baby girl, Maria, was the cutest little baby. All her girlfriends would love to help dress her as both Karen and Sam had boys. As she was only like 4 months old, she was like a real life play doll for the two of them.

Toby and Barbara had gotten married at St. Georges many months ago and they had joined the church at that time, so they knew Father Mayer well, as well as many of the other parishioners. Their wedding was like most other weddings, in one word, it was beautiful. A small simple wedding and reception with her three best friends as her bridesmaids. Barbara wasn't going to pick a best girl, so Toby didn't either. He had three of his friends as his best men and it worked out perfect. Father told them that there was no strict rule to follow on any of this and that they needed to do it as they felt they should.

Her fondest memory of the day was dancing with her father, as not to many girls get opportunities to dance with their father besides at their wedding. When she first found out that she was pregnant, she didn't think it would end up this way, so she picked a long song to dance to with him.

Toby had volunteered to clean the outside of the church windows for the picnic and he had accomplished that with Tom's help on Saturday. Father Mayer always liked to clean the inside of the windows, so Toby didn't have to worry about that and the two of them concentrated on the outside with Tom holding the ladder while Toby washed the windows. There were many volunteers that Saturday getting the church ready for its visitors and Toby wanted the windows to be sparkling clean.

Barbara told the two men that day that she was looking forward to seeing the sunshine create a sparkle from their window cleaning duties.

Sam, Mark and their son, Kyle, who was about 7 years old now arrived next and you could now tell that Sam was pregnant. She was in about her 5th month and her little baby was protruding slightly from her belly. It was hard for Sam to figure out who was more happy when she told them she was pregnant, Mark or Kyle, but she knew who was the most happy.

She was.

Sam had also joined the church after Barbara had taken her with her to confession about a year ago. Father Mayer had suggested to her a little after that day that maybe renewing their marriage vows together at the yearly renewal ceremony would be a wonderful thing for her and Mark. Mark agreed, and they did it and it was like they fell in love again. Her girlfriends all kidded her that it wasn't fair that she had two honeymoons as the two of them went on a little vacation together while Kyle stayed with Sam's mother and father for a long weekend.

She had stopped taking pills for depression and instead made it a point to go to confession once a month even though she had no sin to repent for. It was much better than popping pills and she even got Mark to join her on many of those days.

Her glow was apparent to all of her customers at the beauty salon and she was now truly happy. She had no need to wear a mask. A disguise to keep everyone from knowing your unhappiness about actually nothing. She wouldn't ever need to pretend again as she had found peace. She found peace by talking to God daily and teaching her son Kyle as much as she could about life things. He was now going to school at St. George's and he enjoyed all that the school had to offer.

Mark was an usher there now and he volunteered whenever the head usher, Miguel, would need some assistance. Sam could tell that they truly liked each other, and Miguel was a good influence on not only Mark but also on her son as Miguel's daughter was the same age as Kyle and they had gotten to know each other well and would spend time together at Miguel's or Sam's house.

Miguel had asked Mark to be in charge of making sure there was enough ice for the picnic, so for days, Sam and her three best friends as well as other friends and family, were continually making ice for the picnic. He would store it at his friend's restaurant as they had a walk in cooler and before they headed to Karen's house that morning, Mark and his friend made multiple trips to drop off the ice.

When he dropped the ice off on his first trip to St. George's that morning, Miguel had nicknamed him the "ICEMAN". Mark liked the nickname and after he told everybody that Miguel had came up with that, all of them started calling him the iceman.

One thing Mark and Sam knew about the picnic was that there would be enough ice, Sam had laughingly told Karen and Barbara that morning.

Last to arrive that day was Lori and Mike, they were always a little late at all the events. But nobody cared about that, somebody had to arrive last, they always joked.

The three girls as well as their husbands were peering out the window as they saw his car pull up and Tom said, "I'll bet he's done opening the car door for her anymore."

Everybody nodded their approval on that and they all watched intently as he parked the car. Their husbands didn't open the car door for them anymore, they knew they could do it themselves. But this guy was a little different, so they anxiously awaited to see what would happen.

They were all wrong.

"He's walking around the car to open the door," Sam said, as Mike did just that.

"She's gonna get spoiled," Barbara said as they all laughed together at the site.

"Maybe it's a special day for them, like an anniversary on dating or something," Mark said, "and were going to have to let him know that he's making us look bad by doing that all the time." The other two guys nodding their heads to that comment.

After opening and closing the door for her, Mike grabbed the large bowl of what would be pasta salad and Lori grabbed some other items that they wanted to bring to the picnic. Mike loved to throw the frisbee so everyone knew that would be in one of the bags. Kyle ran out to help them as he and Mike had become frisbee friends.

Mike gave him the thumbs up and Kyle knew right then that the frisbee was in the bag.

Lori was now one year sober. Not a drop of alcohol. She looked like she did when she was playing soccer in high school, running circles around her best friends. They still talked about Barbara's only goal on a sweet pass from Lori.

They all had grown fond of Mike and they all hoped that he would be the one for Lori. It seemed like he would be and they all prayed for that. They had read in the newspaper about her old boyfriend, Adam, and the trouble his drinking got him into and they were so proud of their friend, Lori, for finding the courage that night to come clean and stay clean. It was the old Lori they knew growing up and that's how they wanted her.

They all chatted for awhile and then loaded all their food and supplies into a few of the toy wagons Karen owned and a few she borrowed from her neighbors. She never knew her neighbors well in their other house as the big houses were spaced far apart, but she had gotten to know quite a lot of people on her new street. There was never an issue asking them for anything and she always relished time spent with a few of the neighbors.

So they took off, eight adults, 4 children, one unborn child and four packed little red wagons. They were only a few blocks away from the church and they were going to enjoy the day together.

Ray hadn't eyed his wife's car yet as she was going to pick up Patty and her family so they could all come together. He had a picnic table all set for them and had let Anita know to signal him when she would see Beth.

So Ray kept to the task list that Miguel had made for him and continued crossing items off of it. There wasn't too much more to do, and he was happy about that. The small stage was built, the music was on playing oldies and now he was going to set up the karaoke machine and equipment for the open mic. He didn't like singing, he couldn't remember the words all the time, so he kept laminated copies of the words to look at whenever he played his guitar.

Ray had never played in front of a crowd before, and he wasn't going to change that today. Deep down, he really wanted to play in front of other people, but he was simply too scared.

Evelyn was eager to get to the picnic. She knew that her favorite priest, the priest who had given her the book on heaven at the hospital when her mother was ill, would be there, and they had a special connection. She had talked about the picnic for weeks now and Jeremy wasn't sure if it was because of the children's games, Father Mayer or because she was baking four pies to bring to the picnic.

Lauren and Jeremy had gotten engaged only a month ago and Evelyn couldn't have been happier when I told her. I hadn't seen her cry since her mother's passing, but she cried that day. She cried because she was so happy. She was going to have another mommy and she knew her mother, in heaven now, was good with it.

We were all good with it.

Lauren and Evelyn made the pies together Saturday afternoon and there was no doubt who was in charge of the baking process. Evelyn wasn't bossy, but she wanted to bake them for Father Mayer's picnic she told us. Lauren and her had fun that afternoon and Lauren just did what Evelyn asked her to do. She was getting used to the little girl wanting to help and it brought a smile to Lauren's face.

It brought a smile to my face also seeing the two of them having fun together in the kitchen.

Lauren had always belonged to St. George Church and Father couldn't have been happier than when he saw the three of us together at church the first time many months ago. Evelyn hadn't really been to church much before that and when she saw Father Mayer walk onto the altar that Sunday morning her eyes lit up. She knew the man, dressed in black, and they were friends from the hospital.

Lauren and I were both touched when the usher that same morning, with the nametag Miguel, asked the three of us to bring up the gifts to the altar at the appropriate time. It was as if he knew today was a special day, our first day at church together, the three of us.

Lauren knew when it was time to go to the back of the church to bring up the gifts, so Evelyn and I just followed her. As we proceeded down the aisle, in this packed church, one could see Father's eyes light up with joy at the sight of the three of us. He had known Lauren for a long time and always prayed she would find the right man and he had gotten to know my little angel, Evelyn, very well in a time when she needed a person like him. I needed him then also, but I was to angry to understand that.

So, when we got to the altar, he greeted us with the utmost love.

"Hello Evelyn," he said, giving her a pat on the head as he took the flowers from her that she was carrying. "Hello Father," she responded, as she quickly gave him a hug around his legs and waist. Everyone in the church smiling their approval at Jeremy's little girl.

Father's eyes were like a beacon of love to the three of us that day. It seemed everyone in the church could tell it was special. They had probably seen Lauren at church by herself many times over the years. Father talked to us for a short meaningful time and then we parted ways. As we walked back down the aisle to our seats, I'll never forget the smile on that usher's face, Jeremy remembers fondly. It was a heavenly smile and one he would never forget.

Father Feeney had gone back into his room to work on his sermon, as Father Mayer had asked him if he would give the talk, so Father Mayer took a moment to enjoy one of his favorite things, a cigar. He had smoked cigars for a long time now and one weekend a group of volunteers made a small covered pavilion towards the back of the church grounds and designated that area as the smoking pavilion. Father was there daily and enjoyed his time there talking to the other cigar smokers. It was well kept and there were never any cigarette or cigar butts on the grounds. So after smoking his cigar and chatting with a few of his fellow smokers, it was time to move on.

So he waved bye to his smoke buddies and headed into the vast array of people, food and fun to say hello to as many people as he could that morning.

It was almost overwhelming to him. They all knew his name and he knew theirs but there were so many that he didn't use first names to often as it would take him a few seconds to remember everyone's name. From newborn babies to 95-year-old parishioners. They were all coming. Playpens being setup, makeshift tents, blankets, it was a regular music fest, he thought, as he smiled to himself hearing the music coming from the soundstage.

After slowly making his way through the throngs of people, he eyed Anita, Miguel and Ray talking to his favorite little girl.

Evelyn was just checking in at the gate with her father and Lauren, so he headed that way.

She loved Father Mayer, so as soon as he came over she gave him her usual hug. Father wouldn't have been happy if she didn't.

"That little girl is special," Miguel told Ray and Anita. "She's a blessed girl."

"How are you today Evelyn?" Father asked Jeremy's little girl who was carrying one of her pies.

She just smiled and showed Father her pies.

"Lauren and I made these together for your picnic, Father, and we made sure to make your favorite apple pie!"

Evelyn had made apple pie for Father at least a dozen times since they joined the church and Father always was appreciative.

"I would be honored if you, your dad and Lauren would sit at my picnic table today," Father said to Evelyn.

She just looked at Lauren and her father with a smile you only see at Christmas time when a little child opens up the gift he or she wanted so badly and immediately blurted out, "Yes, we would like that, Father."

They were all happy and chatted briefly and then Father took them over to his table so that they could set their items down there and then take the pies to the food area.

Miguel, watching the little girl walk with Father, just repeated what he said earlier, "She's a blessed girl!"

Charlene seemed to know today was a special day as Peter was over early that day and her mom and him were packing up food and other items and loading them in the car.

Phyllis had made a huge bowl of macaroni salad and Peter had made a large bowl of macaroni and cheese as he knew there would be so many children there and all young children love macaroni and cheese.

They were heading to the picnic at St. George's.

Peter always belonged there and after KEV'S TRANSPORT company got off the ground, the two of them would sometimes utilize it for Charlene. They would schedule her for what the company called a sightseeing tour of the city. Charlene was always happy when they would arrive to pick her up and it would give Phyllis and Peter a little time to themselves and today they were picking her up to take her to the picnic.

The young black man, LeVon, knew Charlene well and she seemed to recognize him after Phyllis answered the knock at the door, and let the young man inside.

"Would you like something to drink, LeVon?" Phyllis asked him as he headed to the family room where Charlene was patiently waiting. She could see the transport bus in the driveway through the front window and she was rocking back and forth, because she was happy, and she knew she would be taking a trip.

"No thank you, Maam," he responded politely, "there will be plenty to eat and drink at the picnic."

"Do you need some help?" Peter asked as he was loading their food, chairs and other supplies into his car.

"No thank you, sir" he replied as he wheeled Charlene out of the house, up the ramp and into the bus after her mother and Peter hugged her. Charlene was totally at ease with LeVon and that made her mother and Peter feel wonderful.

"See you shortly," Phyllis told Charlene as the bus door closed and left for its next destination. "See you at the picnic, LeVon," Phyllis yelled through his window as they took off.

Phyllis loved going to St. Georges and had let Peter know that many times over and over again. She loved the church with its stained glass windows and pretty garden. But most of all she loved the long meandering walkway they had built as well as the large pavilion specially designed for the handicapped. She would drop Charlene off there and volunteers would push Charlene around the walkway over and over again. It was convenient and fun for Charlene and the volunteers seemed to have as much fun as Charlene.

Phyllis's life had changed dramatically over the past year as she grew to love and trust Peter and others who would help her with her daughter. The local daycare center had started up a special needs program and you could sign your child up for a two hour slot where they would have individual care for that time. It would give her just enough time to go to the grocery store without the worries of someone watching Charlene as she didn't want to always bother, Peter, even though she knew it was never a bother to him.

With not only Peter helping out but also KEV'S TRANSPORT and the ABC Daycare facility watching her once in awhile, her life had gotten less burdensome and she got to the point of trusting others with her daughter. She thanked God for all three of them, especially her friend, Peter.

So, after Peter packed up the car with their belongings they were off to the picnic for the day with the sun shining down on them brightly as they left the driveway and headed for St. George's.

It was only a little after 11am when Darlene and her husband

Allen arrived at the picnic. The parking lot was filling up fast but there was additional parking in the street and at the empty plaza across the street. Father had worked out a deal with the plaza owner so there was no problem in parking there. But Al, as everyone called him, found a spot in the lot and the four of them grabbed their supplies which included two large bowls of tossed salad and headed to the entranceway to check in and get some raffle tickets.

Darlene was now working for Ray again at the ABC Daycare and she couldn't be happier. She was making slightly less but since she did not have to pay for her one daughter's daycare it actually made it not only mentally better for her and her family but also financially better. Her son attended St. George School and he would stay there until her work ended and she would pick him up then.

Al was the coach for the boys basketball and baseball teams and was one of the most respected members of the church. He would tirelessly help the kids out whenever needed and that's probably why Ray and he got along so well. When Ray saw them heading toward the entrance he headed that way to help them carry some things and swayed them over to his picnic table area so that their families could spend the day together.

Darlene and Ray hugged as usual and today even Al was in a hugging mood. Everyone at the picnic were leaving their troubles, if they had any, behind them that day as today was going to be a fun enlightening day for those listening.

Just as he got Darlene and her family situated at the right picnic tables, Ray saw Beth and his son Ron and Patty's family walking towards the entranceway, so he let Darlene know and he headed back to the entrance where Anita was greeting everyone in her usual way and selling raffle tickets by the bundles.

Off in the distance he could see his father, Earl, and Miguel talking about something as they were walking around the grounds. It made him smile knowing that he and his father had become closer and that they had both become closer to God. It was of no concern to him what they were talking about because his wife and son were here and he was heading towards them.

Father Feeney appreciated the hospitality of Father Mayer and was so happy that John and he could both make the plane trip together. It made him think how they met on that plane ride just about a year ago. At that time, they were both in need of something and he knew deep in his heart that they had found it. It was always there, he just needed to listen. The bishop had told him that also back then, when he went to the conference, and first met Father Mayer. He was glad he listened.

But it was time to prepare the sermon. He had been thinking about it for some time now as Father Mayer in one of their many correspondences had asked him if he would do that, as he would be so busy preparing for the picnic. Father Feeney agreed wholeheartedly and told Father Mayer he would make the sermon worth remembering and today was the day. Mass at 12:30pm and food at 2pm. He had a little time to go over his sermon as he had started it many weeks ago, so he found a quiet spot and reviewed his notes.

With so many people coming it would certainly be a sermon that would be heard by well over two thousand people, and that would be the most people he ever gave a sermon to. He knew he had the opportunity to touch a lot of lives and that's what he prayed for that morning. He wanted a sermon that everyone could relate to and for those who chose to listen and act accordingly, it would change their lives forever.

John left Angela and her mother and headed towards Alice's parents as they were sitting by themselves in a table towards the back of the grounds. As he walked that way a slight breeze gave him a refreshed cooling feeling as the sun was shining bright and there were no clouds in sight. He knew it was by the grace of God that they would be meeting and he knew that his son, Kevin, had been a part of this. He told himself no more crying as he walked over to the table.

"Hello," John said to the couple at the table, "are you Alice's parents?"

"Yes we are," the man said, standing up to greet the man who he had never met before, "my name is Bob and this is my wife, Alice's mother, Mary."

"Very pleased to meet you," John said.

"My name is John, John McDonald, I am Kevin McDonald's father, and I am so blessed that we have found ourselves meeting today."

Both Bob and Mary were stunned. In front of them, without any notice or inkling that this was going to take place, was the father of the young man whose life was tragically taken in a car accident caused by their daughter.

Again it seemed like minutes or hours before someone would say something as the couple were in a small state of shock.

But it was only seconds before John continued.

"By the grace of God a few minutes ago, I had been somehow, someway given a sign that the young lady pushing the older lady in the wheelchair was Alice. And it was. We talked for quite sometime and she is a wonderful young girl. I believe Kevin made this all possible and I just wanted to come over and say hello and talk a little if that is okay with you."

"Yes sir, I would like that," Bob said, his body trembling a little at what might come next.

Bob and Mary couldn't have expected this, and they asked John to sit down at the table as it was just the three of them. Mary's eyes were tearing as well as Bob's as both her and Bob expressed their sympathy to John and told them how it had affected their family in such a dark way.

"Our best day since the accident was the day Alice brought your letter in from the mailbox," Mary said, "It was truly inspiring and actually Alice had us purchase a frame for it so that she could always remember Kevin and you. There's not a day that goes by, though, that one of us doesn't struggle with the issue. It's been so hard on Alice."

The small tears had turned into outright crying for Mary at this time and her husband comforted her accordingly.

"The words, I wrote in that letter, came from deep in my heart, Mary, and our meeting today only confirms what Kevin wants. He wants total forgivenesss and total love which will bring total happiness."

John wasn't going to cry anymore and he asked them one favor.

"All of us need to leave this behind us now and we don't need to forget Kevin. I can see that your daughter has a heart that can only be compared to an angel, and we need to forgive ourselves and we need to lead our lives with love in our hearts. I was in a dark place also for awhile until I listened to those who were trying to surround me with love, and it wasn't until I listened that I could hear Kevin's words."

Bob was truly amazed at this man. It made him realize how God's

THE PRIEST, THE STEWARDESS, AND THE CHURCH PICNIC

plan may not be the plan we had in our mind but that we need to follow it, no matter what.

As this was all happening, Father Mayer, who had seen the interaction coming, suddenly appeared at the picnic table and sat down with the three of them.

"Hello Father," they all said almost in unison.

"Hello my friends," he said.

"Why don't we say a prayer for Kevin and all that he has given us."

They all said a prayer together for Kevin. The four of them holding hands and only Mary still teary eyed at this point. The suns light shining off the stained glass windows giving a sparkle that shone on all four of them was another indication to John that his son was with them.

"Father, you wouldn't mind if I don't sit with you for dinner as planned," John said to the priest. "I was hoping that there was room at this table for one more today."

A smile came over all their faces as Father got up and told John laughingly that he would forgive him for not eating with him today and that it was truly a blessed day for everyone today, especially Alice, who Father had gotten to know over the past months.

Both Bob and Mary nodded their approval as Father went his way and the three of them continued their conversation. It had turned to laughter now. The three of them talking about their children and the things they did when they were small children.

In the distance, Alice could see the three of them talking and laughing together as she continued pushing her next passenger. It gave her a sense of peace that all was really forgiven, so she held her angel necklace in her hand for a brief moment and continued her duties as Kevin would have liked.

Beth and Patty had gone grocery shopping that morning for their trays to bring to the picnic. At the ballgame the night before they had decided that one of them would bring a cheese tray with all different kinds of cheese and olives and the other would bring a veggie tray. So the shopping went quick as they knew what to get.

They were all amazed at the amount of people at the picnic as it was only a few minutes to noon and that's when the picnic was supposed to start. They arrived at the entrance table just in front of a caravan of red wagons and the families that came with them and were greeted by Anita and her children. They could see Ray heading their way as Beth introduced Patty and her family to Anita.

"Pleased to meet a friend of Ray's and Beth's," Anita said as she signed them into the logbook. Father enjoyed reading through the list of names after the picnic, so Anita knew to get everybody signed in.

The children were happy when Patty handed them a large number of twenty dollar bills for raffle tickets as she told them she really wanted to bring a nice momento home from the picnic to remember this day.

"I will pray you win something wonderful," Anita said with a smile only topped by Miguel's after he arrived and saw all the raffle tickets she had purchased.

Ray introduced them all and then they all headed to the tables Ray had set up for them. Ron and Patty's children took off toward where a number of other children were playing as Beth and Patty took their trays to the overfilled food area. Beth introduced Patty to a number of her friends and she made sure to tell Patty which one's took their children to the ABC Daycare facility. The daycare had seen a 25 percent increase in children since Ray had taken over the facility and she was looking forward to meeting some of the parent's of the children that were in Ray's care.

The red wagon caravan was next to check in and Anita couldn't pass on the opportunity to hold Barbara's little daughter.

"What is your daughter's name," she said, as her oldest child took over filling out the guest book.

"Her name is Maria," Toby proudly said before Barbara could say anything, a smile coming to her face as she knew Toby loved her and her daughter with his whole heart.

"She is beautiful," Anita said as the four men all bought raffle tickets and made sure they were all signed in accordingly.

"I feel she is special," Anita told Toby as she handed her back to Barbara. "She is special indeed."

Toby thanked her and then focused his eyes on the church windows. He was not only proud of his daughter, but today, he was also proud of the 6 hours of work Tom and he did to make sure the stained windows were perfect for the picnic, and today they were perfect. Toby and Tom both nodded at each other as they all took their caravan to an area with empty picnic tables.

Their wives were equally proud of the nice job they did on the windows.

As they headed to find a few tables they could put together, they could all hear someone yell out, "Hey Iceman!"

They looked around and they all saw Miguel, with his thumbs up pointing at Mark. "Thanks for taking care of the ice," he yelled to him, his voice barely audible over the distance he was away from him and the oldies playing on the speakers.

Mark just gave him a nod and a thumbs up sign and Miguel went his way as they found a few empty tables close to each other that they could put together. Mark had definitely gone overboard on the ice. But he knew he had to as it was going to be a hot day. He had made four trips that morning, bringing ice in from his friends restaurant and there was plenty more if needed and it was only minutes away. It made them all feel good knowing they were part of this community and helped as much as they could to make the picnic a success.

They spread their tablecloths out on the tables and set up the playpen for Maria as the beat of the music continued. They all remembered the song that came on next. It was one of the songs they were listening to that day on vacation in the hotel room where they all found peace. The girls couldn't help but dance.

Sam's son Kyle grabbed the frisbee and after saying his name first to get his attention, he threw a perfect strike to Mike, Lori's boyfriend. "Let's go," Mike said and the two of them headed off to an open grassy area where they could throw the frisbee without fear of hitting someone.

Ray's father, Earl, saw the two of them throwing and knew he had to head that way. He told Janice to find Ray and tell him "it looks like we got some more frisbee players," as he headed in the direction they were going. Earl always loved frisbee and he was looking forward to throwing it again with his son and some new friends. He was in pretty good shape, so when he arrived where they were at, he took off running with his hand up signaling throw it here, and Mike knew what to do. He led him perfectly, just like Lori's soccer pass to Barbara many years ago, and Earl caught it perfectly, just as his son Ray had eyed them up. Ray was looking forward to meeting some more frisbee players and picked up the pace a little to get there quicker.

It was high noon and the picnic had officially started. Throngs of people were still lining up to come, some were members others were not. It didn't matter, they all brought a smile to Father's face as he tried to greet as many people as he could. He was thankful for his friend, Father Feeney, who was going to take care of the sermon today as there was little time for Father to prepare accordingly.

After shutting the music off, Miguel gave the inaugural welcome speech, as he had done in the past, per Father's wishes, and after a quick greeting and information to everyone about mass, food and activities, Miguel asked for silence as he led everyone in the Lord's prayer. It was a wonderful rendition of the Our Father and one could only hear the cry's of young babies in the background. It was especially heavenly for John, Alice and her parent's as they all held hands together during the prayer and each of them knew the other was thinking of Kevin.

"Thank you for coming, enjoy the picnic and Mass will begin at 12:30, and Father promised it would be a quick one today," Miguel said laughingly as he turned the music back on slightly higher than the original setting.

Tom was still getting used to the rental van, which sat up higher and was a lot larger than his car back home. But, looking at his daughter through his rear-view mirror, he thought perhaps he should get used to the idea of a van. If they went through with any more adoptions, a van would be practical.

Tom, Jill, and their newly adopted daughter, Kara, had made the trip from Atlanta to Pittsburgh to see Sonya graduate. Though they disliked traveling, they wanted to be there for Sonya on her special day. After all, she was the reason Kara was in their lives in the first place. If Sonya hadn't sat next to them on that plane last year, who knows what Tom and Jill would have done.

The adoption process went quite smoothly for Tom and Jill, thanks in great part to Sonya's advice and guidance. While it was common for some families to wait longer periods for an adoption to go through, Tom and Jill got lucky and only had to wait a little over 10 months. As daunting and exhilarating as the adoption process was, it was also heartbreaking. Jill wished she could adopt all of the children, but she knew that wasn't a realistic option. She just wanted them to all have loving and caring families.

THE PRIEST, THE STEWARDESS, AND THE CHURCH PICNIC

As soon as Jill looked into Kara's dark brown eyes, she knew it was meant to be. Both she and Tom felt an immediate connection to this one year old, who was originally born in Honduras. Over the course of the two months since they first brought Kara home, their bond continued to grow.

Tom was tempted to keep looking into his daughter's beautiful eyes through the rear-view window, but he kept his eyes on the road. Sonya was celebrating her graduation with a party the next day, so the Witchkoff family was heading back to their hotel.

Tom wasn't quite sure how they would spend their day in Pittsburgh. Sonya had wanted to spend it with them, but she had to entertain family that was in town. Jill and Tom didn't mind, however, and decided they would have to find something fun to do with Kara.

As they neared their hotel, a sign on the side of the road caught Tom's eye. It said "FAITH, HOPE, and LOVE AVAILABLE HERE." He remembered a sign like that at the adoption center in Atlanta and he found the words on the sign to be true. He had to pull in.

Up ahead, it appeared as though a local church was having a picnic of some sort; cars were in line to get into the parking lot, and a steady stream of people were making their way toward the field behind the church.

It was such a nice day, and the Witchkoffs didn't have anything planned. Tom and Jill looked at each other, both thinking that a picnic would be the perfect way to spend the afternoon. Ever since they met Sonya, they'd been trying to keep their eyes and ears open to new experiences and opportunities, and this seemed like something they'd regret not going to.

Tom threw on his turning signal and joined the line of cars looking for a place to park. Once parked, Jill got Kara out of her car seat and they joined the queue to enter the picnic. Though they knew nobody there, they trusted they would be accepted with open arms.

Aaron felt like an enormous weight had been lifted off of his shoulders. He practically floated down the hall after exiting the meeting with his doctor. It had been one month since his last chemotherapy session, and his doctor finally informed him of the results of the tests they performed. He was cancer free.

It was hard to believe. This had been the toughest year of his life, but also, in many ways, the most rewarding. He had made two lifelong friends in Joey and Lee, and he had started dating Kate, who was waiting to pick him up outside. Aaron once said it was like being on a boat out in the ocean: parts of the year were smooth sailing, and some of the best times of his life, while others were like being in the eye of a storm with 40-foot waves. Cancer and chemotherapy dragged him down when he felt their presence, but Kate and his new friends helped pull him back up again.

Aaron passed the elevator in the hospital that led to Joey's floor, and he thought of how their friendship had blossomed so much in such a short amount of time. Who would've thought sitting across the aisle from each other on a flight could lead to them going to church together every Sunday?

Aaron's faith was another foundation that had grown over the months of chemotherapy. He had gone to a dark place when he was first diagnosed, perhaps as far from God as he had ever been. He had lost his girlfriend, became alienated from his friends, and chemotherapy wasn't helping, either. Going to church slowly pulled him out of that darkness, and even when he slipped back into it, his faith was like a lighthouse guiding him to safety.

Deep in thought, Aaron almost walked right past his good friend Lee, who was talking to the receptionist in the waiting area. He had almost reached the door when he heard Lee's gruff voice. A middle-aged man, Lee's tan skin and thick, silver hair made him quite noticeable in a crowd; it was a wonder that Aaron almost didn't see him.

THE PRIEST, THE STEWARDESS, AND THE CHURCH PICNIC

"Hey, Lee! How are you doing this fine day?" Aaron asked, smiling. He was excited to share his good news.

"Oh, hey, Aaron," Lee said, turning around to face him. Though a smile was on his face, it didn't look entirely authentic. Aaron might normally catch that something was up, but his excitement kept him from noticing.

They started walking together, making a turn down a hall; sun streamed into the building through enormous windows that stretched from floor to ceiling.

"So, I have some great news," Aaron began.

"Oh? Let's hear it," Lee said, flashing another smile.

"I just got the results of my tests back – I'm cancer-free!" Aaron exclaimed, throwing his arms out for emphasis.

Phyllis and Peter arrived at the picnic just as the transport bus began unloading their passengers. There were many volunteers that day to help in the unloading and "pushing" process as Alice eyed Charlene being wheeled down the ramp by LeVon. She could see a big smile on her face and LeVon singing to her as he carefully wheeled her down and in the direction of Alice. He knew Charlene liked Alice and so did he.

"Bye, Charlene," LeVon said as he greeted Alice.

"Hey Alice, you doing good girl?"

"You bet." She told him as she gave Charlene a quick hug, Charlene rocking back and forth to the beat of the music, smiling like she always did. Alice knew that Charlene was happy, she could sense it, and now she could sense her own happiness.

"Hey, LeVon, would you like to sit with my parents and me for dinner today?" Alice asked. She hoped her parents wouldn't mind, but she enjoyed hanging out with him.

"Sure! I was wondering which table I'd be sitting at later. See you at 2:00," LeVon responded.

Peter was ready to push Charlene but Alice insisted that she would like to push her around the walkway for a little bit. Phyllis totally agreed and pointed Alice to an area that had some empty picnic tables by the handicapped pavilion and told her that her and Peter would be there.

"See you in awhile." She said, as Charlene just looked around at all the people in happy amazement. So many people gave Charlene little gestures of love that it was going to take her awhile. But that was okay.

There was no hurry today. There's never a hurry for love if you have faith.

So Phyllis and Peter grabbed a spot to sit and eat later with friends that they had met at the church.

As Alice pushed Charlene around the walkway, the light, glimmering off the stained glass windows of the church, shone bright on Charlene. Charlene could remember things, and she remembers seeing that light when she was going on an airplane ride about a year ago.

Tom, Jill and Kara arrived at the gate at about 12:15 that afternoon and they were greeted just as Tom thought they would be greeted. They felt guilty not bringing any food to the picnic so instead he bought $50 worth of raffle tickets and then handed them to the children behind him.

"Here you go," he said, to the children, I hope you win something fun, as Jill and Anita nodded their approval.

"Grab a table anywhere and we are having a mass at 12:30 and will be eating at 2pm," Anita told them. "Your baby is so lovely, and I can see that she is adopted. God loves those the most, who sacrifice their time, talent and treasure to help a child, that isn't even their own, in need," Anita continued, "you both are truly blessed."

Tom remembers those exact words from the stewardess on the plane ride when he first met Sonya. He was perplexed that the lady at the registration table would say the exact same words that the stewardess said to them at that time but he smiled, thanked her and gave the children behind them a thumbs up. He laughingly thought to himself that it was probably the first time they ever saw a family like his. A black man, with a white woman and a Hispanic child. Who would have thought it possible, if not for God, he thought to himself.

They felt at home as they headed to a picnic area where there were a number of infant babies laying in blankets. He was glad they had always carried one with them and laid it out for their daughter.

Melissa and Sharon had their hands full on this gorgeous day – Sharon with her grandchildren and Melissa with Julie and Philip – but they were excited to finally arrive at the St. George picnic. The children clambered out of the van and ran toward those waiting in line, while the two women lagged behind.

It worked out perfectly for them. Sharon hadn't been back to Pittsburgh to visit her grandchildren in a year, and Julie and Philip hadn't seen their father in just as long. A joint trip back north from Atlanta made sense for them.

Though neither Melissa nor Sharon belonged to the church, they were invited by Ted, Melissa's ex-husband. Based on what Melissa had been telling Sharon, he had become quite involved with the church in an effort to make up for his infidelity. They didn't know anyone else at the picnic, but Ted said they would be welcomed with open arms.

This was true almost immediately. While they were waiting in line, the man in front of them – Sharon thought she heard his name was Tom – turned around and gave the children a bunch of raffle tickets.

The kids were ecstatic and ran over to the tables containing all the prizes they could win. Sharon and Melissa turned to the kind man and his wife, who was carrying a beautiful baby that couldn't have been more than a year old.

"Thank you so much!" They said in unison. "We've been here less than a minute and you already made their day," Sharon said.

Lee's smile said it all. Though Lee was the one person Aaron had befriended during chemotherapy, everyone at that hospital knew what kind of weight had been lifted off of his chest when he got the good news. Receiving the initial diagnosis, staring mortality in the face, going through chemotherapy – all of those things gave Lee, Aaron, and the others a different perspective on the deadly disease than most people had.

Lee understood the struggle Aaron went through over the past year, especially with the prognosis of a 50 percent chance of beating the cancer. Nobody's life should be determined by a coin flip, but that's essentially what Aaron's past year had been. Aaron frequently credited Joey, Lee, and Kate with tipping the odds in his favor.

"That's fantastic!" Lee said. "Somebody deserves to get some good news around here!"

"Lee, thank you so much for being there for me during my time of need," Aaron said, the expression on his face changed from joyous to serious. "You couldn't possibly understand the impact you've had on me. If it wasn't for you being there by my side week after week and month after month, I honestly don't know what sort of state I'd be in now."

For once, Lee looked speechless. They'd conversed over dozens of coffees, walks around the neighborhood, and through a handful of chemotherapy sessions, but Aaron had never seen Lee keep his mouth closed for more than a few seconds.

Lee's voice cracked as he struggled to come up with a response, but Aaron didn't need him to say anything; he knew what Lee wanted to say. Instead, Aaron took a step forward and embraced his good friend. Their hug conveyed everything that words could not. When they finally broke apart, they just nodded at each other, unsure of where to take the conversation next.

"I'm just glad one of us is getting through this unscathed," Lee said. He had a look on his face that Aaron couldn't quite decipher.

Aaron wanted to ask him what he meant by that, but Lee pressed on before Aaron could get a word in.

"Don't you forget what we've talked about," Lee continued. "I know I blabber a lot, but there was a lot of good life advice in there too."

"I won't, of course I won't," Aaron said, his brow furrowed. What was Lee getting at?

"Take care, Aaron," Lee said. "Don't let this new lease on life slip through your fingers. I'll be watching."

With that, Lee shook Aaron's hand and headed for the exit. If Aaron wasn't so confused, he would have run after Lee to ask him what he was talking about. After a minute or so, Aaron realized the receptionist was peering over at him.

"I wonder what that was all about," Aaron said to her, not entirely sure if she had heard their conversation.

"Well, you see," she said, a little hesitantly, "Lee got some test results today, too."

Realizing what that meant, Aaron sprinted to the exit, the automatic doors not opening fast enough for him to reach full speed. He squeezed himself through the final set of opening doors and out into the bright Sunday afternoon light. The air was humid, more so than it had been all summer, but a slight breeze tickled his face as he looked around for Lee.

Ray and his father threw the frisbee together with their new friends, but it was nearing mass time and they all agreed to meet again after dinner to maybe get a game of ultimate frisbee going. Earl was somewhat sweaty, but he didn't mind, he needed the workout and enjoyed meeting some of the younger members of the church.

Kyle and Mike could hardly see their families through the throngs of people, but they eventually found their way back to their picnic area and found a shady spot together to cool off a bit before mass was to start. Lori enjoyed the fact that her boyfriend, Mike, and Sam's son Kyle liked each other. It made the girls relationship stronger.

Alice made sure to get Charlene back to Phyllis before mass started. Charlene was all smiles as usual and Peter and Phyllis thanked her again. After a short conversation she headed to the table that her parents were at as she weaved her way thru the crowd. It seemed to her that it was like one of those free outdoor musical festivals where everyone was in a good mood and lawn chairs and such were scattered everywhere. She was pleasantly surprised, a happy surprise, when she found Kevin McDonald's father sitting at their table. John had seen her with Charlene and he could imagine in his mind that his son would have been doing the same thing. His boy was quite the man, he thought to himself as they all greeted Alice upon her arrival.

Her parents could sense a peaceful easy feeling surrounding their daughter. They hadn't sensed that in awhile in her so Mary quietly patted John on the back and thanked him again for being with them.

Miguel knew to shutoff the music at 12:20 so he waited until one of his favorite oldies songs ended and then he turned off the music accordingly.

Father Mayer and some church deacons were already setting up a makeshift altar as
Father Feeney wrapped us his thoughts and his notes and headed back out to the picnic area. Mass was set to begin in 10 minutes and

THE PRIEST, THE STEWARDESS, AND THE CHURCH PICNIC

he was ready.

The picnic grounds started to grow silent as 12:30 approached and everybody returned to their respective picnic tables and lawn chairs to await the start of mass.

As people would be coming in steadily during mass, Anita made sure to let them know what was going on as she knew that there would be people coming who maybe had never been to a mass before. The picnic was for everyone. Churchgoers or not. It didn't matter and she was far enough away from the stage, turned church altar, that her words could not be heard from the altar.

Mass started right at 12:30, just like Miguel had said.

There would be no singing as Father wanted the mass to be as short as possible as he knew there were many infants and children as well as all of the other amenities going on at the picnic. The music with members joining in, karaoke, the raffle of all the items, kids' games, food, baseball, frisbee and all kinds of other things. He knew there was nothing wrong with a shorter mass, as they began their opening prayer.

Father Mayer and Father Feeney were saying the mass together and the two of them seemed to be in perfect harmony as a few of the young boys served as altar boys for the two priests who were now good friends.

The opening prayers were over quickly and everyone but Ray's father, Earl, sat down to listen to the first of the three readings from the Bible.

Ray hadn't known his father was going to give one of the readings, but as Earl walked up to the makeshift altar, Ray was never more proud of his father.

Father Mayer introduced Earl and also told the audience of well over two thousand people that Earl Rossi had volunteered the most hours of time the past year towards missions of the church. Ray could see the happiness in his mother's eyes and now Patty also understood how Ray had grown to be the man he was.

His father was a good man.

Earl humbly thanked Father and then began his reading.

Everyone was listening intently as he spoke about the adulteress who Jesus forgave.

In those days, anyone committing adultery were stoned to death according to the laws at that time, but Jesus called for the one without sin to cast the first stone. It gave the crowd that day, and today, something to think about before stoning her and they quickly dispersed as none of them were without sin.

Melissa as well as everyone else listened intently about this story of forgiveness. Deep in her heart she knew she still had some forgiveness to share with her ex-husband and she wasn't going to leave today without totally forgiving him.

Earl ended his reading with the words "your sins are forgiven, go now and sin no more."

There wasn't a person at the picnic who hadn't sinned and they all knew it, so it was good for them to understand God's grace and the power of forgiveness. They also knew that Jesus directed the woman to sin no more and lead a good life and that we shouldn't judge anyone over what we thought were their misdeeds.

It was something many of the individuals at the picnic would struggle with as we all are tempted and due to our human nature, we sin. But they all knew their God was a God of love.

Earl proceeded to walk back to his table where his wife, his son and his family and Patty and her family sat. They all quietly nodded their approval as Earl sat next to his loving wife. Ray could see that the love his mother and father felt for each other had grown over the past year and it could only be described as a good thing, he thought to himself, as he saw his mother give him a small sign of affection.

After a few prayers it was time for the second reading.

Dan had been a little nervous during the first reading as he was rereading his reading that he was going to give. Father had asked him the previous Sunday if he would give the second reading and he agreed. He really didn't like to be in the spotlight, so it was actually a nervous week for him. Joey knew that he was going to be doing this so when the time came, he gave his father a nudge to let him know it was his turn to give the reading and he needed to get up there.

Wearing his favorite Pirate shirt, the one Joey had bought for him for Christmas the year before, he weaved his way through the crowd, up the stairs and onto the stage.

Jeremy, who was sitting close to the stage, thought that he recognized this man but he couldn't quite remember where he had met him before.

Dan had cleared his throat a number of times as he walked up but he did it one more time before starting his reading. With his family watching, Dan started his reading.

Dan's reading was about the good Samaritan who showed mercy and compassion to a man who did not like anybody from Samaritan origins. They were actually almost like enemies. The man was robbed and beaten by thieves and many walked past him that day and did not provide any aide to the man. Even priests from various religions walked past the man and did nothing to help him. They just crossed over to the other side of the street and left him to deal with his own wounds as the man was not of their faith.

Dan continued the reading after looking up briefly and seeing all eyes were on him. He wasn't familiar with doing this but he had a strange sense about him that everyone there was listening intently, so he took a deep breath and continued.

"The Samaritan man, although he knew this man despised him,

stopped to heal his wounds and brought him food and water and then took him to an inn and paid for his stay there for his recovery," Dan said in a clear strong voice.

The Samaritan showing mercy and compassion to someone he didn't even know.

He ended the reading with Jesus' words "Go and do likewise."

"Thanks be to God," those in the audience said as Dan grabbed his reading and headed back to his table. He felt different now, Dan thought to himself, as he walked back to his seat next to Joey. He wasn't sure how or why but, he felt different after giving that reading. He was glad it was over, giving the reading, but he was glad he was chosen.

All those around him nodded their heads at him as he sat down, his son sharing a proud smile with his father and mother.

Father Mayer stood up as it was time for the Gospel and he would be giving that reading with Father Feeney's sermon to come right after the gospel. Everyone in turn stood up with Father as he headed to the microphone to give the reading.

"A reading from the Holy Gospel according to Matthew," Father Mayer said as he then started his reading.

"When Jesus saw the crowds, he went up the mountain, and after he sat down, his disciples came to him. He began to teach them, saying: Blessed are the poor in spirit, for theirs is the Kingdom of Heaven. Blessed are they who mourn, for they will be comforted. Blessed are the meek, for they will inherit the land. Blessed are they who hunger and thirst for righteousness, for they will be satisfied. Blessed are the merciful, for they will be shown mercy. Blessed are the clean of heart, for they will see God. Blessed are the peacemakers, for they will be called children of God. Blessed are they who are persecuted for the sake of righteousness, for theirs is the Kingdom of Heaven. Blessed are you when they insult you and persecute you and utter every kind of evil against you falsely because of me, rejoice and be glad, for your reward will be great in Heaven. The Gospel of the Lord."

"Amen," the crowd said in unison.

Tom and Jill sat in utter amazement at the readings and teachings this church was trying to relay to everyone. Tom knew he wanted to find out more about this faith as he looked at his daughter and knew what God had given him. He wasn't going to leave until he met this priest.

Most everyone there had heard this Gospel before but never outside with the sun shining down on them. Many of those in attendance imagined it was as if they were on the mountain that day, listening to Jesus himself teach his flock. It was a Gospel they would all remember, and the sermon was next.

Father Mayer introduced Father Feeney to everyone at the start of the mass, so when Father Mayer and everyone else at the picnic sat down, he headed to the microphone to give his sermon. Everyone was comfortable in their setting and were looking forward to any words of wisdom this priest, from Atlanta, could give them. They knew Father Mayer always liked to give his own sermons, and this being the biggest audience of the year, they all knew that it was a rather special occasion. It must be a very special occasion, most of them thought to themselves.

"Good afternoon," Father Feeney said as everyone in the audience was peering at Father. Even Anita and those still registering at the entrance paused to listen to his words. She seemed to know that they would be words of wisdom and should not be missed as she told her two girls to pay attention.

Even those who seemed to be homeless and had come for the free food paused and listened intently as Father began.

"There was a man many years ago who had one horse and one son. The horse would do everything for the man and was very important to his families well being. The horse would plow the fields, so he could grow his crops, the horse would haul in the logs from the forest to keep them warm in the winter and it would take them miles into the city and carry back the supplies they needed. It was very important to this man. One day the horse ran away, and all the man's friends came over and told him that this was a terrible thing as he would now be in a big struggle. The man said, well you never know it could be bad or it could be good. They all left wondering how this could ever be good. A few days later, the horse came running back into the corral and with it were ten other horses as it was the leader of the pack. He was going to be a rich man now as with so many horses he could plow more crops and sell them accordingly. He could also haul more wood and supplies and make even more money off these new horses. All his friends came over and told him that this was the greatest thing that could ever happen and that he was going to be a rich man. He in turn told them, you never know it could be good or it could be bad. The next day his son was riding one of the horses to train it and sell it and fell off the horse, paralyzing the young boy. All the man's friends came over and told him how bad this was and that nothing could be worse. The man said, well you never know, it could be bad or it could be good. They all left perplexed as to how this could ever be a good thing. A week later the man's country declared war on the neighboring country, which meant a lot of young men were going to be killed, and his son did not have to go."

Everyone in attendance had been through things in their life that seemed dark and hopeless but with faith these issues turned into wonderful things.

Father paused for a few seconds after ending the story and then continued.

"We must all remember that the Lord sometimes works in strange ways and that sometimes life will be very difficult. Tragedies and bad things will inevitably happen even to good holy people, but we must have faith and trust in him as only God knows what lies ahead for all of us."

He continued commenting on how we must learn to not only

forgive others when they have wronged us and ask for forgiveness, but we must more importantly learn to forgive ourselves. "It is through forgiveness that we will attain God's grace," he said, referring to the first reading. "And," he continued, "like the second reading said, we must help those in need, no matter their color, their origin or their faith. We are all God's children."

Father paused and looked around and he knew with so many people that there was also so much hurt, pain and remorse. He had taken confessions for sins for decades and had heard it all and felt all these emotions himself as he truly loved his congregation. So he knew he had to let them know to be strong. It wasn't written down anymore for him, he was going to wing it.

"Life is not fair, sorrow is right around the corner," he told them, "be pleased with what you have been given, and share as much as possible. Listen to those you trust around you, they love you more than you will probably ever know and remember, Father Mayer wants to help lead you out of the darkness as there is a ray of light behind every cloud."

"Love God, yourself and one another and one day you will rejoice in the light of the Kingdom of God."

He was finished, so he walked back to his picnic chair next to Father Mayer on this makeshift altar and sat down. Father Mayer paused for quite sometime before continuing the mass in order that the words everyone just heard could be digested thoroughly.

There were a number of individuals at the picnic who could not help but be touched in a tearful way. They knew his words, they had lived it and been there and had found the light. They were in a dark place, but they found the light.

Father Mayer then stood up and everyone followed in unison with him and the mass went on and finished in a timely manner as Father wanted everyone to enjoy the day. Enjoy what they had been given. Enjoy what had been taken away from them. Enjoy the company around them, the music and the food.

"Amen" everyone said together as mass ended and Miguel headed to the music system to get things going again. There was a little over a half hour before dinner would be served and the sun continued to shine.

Patty looked at Ray and thanked him again for inviting her family to the picnic as her husband nodded his approval. There were baseball mitts at nearly every table and Patty's husband was looking forward to playing some catch after dinner.

After listening to a number of people tell him how nice he did on his reading, Dan headed over to the baseball field as he wanted to check on it. Yesterday, Dan worked up a sweat making sure the field was ready for the big picnic. Joey's love for the sport helped Dan gain an appreciation for it as well, so he started spending some of his free time managing the field at St. George School.

Over the years, Dan became more meticulous with his upkeep of the field. He prided himself on the field's appearance, and he worked extra hard to make sure everything was perfect for the picnic.

This gave him time to be thankful for all he had been given in life.

Aaron saw Kate parked in the visitor's area, exactly where she said she'd be. She waved at him to alert him of her presence, but his eyes continued to scan the area. There was no sign of Lee; he certainly didn't stick around for Aaron to work out what was going on.

Dejected, Aaron made his way over to Kate's car, the blue paint dull and dusty, badly in need of a wash. By the time he opened the door, a tear was carving a path down his cheek. Kate assumed the worst.

"Your test results," She started. "Were they... were they not what you hoped?"

"No," Aaron said, "they were exactly what I wanted to hear. I'm cancer-free."

Kate continued to stare at him, clearly not understanding his sadness in the face of such amazing news.

"But Lee's not. He's only got a matter of time."

With that, Kate embraced Aaron as he mourned Lee and the fact that he may never see him again. After a few minutes, Aaron composed himself and let go of Kate. He was glad she was there for him.

"I know you're sad," Kate said quietly, "but why don't we head over to the picnic at St. George's? We've missed the mass, but it will be a great day. Joey will be there."

"Yeah, let's do that," Aaron said. "Today doesn't have to be a sad day. Lee wouldn't want it to be. Besides, there's much to celebrate."

Just as Kate put the car in drive, Aaron had a thought.

"Hey, how about we make a slight detour?" Aaron said. "Let's visit Shirley at the corner store. I want to thank her for having "the girls" watch over me."

Kate nodded in agreement, and they were on their way.

After mass was over, the entire congregation dispersed all over the grounds. The children ran to the baseball field to play catch and throw the frisbees, while many of the parents and other adults chatted or browsed the tables full of gifts and baskets for the raffle. Dinner was going to be served in about a half hour, so nobody strayed too far away.

Ray hadn't yet had a chance to look at all the prizes for the raffle, so he went to find Anita to purchase some tickets. He spotted her near the entrance to the picnic talking to Miguel, and as Ray approached with a smile, Miguel started to head off, possibly going to check to see if the dinner was just about ready.

When they passed, Miguel playfully jabbed at Ray's arm. "You got about an hour and a half before your big moment," he said with a smile.

"What do you mean?" Ray said, feeling like he must've forgotten about something.

"I know you're handy with a guitar," said Miguel, "so I signed you up to play during the open mic later!"

"Whoa, I'm not ready for something like that!" Ray said. "I didn't even bring my guitar with me!"

"Good thing I told Beth to bring it along!" Miguel said, smiling even wider. "We both know you've been wanting to play in front of a crowd for a while now. Here's your chance! Don't let it slip by, or you'll regret it."

Before Ray could protest any further, Miguel sped off in the direction of the food tables. Ray was suddenly a huge ball of nerves. He hadn't been planning on this! Unsure of what else to do, he decided to finish his trip to the entrance to purchase raffle tickets from Anita. Perhaps that could distract him from thinking about his big moment for a little while.

It wasn't long before Miguel got the signal that the food was ready to serve, so he made his way to the stage and asked for everyone to quiet down.

"Father has done enough speaking for the day," Miguel said, and the crowd laughed in response. "I've just been informed that dinner is ready to be served, so why don't we say grace and get things underway?"

Everyone was silent and bowed their heads as Miguel led them in a short prayer of thanks.

Not wanting to deprive the hungry crowd of food any longer, Miguel then announced over the microphone that tables 1 through

20 could head over and start filling their plates. There were around 200 tables total, so Miguel had to be extra careful to ensure everyone ate in an orderly fashion. And to think, this picnic used to have just a fraction of the attendees. Father Mayer had done a fantastic job growing the parish.

Kate and Aaron pulled into the parking lot just as dinner was starting. They could see people starting to line up for food, but they had some trouble finding a place to park in the crowded lot. Aaron knew it was a big parish, but the sheer number of cars surprised him.

In the end, their hunger got the better of them and they just parked on a patch of grass and headed toward the well-worn path that led up the hill. The entrance was deserted except for Anita, who Aaron had gotten to know over the past year.

"I wasn't sure if you were going to show up!" Anita said. "You missed mass. Father gave a great homily. What kept you?"

"Well, I never want to miss one of Father's homilies, but I had a very important meeting with my doctor this morning," Aaron responded, smiling. He was excited to share his good news with the entire congregation.

"Oh? So, do you have some good news for us?" Anita asked.

"I'm cancer-free!" Aaron said, raising his hands in triumph.

"That is wonderful news!" Anita said. "Why don't you head on in and grab some dinner. I'm sure your friends will want to hear about the test results."

Aaron followed Kate toward the area where everyone was eating. There had to have been over 150 tables, perhaps even 200, but he was able to spot Joey immediately. His young friend was standing on his chair, looking back and forth, clearly waiting for Aaron to arrive.

As soon as Joey caught sight of Aaron, he started excitedly waving and calling him over. Aaron and Kate exchanged a smile and headed over to their table.

"So, how did it go?" Joey excitedly asked. Dan was sitting next to him, looking anxious.

"I have a clean bill of health!" Aaron announced. "And I have an empty stomach! Why don't we get in line? I can tell you more while we eat."

Mr. and Mrs. McGregor were surprised when LeVon joined Alice at their table for dinner, along with John. LeVon greeted everyone, shaking John and Bob's hands and waving at Mary.

The bond that LeVon and John shared, and the attention Alice was giving LeVon, did not go unnoticed by Bob. He was wary of any boy who got his daughter's attention – he was old school – but if there was someone he could trust to take care of his daughter, it'd be a boy who invested his time helping others like LeVon did.

Mary looked past her table to see Father Feeney, the priest who had given the homily, speaking with an interracial couple she had never seen before; she figured they must be new to the parish or just passing through. The wife was carrying a beautiful little girl, and Mary was reminded of the miracles that love can produce.

As Alice and LeVon started talking about their favorite parts of Father Feeney's homily, Mary put her arm around her husband and rubbed his back. Their daughter had made her mistakes, but she had grown into a fine young woman and they were excited to see the twinkle in her eye as she looked at her friend.

"So, how's the business going, LeVon?" Bob asked.

"It's been going very well, sir," LeVon said, walking over to Mr. McGregor. "We recently started working with ABC Daycare, so we needed to hire two more employees. We have 12 now!"

After a little small talk between LeVon and her husband, Mary had an idea. "LeVon, what are you up to next Sunday?"

John was listening intently from the other end of the table.

"Nothing too much, Ma'am, other than going to mass. Why do you ask?" LeVon said.

"The three of us were thinking of going to the Pirates game," Mary said, gesturing to her husband and daughter, "and I'd like to make it a foursome if you're available."

A hesitant smile flashed across Alice's face as she looked to her father to gauge his reaction. John was smiling and nodding his approval, while Bob looked at his wife in mild surprise before turning to LeVon and giving a curt nod. "We would all like you to be there," he said.

"Count me in!" LeVon said, slightly taken aback by the offer. "Who's driving?" he said with a laugh.

The McGregors hadn't seen Alice look this happy in a long time, and the two of them were truly looking forward to what next Sunday would bring.

Father Mayer's table was always the last to eat at the picnic. He liked to make sure all of his parishioners and others in attendance got to eat first, and the rest of his tablemates were kind enough to wait with him. As soon as the first tables started grabbing their plates, Father knew it would be the perfect time to take a little walk with Miguel and Evelyn.

Father Mayer gestured to Miguel, who stood up immediately, and he leaned over to Jeremy to ask if Evelyn could walk with them.

"Of course, Father," Jeremy said. "I'll wait here, and we can eat when you return."

Father joined hands with Evelyn, who in turn joined hands with Miguel, and they set off along the pathway that led past the church's beautiful garden. As they walked, Jeremy could see them talking and laughing animatedly and he wished he could be a fly on the wall for their conversation.

"Miguel talks to angels just like you do, Evelyn," Father told the little girl, "and if you ever need someone to talk to about all this and I am not around, talk to Miguel, he loves you like your mom and I do."

She looked at Father and then Miguel and said, "Silly Father, when I talked to mommy this morning she told me about Miguel and that I could trust him and that he is a good person, so I already knew that," as she clutched both their hands. "Mommy says he is a blessed man and that the two of us are going to be good friends for a long time."

The trio returned after a short time, and their table joined the end of the line to get their dinners. Jeremy now held one of Evelyn's hands and her other hand clutched the raffle tickets he bought her earlier; she seemed even happier than usual after her walk, and Jeremy asked what was on her mind.

"Oh, it's just that mommy is very happy today," Evelyn said. "She's watching over you, Lauren, and me as we celebrate Father's picnic."

They were in line behind a group of people from the parish's outreach program. All of them took a turn thanking Father Mayer and Miguel for putting together such a perfect picnic. They offered to help clean up at the end of the picnic, so Miguel thanked them and told them to see him around 6:00 pm and he would give them some direction.

Even after all the guests had eaten their fill, there was plenty leftover. Some parishioners periodically got up to get another plate or perhaps have some dessert, but it was clear that there would be plenty of food to donate to those in need.

Ray sat back in his chair, his pants a little bit tighter now that he had cleaned his second plate. He looked over at Beth, still a little shocked that she had brought his guitar here today. She knew he had been trying to work up the courage to perform in front of a crowd, but now she was forcing his hand a little bit.

"I don't know whether to thank you or not for bringing my Les Paul with you," Ray said, beginning to feel the butterflies creep into his stomach, even though it should have been full of food.

"This has been a long time coming, Ray," Beth said. "You want to do it, but you needed a little push. So here it is. You'll do great, I know it."

Mike and Lori finished eating before the rest of their table, who were busy fussing over their children. Lori was stuffed, so Mike suggested they take a brief walk to work off some of the food. He told her he wanted to see the stained glass windows that Toby and Tom had been telling him about. They excused themselves from their table and Mike gestured to Lori to lead the way.

Ted wasn't lying when he said everyone here was friendly, but Melissa was still glad when he collected her, Sharon, and the children as they made their way into the picnic. Melissa introduced Sharon and her grandchildren to Ted, who was excited to finally meet them after hearing so many stories over the phone from Julie and Philip.

Over the course of the afternoon and throughout dinner, Melissa and Ted got caught up with what they'd been up to over the past year. After dinner was over, all the kids were full of energy and couldn't sit still at the table.

"Hey, kids, why don't we run on over to the field and play a game?" Sharon said, much to their delight. Melissa and Ted watched as they all sprung up out of their chairs and sprinted in the field's direction, arguing about who would get there first.

"I'll watch the kids for a while, Melissa," Sharon said, looking back and forth between the ex-couple. "You two can come over and join us in a bit."

Even though their table was in the center of the crowd of people, the absence of the children made everything seem much quieter. Ted and Melissa considered each other a moment; this was the first time they'd been alone since the divorce.

"I'm amazed by how many people you know here," Melissa said, breaking the short silence. "Julie and Philip mentioned that you were involved with a church up here, but I wasn't sure if I believed it until today."

"Well, I've had a lot of time to reflect on my behavior and where my life was going," Ted said, unable to meet her eyes while talking about his infidelity. "It's a shame that I let myself stray so far from the light, but I was slowly able to work my way back."

"All these people here," Ted continued," helped me along the way. I don't know where I'd be without them – especially Father Mayer."

"Yes, it truly seems like everyone here knows you. I saw Father give you a hug after mass, and it finally started to get through to me that you really have changed for the better."

"Julie and Philip need a father figure in their life that they can look up to, and I wasn't that guy for much too long," Ted said. "But I'm working every day to make sure I can be someone they will be proud to call their dad, even if I can't be there for them every day anymore."

"I've been thinking about that, actually," Melissa said. "I never wanted you to be on the outside looking in, and you know why you are, but the mass today really helped me get to a point where I can start to leave this darkness behind me. It might be hard for you to visit often when you live so far away, but I'd like it if you could be there for Julie and Philip more often."

"I'd like that, too," Ted said, tears forming in his eyes as he realized what Melissa was saying.

Karen and her friends had been laughing all through dinner,

reminiscing about memories from their last trip together. The trip was a turning point for all of them, and they were thankful every day for how it had gone.

Across the picnic, Karen noticed Charlene, one of her favorite children at her new job, who was sitting with her mother. Charlene had a smile on her face, just like she always did, but Karen couldn't help but feel bad that she wasn't joining all of the other children heading to the field to play together.

"I'll be back in a bit," she told her husband and her friends. "I'm going to go say hi to someone."

She squeezed herself between two chairs and hurried off in Charlene's direction, making a slight detour when she saw Ray and Patty, who were both important people at ABC Daycare. She had never met Patty, but Ray hired her and she saw him from time to time.

Finding a way through the huge cluster of tables felt like trying to get through a maze; people and chairs blocked some of her turns, but she eventually made it to Ray and Patty's table.

"Hey, Ray!" Karen said, not pausing to talk. She saw he was in conversation with Patty and didn't want to interrupt.

"Oh, hi, Karen! Good to see you!" Ray said, waving back, before returning to his conversation.

Charlene's table wasn't too far away from Ray's, and Karen was there in a flash. She talked to Phyllis and her boyfriend Peter, who she had gotten to know over the last few months and gave Charlene a long hug.

After a little more small talk, Karen picked up "Heaven," Charlene's favorite book, and started to read it to her. She'd read it to her countless times, but it never failed to brighten up the girl's day. Truth be told, it brightened up Karen's say just as much.

A few tables away, Ray watched Karen interact with the young girl. Based on the expression on their faces, he could tell they enjoyed each other's company.

He'd evidently been looking for a while because Patty soon looked over at the woman who had waved at Ray.

"Who is that?" Patty asked. "She's doing a great job with that young girl."

"That's one of our newer employees, Karen," Ray said, his chest swelling with pride as he watched her interact with Charlene. He had a hand in hiring every new employee in Pittsburgh, so it felt great for Patty to pay Karen such a nice compliment.

Patty could see why ABC Daycare's Pittsburgh branch had seen such a dramatic increase in business over the past year, both in employees and new children. The chance meeting with Ray on that flight constantly proved to be a blessing; he was a great man who cared greatly about the children and made sure every employee matched his enthusiasm.

The sun was high in the air, and the grounds around St. George Church were alive with activities. Though a large group of parishioners still mulled around the dinner tables, there were people checking out the raffle prizes and kids and adults alike playing frisbee, baseball, and other games throughout the picnic area.

Miguel cut the music that had been playing throughout dinner and got on the microphone.

"How are we all doing?" Miguel said, getting everyone's attention. "You're probably all full of that delicious food, but I hope you all have room for one more treat! In just a few minutes, we will be having an open mic for those of us who would like to sing or play an instrument."

There was a smattering of cheers and applause throughout the crowd as a few parishioners got up to retrieve their instruments and head toward the stage.

"After the final performance, we will be announcing the winners of the raffle, so make sure to buy tickets if you haven't yet!"

As Miguel was speaking, Ray's son, Ron, returned from the car with the Les Paul and presented it to his father. Up to that point, Ray had been enjoying dinner and everyone at his table, so he had completely forgotten that his wife had brought it.

"I didn't know you played guitar, Ray," Patty said, looking impressed.

"Well, I've never performed in front of a crowd," Ray said, getting nervous again. "Beth brought my guitar, but I don't think I can play without my song sheets."

"Good thing I brought those, too," Beth said, fishing them out of her purse. "I chose a favorite of mine: Peaceful Easy Feeling."

"I tuned your guitar myself this morning, Dad," Ron said, still holding onto it. "We've heard you play hundreds of times. I know you're nervous, but you're gonna kill it up there!"

Ray nodded at his loving wife and son, unable to speak at the moment. The butterflies he felt earlier were back in full force, but he knew deep down that this was the perfect time and crowd for his first live performance.

"Ok, first up to perform is my beautiful wife, Anita!" Miguel announced a few minutes later. "Don't worry, she'll be back selling raffle tickets in just a bit. Here she is, performing Amazing Grace!"

The crowd surrounding the stage grew quiet as Anita took the mic from Miguel and gave him a hug. She performed every year, so the parishioners knew they were in for a treat. As soon as she began to sing, even those far away at the baseball field paused their games to listen to her beautiful voice. She had a true gift, and everyone was grateful that she sang during mass every week. Still, this rendition of

Amazing Grace was special, even for Anita, as if it was a gift straight from heaven.

When she finished captivating the crowd, applause rang out for over a minute. Miguel finally took the mic to quiet the crowd and announce the next performer. The parish had some wonderful singers and musicians, so the picnic almost seemed like a festival instead of a religious gathering.

A few performances later, after a violin rendition of America the Beautiful, Miguel announced that Ray Rossi was up next, playing his guitar and singing Peaceful Easy Feeling.

The stairs creaked as Ray ascended to the stage and the crowd politely clapped. His hands shook slightly from the nerves, but he gripped his guitar tightly and made his way to where Miguel was standing. Holding his guitar in one hand, Ray threw his other around Miguel and brought him in for a tight hug.

"I still can't believe you got me to do this," Ray said into Miguel's ear as they embraced. "But I'm also thankful. It's time I finally do this."

"You'll do great!" Miguel said, smiling from ear to ear.

Miguel let go of Ray and tried to walk off the stage, but Ray kept hold of Miguel's shirt and pulled him back.

"I'm not going to do this alone, though," Ray said, smiling. "We've sung this song together dozens of times, so what's one more?"

Ray grabbed the mic and looked out over the crowd. Everything looked a lot different from up there; hundreds of faces were looking right back at him, but, surprisingly, all of Ray's butterflies were gone. This was his moment, and he wanted Miguel to be a part of it.

"Good afternoon, everyone!" Ray said. "For those of you that don't know me, my name is Ray Rossi. This is my first time playing in front of a crowd, so go easy on me."

The crowd chuckled at Ray's joke, and he continued.

"I'm not going to be singing alone, though," he said. "Believe it or not, my good friend Miguel here has a great voice, too, and he volunteered to help me out."

Miguel's mouth hung open in surprise at Ray's trickery, but it quickly turned into a laugh. He could think of nothing better than being by Ray's side for his first performance.

Ray placed the song sheets to Peaceful Easy Feeling on the music stand and, with a wink at Miguel and the mic in between them, Ray started the first few chords of the song.

By the time Lori and Mike got through the crowd, Miguel had started the open mic portion of the event. Though the music and singing was beautiful, Mike was hoping to have some privacy with Lori and steered her toward the church's flower gardens, which appeared to be deserted.

"Are you doing ok?" Lori asked Mike. "You haven't said much since dinner."

"Oh, I'm doing great," Mike replied, trying to sound casual. "This is a beautiful picnic, and I'm just trying to take everything in."

Nerves were getting the best of Mike; he kept fidgeting slightly and he had to frequently wipe his sweaty palms on his shirt.

The further they walked, the quieter things became. The garden was around the side of the church, so most of the sound from the concert was cut off, though they could still hear what was going on. The area was filled with colorful flowers of all different kinds, and the left side was framed by the most beautiful stained glass windows Mike had ever seen; the sun danced off of the glass. Mike made a mental note to tell Toby and Tom what an excellent job they did.

"So why did you bring me over here?" Lori asked, turning to Mike and smiling up at him.

Mike stared into her eyes, unsure of how to start. After a few seconds of silence, he heard the first notes of Peaceful Easy Feeling, one of his favorite songs, start to drift across the garden. He knew it was now or never.

"Well," Mike said, "I wanted to ask you something."

With that, Mike got down on one knee and pulled a ring out of his pocket.

The past few hours had been a whirlwind for Tom and Jill, who were stymied by the hospitality everyone at St. George's parish showed them. Though they loved their home in Atlanta, they both wished they had a community like this to take part in.

Jill had hoped to stay until the raffle prizes were announced, or at least until the end of the open mic concert, but Kara was getting fussy and she decided it was best to head back to the hotel to put her down for a proper nap.

Tom led the way toward the parking lot, but he made a slight detour when he saw the priest who gave the sermon at mass earlier. It would be rude, he thought, to leave without properly thanking him for the hospitality shown today.

"Excuse me," Tom said, leading Jill and Kara over to the priest. "I just wanted to stop by before we headed out and thank you for letting us join your church's picnic."

"Of course," Father Feeney said. "All are welcome here."

"Your sermon today was very eye-opening," Jill added. "We are just thankful we could be a part of your parish, even if it's just for today."

"I'll pass on your kind words," Father Feeney said, smiling.

THE PRIEST, THE STEWARDESS, AND THE CHURCH PICNIC

"Though, this is not my parish. I'm a visitor as well. My church is in Atlanta."

Tom and Jill exchanged a look of surprise. What a coincidence that he would be from the same city.

"We are from Atlanta, too," Tom said. "We are just here visiting our daughter's god mother, Sonya, who graduated from college today."

"You don't say!" Father Feeney said, also surprised at how their paths had crossed. "Well, if you're interested, my parish in Atlanta is Blessed Sacrament. You'd be welcome to join us for mass any time!"

"I'm sure our paths will cross again soon," Tom said, shaking Father's hand. By the time they made it back to their car, Tom and Jill had decided to visit Blessed Sacrament for mass the following Sunday.

The baseball field was packed with people of all ages; fathers, sons, and friends were playing catch, running around, or just spectating. This was exactly what Dan had envisioned when he was working on the field in preparation for the picnic.

He was playing catch in a big triangle with Aaron and Joey, who had brought the baseball Aaron caught for him last year. After a while, Dan thought it might be fun to get an actual game of baseball started. Removing himself from the game of catch, he quickly counted how many kids were on the field. They had more than enough for two teams.

A few yards away, Dan spotted another father playing catch with his son. The man had a very good arm, and Dan could tell he knew the game of baseball.

"Hey, what do you say we get a game going?" Dan called over to the man. "I have access to the equipment shed. We have gloves, bats, catcher's equipment – everything we need."

"That'd be fun!" Dylan called back. "Why don't you get the equipment and I'll round up everyone who wants to play?"

Dan was excited that a real game would be taking place on the field he'd meticulously prepared. It only took a few minutes to get the equipment from the shed, but Dylan had all the boys and their fathers divided into two teams when Dan and Aaron got back to the field.

"You're on my team, Aaron!" Joey said. "I made sure we weren't split up."

"Great!" Aaron responded. "I'm not too great at baseball, though, so you're going to have to give me some tips."

Dylan decided to be the full-time pitcher and Dan volunteered to do the catching.

"Does anyone have a good ball we can use?" Dylan asked the crowd around him.

A few boys raised their hands, but Joey shot over to him and handed him the ball Aaron had caught for him the year before. "This is a big league ball!" Joey said with a proud smile. "My friend Aaron caught it for me."

"Ok, that's settled," Dylan said, looking at the National League inscription on the ball. It reminded him of his playing days. "Let's play ball!"

Ray and Miguel had only ever sung together in the cab, but their first time in front of a crowd was as natural as if they'd been on stage together for years. As soon as the song ended, the crowd erupted in applause and Ray made eye contact with his wife and son in the crowd.

Performing in front of a crowd was a dream come true for Ray, but he could tell that Beth and Ron were even happier than he was. Before leaving the stage, Ray turned to Miguel and gave him a big

THE PRIEST, THE STEWARDESS, AND THE CHURCH PICNIC

hug. He wouldn't have wanted his first performance to have gone any other way.

"Give it up for Ray!" Miguel said, returning to the mic. "Next up, we have our favorite teenage twins, Janet and Jane, performing an original song!"

It took a few minutes for Ray to make his way back to his table – everyone kept stopping him to compliment his guitar playing – but nothing felt better than being greeted by his family and friends.

Throughout the open mic concert, Father Mayer walked from table to table, thanking everyone for attending the picnic. He truly appreciated the support everyone showed his parish. Before long, he noticed Phyllis and Charlene, two of his favorite parishioners; though he always told himself he didn't really have any favorites.

Karen, a newer member of the church, was reading a book to Charlene, who looked happier than ever. When Karen finished reading to Charlene, she closed the book, and Father Mayer immediately recognized the cover; it was the book he had given to Evelyn, who in turn must have passed it on to Charlene.

Struck with a sudden inspiration, Father Mayer looked around for Evelyn and spotted her playing tag with some other children next to the tables. He didn't want to interrupt her fun, but he knew she would appreciate another chance to see the girl she had given her book to.

"Hey, Evelyn!" Father Mayer called. "Come over here for a minute! I have something to show you."

Evelyn told her friends she would be back and ran over to Father Mayer, panting slightly from the game she had been playing.

"What is it, Father?" she asked.

"Do you remember that book about heaven I gave you?" he asked her.

"Of course I remember, Father. It was my favorite book!" Evelyn said. "But I knew it by heart, so I gave it to someone who needed it more than me."

"That's awfully kind of you," Father said. "You know, I think the girl you gave the book to is right over there and I think she and her mother would love to say hello."

Evelyn looked in the direction Father was pointing, and a smile lit up her face. She grabbed Father by the hand and dragged him toward Charlene and Phyllis.

Phyllis was taking in the concert when she saw a little girl dragging Father Mayer toward her table. It took her a second, but she recognized the girl as the one who had given Charlene her favorite book on the plane the year before. She was a little taller but she had that same aura surrounding her.

A smile came to her face as she watched the pair approach. Phyllis stood up and turned Charlene's wheelchair to face them, so she could see them coming, too. Charlene immediately started rocking in her seat, more than she ever had before. She still had the book clutched in her hands, and she raised it in front of her as Evelyn and Father Mayer got to their table. Charlene had never done something like that before.

"I believe the three of you might know each other," Father said as he approached the table, still being led by Evelyn.

"You're the little angel who gave Charlene her favorite book on the plane a year ago, aren't you?" Phyllis said.

"Yes, I am," Evelyn said, smiling back at Phyllis. She walked right up to Phyllis and gave her a big hug and then did the same to Charlene.

"It was my favorite book. Is it your favorite, too?" Evelyn asked Charlene, who was still rocking.

THE PRIEST, THE STEWARDESS, AND THE CHURCH PICNIC

Charlene couldn't vocalize her feelings, but, for the first time ever, she opened the book herself and pointed to Evelyn's name which was written on the first page. Phyllis and Peter, who was observing the scene in amazement, couldn't believe what was happening.

All of this happened without anyone speaking a word. Nobody really knew what to say or what to do next, but the silence was broken when the sound of a boy's voice called out "Evelyn! Evelyn, it's your turn to start the game!"

"I guess it's my turn for tag!" Evelyn said. She hugged Charlene one last time and took off back toward her friends.

Phyllis turned to Father and said, "She sure is a special little girl!" Father Mayer could only nod in agreement as he watched Evelyn return to her game.

Just as the final performance of the night took the stage, Lori and Mike returned from their walk across the grounds. They both had smiles on their faces, though Lori's eyes were a little red, almost as if she had been crying.

"What's up with you two?" Barbara asked, as everyone turned to look at the arriving couple. "Lori, are you ok?"

"Well," Lori began, clearly unsure of where to begin. She struggled over her words for a few seconds before giving up and thrusting her left hand toward her friends, exposing a brand-new diamond on her ring finger.

There was an eruption of cheers from their table as all the girls rushed at Lori and the guys got up to shake Mike's hand and pat him on the back. They were so loud that the surrounding tables all looked over to see what the commotion was about. Even Miguel and Anita overheard, as they were nearby talking to a few friends.

"You know what this means?" Tom said to Mike, arm around his shoulders. "You don't need to open the car door for Lori anymore!"

Their table erupted in laughter, and even the women couldn't keep from chuckling at the joke.

A few minutes later, Miguel got up to wrap up the last performance of the night and get the raffle started. Walking past Lori and Mike, Miguel gave them a quick thumbs up and continued toward the stage.

"Give it up for Janet and Jane!" Miguel said, retaking the stage as the final performance of the night ended. "And let's give another big round of applause for all of our performers tonight."

The crowd cheered once again, some even standing to show their appreciation.

"Before we begin the raffle, which I know you've all been waiting for," Miguel said, "we have some wonderful news! A young couple just got engaged! Lori and Mike, stand up on your chairs so everyone can see you."

Once everyone at the baseball field heard that the raffle was about to begin, they finished their game, put the equipment away, and everyone ran back to their seats.

Dan, Aaron, and Joey were the last to leave the field. Dan needed to lock the equipment shed, so they headed back together.

"So, Joey, where and when's your next stadium trip going to be?" Aaron asked, looking over at Joey who was still full of energy from the baseball game.

"We're going to go to Wrigley Field in Chicago!" Joey said. He was clearly excited to visit this historic field.

"Well, if you and your dad don't mind," Aaron began, "would it be ok if I tagged along with you?"

"That'd be the best thing ever!" Joey practically squealed. "Dad, can he come with us?"

"Of course he can, buddy," Dan said, patting Aaron on the shoulder. "We'd love it if you came, Aaron."

Mark and Tom helped Lori and Mike climb up onto the picnic table. They both blushed at all of the attention – all eyes were on them – but they enjoyed the celebration, and Lori even brandished her ring for everyone to see.

It took a few minutes for everyone to quiet down, but Miguel was eventually able to get the raffle under way. Dozens of parishioners had donated prizes and baskets for the raffle, and thousands of tickets had been purchased throughout the day.

Miguel knew the children loved helping out, so he enlisted some of them to bring the prizes on stage, select the winning tickets, and call out the numbers.

"First up, we have a beach basket," Miguel said. "This has everything you need for a perfect day at the beach. What's the winning number, Allie?"

Miguel crouched down to give the microphone to the little girl, who was clutching the big jar of tickets. "1738!" she called out, and a man in the back of the crowd jumped up, shouted "That's me!" and headed to the stage to get his prize.

After that, the raffle continued on without a hitch for the next hour.

As soon as the raffle started, LeVon knew it was time to load up the leftover food and take it to the local food bank so it could be distributed to needy families.

"Duty calls," LeVon said, getting up out of his chair. He would've preferred to stay with Alice, her parents, and John – he was really enjoying the afternoon with all of them – but he didn't want the food to spoil in the heat.

"Do you need any help delivering the food?" Alice asked, getting up as well so she could say goodbye.

"No, me and the guys have it covered," LeVon said. "Just keep an eye on the raffle and let me know if I win anything!"

"It was great seeing you, LeVon," Mr. McGregor said, getting up to shake his hand. "I'll make sure Alice gives you the details for next weekend."

"Yes, sir!" LeVon said, before turning to give Alice a quick hug.

"I'll be right back," John said. "I'm gonna walk with LeVon to the van and help him load the food."

LeVon and John walked off in the direction of the food tent, and Bob couldn't help but admire this young man his daughter was getting to know.

Melissa was enjoying the raffle when she first noticed some ominous clouds approaching in the distance. Thinking about how long it would take to pack up the van and get all of the kids in order, she wondered if it would be best to get started now.

Peeling her eyes away from the stage, Melissa saw that the kids were much more subdued than they had been all day. The food, sun, and all that running around must've really tired them out. Julie and Philip were slumped in their chairs, clearly struggling to stay awake.

"Sharon," Melissa called softly over to her friend. "Why don't we start to get packed up? The kids look exhausted and I don't like the looks of those clouds over there."

Sharon agreed, seeing that her grandchildren were also getting tired. She figured it'd be best to get going before they all fell asleep; she didn't fancy having to carry them all back to the van.

"Ted, would you mind helping us get everything back to the van?"

Melissa asked.

"Of course," Ted said. "I don't mind at all. I'll grab all of your things, and you and Sharon can lead the children over and get them buckled in."

With that, Melissa and Sharon roused all of the children and had them start walking toward the car. Melissa couldn't help but chuckle as she watched Julie and Philip drag their feet, clearly tired from all they did that day.

When they got to the van, Ted had just finished loading everything into the trunk. Julie and Philip perked up momentarily when he hugged them goodbye, telling them he would make sure to call them more often. He loved hearing about their daily lives.

"Melissa, I can get them all buckled in," Sharon said, looking meaningfully between her best friend and Ted. "You two can say goodbye."

"Thank you again for inviting us today," Melissa told Ted. "It was really great seeing you, and I know the kids loved it, too. It felt just like old times."

"Of course!" Ted said. "I'm glad you were able to visit for this. You know, I'm really trying to be a better father to Julie and Philip. This church has been my safe haven. It's really helped me turn things around."

"I couldn't agree more," Melissa said. "Julie, Philip, and I want nothing more than for you to be there for them. If you have the time this year, it would be great if you could come visit. I know the kids would love it."

"That would be great," Ted said. "I'd love nothing more than that."

By now, the children were all buckled in and Sharon was climbing into the driver's seat of the van. Melissa knew it was time to go.

"Well, goodbye," she said, before throwing her arms out and giving Ted a nice, long hug.

In the car, Philip was already sound asleep. He had been running around the baseball field so much that he barely had the stamina to walk to the van. Julie, on the other hand, still had her eyes open. She couldn't hear what her parents were saying, but she saw her mom pull her dad into a big hug right before she got into the car. With a smile on her face, Julie finally drifted off to sleep.

Near the end of the raffle, Miguel had asked Anita to find Ray and have him come to the stage. There were some looming storm clouds that Miguel didn't like to see, and he wanted to ensure everything got wrapped up before the rain started.

Ray appeared at the edge of the stage just before the final prize of the night was to be announced, and Miguel took a quick break to go talk to him.

"Hey, Ray, could you do me a favor?" Miguel asked.

"Sure thing, Miguel," Ray said. "Anything for my singing partner."

"I'm about to finish the raffle, and then I'll give a closing speech," Miguel said. "But right after that, I have to get going. I hate to do this, but could you oversee the closing of the picnic?"

"That's not a problem, Miguel," Ray said. "Just let me know what needs done."

Miguel handed him a task list with a few remaining items on it. "I let everyone know you'd be in charge once I leave. Thanks again. I really appreciate it!"

After patting Ray on the back, Miguel returned to the center of the stage to present the final prize of the night. It was a 10 game, 4 ticket package for the Pittsburgh Pirates – a really nice gift!

THE PRIEST, THE STEWARDESS, AND THE CHURCH PICNIC

The girls called out the number for the winning ticket: "5985!"

Instead of hearing a cheer from the crowd, Miguel only heard mutterings. Perhaps the winner had already left for the night. He had the girls call out the number a few more times.

Darlene Oliver had been deep in conversation with Patty and her husband, Dylan, during this whole ordeal and had completely missed the winning number.

"Wait, what was that winning number?" Darlene asked everyone at her table.

"I think it was 5985," Ray said from a few seats over. "Is that yours?"

"Let me check," Darlene said, her hands shaking slightly as she sorted through her tickets. "Yes, it's me! I won!"

Her whole table erupted in cheers, and Darlene jumped up and ran to the stage to collect her prize. She was a little embarrassed for not paying attention, but she was so excited to have won. Her husband loved baseball, and so did her kids.

Thanks to John's help, LeVon was able to get all the food packed up in no time. Good thing too, John thought, as the clouds closing in did not look friendly.

"It's a shame your brother had to miss the picnic," John said to LeVon. "But hopefully James' baseball team won their playoff game today. Where was the game again?"

"It was up in Erie," LeVon said, as he packed the last box of food into the truck. "I told him he'd be missing out, but he couldn't let the team down. Hopefully he can come next year."

"Well, you take care," John said. "I'll Face Time with you and James sometime next week. Sound good?"

"Yes, sir," LeVon said, giving John a hug. "Have a safe trip home. Thanks for coming to visit!"

With that, John set back across the grounds toward the McGregor table.

After Darlene finally made her way to the stage to collect her prize, Miguel returned to the mic to wrap things up for the night.

"Ok, that about does it for us tonight!" Miguel said to the crowd. "Father Mayer said he does enough talking on Sundays as it is, so he passed the duty of closing the picnic to me"

There was a chuckle from the crowd and everyone turned to Father Mayer, who mouthed "thank you" to Miguel from his seat. Evelyn was sitting right next to Father, and she turned to him, smiling along with the crowd.

"Once again, everyone here at St. George Parish would like to thank you all for coming out and supporting the church. Today was a huge success by all measures. We had more than enough food, and all of the leftovers are being hand-delivered to the local food bank by KEV'S TRANSPORT, so let's give a hand to LeVon over there and to everyone who prepared food for today."

There was a loud cheer and applause from the crowd.

"Let's also give a round of applause to everyone who donated prizes and baskets for our raffle this year," Miguel said, with the crowd clapping in response. "I'm jealous of everyone who won tonight! We don't have the final numbers, but I can tell you right now that Father Mayer will put every penny to good use."

"I also want to thank everyone who performed at our open mic! It started out a few years ago with a single performance, and look at it now!" Miguel said. "We'd like to see even more parishioners perform next year, so don't be afraid to sign up."

"Remember to not be so hard on yourselves, treat everyone with respect and honesty, and its unfortunate, but sometimes you have to wash the sand off of your sandals and move on as you can only forgive those who ask for forgiveness."

"Lastly," Miguel said, "I'd like to thank all of you for attending. A parish is nothing without its people, and this picnic highlights that on every level. God bless you all for everything you do for this wonderful community."

Miguel paused to look up at the clouds looming overhead; the storm was going to be starting sooner rather than later.

"Ok, that's all I have to say," Miguel said. "We have more than enough volunteers helping us pack up, so please head on out whenever you're ready. It looks like we have a nasty storm incoming, and I don't want to see anybody caught in it."

The crowd gave Miguel one last round of applause – perhaps the biggest of the night – for everything he did over the course of the picnic.

"So, what do you say?" Barbara turned to Karen after Miguel stepped off the stage. "Should The Karen and Barbara Duo make a comeback at next year's open mic?"

"Gosh, it's been a long time since I've heard that name," Karen said with a small laugh. "But I'm in if you are."

The girls had been discussing preliminary wedding plans for Lori while the guys got all of the wagons packed up for their trip back to Karen's house. They had four wagons in total. Mike led their little red caravan away from their table, a smile still plastered to his face. The day had been perfect, and he couldn't wait to share the good news with his family.

Miguel walked through the crowd, pausing every now and then when people stopped to thank him for putting the picnic together. He took the longest pause at Father Mayer's table, who reached out to shake his hand.

"Thanks again for giving the closing speech," Father Mayer said, "and for all your other work today."

"Of course," Miguel said. "Anything for you, Father. I've gotta go meet someone, but I'll see you at next week's meeting."

Miguel waved goodbye to Jeremy and Lauren, but stopped to say something to Evelyn that nobody else could hear, though she smiled in response.

John got back to the McGregor's table just after Miguel signed off for the night. The picnic really had been perfect, but he was worried about the oncoming storm and decided to head out after one last goodbye to his new friends.

"Well," said John, "I think it's just about time I head out. I don't plan on getting rained on today."

"We were thinking the same thing," said Bob, as Mary and Alice got their things together.

"It was great finally meeting you all," John said, shaking Bob's hand. "Especially you, Alice. It's been an interesting year, but talking to you and finally seeing you in person has been the final step of my healing experience."

Alice looked to the heavens, not because of the storm clouds, but because she knew all of this was only possible thanks to a higher power. She still felt like she didn't deserve to be forgiven, but she knew all things were possible through God – from meeting John, to her parents' acceptance of LeVon, her black friend.

"I'll be sure to keep in touch," Alice said, hugging John as they said their goodbyes. "I know you like your letters, but texting might be easier now that I have your number."

By the time Ray made it back to the table where his family, Patty, and Dylan were sitting, Ron had gotten everything packed up and

THE PRIEST, THE STEWARDESS, AND THE CHURCH PICNIC

ready to go.

"Hey, you all should probably head out," Ray said, looking at all of them. "Miguel has to leave early and he asked if I could stay to watch over things."

"Not a problem, Dad," Ron said. "I've got everything ready to go, so no need to worry."

"Thanks, Ron," Ray said, swelling with pride. His son was turning into a responsible young man. "Patty and Dylan, thank you again for coming with us. I'll see you back at the house."

"Of course!" Patty said. "Today was amazing, and we can't wait for next year's picnic. Did Miguel leave already? We wanted to pass on our gratitude for his hospitality."

"Actually, you still might be able to catch him," Ray said, pointing over at Miguel, who was a few tables away, saying goodbye to his family.

Patty hurried on over to catch Miguel before he headed for the parking lot.

"Excuse me, Miguel?" Patty began. "Hi, I'm Patty, and that's my husband, Dylan, over there."

"Nice to meet you," Miguel said, flashing his friendly, crooked smile.

"Ray and Beth invited us here today," Patty continued, "and I just wanted to say thank you for welcoming us with open arms. This was a beautiful picnic. You did a fantastic job hosting everything. We aren't from around here, but we will definitely be coming back next year. Even though I didn't win anything in the raffle, I'm leaving with much more than I came with."

"Well, I'm happy to hear that," Miguel said. "It was a pleasure finally meeting you! Ray has told me so many good things about you, and I look forward to seeing you next year."

With that, Miguel continued his trek to the parking lot and Patty headed back to Ray and everyone at the table. Ray said his goodbyes before heading back to the cleanup crew gathered around the stage, and Ron and Beth led the rest of the group toward their car.

"Thanks again for letting us use all your equipment," Ray said to Stan, who had his own recording studio. "We couldn't have done this without you."

"No problem," Stan said. "I'm always down to help out friends who enjoy music as much as I do. Was that really your first performance? I thought you played great!"

"Yeah," Ray said, a little embarrassed by the praise, "that was my first time. I've been playing for years, though."

"Well, if you ever want to jam out or do some recording, you're welcome to stop by the studio," Stan said. "I play the drums, and I know plenty of other musicians who like to get together and play."

"That sounds great!" Ray had been waiting for this opportunity for years. "You just tell me when, and I'll be there."

Lightning flashed and the sound of thunder quickly followed. The storm was nearly upon St. George Church, though most of the crowd had gone by this point. The only people left were those who had volunteered to clean up, and even they were starting to run out of things to do.

"Can I book you to do next year's sermon already?" Father Mayer said, walking up to Father Feeney and clapping him on the back. "I've heard a number of people compliment you today."

Father Feeney smiled at this offer. "Count me in. Today has been very enlightening for me, Father."

Just one year before, Father Feeney was feeling lost in his

vocation. His job was to guide his parish, yet he hadn't felt like his sermons were getting through to anyone. Every day passed with him wondering if he was having any positive impact at all.

But everything that happened over the past year reminded him that he needed to listen as well. He was so focused on spreading the good word that he hadn't spent the time to take the good word in as well. Once he opened his heart and his mind to others, he found what he thought had been missing. It was always there, but he had somehow lost sight of it.

The sermon today had gone well – he had received his fair share of compliments – but his own parish had reinvigorated him and he was at peace with his place in the grand scheme of things.

"I'm going to make sure Ray has everything covered," Father Mayer said, looking up at the sky. "Then I'm going to have one final cigar before the storm hits."

"Sounds good, Father," Father Feeney said. "I'll see you in the rectory in a little while."

Ray crossed another item off Miguel's list and then reviewed it one last time; the only thing left was to report to Father Mayer. Miguel had organized the whole picnic so well that cleaning up had been a breeze.

Ray let the final volunteers head out before he headed to the smoking pavilion, which was Father Mayer's favorite place to have a cigar. The pavilion was surrounded by a row of hedges for privacy, but Ray saw a small cloud of smoke in the back corner and made a bee line for it.

"Well, Father, I've completed everything on Miguel's list," Ray said, flashing the paper at the priest.

"Ray, thank you so much for all your help today," Father said as they shook hands. "And thank you for that beautiful rendition of Peaceful Easy Feeling; it's one of my favorites."

"Of course, Father. I'm always happy to help," Ray said. "And thank you for the kind words."

"I'd love to stay and chat," Father began, "but this storm is going to start any minute. Why don't you run to the parking lot before you get soaked? The walk to the rectory is much shorter."

"Yeah, I think that's smart," Ray said, taking one last look around the grounds.

With one last goodbye, Ray ran out of the smoking pavilion and across the grounds. With all of the tables out of the way, he got to the parking lot in no time at all. Breathing heavy from his short run, Ray reached out a hand to open his car door just as a drop of rain hit him right on the forehead. He climbed into his car just as the heavens opened and thunder cracked once more.

The picnic was over.

CHAPTER 14: THE RIDE HOME

Large droplets of rain danced off the hood of Ray's car as he put it in gear and its headlights flickered on, exposing the rapidly darkening parking lot. Ray had taken his usual parking spot in the back corner of the lot; he didn't like to steal a close spot from someone who needed it more than he did.

Steam rose off of the asphalt of the large, rectangular lot that had just recently been full of hundreds of cars. Ray drove right down the middle of it as his windshield wipers shoved torrents of water out of the way. He felt happy and content knowing the day had been a success.

Stopping at the mouth of the parking lot and flicking on his left turn signal, Ray took one last look around. Through the sheets of rain, Ray could still see the glow of embers from Father Mayer's cigar in the smoking pavilion. He chuckled and pulled out onto the road, wondering how long Father would be stranded in the tent as he waited for the rain to die down.

Ray kept the radio off, preferring to listen to the storm instead; there was something peaceful about a thunderstorm that made it easier to think and reflect. Memories and feelings from the picnic continuously danced through Ray's mind while he drove, his car splashing through the rapidly forming puddles.

Getting up on stage and playing his Les Paul, singing with Miguel, and feeling the eyes of everyone in the crowd focusing on him; it was a pure adrenaline rush, exactly what he had always imagined. It was such a small taste, he had to go back for a bigger bite – and soon. He'd be getting in the recording studio with Stan as soon as he had the free time.

Storm clouds blanketed the sky by this point, though Ray could see one spot in the distance where light was shining through the clouds. It looked kind of like a spotlight, but instead of reaching for the sky, it was shining down somewhere over the hills.

About two blocks away from the church, Ray rolled past a truly entertaining sight: A caravan of red wagons led by a small group of men and women was dancing along in the rain. Children filled the wagons, splashing in the water that had collected in them, while the adults jumped in the puddles that lined the sides of the road.

It was impossible to tell who was having more fun. They must've been returning home from the picnic and decided to make the best of the weather change. Ray passed by, giving them a wide berth, though he was tempted to drive through a large puddle to join in their splashing.

The view of the people and their wagons faded in the rearview mirror, but the smile did not leave Ray's face. Seeing the children in the wagons made him think of his son, Ron, at first. Ron would always be his little boy, but the events of the day showed just how mature his son was becoming.

Just from observing him cleaning up the picnic table and taking care of the Les Paul, Ray couldn't have been more proud of whom his son was becoming. But it was an interaction he saw earlier in the day that really made Ray realize times were changing. Instead of following many of the other boys to the baseball field like he usually would have, Ron had been seated at a table talking to a few girls that were around his age. It looked awkward, just like most interactions at that age were, but that was part of life.

Another interaction at the picnic caught him by surprise. When he was in line to get dinner, one of the volunteers dishing out food and beverages was the vice president of his old stockbroker firm. Ray almost dropped his plate at the sight of him. It had been over a year since he'd last seen Mr. Brunner, and this was the last place he had expected to see him.

When Ray got back to his table, he mentioned the sight to his father, who informed him that Mr. Brunner was a frequent volunteer and a big contributor to the church. "I sure judged him wrong," Ray thought to himself while reliving the memory.

By this point, Ray was in the middle of town, still a ways from home; on his left, a large billboard for the Pittsburgh Pirates momentarily flashed bright from the storm and Ray remembered Darlene's big win in the raffle. It was the perfect end to the picnic for their table – they were all huge fans of the team. Darlene promised to invite Patty to a game, as well as Ray and Beth, when she was next in town.

The rain continued to plink against the roof of his car, and his windshield wipers worked overtime trying to keep the droplets out of his line of sight. Up ahead, Ray could make out the blurry green light of a traffic stop; he slowed his pace to try and maintain better visibility, and the blurry light rapidly switched to yellow and then red. Coming to a stop, Ray relaxed his grip on the wheel and sat back in his seat; driving in this weather always made him tense.

Drawing a deep breath, Ray cast his eyes around the intersection; it was a familiar place to him – he always drove this way home from church. To his left, everything was bathed in darkness and rain. The only signs of life were a few cars retreating into the distance.

Casting his gaze from left to right, Ray paused as he got to the far corner of the intersection. The ray of light he saw earlier was shining right on the old café that occupied the building. Its sign wasn't lit up, but he knew it was named something generic.

As his windshield wipers whipped back and forth in front of his gaze, Ray caught sight of a couple sitting in the closest window of the café. They looked familiar, but he couldn't quite remember where he knew them from. The woman was facing him, her dark hair ran down past her shoulders, and he could see kind eyes and a big smile, even through the rain.

She was with a man – Ray could only make out his side profile – who he also thought he recognized, but he didn't turn to show his full face. Ray wasn't sure how long he had been staring at the couple through the window, trying to unlock the puzzle in his brain to remember who they were.

After a few more seconds – it felt like an eternity – the woman looked out the window and over at him. They made eye contact and, combined with a brief break in the rain, Ray had the clarity he'd been seeking. It was the stewardess from the flight he had taken just over a year before, Maria. It was her idea to have Patty sit in his row, sparking their conversation.

Maria smiled at Ray, as if she recognized him as well. She couldn't possibly make out his face in his dark car, could she?

Just as quickly as she had smiled at Ray, she returned to her conversation. Who was it she was talking to? He had to know, but the man still wouldn't turn. Maybe Maria would tell the man to look over-

HONK

Ray spasmed in surprise. His whole being was pulled out of the café and returned to his car in the intersection. Headlights and an angry face flashed in Ray's rearview mirror. The light was green again, and he'd clearly been sitting there too long for the driver behind him.

He took his foot off the break slowly, inching into the intersection as he attempted to get one last look at the couple in the café, but the magic seemed to be lost. Maria was no longer looking at him, and she seemed completely engrossed in her conversation with the unknown man.

Ray gave up the fight and finally started to accelerate, making it through the intersection before another sight caught his eye.

Parked at a meter in front of the café was a yellow and black cab. Ray's mind went into overdrive and he started to connect the dots. He recognized that cab.

Everyone knew that familiar cab.

Made in the USA
Middletown, DE
21 December 2018